GUARDIANS OF ATLANTIS
CRYPTO-ADVENTURES BOOK 1

RICK CHESLER

SEVERED PRESS

GUARDIANS OF ATLANTIS

PROLOGUE

February 1939, Antarctica

The crunch of a metal flagpole penetrating the ice-covered ground was quickly lost in the vastness of the windswept shelf. A plateau of land on the edge of a continent that remained almost entirely unexplored, the object marked the rare presence of humans hoping to claim part of this forbidding new land as their own. Hans Lange glanced up at the flag fluttering in the wind atop the newly planted pole.

A red background set off a white circle containing a black, right-facing swastika, the hooked cross. Though Hans was filled with pride at being chosen to serve his country as part of this elite team, this was the tenth such flagpole he had jammed into the ice today, each a kilometer apart across the frozen wasteland, and profound weariness had long ago overtaken him.

Yet knowing he was an integral part of Heinrich Himmler's elite new unit, and that furthermore he was chosen to represent that unit on this most auspicious of expeditions to the very bottom of the world—to a land Germany was calling New Swabia in hopes of claiming it for their own-- spurred him on like no caffeinated beverage, or like no night of sound sleep ever could. The *Ahnenerbe*. It roughly meant "ancestral heritage" in English, but to Hans, it signified that he was charged with upholding the doctrines espoused by none other than the *Führer* himself. Hitler had charged his number-two-in-command, Himmler, with sending *Ahnenerbe* expeditions all over the world, including both the Arctic and the Antarctic, to find archaeological evidence for the supremacy of Germanic culture, as well as the more straightforward objective to map and claim new territory for the German homeland.

Hans looked over to his nearest associate, who now attempted to take a photograph of the newly planted flag. Proof of their land grab for the *Führer*. "I think we should get back to the ship now. The last flag requires us to cross a crevasse, and it will be getting dark soon. The weather is worsening. We can do it tomorrow."

Apparently, the austral summer's 9F temperature without wind chill was greater than photographer Kurt Bauer's need to further prove his valor. "That is fine. Just let me finish my photographs of this site, and we will turn back."

Hans signaled his approval, voice already hoarse from shouting over the wind all day. Although he wished he could plant the last flag today, thus completing the prescribed pattern, he would be glad to return to the cozy confines of the ship after such a physically demanding day's work.

Kurt finished his shots and packed up his camera gear. He and Hans placed it on their small sled, which was drawn by a pair of Greenland dogs they had acquired in Buenos Aires, Argentina, their last major port of call before crossing the Southern Ocean to the mysterious continent of ice. The breed of dog originated in Siberia nearly a millennium prior to the expedition, at some point spreading to North America by way of the Inuits' ancestors, the Thules. Extremely well suited to polar environments due to a number of adaptations, the canines boasted powerful legs with short fur, small ears for their size as well as a double coat—all characteristics that combat frostbite.

With all the gear loaded on the sled, Kurt secured it in place with ropes while Hans was charged with attaching the sled leads to the dogs' harnesses. While the canines were both the same breed and of about the same size and weight, one of the dogs was mostly tan in color while the other's coat was a patchy brown and white. The tan dog, which the ship's crew had named Shila, stood still and accepted the tether. The other animal, Arrluk, lunged forward, away from Hans just before he could attach the lead. Hans called the dog's name, issuing the voice command that he used to tell the animal to stop. Unlike every previous time he'd uttered it, this time the dog did not stop. Hearing the noise of four legs scrambling over the snow-covered ice, Kurt looked up and also tried calling the dog's name. "Arrluk! Stop!" But still the beast ran away from them. Shila strained at her harness, whimpering with excitement.

Hans eyed Kurt intensely, a piercing stare that ignored the goggles they both wore to protect from reflected sun as well as driving wind and precipitation. "We need that dog to complete our work."

"Isn't there one other dog on the ship?"

"There was, but it fell off an ice floe yesterday chasing birds while no one was watching, and drowned."

Kurt scratched his thick beard. "How did I not hear of this?"

Hans gave an irritated shrug. "I don't know, perhaps because you were sleeping off your Jägermeister hangover." Kurt sighed in defeat but still Hans hammered his point home. "Without that dog we will not be able to transport our equipment to the final survey marker."

Kurt pointed to the wayward work dog, still galloping away from them. "Then maybe we should just finish the last marker today, since by the time we catch him, it looks like that's about where we'll be."

Frustration welled up within Hans and for a moment he closed his eyes and took a deep breath, a trick his mother had taught him long ago. He could feel the cold settling into his bones from lack of movement. "We need to catch the dog *and* transport our equipment to the remaining site."

Kurt shrugged. "Either we leave the gear here, chase after the dog on foot, bring her back here and then sled the gear, *or*…"

He was interrupted by Arrluk barking furiously in the distance, now almost out of sight.

Hans gave Shila the command to start pulling the sled. "Or we have Shila pull the sled the remaining distance to the last site. She can do it from here. You guide Shila and the sled, and I will run ahead to the site."

Kurt nodded but gave his associate a grave stare. "Be careful, Hans. You know it is not safe to run in this land."

Hans returned the nod and then took off at what for Antarctica was a run, but in reality, burdened with a cold weather survival outfit, was more like a slow trot. Even so, it was faster than the rate at which the single dog hauled the equipment-laden sled, alongside which Kurt trudged.

The wind picked up as Hans ran and soon he could no longer see the loose dog, though he could hear it barking. He pressed on, knowing that Kurt was indeed correct that he was jeopardizing his safety at this pace. But the thought of disappointing Himmler himself, of letting down his great nation in the important task with which he had been charged, spurred him onwards against his better judgement. Craning his neck to look back, he soon found that he could no longer see Kurt and the sled, nor was he able to see Arrluk somewhere up ahead.

Then the dog's barking transitioned to a whine, and Hans pressed himself to move even faster. He cursed the lightly falling snow as it blanketed the ice, covering the telltale cracks that indicated danger in the form of unstable ice that overlay a crevice. Many an explorer had perished on this continent by falling through the ice into some undiscoverable chasm. No, he had no desire to die in order to plant a flag on an area of the Earth 99.9% of his countrymen would never visit. Yet the military, scientific and logistical advantages of staking a claim here had been drilled into him since joining the *Ahnenerbe*.

The missing dog, still out of sight somewhere up ahead, let loose a sharp whine. Hans cupped his hands to his mouth and called the animal's name, hoping that the mere sound of a human voice might calm it. But if it did hear him, it did no good. If anything, its howling intensified with the wind. Hans squinted in the direction of Kurt and the sled, but could no longer see him. He looked to his right, hoping to catch a glimpse of their tall ship anchored in the bay, but they had trekked too far inland.

Wondering if he might be making a mistake, Hans resumed his progress toward the runaway sled dog. Snow flurries cropped up here and there as he hiked, causing him to pause more often to wipe his goggles clear. He hoped that Kurt was able to keep up, since it would be a shame to reach the dog, who was now somewhere near the last marker point, only to not have access to their equipment. Innumerable footsteps later, it dawned on Hans that the dog was no longer moving further away from him. He was getting closer to it, which had to mean that it had stopped moving, or at least stopped running. He considered calling the dog's name again. He didn't want to trigger a game of chase, but on the other hand, if the dog was lost, it might take comfort in hearing his voice.

But the incessant canine whining told him it wouldn't make much difference, and so he picked up his pace without calling out. Hans was focusing on what he thought to be a patch of color (a rare enough thing in itself amidst this backdrop of near perpetual white) that might be Arrluk, when his leading foot broke through ice to the knee. Instantly, Hans splayed the rest of his limbs outward in an attempt to distribute his weight over as wide an area as possible. Falling all the way through here, completely unobserved, would be tantamount to a death sentence.

He pulled up on the foot that had penetrated the ground and found it to be immobilized. Removing a small ice pick from his pack, Hans used the tool to carefully break away just enough of the ice so that he was able to wiggle his foot and ankle. From there he was able to pull the imprisoned leg free, and then to backwards crabwalk away from the weak spot in the ice.

A close call. He breathed heavily in the aftermath of his thankfully short-lived predicament. *Shake it off,* he told himself. *Don't let it get to you. Keep moving.* Hans got to his feet and stood there a moment while scrutinizing the ice that lay ahead for any signs of instability. He didn't see anything that looked dangerous, but then again, he told himself, he hadn't noticed the weak ice that he had just fallen through, either. He scoured the landscape carefully, then proceeded by walking slowly in an arc to the left of the hole in the ice.

The wind picked up some more, enough so that he had to lean into it in order to walk. The incline also became much steeper as he neared the base of a mountain range. His walking pace—if the torturous leaning and calf muscle straining activity he endured in order to push himself forward could be called a *walk*, was much slower than his run, and with just as much effort. That was Antarctica, Hans knew, that fickle mistress-- seductive and beckoning one moment, cold and treacherous the next.

For all his trekking, it was Arrluk who came to Hans. The Greenland dog bounded up to the explorer with its tongue lolling out of its mouth, eyes sparkling with interest and recognition. But the dog was also trying to tell Hans something. It jerked its head and body back toward the way it had come from, and then ran back to Hans only to repeat the process.

"What is it? What is it, boy?" Hans queried the animal. In response, the canine wagged its tail harder and galloped a few feet away before stopping and turning around to see if Hans was still following. The German kept up his pace, battling the wind, to which the much lower- profile dog seemed immune. Man and dog continued pushing their way along the vast ice shelf, with Arrluk circling nervously around Hans every few feet before forging onward. Hans grew too tired to twist his neck around to look for Kurt, so he had to content himself with listening for him above the wind noise, which he knew was all but fruitless. *I'll turn around when we reach the waypoint*, he told himself. *We should be almost there.*

Sure enough, no sooner had he completed the thought than Arrluk suddenly flattened his body into the snow while facing forward. He began to growl. To Hans, the visible landscape before them looked no different from any of the rest of it. Realizing that he had the map in one of his fur jacket pockets, Hans stopped moving and fished it out. He unfolded it and noted the careful navigational markings he had made on it earlier. He was able to confirm that the marker point was not far ahead, perhaps a sixteenth of a mile. Still, on this continent, even small distances could be deceivingly difficult.

He put the map away, taking some satisfaction in feeling the wind die down, if only for a few seconds. Yet the dog still hunkered down in the snow, whining. *But wait*, Hans thought, observing the animal. Now Arrluk crept forward, slinking through the snow away from him.

"You see something, Arrluk?" The dog continued the slide forward on its belly while alternately emitting a low pitched growl and a high- pitched whine. Hans had never heard it do that before. "Where are you going, buddy? You know this is not the time to—"

Suddenly the dog disappeared down into some gap in the ice. Hans felt the hairs on his arms stand up, for it wasn't as if the ice cracked and the dog fell straight through, or a chunk of ice began to subduct below another, which could create a sudden incline. No, it seemed to Hans that Arrluk was *grabbed* by something and pulled down into a crevasse or crack.

He put himself into motion in order to find out, while calling the dog's name. He wanted it to have something to home in on, and to not feel abandoned. He kept his own pace deliberately slow and measured, since regardless of how the dog fell into it, there was obviously a gap or opening of some kind in the ice mere feet away. A few cautious feet later, Hans' heart jumped into his throat when he heard Arrluk yelp. Not because of the yelp itself, but because of how far away it sounded—how far down into the ice the dog must be for it to sound so faint.

As he neared the crevasse—it had to be there although he couldn't actually see an opening yet—Hans got down on his belly to distribute his weight more evenly. He low-crawled toward the crevasse, pressing down with his elbows before committing his full weight. "Coming, Arrluk— hang tight!" He cautioned himself not to put his own life in too much danger for the sake of an animal, even an animal in service of his country. But deep down he knew that the real reason he persisted was to get that last marker down now that he had trekked all the way here. To accomplish that and return back to the ship before nightfall, he would need the dog. To be out here at night was suicidal. So he wormed his way toward the still unseen gap in the icy ground.

Just as he was about to conclude that the dog had slipped through a micro-crevice that had already been re-covered with snow, Hans saw it: a cleft of rock set down about ten feet from the snow-covered ground. Nothing more than a small break in the ice. And yet the dog had for some reason gone down into it—*or was dragged into it. Perhaps there was a mini-avalanche*, Hans speculated to himself as he slithered forward a little closer.

Peering down through the rocky cleft, he found he could hear the dog again. Barking this time, like a regular junkyard dog yapping at an intruder. *Probably just panicked at being stuck down here*, Hans thought, and with good reason. He wasn't going to risk his life for a dog, one that would allow him to complete his honorable mission or not. But he would see if there was something he could do. Peering back in the direction he came from, it concerned him that he still saw no sign of Kurt and the sled. Once Hans disappeared into the cleft, he would be, for all intents and purposes, vanished. Although Kurt had a radio aboard the sled to be able to contact their ship, that was the only radio their team had. Due to their bulk—basically occupying an entire frame backpack-- individual portability was not an option, which Hans now regretted.

He turned his attention back to the cleft of rock and sucked in his breath as he took in a new detail, a formation of some sort off to the left. It was deep down into the cleft, and seemed to be made of smooth rock. Hans belly-crawled to the edge of the slope, where to go any further meant to slide down into the abyss. Yet somehow the dog had found a resting place without falling completely out of sight. His gaze was torn between the odd structure to the left and the drop-away in front of him, where somewhere far below, the dog's barking echoed about the chasm walls.

Hans mentally reviewed his limited inventory of climbing equipment he carried on his person. They had a collapsible ladder for crossing ice crevasses such as this one, but, although the marker point was just on the other side of this gap, crossing it would have to wait until he had dealt with the canine situation.

And that situation did not look good. With the use of safety ropes, Hans figured he could get at least a little ways further down, and then assess the situation and go from there. But first, he needed to make sure Kurt could find him. He decided he would have to use his marker flag and pole, even though he was a few meters shy of the intended placement site. He backed up until he felt he could safely crawl up to level ground again. He eyed the ice plain in the direction he had come but still saw no activity.

Hurriedly, Hans removed the collapsed flagpole from his pack, extended it to its full length and attached the German flag. Then he held it upright and rammed it into the ice. He didn't go to the trouble of pounding it into the ice as well as the others, since it wasn't meant to be permanent. It only had to last for a few more minutes, when Kurt would get close enough with the sled and the other dog to see it. It would stay put until then, he thought, closing a gloved hand around it and giving it a couple of shakes. Satisfied he could now be found once Kurt came into view, Hans went back to the crevasse.

He could still hear Arrluk whining somewhere far below. Working quickly, but at the same time mindful that a mistake could easily prove deadly, Hans set about using a climbing harness, metal stakes and an ice hammer to rig a safety line anchored in the ice. "I'm coming down, Arrluk!" he called out, hoping to calm the dog. If he did manage to reach it he wouldn't want it to be in a panicked frenzy.

Hans began his descent. It wasn't long before he came to what would be a no-go had he not been tethered in. The sides of the crevasse became too steep. His helmet lamp allowed him to see down into the dimness of the narrow, vertically oriented environment. The sight was not comforting, and yet was fascinating to him all the same. Further below he could pick out a ledge wide enough to stand on. It ran for perhaps twenty feet or so before rejoining the smooth ice walls of the crevasse. After a minute of looking, it dawned on him that there was a whole series of these formations, extending as far as his light beam's rays would reach.

On one of them, amidst the dimmest rays of his light's reach, sat Arrluk, nose up to the distant surface air, howling. Hans took a deep breath as he considered the daunting vertical distance to the dog. He thought he had enough rope, and enough extra gear to rig a harness for the beast and be able to haul them both back up. With any luck he'd have some help from Kurt for the return trip up, but he couldn't count on that, especially once he was down there. He stared down into the abyss again, this time looking beyond the dog's ledge.

He could swear he saw another of those odd structures, so smooth, with such non-natural lines. What was that? A glint of light, as if from metal? *Probably just ice,* Hans told himself. But then he looked at the structure that was higher up, the one he saw first. That wasn't ice. And now that he eyeballed it again, he thought it might actually be metal. *That would explain the light reflection,* he thought. He aimed a handheld flashlight down onto it, and sure enough, was rewarded with the reflection of light in a way that rock or even ice couldn't do.

Hans descended into the crevasse, towards the metallic structure. Halfway down to the first normal rock ledge, Arrluk abruptly stopped howling. Hans slid down the rope as fast as he dared. When he planted his booted feet on the snow-strewn ledge, he turned around, facing away from the wall, and looked down.

Arrluk? He thought it before he shouted it. But regardless of how he expressed himself, the dog was no longer there. He glanced around the other ledges to make sure he hadn't latched his gaze onto the wrong one. Nope. "Arrluk? *Arrluk!*" he shouted down into the void, but his only response was his own voice echoing back up at him, mocking his solitude.

He glanced around the forbidding, claustrophobic environment. Looking up, he could see only the barest sliver of sky, about a hundred feet above. He did not have sufficient ropes to continue down much farther. Eyeing the crevasse walls laterally, he saw that he was almost in line with one of the odd metallic structures he'd sighted from above. To get there meant rigging more ropes and driving more stakes into the wall—which, at this depth—was solid ice as opposed to rock. Which made it even more odd that something metallic was down here.

Hans tested his newly rigged equipment, double-checking knots, kicking the stakes in the ice to make sure they wouldn't budge, eyeballing the chain of gear to make certain he had rigged every part of it properly. He had absolutely no backup, which meant any error on his part could be fatal.

Standing on the edge of the ledge, Hans took a deep breath and put his back to the abyss. Then he pushed out from the cold wall and allowed himself to jump while the rope slid through his hand. When he bounced back onto the wall, he sprung off again, essentially bounding down the face. When he was perhaps half the vertical distance to the peculiar platform, he kicked off toward the right. As he neared the oddity, he was so taken aback by the increasing level of detail visible to him that he didn't notice he was at the end of his rope.

Metal! This platform was definitely made of metal. Hans kicked off of the rock below it and swung out and back again, this time generating enough momentum to drop onto the platform, his rope barely reaching. He was at a loss for words on touching down on the smooth metallic surface that was somehow devoid of snow or ice. Hans looked around but could find nowhere to attach his climbing rope once he unclipped it from his person. He had to do that to explore this new area, but couldn't risk the rope falling off the edge, pulled over by its own weight. So he dug something heavy out of his pack—a book of Antarctic maps—and set it on top of the rope to keep it in place. Staring at it as he backed away since if it failed, he would be stranded for the remainder of his short life on this odd metal shelf, Hans satisfied himself it would hold and then turned around to investigate his new surroundings.

Looking up, he saw only the smooth face he had just descended, reaching all the way up to that now distant sliver of grey sky. Down, however, he saw that the platform on which he stood was a lip that extended out over….he crawled to the edge and lay on his belly for a better view of what lay beneath.

His helmet light picked up movement far below. He instinctively pulled his head back from the edge. After taking a breath, he peered over the edge again. This time he forced himself to remain calm and logical as he watched the points of light dancing below. It took him a few seconds to understand that he was staring at the reflections of his headlamp off of water. He figured it was ocean water, since although most of Earth's freshwater was in Antarctica, it was locked up in ice.

"Arrluk?" He called the dog's name out again as he now considered that it may have fallen into the freezing sea below. No reply from the canine came. His mind reeled with the fact that he had lost the dog, and now he must get back to the surface alone. As his thoughts about how exactly to do this blurred from one half-formed idea to the next, he began to recognize shapes and patterns in the snow and ice. He reached out a hand. Was that light? Glowing lines traced through the thin layer of snow that blanketed the ice shelf separating him from a long fall into icy water.

Hans heard a faint *click* and then heard a rumbling, grinding noise behind him. He whirled around in time to see a section of ice slide open in the crevasse wall. He froze in place, not trusting his own sensory inputs. He was aware that those lost on the Antarctic plains were prone to suffering hallucinations, much like the famed mirages seen by thirst-weary desert travelers. And yet this seemed all too real, and somehow beautiful. He reached out a hand to trace the glowing lines but found they were always ahead of his fingertips, dissolving and reappearing closer to the opening in the crevasse wall. Peering into the gap in the wall, he was unable to see through a swirling mist.

The explorer took a tentative step forward, then another. He walked to the edge of the opening in the wall and reached out an arm, waving his hand back and forth in an attempt to dissipate the thick fog. It parted just enough to see that there was ample space inside, and so he took another step forward, crossing the threshold. Instantly he felt warmer. He almost didn't recognize the sensation, so foreign it was to this frozen world. For weeks he'd been exposed to the elements, and had become inured as long as he wore his furs. But now, sweat beaded on his skin, and he felt uncomfortably itchy and warm.

Suddenly he felt a prickling sensation on every one of his skin pores, like an electrical charge. It intensified rapidly from a mild pinprick to a *stop-this-at-all-costs* demand from his central nervous system. He had just gotten one arm free of his seal skin coat when he felt the ice floor give way beneath his feet. He free-fell three feet until his backside slammed hard against more ice.

Hans began sliding downward at a scary speed that gave him no time whatsoever to assess his situation or to try to understand what was happening to him. One second he was standing there, prickling, and the next he was sliding down an amusement park-like chute. But the electrical sensation had stopped! That was the only positive thing about it, though, for now he was barreling feet first through the dark, almost straight down.

On the way he caught glimpses here and there of illuminated hieroglyphics, strange runes and symbols seeming to glow of their own accord. To Hans they appeared the same color as the bioluminescent algae that sometimes sparkled in his ship's wake. Down, down, down he went, smoothly and without much discomfort, owing to the slick ice.

After an indeterminate amount of time, he processed the fact that he could see natural light from above. Then with terror, he realized it was because he stared out over the water at the bottom of the chasm, where out in the middle of it a narrow swath of sunlight reached. The daylight gave him hope, and he was drawn in that direction. He stopped short of the water, perhaps six feet away.

Gazing out across the chasm's watery bottom, he fixated on the sunlit section in the middle, for that closest to him was too dark to see. His senses were overloaded as his fatigued mind struggled to make sense of all that surrounded him: the strange lights in the ice, the water a few feet away, the sun out in the middle of the water, the ice shelf on which he now stood at the bottom of the crevasse....

...as well as the *sounds*—ice cracking and creaking, water slapping against the ice shelf, and, in the distance, a dog's frenzied howls. This snapped him out of his trance-like state and he turned his head right, trying to follow the vocalizations. He walked a few feet in that direction, watching the ice beneath his feet carefully. A little too carefully, since he failed to notice the sleek shape approaching him from the water. Hans then became distracted by a noise from above. A human voice. Craning his neck skyward, he could just barely make out the yellow point of a flashlight. Kurt had arrived!

He sucked in a great breath and had just begun to shout when a massive, sleek shape erupted from the black waters of the crevasse. A maw gaped open, water cascaded from fins, and the only thing that made it not so horrifying to Hans was the sheer swiftness of it all. The entire man was gone from the ice in one second, his body engulfed by a force of nature inescapably larger than himself.

CHAPTER 1

Present Day: Cairo, Egypt

Dan James stared wistfully at the bar, knowing it would be his last time here. The bartender, a local Egyptian he knew only as Nour, slid an open Stella lager his way. "I'll add it to your tab. You gonna pay it tonight?" he asked in accented English accompanied by an accusatory stare. "Owner's been getting on my case about it."

Dan's smile tightened a little as he nodded. Nour returned the nod and left for the end of The Cairo Jazz Bar, where a pair of twenty-something women, dressed for a night of dancing, waited for drinks. Behind them, a small but modern dancefloor thumped with the sounds of electronic music curated by a female DJ in a booth shaped and decorated to look like the head of the famous Sphinx that lay only a few miles away in the desert sands. The Friday evening was young enough that it was still mostly empty, but Dan knew from experience that would soon change. He stared at the two women until he caught the eye of the one not ordering from Nour, the one who he saw as slightly more attractive. She quickly looked away and started chatting with another man who had just walked in. Dan sighed and turned away from the bar.

Time to head for the old guys' section, he thought, sliding off his stool onto the floor. He wasn't old, but he felt like it. Losing his job yesterday had taken the wind out of his sails. He'd barely been making it paycheck to paycheck anyway, even with his low paid gig as a tour guide at the pyramids. He wasn't an archaeologist, had never even gone to college for anything. After living and working here for about a year now, he had nevertheless come to be fascinated by the ancient Egyptian culture—the heritage, myths, legends and architecture that had endured for so long in the world's collective consciousness. When mixed together with the contemporary urban scene of Cairo, nearby Giza and the country itself, Dan had become completely enamored of all things Egypt.

But now all that was coming to an end. Back to the States, where he'd find a job as a barback in a busy place if he was lucky. Like it or not, his world travel period was coming to an end after just shy of four years. He supposed he should be grateful for being able to take such an extended trip at all. That fact was not lost on him as he looked about surroundings that, while exotic to most people he knew, Dan had come to take for granted. Most high school graduates who decided to travel opted for one year abroad backpacking Europe before returning to their country to attend college. The thing was, Dan was able to take four years instead of one precisely because he had nothing to go back home *to*. No university to attend. No training program of any kind. He'd briefly entertained the notion of joining the military, and even went so far as to physically visit a recruiting office and express interest. But his history of asthma made him ineligible for service.

He moved to the quietest, most out of the way section of tables and chairs in the corner. By the time he was seated with his Stella on the table in front of him, he was already eyeing the cute woman again, but she was still flirting with the newcomer. Just as well, Dan thought. No point in getting involved with anyone when I've got to spend my last dollar on the plane ticket back home. Four years of aimless globetrotting—not the luxury kind either, with cruises, side-trips, resorts and Michelin star restaurants--but of dodgy hostels while working various unskilled jobs—whatever he could find that was legal—and taking busses and trains from country to country throughout Europe, solo. He'd hit all of the U.K., and then came Germany, France, Spain, and Portugal. Egypt was as far south as he'd made it, and the fact that it was actually part of Africa made it all the more alluring, expanding his travels to two continents. Not bad for a guy who'd been hoping to score a bartending gig in Virginia four years ago.

He sipped his Stella and thought about his friends back home. Some of them would have completed degrees during the last four years, or at least some kind of technical or vocational training that allowed them to make a decent living. And if not that, then they were meeting the loves of their lives, starting families, entrenching themselves within their communities. As much as Dan had hoped to find a kindred spirit in his travels, he'd only managed a couple of "hook-ups" here and there. The ones he really wanted, or at least thought he did, always got away. He vowed to himself that he would save up more money and then, in a couple of years or so, be able to head out on another adventure, but he knew anything could happen with dreams like that.

He nursed his beer in the corner, trying to decide what he was going to have to do without in order to pay his bar tab at the end of the night—almost two months' worth. And Nour didn't yet know he'd lost his job. If he did, Dan knew, he wouldn't be floating him drinks tonight. And Dan wanted tonight to be fun since it would be his last night abroad.

His thoughts were interrupted by a gaggle of boisterous people entering the establishment. He couldn't help but notice that one of them swigged from a flask as he walked in, a real bonehead move, Dan thought. Sure enough, Nour's voice boomed from behind the bar: "Hey buddy, nuh-uh." Nour pointed his finger forcefully toward the door. "Try that again. You come in without the flask or you don't come in. Go back out, come back in!"

Dan shook his head at the leniency. He'd never see that where he was from. But *This was Africa*, he'd heard people say. *Indeed*. He watched as the guy wheeled back out toward the sidewalk, causing a lady walking her big fancy poodle dog to jump out of the way. Then the man shoved the flask into the pocket of his black leather jacket and walked back to the entrance, where his friends waited for him in a knot, conversing loudly about other things, as though nothing at all had gone wrong with their entrance.

The group of men, five in all, fanned out along the bar and ordered from Nour. Dan could see that the bartender had some additional warnings, especially for the one in the leather jacket, but all of them were served, nonetheless. Dan sipped his own drink and cringed as he saw them pointing to the group of empty tables next to him. He wanted to wallow in pity alone, not have to interact with a bunch of drunks he didn't know, but already the guy in the leather jacket was asking him if any of the seats were taken. Dan signaled with a casual wave of the hand and shake of the head that they were not, and the rowdy group proceeded to make themselves comfortable.

Side-eyeing them as they moved past him to sit down, Dan noticed that he recognized one of the newcomers as a pyramid guide who worked for a competing company. They'd see each other now and again coming in or out of the Great Pyramid with a tour group, exchange pleasantries and even small tidbits of information like areas of high pedestrian congestion, construction progress or issues with standing water, certain passages that were closed for renovation, new archaeology groups coming through, that kind of thing. The others, he couldn't place. Two of them, including the one he'd met, were Egyptian, locals who made a living off of the thriving tourism industry. One was British, Dan guessed by his accent, while another appeared to be some type of Middle Eastern extraction, olive skin with thick, dark hair and a black beard. Dan didn't think he was Egyptian. All spoke English, which was not unusual for Egyptians, especially those who worked with or among foreigners.

Dan watched as the woman he'd been observing left the bar for the dancefloor with the gentleman she'd been talking to. As he watched her sashay past the tables to the dance area, he drained the last of his beverage and set the bottle on the table. He became distantly aware that the men seated next to him had begun discussing the pyramids, something about a secret passage. Dan had heard reports of many passages in the pyramids, secret and otherwise, some substantiated and some not. New ones were always being discovered as technology, such as LiDAR and Ground Penetrating RADAR emerged and improved.

These guys were really into it, Dan found as he turned to face them. Their discussion was turning heated, with the leather jacket guy insisting that what he had heard was true. He downed an amber-colored liquid from a shot glass and then slammed it on the table while widening his eyes to say, "It's called the Hall of Records! Under the sphinx's right front paw. There may even be a second sphinx, also buried, as the first one was for some time."

The man Dan knew to be a guide responded. "I've never heard of a passage there, but it's true that new projects are always being approved. This is Egypt. If you pay the right people, your team may be allowed to dig somewhere no one else has been."

"And how do you know about this, this Hall of Records passage?" one of the other Egyptian guides asked the leather-clad drinker.

"I am from the United Arab Emirates. I know Prince Abdullah Mohammed personally, and he has told me of his archaeological projects that he funded in Egypt."

At this, the other men shrugged and sipped their drinks. It could be true, Dan thought to himself, not really caring.

The guide known to Dan persisted. "If you are friends with him, why would you want to possibly sabotage his dig site by giving up its location to rival professionals such as ourselves?"

At this, Dan found himself turning his head to watch the Emirati man's response, which was measured and calm, albeit with a tumbler of Auld Stag whiskey held in one outstretched hand. "I said I know him personally. I didn't say he was my friend."

At this there was an initial period of silence while those at the table watched each other's expressions. At length, one of the guides said, "He banged your sister, didn't he?"

Uproarious laughter ensued, with even Dan unable to contain his reaction. He caught the eye of the guide he knew while they both laughed.

"What's the matter with you, man?" one of the other drinkers said, shaking his head, but he was cackling even as he said it.

"What, have you seen his sister? She's hot! Hey, Khalif, let these guys see the pic you showed me of your sister!"

Dan watched the man he now knew was called Khalif smile and shake his head slowly before consuming about half of what was left in his glass. "It has nothing to do with my sister, I can assure you. Suffice it to say, gentlemen, that I know what I speak of to be true. If you, as longtime guides at the Great Pyramid, might be able to make use of this information and take me to the new passage before Prince Abdullah's archaeology team begins their work—which I happen to know will be any day now—then it may come to pass that *we* will be the first humans to step foot into the legendary Hall of Records since it was created untold thousands of years ago."

"What if it's cursed?" one of the guides Dan did not know asked, quieting the table once again.

The Egyptian who'd brought up the sister said, "Then, for the rest of your life…" He looked around the table dramatically before continuing. "You will have to share Khalif's sister with the Prince! She will never be all yours--you're cursed!"

Another round of uproarious laughter made its way around the table while Khalif shook his head, smiling good-naturedly. He spotted a passing server who had just started on duty as the dancefloor traffic picked up, and hailed her over by holding his empty glass aloft. He made it clear that he wanted another drink, but he couldn't stop those around him from continuing the conversation.

"Khalif, Khalif, Khalif!" the guide Dan knew pleaded. "Even if we agreed to accompany you to this so-called dig site, the passage to get to it—an offshoot of the Osiris Shaft—is a locked gate. A permit is required to obtain the key from the Ministry of Antiquities. So we cannot even get back there to the Osiris Shaft that leads to beneath the Sphinx."

At this, Khalif became less animated as he addressed the others. "You mean, none of you know of a way to access the tunnel I am talking about?"

Between a few shrugs and those who chose not to answer the question in favor of ordering more booze from the waitress, Khalif's query seemed destined to go unanswered.

Until Dan spoke up.

"I know a way to get into that sub-sphinx corridor."

At this, everyone turned to stare at him with the exception of one man ordering a mixed drink from the server.

Khalif aimed an ear-to-ear grin at the American. "Is this true?"

Dan nodded in a way that he hoped exuded confidence. He did know where it was, at least in a general way. He'd been there once, but it was a few months ago, the drunken meanderings of a late night spent in the pursuit of…something interesting, he supposed. The urge to explore his world, which was what had led him all the way to this part of the planet in the first place. "Yes, I know a way there."

Khalif's visage took on a more skeptical tell. "You are American? How is it that you are so familiar with the Great Pyramid and the Sphinx?"

"Yes, I'm American. But I've been working here full-time as a tour guide at the pyramid for the last year. Let's just say that I've been on a few…side trips…during that time. I've never told anyone about them."

"Well, if this is true—" Khalif was cut off by the guide Dan knew.

"It is true. Dan James, here, is—or should I say *was*—a pyramid guide."

Dan felt his cheeks flush at the use of the past tense. Word got around already? He supposed the professional Egyptology tour-guide community was small enough. He knew everyone would find out pretty soon, but he was hoping to have left the country by then.

"Oh hey, Rashid. Long time no see. How's it going?" Dan tried to act like it was no big deal.

"Still have my job, so, better than you, I expect!"

"Ohhhhhhh," came from those seated with Rashid. The server turned to Dan. "Sounds like you could use another?" she said with a smile.

Dan nodded, and was about to simply ask for another Stella when he turned and made eye contact with Khalif, who immediately took the bait.

"Let this one be on me, my new friend!" He eyed the server and began nodding but Dan held up a finger in his direction.

"Tell you what: You want me to take you there?" he asked, being deliberately vague by not using the word "pyramid" or "sphinx" or anything that would give away to the server they were talking about off-limits parts of the guided tours.

Khalif nodded eagerly in response. "Yes, I got this one, no problem!" He nodded to the empty beer bottle in Dan's hand. But Dan said to the server, "Stella, on my tab, please."

She nodded and left the table while Khalif held up his hands. "Dan, Dan,…I said I would—"

"Tell you what," Dan said. "That'll be my last drink. You pay my bar tab, and I'll go with you right now to the Sphinx. Show you the passageway that leads to the Osiris Shaft and the new dig project."

Dan saw Rashid hold a hand up to his face while he snickered, but Khalif seemed unfazed. "You got a deal, my American friend. Let's go do this! Are we all ready?" He had to raise his voice now to be heard over the dancefloor music, which had steadily been increasing in intensity.

The men chugged down the last of their drinks and gathered their things from the table, talking loudly as they did so. "Let's do this, then."

"We can always hit Sands Club in Giza if it doesn't pan out."

"Hey, maybe I can get one for the road?"

Khalif told everyone, "Go ahead on out, get the cars, I'll pay the tab and meet you outside."

Dan quickly made his way toward the exit, leading the way for the rest of the group, while Khalif made a beeline to Nour at the bar. Dan had almost reached the end of the bar that was closest to the main exit when a commotion broke out.

"I said don't touch me, creep! Get away!" The shrill voice of an angry woman pierced through the high level of background noise. Dan turned to see a small throng of people, including the female friend of the woman he had briefly tried to get to know at the center of it all, separating her friend from the man she had chosen to flirt with.

"What the hell's wrong with you?" the guy was yelling back, but he was taken by security guards and pushed roughly out the exit. At the bar, where both Nour and Khalif had paused to watch the action unfold, Nour pointed to Khalif and said, "What can I do for you?"

Khalif pointed to Dan, who smiled at Nour and then hurriedly turned and followed the security guards out the exit. "I wish to pay Dan's tab." Nour raised an eyebrow at the customer before holding up a finger to indicate he would be right back.

Meanwhile, Dan and the rest of Khalif's party made their way out of the club and onto the sidewalk, where a warm zephyr circulated the dry desert air. The weather, the scents of falafel, Shawarma meats, roasted chicken, Kofta Kebabs, and incense, the streets of Cairo, the sounds of prayer bells and Arabian music—they all reminded Dan that starting tomorrow he would need to make his way away from here and head back home.

A car slid up to the curb and one of the bouncers said to the man who'd been kicked out of the club, "Here's your Uber. Don't come back tonight." The ejected patron flipped the bouncers the bird before hopping into the back of the car, a late model blue sedan. Rashid pulled up behind the sedan in his dusty Toyota pickup truck, waving his friends over while he flung open the passenger cab door.

At that moment, Khalif emerged from the club, withdrawing his flask from his jacket pocket and taking a pull. He spotted Dan and wagged a crumpled receipt at him. "Hey Dan, you didn't tell me you had two months' worth of unpaid tab! This better be worth it, my *friend*!"

Presently, the woman in the fracas opened the door but paused in the doorway, the hand of her female friend on her shoulder, trying to get her to stay inside.

"I just wanna get out of here. See ya later. I don't know where--home, another club? Anywhere's better than here." She pushed her way outside and the bouncer said, "Whoa, no, hey—what are you doing? Go back inside until he leaves."

"C'mon, baby—my place, remember?" her former dance partner called.

The angry woman glared at him. "Hey, that's *my* Uber!"

"We can share, baby! Calm down and let's go for a ride!"

Dan, Khalif and the others reached Rashid in the pickup. Dan passed the woman on the way, saw she was frustrated by having her ride stolen, and asked, "Hey, you want to come with us? Plenty of room!" He motioned to the empty pickup bed.

She eyed the dirty truck, then Dan again. "Where are you going?"

The rest of the group was hopping into the back now, with Khalif taking the shotgun seat in the cab. Dan reached the truck bed and hopped inside, looking back at the woman, feeling the effects of the beers he'd had.

"Giza. We're going to the Sphinx, to find the secret hidden room beneath the right front paw!"

At this the security guards laughed. "Sure you are, buddy. Sure you are."

To everyone's surprise, the woman flipped off the guy in the waiting Uber and walked to the pickup. "Sounds fun. Take me with you!"

CHAPTER 2

Dan extended a hand to the woman and pulled her up into the bed of the pickup. "My name's Dan James, nice to meet you."

"Hi Dan, I'm Jami Stratton. Pleasure to meet you under such awesome circumstances!" She shook his hand and gave him a sarcastic smile that warmed him more than the alcohol ever could. The bed of the pickup was crowded for four people owing to the sacks of wheat stacked up against the cab, but they made the best of it. Dan created a cushy space for Jami up against a sack of wheat while he sat next to her, and the two Egyptian tour guides sat on the other side of the bed chatting in Arabic. They rumbled through the stop-and-go traffic of Cairo, breathing in the nighttime air. Dan smiled to himself, happy to have paid off his hefty bar tab, and even happier to now be in the presence of such a beautiful woman. He was glad he had decided to go to the bar rather than sit in his room and sulk over his lack of options. He eyed Jami now while she watched the club and her unfortunate experience there fade into the distance.

Shoulder length, wavy auburn hair. Sparkling green eyes, a perfectly symmetrical face with slightly upturned nose. He wasn't about to ask, but guessed her to be about his same age, mid-twenties. He stood six feet on the nose, and she was only a couple of inches shorter than him. He continued to eye her surreptitiously. Athletic figure, toned, he could see. She must workout at least semi-regularly. His observations were interrupted when the truck stopped at a red light and the two Egyptians in the back suddenly jumped out.

"What's up?" Rashid called out the window from the driver's seat.

"We're going to hit the After Eight club. You guys have fun!"

"You don't want to go with us?" Rashid asked, holding his hands palms up.

The tour guide shook his head. "We'll be back at the Sphinx the day after tomorrow for work. Why do I want to see it on my day off?"

"You don't want to look for the Hall of Records?" Khalif asked through the open window.

"The only records we want to find tonight are the phone numbers of hot women!"

While Jami laughed out loud, Rashid waved good-naturedly, shrugged and pressed on the gas as the light turned green. "Looks like it's up to us."

Even though there was now more room in the truck bed, Dan made no move to get farther away from Jami. She didn't seem to mind, and so they stayed where they were as they drove on through the streets of Cairo. They chatted about her negative experience with the guy at the club, and before long they left the city behind, heading through the desert on a highway to the town of Giza, the jumping-off point for the Great Pyramid and the Sphinx. The night air was warm and pleasant, with a perfect half-moon lighting up the sky.

Dan changed the subject from the club to Jami the person, and asked her if she'd been to the Sphinx before.

"Haven't been to the Sphinx or the pyramids," she said with a smile. "Been meaning to, just haven't got around to it yet. Part of the reason I accepted your offer of a ride."

"Part of the reason?" Dan inquired.

She smiled coyly. "Well, and I wanted to get away from that sleazy creep. And you seem nice!" She flashed a winning smile that melted Dan's heart.

Dan groaned as they hit a pothole and his shoulder blade bumped into the lip of the truck bed. "So what do you do for a living?" he asked Jami.

"I'm a zoologist."

He wasn't sure what he had been expecting, but it wasn't that.

"A zoo—"

"Yeah, I study animals. That's how I know one when I see one," she spat, jerking her thumb back toward the Cairo club. "Well, that's what my degree is in, anyway. And I do work with animals, at the zoo in Chicago where I'm from."

"You're from a zoo?" Dan smiled to show he was joking.

"I'm from Chicago and I work at a zoo there." She swatted him playfully on the top of the head.

"So what made you want to go to Egypt?"

She shrugged, looking around at what she could see of the flat desert scenery on either side of the highway. "I'm taking a gap year between earning my bachelor's degree and starting grad school."

Dan looked at her, impressed. She was all dolled up to go clubbing and he never would have guessed she was one of those year-off-from-school types.

"Wow, cool!" was all that translated to.

Again, Jami shrugged as they bounced along the dusty highway. "I think so, but tell that to my parents. And my professors. They all wanted me to go straight into grad school, to just keep going."

"But you didn't want to?"

"No, I need a break. There's more to life than just work, work, work, you know?"

Dan nodded sagely. "Believe me, I know."

"Next month I'm supposed to start my master's program at Northwestern and I'm just trying to wrap my head around it. It doesn't seem real."

"Well right now you're bouncing around in the back of a pickup truck in Giza headed for the Sphinx to look for a secret chamber, so…what's real?" Dan posed.

Jami laughed and shook her head. "I guess we'll find out." They rolled on in comfortable silence through the city streets, smaller than Cairo but seemingly with the same amount of traffic. "First time in Giza?" Dan asked.

Jami nodded. "Yes, been in Cairo my whole time in Egypt so far."

"Well it's good you'll get to see the Sphinx and the Great Pyramid, at least. Chalk that off the ol' bucket list before you get back to Real Life, right?"

"Absolutely! Thanks for taking me."

"No worries." Again, they lapsed into a relaxed calm that lasted until they reached the outskirts of the city. There, on the edge of the Giza Plateau, Dan pointed off to their left as the pickup rolled toward the open desert. "Behold, the Great Pyramid of Egypt….and the Sphinx!"

Jami turned her head and literally gasped at the sight, for in the distance, the Great Pyramid was visible, its pointed tip bathed in colored light. Nearby, the Sphinx was also illuminated in otherworldly colors.

"Laser light show, happens every night," Dan explained. "Really cool, right?"

"Oh yeah, I heard about that! Heard it's expensive to get into?"

Dan smiled. "Don't worry, I'll take care of that. Perks of my tour guide job."

Suddenly a peddle-drawn cart tipped over in front of them and Rashid lay on the horn as he swerved to the right. Jami was thrown forward and to the left, and Dan reached out an arm to steady her. He held her until Rashid got the truck back under control.

"Sorry!" the driver called back through the open cab window. "Crazy cart driver pulled in front of me!"

"We're okay!" Dan called back. Then, in a softer voice, he asked Jami, "You are okay, right?"

She nodded. "I'm fine. But look at the street!" She pointed behind them. In their wake, all manner of debris littered the road, much more than the single cart they had almost collided with. Fruits and vegetables from uprooted stands rolled across the roadway. A horse-drawn wagon lay in the street with a broken wheel. On the side of the busy thoroughfare, numerous shanties had collapsed to the sand. The road itself had a buckle in it that ran for several feet.

"What the—" Dan started, and then Khalif's voice came from the cab. "On the radio they're saying we had an earthquake! 5.2, a few miles west of Giza!"

"Wow!" Jami said. "I didn't know they had earthquakes in Egypt?"

Dan nodded. "Actually, yes, I know they do because one of my tour spiels talks about how they affected the pyramids. Most recently, there was a 5.9 in 1992. And then way back in 1847, and I'm told there was one in the 1300s."

"You know a lot about the pyramids, don't you?" Jami asked, blinking her big green eyes at him.

Dan shrugged. "I guess so."

"So do you really think we'll find this mystery room in the Sphinx?"

Dan leaned in closer to her and lowered his voice to a conspiratorial whisper. "Don't tell Khalif this," he said, nodding toward the driver, "but the chamber he's looking for—it's called The Hall of Records—is not a new idea. In 1932 a man named Edgar Cayce claimed that the Sphinx was built much longer ago than previously thought, and that it was related to the mythical civilization of Atlantis."

"Wow, the underwater city?"

"That's the one. And in 1978 the Cayce Foundation sent an expedition to look around under the Sphinx for the hidden chamber."

"And what did they find?"

"Nothing."

"So if you don't believe there's anything to be found, why are you helping Khalif look for it?"

Dan chuckled. "Because I wanted to get my bar tab paid before I—" He hesitated, aware that he hadn't yet told Jami he was planning on leaving back to the States tomorrow. Now he wasn't so sure he wanted to.

"Before you what?" she prompted.

Dan was relieved to see Rashid's face turn toward them from the cab. "Hey Dan, which entrance you think we should use—South or West?"

Dan stood up in the cab. "I think west is the way to go."

"Go west, young man!" This from Khalif, and the truck swung around to the left. Jami reached an arm around Dan for support.

"Are you ready to see the ancient wonders of Egypt?" he asked her.

She laughed. "Hell yeah, bring it on!"

They fell in with a line of vehicles heading toward one side of the Great Pyramid, many of them playing music filled with people going to see the laser show. When they reached a parking area with the pyramid towering above in the background, an attendant greeted Rashid by name. After a brief and, to Dan's ears, pleasant-sounding conversation in Arabic, the attendant lifted a velvet rope and waved their vehicle through before replacing the rope again.

Jami pointed to the mass of cars they were leaving behind. "What, we get our own private road right to the pyramid?" While there were in fact a couple of other cars travelling the same road up ahead, it was far less crowded than the parking lot.

"Perks of the job," Dan said with a shrug, to which Jami replied, "Cool!"

Rashid turned around in the cab to face them through the open cab window. "He said the earthquake is not going to stop the light show, which is good since it will provide us with a distraction."

"A distraction from what?" Jami asked. "I thought you work here and so can go anywhere?"

Dan met her gaze. "Everywhere the public tours operate, which is limited to the known areas of the pyramids and Sphinx. Not the special areas of archaeological or geological investigation, one of which we will try to visit this fine evening."

She raised an eyebrow suggestively. "I won't tell."

He surprised himself by winking at her. "Thanks. We'll be all right."

The truck rolled slowly down a slight grade to a flat sandy area. Dan pointed to the Sphinx, which loomed tall in front of them about a football field away. "This is as close as vehicles can get to the site without a special permit, so we'll be parking...." He cupped a hand around his mouth and yelled into the cab, "...as soon as Rashid finds us a parking spot!"

"Right up here," the driver called back, pulling the truck to a stop next to another parked vehicle.

"Game on!" Dan said, jumping out of the truck bed. He reached up a hand to help Jami down. She took it and gracefully landed on the sandy ground. "Welcome to the Land of the Sphinx," Dan said solemnly.

"Thanks," she said, shaking some sand out of one of her pumps. She pointed up to the glowing face of the ancient stone lion, bathed in shifting artificial light that faded from purple to turquoise and beyond. "Where's the dance floor?"

Rashid answered her as he and Khalif walked over to them. "I would think you've had your fill of those for tonight, no offense!"

"None taken. You're right. Just curious."

"They don't actually have one, anyway," Dan said. "It's just a light and sound show." The psychedelic strains of Pink Floyd pulsed in the distance while Dan addressed them all.

"Before we get going, allow me to give Jami some quick facts," said Dan with a smile. "After all, this is her first visit here. We are standing before the Great Pyramid Complex, built about 4,500 years ago. It contains the three pyramids, the largest of which is a tomb for Pharaoh Khufu, while the other two are for Pharaohs Khafre and Menkaure. There is also the Sphinx, built to protect Pharaoh Khufu in the afterlife."

"Okay. Are we ready?" Khalif asked, holding his hands palms up.

"Relax," Rashid said, clapping him on the back. "Whatever's down there has been down there for thousands of years already. It's not going anywhere."

Khalif nodded in acceptance. "Yes, you are right, of course. I am just impatient. However, there is the matter of the Prince's team beginning work on the site. Once they do, we will be shut out, so now is our chance."

"Let's do this, then." Dan pointed to the Sphinx's hindquarters and then looked at Rashid. "Entrance 5."

Rashid nodded. "That should work. Let's check it out, we can always try 7 if that's no good. Hold on, before we go, let me get one thing. I notice none of you have any gear with you." He went back into his truck cab and returned with a simple, student-style backpack and a shrug. "At least we'll have a few things."

The four of them began walking across the sand to the Great Pyramid. Dan explained to Jami that there is no direct opening into the Sphinx, but that the pyramids do have various passageways and chambers, some of which are open to public tours. Jami noted that, even at night, the sandy ground was still warm.

"It's nice and cool in the pyramid," Rashid promised.

They reached a gated area where they had to unlock a metal gate set between two stone walls. Rashid produced a key from a large ring of them and they passed through, after which he locked it behind them.

"It's like a maze in here," Jami said, looking around at the corridors leading this way and that between high walls. "This leads into the pyramid?"

Dan explained that there are multiple entrances to the Great Pyramid and some to the two smaller pyramids. Rashid added that some of the passages led to additional archaeological sites surrounding the pyramids and Sphinx.

"I'm glad you guys know where you're going," Jami said, "because I would get lost here in a minute."

They walked down a corridor until it reached a stone stairway that led down, beneath the ground. When they got to the bottom of the steps, they found themselves on a stone tile floor, with walls of limestone block, similar to those of the pyramid itself. In front of them, a dark opening yawned.

"Is this part of the secret areas?" Jami asked.

Dan and Rashid exchanged amused glances. Dan smiled at her. "It is now, after hours, but during the day, inside here is part of the tour."

"The first part of what's inside here," Rashid clarified. "'In here' is a vast place, as you will soon see."

Jami appeared confused. "I thought inside the pyramids was just one room, to house the coffin, or sarcophagus or whatever you call it, for the mummy and a few treasures for the afterlife? And the rest is just solid blocks that form the shape of the pyramid?"

Dan shook his head. "A common misconception. In reality, the pyramids—particularly the Great Pyramid that we are about to enter--- have many chambers, passageways and voids—that is—space of some type—some of which remain unexplored to this day."

"Wow, cool. Let's check it out!" Jami said.

"Yes, yes, let's go!" the impatient Khalif seconded.

With that, they entered the last remaining intact ancient wonder of the world.

CHAPTER 3

"I'm sorry that we can't give you the regular tour right now," Dan said to Jami, "but we need to be quick about it in here."

"No worries. I understand completely. I've given the same type of after-hours 'tours' to my friends at the zoo I work at before, so I know the feeling. Besides, being inside any part of the Great Pyramid is plenty awesome." She looked around at the massive stone block walls. "So cool!"

"Even cooler," Khalif felt the need to point out, "is that many think it still contains untold treasures of incalculable worth!"

Dan couldn't hold back his sarcasm. "Somebody must have calculated that it was worth it to fund an expedition to go after them."

Khalif gave him a knowing stare as they walked down a narrow passage constructed of solid stones, including the floor. "Yes, well ostensibly, the expedition is for scholarly purposes, to advance humankind's understanding of our shared ancestors' wondrous creations," he said, waving an arm about the interior pyramid space. "But I get what you're saying. They can do that *and* make a profit for themselves."

Rashid nodded, before adding, "And perhaps we can make a profit for ourselves, if you're right about there being something unexplored and valuable down here. I personally find that hard to believe, though. As tour guides, we have not only never seen, but not even heard of it." He held up his hands in a mock gesture of self-defense. "But we'll see! Maybe I'm wrong!"

Dan stopped up ahead of them at another wrought iron gate meant to restrict access to certain areas of the Giza plateau complex. "Here's the Osiris Gate."

"Osiris Gate?" Jami walked up next to Dan and stared through the bars at the dark space that lay beyond.

Dan removed a keyring from his pocket and flipped through the keys while saying, "Rashid, you have a flashlight in that pack? You know how it is down there."

"Actually, I don't really know how it is down there, since it's not part of the tours, but I do know that there is no artificial lighting and so it is completely pitch dark." He started to take off his backpack to get the light and then paused. "How do *you* know how it is down there, may I ask?"

"Had a fun night a few months back. Had nothing to do with looking for artifacts or anything like that."

"Well then, what were you doing down there?" Rashid pressed.

Dan shook his head and laughed while his key clicked in the lock. "Having fun, Rashid. You know, with members of the opposite sex. You should try it sometime."

There was some guffawing, but Rashid was quick to recover. "At least I don't need the seventh wonder of the world to get laid!"

"No need for the seventh wonder when you've got the eighth wonder right in your pants, am I right?" Khalif started to laugh before he finished the joke.

"*Ahem*....boys?" This from Jami, who stood with a hand on her hip looking from one man to the other.

Dan, knowing that Jami might be starting to think Dan was using his access to the pyramid to charm yet another woman, decided it best to change the subject.

"Okay, enough you clowns, How about you step through the gate."

"My apologies," Khalif offered. "Clearly we are not used to being ourselves in the company of such a beautiful woman."

"That's because they have to cover their faces where you're from," Dan said.

"Not really," Khalif defended. "Well, the Emirate women, yes, but not the tourists. They—"

"Can we please get on with this?" Rashid flicked on a small but powerful LED flashlight before walking into the shaft entrance. Khalif eagerly moved through the gate at a near trot, while Dan closed the gate and made sure it was locked once again, leaving no trace of their entrance. Or so he hoped.

But then they heard voices.

"Hey, who's down there?"

"Let's go!" Rashid hissed. "I'm not going to lose my job over this! I can't just fly back home like you, Dan. This *is* my home. I cannot lose my job. Tell us where to go!"

"This way." Dan walked at a brisk pace to the center of the square room, where a smaller square opening was set in the middle. "Down here, follow my steps exactly—do not fall, it's high!"

With that warning, Dan walked down an inclined ramp set into the side of the inner square that switchbacked all the way down into the darkness. When Rashid caught up to him, which wasn't long, his light beam illuminated a stone tile floor perhaps fifty feet below. Dan walked down in a descending square pattern. The others followed suit, Jami right behind him, though she tottered a bit in her pumps, then Rashid who shone the only beam, and lastly Khalif, whose face belied the mixture of excitement and fear they all felt.

Dan had just begun his third square cycle downward when a powerful search beam, one both Dan and Rashid knew to be a full-size mag-lite similar to the ones cops used that could double as a club when the need arose, bathed the upper floor of the square chamber in harsh white light.

They heard male voices talking loudly above, in Arabic, and then came a shout, in English. "Stop! This area is off-limits. It is very dangerous! Come back up immediately or face arrest!"

The words were repeated in Egyptian, an indication to Dan that they didn't know exactly who they were dealing with, for which he was glad.

Dan picked up his pace as much as he dared, given the twelve-inch platform on which they had to make their way down. To fall from here meant probable death and certainly very serious injuries, given the stone floor forty feet down.

"Go, go, go!" Khalif quietly huffed to no one in particular as he pedaled his feet around the descending squares, his right hand tracing the stone wall like a surfer in the tube of a big wave. About halfway down, the bright light from above shone directly down on them. "Halt, by order of the Egyptian Ministry of Antiquities! You are in grave danger!"

"Don't stop!" Dan reiterated in the face of the renewed command. The harried quartet continued their precarious descent. Jami snapped a pump strap. She kicked both shoes off and they fell through the air until they clattered on the stone floor, now about twenty-five feet below. She continued hugging the wall, barefoot, with Dan about ten lateral feet ahead of her.

That was when Rashid slipped and fell, managing to save himself from dropping the rest of the way down by snaring the edge with the fingers of one hand. Being last in the procession, he had no one behind him to see it, and the others continued on for some ways until they heard him calling out. Khalif was directly in front of him but his considerable bulk made it impossible for him to turn around on the narrow ledge. He faced the wrong way—toward the wall—to be able to assist Rashid by grabbing his hand and pulling him up. Jami had no trouble turning around but was roadblocked by Khalif's body.

"I'm falling!" Rashid said.

Then, from above, a booming male voice: "Your location has been noted. You are being tracked. Come back up immediately or be prosecuted!"

Dan froze on the narrow shelf just as he was about to make the turn onto another square side. He looked back and saw Jami trying to help, barefoot and blocked by the hefty Khalif. *She's having one hell of a night*, Dan couldn't help but think. *And so are we all.*

Rashid's fingers slipped from the ledge and he fell. Dan watched him drop and any hope he had for a smooth landing was instantly dashed when he heard a crack followed by Rashid howling like an injured animal, which at that point he absolutely was. With silence and stealth out the window, Dan called out to the others, "Move it--to the bottom—safely but fast, let's go!"

"Surrender!" came the order issued from above. Dan wanted to glance up to see if they were coming down after them, but didn't want to risk being blinded by the light beam and losing his night vision, so he just kept moving. What at first had been an awkward sidestepping motion was now a practiced and smooth specialized gait that moved him efficiently along the narrow precipice. His concern for Rashid was beginning to interfere with his clear-headedness, however, since the agonizing moans echoing throughout the shaft shattered his concentration like an armor-piercing bullet through medieval chainmail. He did his best to block the external things—Rashid's injury, their pursuers, how Jami might be taking all of this—from his mind so that he could keep moving. He knew that if he stalled, Jami and Khalif's resolve would start to crumble. They would all be caught like deer in headlights, one of them roadkill. For the first time since this little adventure began, Dan began to question whether it was worth getting his bar tab paid.

Too late now ran through his head and he kept sliding his feet along the edge, tracing squares lower and lower while Jami and Khalif did their best to follow. Somehow in the back of his consciousness he registered that something was different about the walls themselves as he drew nearer to the bottom level. Now he discerned various patterns etched on them. As he wound down and around, he could make out a variety of animal figures—maybe a goat here, and a falcon there, and was that a lion? He had no time to really make any true sense of it, and the only reason he could see them at all was because Rashid's flashlight had come to rest on the floor against his broken body, pointing up.

Dan felt no sense of relief on reaching the bottom. If anything, he was even more pressured to reach Rashid now that he could see him lying there crumpled on his side, clutching a knee with both hands, writhing in obvious agony.

"Rashid, how bad is it?" He rushed to his friend's side and knelt. In the dimness he couldn't see any obvious damage, but it was plain to see that the downed man was making no attempt at getting up. Meanwhile he could hear the clamor of Khalif and Jami making their way down the ledges, with the authorities still hollering down at them to stop. He had no idea what he was going to do. They still had a long way to go to get to the new dig site. He hadn't anticipated anything going this far wrong. The squares weren't that hard to walk if no one was chasing you. Now he was beginning to regret making it known that he could lead the way to the site. He'd even taken a form of payment to do so, meaning that he was profiting from this, which would make things even worse for him in the eyes of the law.

"It's bad. I'm sure I broke a couple of things. I don't think I can walk."

"You don't need to walk. I'll take you. Let's go, we've got to move on."

Rashid sensed the transfer of the balance of power between them and glared ever-so-slightly. As a more senior guide and native Egyptian, he had always been the leader in their relationship until this point. But now he had no choice.

"Okay." He let the American hook his arms under his and pull him to his feet. He winced and grimaced and gritted his teeth with the pain but did not allow himself to scream. By the time Dan had him in a position where they were ready to move forward, Jami and Khalif had completed their descent of the squares and joined them in the middle of the stone floor.

"Where do we go from here?" Khalif gasped, looking around with his hands on his knees.

Without hesitation, Dan pointed to a narrow, hallway-like exit. "That way. It leads to the second portion of the Osiris Shaft." He eyed the flashlight, still somehow clutched in Rashid's hand, and took it before handing it to Khalif. "Let's move. Khalif, you take this and go first with Jami. Wait for us in there at the top of the next shaft. I'll bring Rashid."

Khalif and Jami took off to the passage while Dan and Rashid began a slow hobble. Meanwhile, from the noise of their pursuers it became clear that they were descending the ledges after them. Dan said to Rashid, "I know you're in pain, buddy, but we need to move kind of fast, okay?"

"Oh…" He grunted as he took the first step before finishing the word, "—kay."

In the last of the artificial light before Jami and Khalif disappeared into the corridor, Dan caught a glimpse of the fat smear of blood Rashid left on the stone tiles, clearly marking their progress. He had no time to clean it up, for that would mean setting Rashid down and picking him up again, something he wasn't sure they would even be able to do. His only saving grace was that he knew the entrance to the new site was difficult to find, and yet he knew exactly where it was. Leading to it was a rubble field that would not retain the blood smears in such an easily traceable manner. While thinking these tactical thoughts, he continued dragging Rashid until they found themselves inside the corridor. Up ahead they saw the light held by Khalif. It moved erratically, as if being guided by an unsure hand.

"Hieroglyphics!" Rashid panted, eyeing carved inscriptions on the wall for the fleeting seconds they were illuminated by Khalif somewhere up ahead. "We'll have to check them out later." Dan dragged the Egyptian along, noting that he thought he could see bone sticking through his ankle. He hoped he was wrong, but given the amount of blood, he didn't think so. He had no idea what he was going to do and considered giving themselves up to the authorities behind them. Nothing down here was worth dying for, though he was aware that many over the centuries and in recent decades had done exactly that. The lure of riches, the siren song of discovering tangible historical connections--whatever it was, Dan knew it had caused many people to abandon reason in their pursuits.

They emerged from the corridor into a new chamber. It was basically a smaller version of the last, complete with a square opening in the center and no other visible exits.

"Another stepwell leading down," Khalif said, confirming Dan's suspicions.

"This one is smaller, though," Dan said. "Let's go. At the bottom is where the site is."

"Are they still coming?" Khalif asked, looking back toward the corridor.

"Yes," Dan snapped. "Don't shine your light this way, please."

"It's my light," Rashid for some reason felt the need to remind them.

"Don't shine *any* lights this way. Yes, they are still coming for us. We need to go down there right now." He continued his awkward half-carry, half-drag of Rashid until they reached the center of the room.

"What is this place?" Jami asked, showing interest in their unique surroundings at precisely the wrong time.

"Osiris Shaft, Level Two is what I call it, but there's no time to explain now." Dan pointed to the concentric square ledges leading down into darkness. 'Let's go see Level Three."

Khalif led the way with the flashlight while Jami followed closely behind him. Dan and Rashid paused at the edge. Rashid shook his head as he eyeballed the narrow ledge.

"No way I can do it," he said from behind tightly clenched teeth.

Dan addressed Rashid with what he hoped was an appropriate level of seriousness. "Look, Rashid, maybe we should just get you some help. I know you don't want to lose your job, but you're hurt bad."

"If I lose my job, I lose my health insurance. It's not that bad. I'll walk it off." He even managed a feeble grin with the joke, but Dan didn't see the humor in any of it.

"Rashid, it's not something you can just walk off. The bone needs to be re-set."

"Well like I said….insurance."

Dan looked down the tight stepwell and shook his head. "No way can—" His eye caught an object in the light beam held by Khalif down below as he aimed it up. A rope hanging from a scaffolding of some type that had been constructed in place to aid an archaeological dig effort.

"Maybe we can lower you down, without having to walk along the edges. Hold on…" Dan set Rashid down on the edge of the opening and moved to the scaffolding. He noted that a decent length of manila rope was coiled and hanging from one of the scaffolding bars. It was tied to the bar from one end, so he quickly undid the knot and pulled the rope free.

"Nice and long," he said, running back to Rashid.

"That's what she said."

"Your voice sounds almost as weak as that joke, buddy. Just take it easy and let me rig up a harness to lower you down there."

They could hear the scuffle of footsteps now somewhere behind them, accompanied by inaudible conversation. Dan wrapped the rope around Rashid's midsection several times and brought an end under each arm. "I'll stay up here and hold the rope in place while you get lowered down to Level Three. Here we go. Do your best to stay quiet."

Dan planted a shoe on one end of the rope and held the other so as to let out slack while he lowered the injured man deeper underground. He began paying out slack and then heard Khalif's voice from down below: "This is incredible. My God!"

"Shhhh," Dan reminded him. He recalled the first time he'd seen Level Three of the Osiris Shaft and so he was empathetic with the reaction. Nevertheless, he was hoping that at a certain point the descent would be too much trouble for their pursuers to bother with, and so they didn't need to make tracking them any easier.

Rashid, for his part, was silent during the descent, being that his upper body was uninjured and he had one good leg that he used to bounce off the wall on the way down. A small miracle, Dan thought, but one he was glad for, nonetheless. Though tiring quickly of holding the rope, Rashid made good time and before Dan's muscles gave out, the Egyptian was planting his good foot on the solid stone tile of Level Three.

Up top, Dan began the same sideways slide he had used to negotiate the larger stepwell, this time proceeding even faster. He knew it was unsafe, and after witnessing the gruesome injury Rashid had sustained doing the same thing, he couldn't deny that it gave him pause, and yet he didn't want to be caught by the authorities. Spending the night—the next week, month?—in an Egyptian jail while waiting for a court date wasn't appealing at all compared to hooking up with Jami for an adventurous last night in Giza before catching a plane home tomorrow. He told himself to stop thinking about Jami—without his full concentration there were too many unpleasant ways that things could go wrong, not limited to falling and breaking something or simply getting lost. Not to mention what he was going to do if the authorities actually did follow them all the way to the dig site entrance. They were almost there, after all.

By the time he drifted out of these distractions in his head, he was staring at more elaborate hieroglyphics and cave-style paintings on the wall, now illuminated by the flashlight on the Level Three floor. He saw fearsome predators—was that a saber-toothed cat here? A wooly mammoth being speared by men there? Sea creatures, too—a giant fish— probably a shark, lunging after a capsized reed boat, its crew flailing their arms as they fell into an angry sea.

Dan's gaze did not linger on the ancient art as he negotiated the descending right angles. On seeing he was ten feet from the floor, he dropped the rest of the way, landing in a controlled crouch with an accompanying loud slap as his soles hit the tiles.

Looking around, he dimly recalled the surroundings but was embarrassed to admit that much of it was new to him since he had partaken of certain libations on his previous visit. All around them were jars of red clay and various other pottery.

"This is so amazing!" Jami said, eyes wide as she approached him. "I can *feel* the history in here! And what are those?" She indicated two large oblong objects occupying a good portion of the available floor space.

"Those are sarcophaguses," Khalif answered. "I do not think we should touch them. They may still contain ancient, mummified bodies."

"Do not touch anything," Dan said, a little louder than he needed to because that was something he wouldn't mind the authorities overhearing. He stared into one corner, confused, while the others all pointed to the obvious: a section of floor against the wall that had been opened up to expose a tunnel leading downward. Barricaded with boards and tape reading "Ministry of Antiquities," it also was festooned with

KEEP OUT, AUTHORIZED PERSONNEL ONLY signs, as well as SANCTIONED ARCHAEOLOGICAL DIG IN PROGRESS.

"So this is the site of the Prince's dig?" Khalif said it more than asked, though he looked to Dan, who nodded without turning his head to look.

"Dan?" Khalif prompted.

"Yes, that's it. I'm sure of that. Through that tunnel is who knows what? Perhaps the Hall of Records?"

"Then why are you looking over there?" Khalif asked, pointing to the corner Dan was staring at.

After a pause, Dan responded. "Because that opening wasn't there before."

"A new dig site?" Rashid asked, breath ragged.

Dan shook his head. "No, it looks awfully rough and unfinished to be any kind of organized excavation."

"Then what is it?" Jami asked, inching closer to the mysterious aperture in the stone construction.

"If I didn't know any better," Dan said, also moving closer to the opening, "I'd say it looks like it was caused by the earthquake."

CHAPTER 4

The four of them surveyed the second, smaller opening in one of the Level Three walls. Unlike the blasted opening that clearly was engineered recently, this break in the wall, while also recent, was messy. Broken blocks and bits of rubble were strewn about the floor beneath the hole, and the outline of the hole itself was irregular and jagged. Khalif shined the light beam into the opening. Inside was a small chamber or large tunnel, equally strewn with rubble.

And then the voices from above came again, in English: "We know you are down there! Remain in place until we reach you! It is dangerous to be in this area. Do not enter the dig site that is marked unauthorized!"

Rashid appeared concerned. "It seems like they know an awful lot about the new site." He turned to Dan. "You said you've been here, to this very spot before."

He nodded. "Yes, except *that...*" he pointed to the jagged opening, "...wasn't there."

Khalif gave a hurried nod to show he'd heard what was said. "Yes, but were you pursued this vigorously?" He cocked his head toward the approaching commotion.

"No, but perhaps we weren't seen when we entered. I have no way of knowing."

Khalif shrugged. "Wouldn't surprise me if the Prince bribed the local authorities for additional security. This doesn't seem like an area a lot of people would venture down to."

Rashid managed to speak up. "The Hall of Records is a powerful draw. It is rumored to hold many antiquities and secrets that define ancient Egypt itself."

Dan addressed them all while pointing with one hand at the jagged aperture, and the other at the opening dug by the United Arab Emirates Prince's archaeological team. "Lady and gentlemen, it appears we have a choice: The Hall of Records through Door Number One, or the Complete Unknown behind Door Number Two. What's it gonna be?"

"Before we go anywhere, does anyone have any pain medicine?" Rashid asked through clenched teeth.

Dan and Jami immediately shook their heads, but Khalif began searching his pockets. "I think I have some Tylenol, I know that's not much, but...."

Rashid nodded eagerly. "Anything, please. The pain is growing unbearable."

"I'm not sure you want to take those," Dan said. "They're blood thinners, and you're bleeding heavily already. It'll just make you bleed easier."

"What are you, a doctor?" Rashid asked with a glare.

"No, but it's just common sense. Take them if you want. If he has them." They all looked to Khalif, who pulled a small white bottle from his pocket.

Dan shook his head. "A flask, some pills—what else do you walk around with?"

"Not a flashlight, apparently," Rashid pointed out, "since he needs mine."

Khalif leveled a hard stare at Rashid while holding out the Tylenol bottle. "I'll trade you these for your light, how about that? Deal?"

"Deal!" Rashid barked. Khalif tossed him the bottle, which he caught before promptly removing the lid and pouring some capsules into his palm. He gobbled them down dry and pocketed the bottle.

"Back to the question at hand," Khalif said. "I say we check out the brand new passage. Who knows what it holds, and we will not be trespassing on or interfering with a sanctioned dig."

Suddenly a rope came into view. Dan's first impression was that a man was rappelling into the chamber, but in fact an electronic device of some kind dangled from the end of the line.

"I think it's a camera," Jami said.

Dan started to move. "In here, let's go, we don't want them to get our pictures!"

"Or start spraying us with poison gas. Who knows what it is?" Khalif added.

Dan stooped to fit beneath the jagged entrance to the unknown tunnel. Jami followed, and then Khalif. Rashid got down on his hands and knees and crawled into the opening, dragging his bad leg behind him like a wounded animal. It became abundantly clear to Dan that this passage was raw, freshly created by natural forces. This meant it would be unexplored, as it consisted of jumbles of loose rock with zero evidence of engineering to prop up the tunnels such as buttressing, scaffolding or structural reinforcements of any kind, which were common in other excavation areas.

He paused to turn back to the others. "I need the light up here."

"Careful, don't drop it. There's a lot of nooks and crannies in here for it to disappear forever into." With that warning, Khalif passed forward his light to Jami, who then pressed it into Dan's waiting hand. He thought he felt her fingers linger perhaps a second longer than was necessary in order to pass the light, and wondered if he was reading too much into it. He aimed the beam ahead of him and the shock of what he saw changed his thoughts completely. About ten feet ahead, the jumble of rock dead-ended except for an opening in the floor that led to a down-sloping rock pile. At the bottom of that, Dan could see what appeared to be an impressive subterranean vista. The single flashlight didn't allow him to be certain of what he was looking at up here, but it looked like a very large space lay below. To reach it, they would have to negotiate the rock pile, but while not easy, it looked doable even considering Rashid's injury. He waited for the others to catch up and then presented them with the view.

"Water? Is that water?" Jami asked in disbelief.

"Sure looks like it," Khalif said.

"It is water," Dan said. "Want to check it out?"

"I think we have to check it out," Rashid said, through clenched teeth. "They're coming!"

"You guys start in this way, I'm going to throw them off our trail a little bit." Dan backed out of the passage and paused, looking for the camera or whatever device it was dangling from the rope. But the rope itself was no longer there. Reasonably satisfied he would be unobserved, he bolted back over to the other exit from Level Three, the opening to the Prince's dig site. He pulled off the RESTRICTED KEEP OUT tape and left it on the ground before returning to the newly opened passage and rejoining the others inside.

"Let's get down there. Hopefully, I threw them off the trail a little bit."

"This is really weird." Rashid crawled slowly but steadily forward to the edge of the jumbled boulder passage. "I could not have imagined such a large unknown chamber beneath the Sphinx!"

"Let's check it out." This time, Dan gave Khalif the light and told him to take point so as to put the light source which could give them away to their pursuers as far away as possible in case Dan's ruse didn't work. Dan brought up the rear so he could help Rashid, with Jami in between them and Khalif.

They picked their way down the jumble of rock—very slowly, especially Rashid. Dan glanced at him when Rashid wasn't looking and thought that he looked terrible. He could not understand why he refused medical assistance but maybe it was worse than it looked. But he was still bleeding some, and his skin pallor had taken on an ashen appearance when he shined the light directly on him, which he didn't like to do for fear of making Rashid self-conscious about his injuries.

Downward they went. Dan was pleased to see that Jami appeared to have no problems at all, easily negotiating the rocky obstacles in her path, even though she was now barefoot. *Our crew is all right for now*, he thought. Yet a darker concern lurked. The opening to this area had been created by that night's earthquake. He was certain of that. He only hoped that the overhead environment hadn't been rendered unstable enough to pose a cave-in hazard. Shining the light up, he saw nothing that was obviously unstable and ready to come down on them, but it was hard to tell since the ceiling here was that of an irregular, natural cave formation rather than the smooth-stoned, repeating pattern construction of the ancients.

The most pleasing thing about the descent of the jumbled boulder passage to Dan was that they no longer heard signs of their pursuers. That, Dan thought, and the dawning realization that there was not merely some water down here, but a lot of it. In fact, as he reached the bottom of the jumbled passageway and cautiously shone the beam out into the great subterranean space that lay before them, he'd have to say it was a lake, and a sizable one at that. A lake with a shoreline of cluttered boulders on this side, but what looked like flat, level ground on the opposite shore. That shore seemed to feature smooth, graded stones and what could be, at least from this distance in the dim light, a human-made edifice of some kind.

After much effort, the group assembled on the shore of the subterranean desert lake with Rashid's bad leg propped up on a rock. The injured man speculated that the source of the water was from the same water table that fed the mighty Nile River.

"Longest river in the world, right?" Jami asked.

Khalif nodded. "It is the longest, but the Amazon is largest by volume."

"Let's focus, shall we?" Dan reminded them. "We need to get a game plan." He shone the beam of the flashlight around their new surroundings, slowly and deliberately illuminating the vast confines in which they now found themselves. A natural, cave-like ceiling loomed overhead, cathedral style, while the still waters of the lake reflected the light below. To the right and left, the lake lapped against the cave walls with no obvious features eliciting curiosity.

"Well I hate to say it," Dan said, "but it looks like anything of real interest is going to be on the opposite shore of this lake."

"Of course!" Rashid moaned.

"Or underwater," Khalif speculated, glancing at the dark, foreboding subterranean waters.

"So how the heck are we going to get to the opposite shore?" Dan pleaded, holding his hand up while looking across the lake. Underwater exploration was of course out of the question, so he focused on what they might be able to discover on the lake's shores.

A moment of silence transpired as the group pondered this. Jami said nothing, but broke the conversational lull by walking across the loose rock until she reached the water's edge. She bent over and put a hand in the water. "It's like my Mom's swimming pool in Ohio in the summertime," she declared, standing upright while wiping her hand on her pants.

Khalif made a face that suggested it wasn't so bad. "Could be worse," he verbalized.

Dan eyeballed him. "Are you saying you would swim across?" He swiveled his head and aimed the light beam to the opposite shoreline. "How far do you think it is?" Dan posed.

"I don't know, I left my laser range-finder at home," Rashid quipped, "but if I had to put a number to it, I'd say…about a hundred meters."

"So like about three hundred feet," he roughly converted for the benefit of himself and Jami.

"I can swim it, if you want," Jami said, with a shrug.

"Rashid?" Dan levelled his gaze at the crippled man.

Rashid eyeballed the lake before saying, "Once I'm in the water I should be fine. And the shore on the other side looks easier to get out on than this." He waved an arm at the jumble of heavy rock in which they found themselves.

"And you, Khalif?" Dan asked, turning his head.

"I'd like to check it out," he said while staring out across the lake.

Behind them, up the rocky incline, they heard human voices.

"They reached Level Three," Dan stated, realizing that they had probably pulled the rope back up with the camera on it in order to use it for rappelling down themselves. "Ready for a swim?"

"We'll all be wet on the other side," Khalif pointed out. Rashid indicated his pack. "We can each take our shirts off and put them in here, if someone besides me can hold it up out of the water while they swim."

Dan held out a hand. "I can do that." The other men took their shirts off and handed them to Dan, who stuffed them in Rashid's pack. He had expected Jami to remain fully clothed, but she surprised them all by pulling her top over her head to reveal a stylish black bra. She handed her shirt to Dan with a smile, turned, and walked to the water's edge.

"Looks deep," she said, pausing for a moment while the others made their way toward her. "Last one to the other side's a rotten egg."

And with that, Jami dove into the subterranean lake. "Oooh!" She couldn't suppress the outburst as her head broke the surface after coming up from her dive.

While she acclimated a few steps from shore, Dan and Khalif assisted Rashid into the lake until he was deep enough to float. "Too cold for you?" Dan asked.

The lakebed in the shallows consisted of a random array of flat stones and rock, like castoff building materials, angled this way and that. Due to the clarity of the water when viewed with the flashlight, they could plainly see that the bottom sloped off rapidly into an unknown deep none of them wanted to contemplate for long.

"You good, Rashid?" Dan asked.

"Swimming is much easier for me than walking right now. Let's get to the other side."

With that, the four of them began kicking into deeper water. Jami led the way with a confident yet quiet breaststroke, with Dan and Khalif flanking Rashid to keep a close eye on him. Dan held the light to make sure they wouldn't be separated, even though it meant that should their pursuers make it as far as the lake, they would easily be seen. Right now he couldn't hear any sign of them.

Quietly, they made their way across the lake. With Rashid injured and Dan able to swim with only one hand while he held the light and backpack above water with the other, the going was slow yet steady. The couple of times Dan shone the beam down into the water, he saw nothing but endless black. The closer they got to the opposite shore, the more intriguing the details they could see became. Hallmarks of classical architecture such as pillars or columns, and large expanses of smooth flooring provided tantalizing glimpses to what lay ahead.

About three-quarters of the way across, they spotted a disturbance in the water ahead of them.

CHAPTER 5

"What is that?" Jami cried out, now treading water, all thoughts of forward progress temporarily abandoned.

Dan, also treading, whirled around and faced the shore from which they had come, thinking that maybe their pursuers had caught up with them and were shooting at them. But they hadn't heard any shots and there was no one there. He turned back to the disturbance, focusing his flashlight beam on it. He squinted his eyes at the bright pinpoint of light amidst the ambient darkness and tried to discern a shape from it. All he saw was a lot of quick motion and some whitewater. Then a shape materialized just outside the light, where it was mostly shadow but still light enough to see a triangular form slicing through the water's surface.

The first word that popped into his head had the greatest likelihood of being the correct one, Dan knew. And yet, he didn't trust it, couldn't trust it because it made absolutely no sense.

Shark.

What? How could there be a shark somewhere under the Sphinx? And yet, Dan thought as he eyeballed the fin, there it was. The classic killer shark profile. He stifled the urge to yell "Shark!" at the top of his lungs and instead said calmly, "It's a shark. Keep moving toward shore, no splashing."

"Is this some kind of joke?" Khalif asked, fear evident in his shaky voice. "Because if it is, it's not funny."

"Does that look like a joke to you?" Rashid said, pointing to the now circling fish.

"Not a joke!" Jami said. "Bull shark."

"How do you know?" Rashid asked.

"Dorsal shape is right, for one thing. For another, this is freshwater. Not a whole lot of freshwater sharks out there that are this big, with that dorsal shape. I don't see how it could be anything other than a bull."

"Who cares what kind it is right now?" Khalif said. "Like Dan said, keep swimming—quiet! No splashes!"

Dan wasn't sure if it was because he wanted to explore the other side of the lake or if he was truly terrified of the shark, but Khalif stroked around the shark, which, while keeping its distance from him, also did not move out of the immediate area. Dan and Jami also began swimming.

As Dan's light caught the angle of the water just right, he could make out a reddish tinge to it and realized they were swimming behind Rashid. The Egyptian was bleeding badly, so Dan knew it had to be his blood they were swimming through. No wonder we're attracting sharks, he thought, moving as disturbance-free as possible away from the shark, which seemed to follow Rashid in a tightening circle.

Dan could only hope that what was in the water with them wasn't really a shark, that it was some other kind of fish, a harmless one. But then Jami had sounded so confident, and she was a zoologist, after all. He could hear her swimming strokes up ahead—hers and the louder Khalif's. He angled his light away from the water—maybe it attracted the shark—and trained it on the shore. They were close to it now, especially Jami and Khalif.

"Come on, Rashid, we're almost there."

Dan had just finished uttering the sentence when Rashid cried out in pain, or surprise, or both.

"What?" Dan said, already fearing and knowing the answer.

"Something hit my leg. The bad one."

Dan felt he had to see what was happening to Rashid, so he turned his flashlight back on the water. A flurry of fins and tails disappeared beyond the cone of light and into the deep. He didn't know if he should tell Rashid what he saw, or if it would make things worse.

"What was it? What do you see?" a panicky voice came from Rashid.

"Could be the shark, not sure. Keep moving toward shore. I got you, let's go." Dan grabbed a hold of Rashid's arm, up by the shoulder, with the hand not gripping the flashlight, which he now aimed on shore. Dan tried to make sense of the greater detail he could now distinguish, but his mind was silently reeling from what he had seen underwater. Rashid's leg had been feasted upon by sharks. He was certain of that. It now bled heavily, leaving a visible fresh trail of blood in the water. He distracted himself from the grisly sight and grim prognosis for his friend—how would they get him out of here in time to save his leg, or even his life?—by considering the source of the sharks and the reason for their being here.

This was freshwater. The nearest major source of freshwater was the Nile River, five miles away. He knew there was also a major lake nearby that used to be freshwater, but was now salt. Other than those two bodies of water, there was only the Red Sea, eighty miles away, and then the Mediterranean, about a hundred miles distant. He reasoned that the sharks must be coming from the only freshwater body of water, and the one that was closest—the Nile.

He called out to Jami by name. "Are there bull sharks in the Red Sea or the Med?"

"I don't think so. Maybe in the Nile? Hold on, we're almost there, need to check out some obstacles. We might need to wait for you to catch up to us with the light."

"Probably safest. We'll be there soon."

"I hope so," Rashid surprised Dan by answering. "I'm starting to feel dizzy. I'm afraid to feel my leg."

"Don't touch it. Just concentrate on getting to shore, then we'll take care of you, okay?"

Rashid didn't answer, but he kept paddling through the water with Dan's help.

Again, Dan saw no need to comment for fear of panicking not only Rashid, but also the others and even himself at this point, but there were definitely multiple sharks of considerable size in the water around them. And they were becoming increasingly agitated, no doubt fueled toward frenzy behavior by the powerful scent of Rashid's blood in the lake. Keep swimming, he told himself as he towed Rashid along. Slow, steady, no splashing. At least Jami and Khalif were right at the edge of the lake, hopefully shallow enough to be out of the sharks' way.

Suddenly Dan felt Rashid be pulled out from under him. Heard a gasp for breath that was cut short as he was dragged underwater. And then, even worse, he lost contact with Rashid. Dan swiped his left hand, the hand not holding the light, beneath the water's surface and gasped when his fingers brushed across a rough, sandpapery surface that he knew had to be a shark's hide. If the sharks were dragging Rashid under, he knew he had very little time in which to act. Rashid was down there with one incapacitated leg and weak from loss of blood before the sharks were even involved. He had to do something. He stuck his head beneath the water and opened his eyes. Straight down, nothing. But angled down out in front of him, a flurry of commotion. Swirling bodies, both shark and human. Rashid! But the tangle of flesh was spiraling farther into the depths. Dan had no more time to think about it. He took a deep, full breath while bending at the waist, kicked his legs up into the air, and then allowed his body weight and gravity to send him into the water's depths. The light was going down with him, not much choice about it. He hoped it would last long enough to at least locate his friend.

Dan kicked downward, fanning the water with one hand while aiming the light with the other. He could see the mass of swirling activity perhaps fifteen feet farther below, and descending. He kicked harder, scratched harder at the water separating him from Rashid. He knew he wouldn't be able to stay down here much longer. The exertion of simply getting here had worn him out. And once he had to surface, he knew that with Rashid being dragged even farther into the depths, he wouldn't be able to hold his breath long enough again. So this had to be it, he told himself. *You've got to pull him up now!*

His lungs were feeling the burn of not having enough oxygen by the time he reached the blurry form of Rashid's body. Bloody clouds in the water obscured Dan's vision, making it difficult to tell if Rashid was moving about under his own power. Was he already dead and simply being rag-dolled by the finned predators?

Unfortunately for Dan, the only way to find out was to dive a little bit deeper. As he neared Rashid, he thought he was close enough now that he would be able to grab him, but the sharks weren't dispersing. He knew it would be hopeless to try and stick his arm into the seething mass of aquatic marauders. He need a way to scatter them, even if just for a couple of seconds, so that he could safely retrieve Rashid. *Rashid*, he told himself, and not Rashid's body. *Rashid.*

And then he was screaming, out into the water, even though it was the dumbest thing he could do in terms of conserving what little remaining oxygen supply he had left in his body. *"Rashiiiiiiiiiiiiiiid!"*

He clenched his muscles in a fit of anger about what was happening, and then, quite by accident, his thumb pressed the flashlight switch hard enough to turn it off. He pressed it again to turn it back on, and noticed that when he did the sharks had changed position. They had scattered during the light outage. Encouraged, Dan flicked the light off and on again in rapid succession for a few more seconds. When he flicked it back on, he was excited to see a large enough gap in the water that was free of sharks for him to quickly dart in and grab Rashid. His left hand shot out. He gripped the troubled swimmer by his shirt and yanked him upward.

The movement dragged Rashid up, but had the consequences of simple physics to also pull Dan down. For now, Rashid was up and out of the thickest swarm of sharks. Dan took advantage of the lull and kicked toward the surface until he could continue hauling Rashid higher up through the water. He couldn't tell whether the man was still conscious. He didn't seem to be moving in a coordinated way. With only one hand free, and the other handicapped by having to hold the flashlight, Dan kicked and kicked. After a few seconds, scared that any moment now he would feel the sensation of razor-sharp teeth controlled by powerful muscles, Dan rapidly flicked the light on and off as he had done before, hoping it would still have the startling effect. He didn't bother to look down and check that it did, knowing that it would interrupt his upward progress. He just kept kicking up.

Dan's head was just breaking the water's surface when he felt Rashid's body tugged sharply downward. He clenched his fingers tighter on the shirt, rumpling it into a ball in his fist. He felt the opposition to his movement--the sharks grabbing Rashid, until the shirt started to rip. Dan pulled one more time, knowing he was about to lose his friend but having no other option.

He felt the resistance stop and then Rashid's body was rising up to the surface, pulled by his torn shirt. Dan gulped air in the most desperate fashion he had ever experienced. Never before had the cells of his body been so completely oxygen deprived. Even though his eyes were wide open, he was seeing weird shooting stars that he knew were not real, that were nothing more than the oxygen-starved cells in his brain dying off. For a moment he couldn't do anything except inhale air while he clung to Rashid's shirt, unable to hold Rashid's head out of the water until he himself had taken in sufficient air to avoid unconsciousness.

As soon as he realized he was still breathing, Dan turned his attention to Rashid, who floated face down next to him. He rolled him over and shone the light on his face. Eyes closed. "Rashid! Rashid, wake up." In the back of his mind he heard other voices, those of Jami and Khalif, but he was too fully focused on saving Rashid to pay them any mind. He was starting to think about in-water CPR, not that he was even trained in it, or if he should wait long enough to drag him up onto whatever land awaited them on this far side of the sub-pyramidal lake when Rashid's chest heaved and a plume of frothy water was ejected from his mouth.

"That's it, buddy! You got this, Rashid. Hang on, I'm gonna get you out of the water."

Jami was yelling to him now, louder than ever: "This way, right here!" Dan swept the flashlight beam toward the sound of her voice until her still wet form was visible in the light. Khalif walked up behind her, waving frantically. Dan veered to the right, dragging the still unmoving Rashid with him. Around him he could feel the water changing, becoming more placid, shallower. Even the color of it changed as the depth decreased, his light reflecting more of the hues of the underlying stone. For a split second, as he moved the hand with the flashlight into the water to be able to swim up onto an angled stone shelf, he saw a petroglyph on the underwater rock. A man running, it looked like, through a field or maybe some woods.

Then Dan's knees were hitting the bottom and he knew it was time to stop swimming. He knelt on the flat, inclined stone and pulled Rashid's inert but breathing body up onto the slab. Somewhere around him he could hear Jami and Khalif splashing through shallow water to reach him. "Is he okay?" they were both asking at once. But as the light beam passed over the shallows and Rashid's leg, they all knew the answer. Dan heard Khalif suck in his breath and Jami choke off a cry of surprised horror.

"He'll be all right once we get him out of here." The confidence Dan had tried to marshal with his voice was simply not there. Rashid's leg had been completely shredded below the knee. Dan lifted Rashid by the shoulders to move him, and made the mistake of shining the light on the wound. He got a detailed look at it before he turned away to vomit. He saw white tendons, bone, heavy flaps of red meat waving in the currents, barely attached to the leg, even bits and pieces of flesh wafting about in the water.

"We've got to get him out of here, to a hospital right now. Never mind getting busted for being down here. Shout for help--we want them to find us at this point." While Dan began dragging the still unconscious Rashid out of the shallow water onto the flat rock, Jami and Khalif yelled for help. Jami's voice was louder, Dan noted, but he had no doubt that the racket both of them made together carried for quite a ways. He was sure that if the security team was anywhere near the Osiris Level Three floor, that they would hear it.

But right now Dan's main focus was extricating the stricken Egyptian from the lake. He hauled him up the slab, sloshing water with his feet as he went. Jami and Khalif continued calling for help, their voices echoing off the lake. When Dan got Rashid to the top of the slab and the edge of the shore, the shouting stopped. Dan looked up, hoping that maybe they heard a response, but instead Jami and Khalif were staring open-mouthed at the grave extent of Rashid's leg injuries. And the leg was the only thing he could see, Dan realized. Hopefully, he had no additional injuries, but it was hard to tell with him still partly in the water and on his back.

Jami held her hands up to her mouth, her eyes wide open. "Oh my—" but she stopped herself.

"Help me get him over to where you are," Dan commanded, knowing he needed to give them something to do in order to keep them from losing their minds. "Are either of you wearing a belt? We're going to need to make a tourniquet."

Khalif reached for his waist and undid a belt buckle. Jami walked up to the edge of the slanted slab, the first piece of dry ground Dan would be able to reach. She asked Dan how she could help.

"Help me ease him onto the dry ground. As soon as we do, we're going to need that belt."

"Got it." Khalif pulled the belt free from his pants, held it out to show he had it and ran over to Dan.

"Both of you help me ease him off. On three: One, two…"

Dan hauled Rashid's upper body up to the edge of the slab, where he was supported by Jami and Khalif. Together, they eased him down to the ground. Dan was horrified to see a thick smear of blood covering the rock after he had cleared the slab. The three of them eased Rashid onto the nearest section of flat, dry ground. Khalif handed his belt to Dan who exhaled heavily as he tried to figure out where exactly to place it. The entire leg was so messy. The bleeding had to stop, though, so Dan bent down with the belt and reasoned that it was better to err on the side of placing the tourniquet too high rather than too low. He put his hand beneath Rashid's lower thigh to lift it, and felt raw meat separate there, so went higher until the flesh was intact. Then he encircled the leg with the leather strap. He cinched the belt tight and fastened it using the buckle.

Suddenly Rashid's eyes opened and he began to scream.

CHAPTER 6

"It hurts! Hurts! It…" Rashid's words trailed off into indecipherable wailing as his body was overcome with pain after Dan cinched down the belt.

"Should I loosen it?" Dan asked Khalif and Jami. Both of them shook their heads.

"It needs to be tight to stop the bleeding," Khalif said. Beyond the flat stones at the edge of the lake, they heard splashing. Looking into the shallows from where Dan and Rashid had just emerged, they saw a number of fins and tails disturbing the water's surface as the creatures thrashed about in search of the source of the blood that overwhelmed their olfactory senses.

Dan turned back to Rashid and placed a hand on his chest. "Rashid, listen to me." The wounded man continued to howl and thrash about. Dan patted him on the chest. "Listen to me, okay?" Rashid quieted the volume of his cries while making red-rimmed eye contact with Dan.

"You've been bitten very badly by sharks on your leg—the same one injured in the fall."

"Sh—sharks? But…"

"I don't know how they got here, either, but right now that doesn't matter. What does matter is that we need to get you to a hospital as soon as possible to save your life." He turned to the others. "Any sign of the authorities?"

At this, Khalif and Jami both turned toward the opposite shore of the lake and shook their heads. "Don't see anything," Khalif said.

"Don't hear anything, either," Jami added.

"Keep shouting for them. At this point, they would make things a lot easier for us," Dan said, before turning back to Rashid.

Jami and Khalif stepped a few feet away and continued calling for help. "Hey, can anybody hear us? Help! We need help!" Khalif delivered the message in Egyptian, while Jami used English, but the only reply came in the language of silence.

Rashid started to bend at the waist in order to get a look at his ruined leg.

"Don't. Save your energy." Dan pushed him gently back down with the hand on his chest.

"I just want to see how—"

"It's bad, Rashid. You don't need to see it right now. Just rest and we'll get you out of here."

Khalif and Jami shouted for help some more and then paused to listen for any results. "If they're there, they're not answering," Khalif said with a shrug, eyeing Rashid dubiously.

"Then we're going to have to get him out of here ourselves," Dan said.

Jami pointed to the sharks still churning the water to a boil a few feet from the stone slabs. "We can't swim back across the lake. No way."

"How are we going to get back, then?" Khalif wondered aloud.

Dan aimed the flashlight toward the odd structure further from the lake. "Maybe we can find something to build a raft out of."

"Well we need to hurry," Jami said. "He needs medical attention."

At that moment, the flashlight began flickering. Dan whacked it with his hand and it came back on steady, but noticeably dimmer than before. "We need to hurry anyway. This is our only light, and without this, it's pitch black down here." He cupped his hand over the light to make the point, and they were plunged into a solid, unrelenting darkness. "I don't think I need to tell you that our situation would be very difficult without this, so let's try to move fast to find what we need to get back across the lake. Keep calling for help, too."

Dan flicked the light back on, and if anything, its beam was even more feeble than before. "I think, to speed things, up, we're going to need to leave Rashid here while we three search the area for materials, and continue to shout for help. You never know, those people could—"

"You must take me with you," Rashid's voice was oddly clear and strong.

After a brief pause, Dan said, "Rashid, it will take too long if we bring you. The flashlight would burn out before we get back."

"Ra the Sun God will light our path."

Dan, Jami and Khalif all exchanged concerned glances. Talking behind his hand, Khalif said, "He's hallucinating, gone into shock."

Dan flicked off the light again. "Really? Ra the Sun God? Because this is how it's gonna be down here once these flashlight batteries go dead." Without the flashlight's beam, they were once again plunged into total darkness. "I don't see any other light down here so far, do you? Should we start practicing how to walk across these stones? Because this it what it's going to be like!"

"Dan, ease up, he's hurt bad." Jami put a hand on his shoulder, an attempt to calm him down.

"I know about this place." Rashid's chest heaved with his breathing.

Dan sighed heavily. "I'm just going to save battery power until we're actually ready to move. We can talk in the dark. So Rashid, what is it that you know about this place?"

"I know it to be a gateway."

"Gateway to what?" Dan asked.

"You must take me there."

Suddenly Dan turned the light back on, causing all of them to blink. "I'm sorry, but we don't have time to debate this any longer. I'm taking the light over there to see what's there. If I find stuff to build a raft I'll bring it back. The rest of you can stay here if you like, I'll be back soon, with or without supplies."

Khalif spoke up. "How about Jami, you stay here to watch Rashid, and I will go with Dan?"

Dan eyed Jami to see if she seemed unhappy at the suggestion they separate, but she merely shrugged and said, "As long as I can see your light, fine by me." She nodded to Rashid. "If we can no longer see your light, we'd get worried."

Dan nodded and then looked to Khalif. "Let's go."

The two of them started rock-hopping farther away from the lake, sloping upward toward the strange structure. The light beam bounced crazily about with Dan's movements, which involved an active combination of jumping, walking and climbing. "Be *careful!*" Jami called after them.

A little further on, Dan hauled himself up onto the smooth flat surface of a raised stone block, and took a look around. He aimed the light beam further from shore, where a structure of some kind formed a wall or end of the subterranean space the lake occupied. It was a long stone structure with what looked to be partially crumbled pillars or columns at regularly spaced intervals.

"That type of architecture doesn't look ancient Egyptian," Khalif noted.

Dan agreed. "Let's check it out. Careful, watch your step. Would be really easy to twist an ankle."

The two proceeded to navigate the jumble of massive stone slabs as they made their way toward the edifice. It was slow going as they had to climb down into narrow cave-like spaces and then climb up and out of them to trek across more smooth stone before getting to another gap that required climbing. The sounds of their feet and labored breathing were occasionally punctuated by Jami's calls for help across the lake, which went unanswered.

By the time they were close enough to the unknown construction to make out more detail, they could barely hear her calls. Dan noticed the flashlight was even dimmer now, and he had to try hard to push aside the fear that crept over him as he stared at the daunting distance across the piles of stones back to the lake shore.

"Which part should we check first?" Khalif wondered.

Dan considered their alternatives as he turned around to study the huge structure. He was mystified by its sheer size. It was very large, almost a football field wide, Dan guessed. It was one of the largest buildings he'd ever seen. The light was now too weak to illuminate much detail except for straight ahead of them, so Dan suggested they make their way to the central portion of the building that was right in front of them. They climbed up to a smooth stone ramp that led to a flat area fronting the building or whatever it was. They saw only smooth stone with no sign of vegetation this far underground.

"I doubt we'll find any trees, but look for anything we can use to float across that lake," Dan said as they walked up to the massive stone apron that fronted the edifice.

"We are really in trouble if we can't find anything. You know that, right?"

"I sure do. But don't give up. Let's look around."

Dan shone the light up toward the cave ceiling. It was hard for him to discern where the natural cave ceiling ended and the roof or wall, or whatever it was of the structure, began.

"I don't see any entrances that lead anywhere," Dan said, with a nervous edge to his voice. They both knew that once the flashlight died, there was a good chance they would die. Dan cursed himself for getting them all into such a terrible predicament. He told himself he should have stayed in the bar, had an ordinary last night on the town in Egypt and flown home tomorrow like he had planned. Bar tab be damned. He could have sent payment later after he got back to the States. Instead, here he was deep underground trying to figure out a way to survive.

"It's not much, but I see a crack, or some kind of break in the wall over there." Dan aimed the light to their left, near the end of its reach.

"Let's check it out." Khalif walked that way, eager to find a way out. He reached the spot first while Dan shone the light on it from behind. Dan knew from Khalif's excited outburst that they had found something out of the ordinary.

"It's more than just a crack! It's an actual opening, like a gap between two walls."

"Like it was designed that way," Dan said. He caught up to Khalif and shined the light through the break between the two walls. It was just wide enough for them to slip through standing sideways. Directing the light up, Dan could see that the channel between the two walls extended all the way up to the chamber ceiling high above. "The spacing between the walls is perfect all the way up," he noted.

Khalif nodded. "The same precision engineering with which the Great Pyramid itself was made. It's a very grand construction, whatever this is," he said, truly marveling at the edifice before them in spite of their rough situation.

"Let's move in. I'll go first." Dan slid into the passageway and sidestepped until he was deep enough in that Khalif could follow. The slightly larger man had a tougher time squeezing through, but he managed to fit.

"Good thing I only had a salad for dinner."

"I can see something up ahead. Looks like a wall."

"Great, all the way in here for a dead end?"

"We'll just have to see." They continued to slide through the narrow space. Dan thought it was in fact a dead end, until he was about five feet away, but he could see that it was the same type of tightly designed construction allowing for a new passage—just as narrow as the current one—that led off to the right.

"You feeling like a rat in a maze yet?" Khalif asked as he made the turn.

"Hopefully, the piece of cheese at the end is not a piece of cheese, but something we can use to get out of here." Dan picked up his sideways slide, now having very little faith in the feeble light beam. Even in the weak light, he could see that something about the walls was different here. Hieroglyphics began to appear, only a few at first, and then, as they traversed the narrow corridor, the walls became more richly decorated with them. Dan didn't pause to examine them, but the glimpses he saw appeared to show intimidating depictions of crocodiles in pits devouring men and their severed body parts. After the crocs there was a landscape of stick-like plants, with a stick figure drawn as being taller than them, and Dan realized it was a field of reeds or some type of vegetation.

He continued walking until the reeds ended, and then the drawings expanded to a full mural depicting a crowd of people apparently having a good time, hugging, dancing, sitting at a table piled with food—a picture of peaceful serenity. He was trying to make out more details when his light faltered and blinked....

And then stayed dark.

CHAPTER 7

It had been a while since Jami saw Dan's flashlight. Or any light, since it was pitch black on the subterranean lake shore. She called Dan's name again, screaming it at the top of her lungs while facing the direction in which he and Khalif had gone. No reply came.

"They can't hear you," Rashid whispered.

"How do you know?"

"They entered the structure. The Gateway to the Realm."

She was about to say something about equine fecal matter when she reminded herself that she was talking to a dying man. "What's that? How do you know what's down here if you've never been before?"

"I always knew it existed, but thought it to be inaccessible."

"But how do you know this is it?" She waved her arms at the open space around them and then laughed at herself for forgetting that in the darkness, Rashid could not see her gesturing.

"It has to be. Nothing else needs to be down here but the Gateway. I have arrived at where I belong. I am an Egyptian. My destiny is to die here and be forever at peace."

"Stop it. You're not going to die here! None of us are!"

"None of *you* are if we pass the test. But I am. I am surely going to die here. Soon. You must listen to me. I will tell you what you must do after I am gone."

"Please stop it! You're scaring me!"

Rashid's voice became both calmer and weaker at the same time. "I do not mean to scare you. But I am certain that my death offers all of you a way out. My heart is good. I know it is. I know I will pass the test, and by me being granted access to eternity, the rest of you, as my shepherds, will be granted the freedom to continue your journey in this life."

"Rashid, I think you're in shock. Just try to get some rest."

"I am about to rest for eternity. It is you who should rest for what lies ahead. When the time comes, you will know what to do. And I implore you to do it. It will seem unpleasant. Even grotesque. But you must do it."

"Do what? Must do *what*?"

But no further words came from the Egyptian's mouth. Jami scrambled around in the dark until she found the man's left wrist. Felt for a pulse. Again, felt for that weak pulsation that would indicate pumping blood.

Nothing.

* * *

Dan rapped the head of the flashlight with his palm in an attempt to get it going again, but that produced no effect.

"What happened?" Khalif asked, panic already evident in his voice.

"It's out." Dan gently tapped it against the stone wall in an attempt to get it to come back on, but this also yielded no results.

"Let me see it." Dan felt Khalif's hand groping in the darkness and brush against his arm. He pressed the now useless flashlight into his hand. "Sometimes if you just wait a while," Khalif said, "the batteries naturally recharge and we can get a little more light out of it, but let me try twisting the battery compartment...."

Dan looked around while waiting for Khalif to try things with the light, but there was nothing to see but total, absolute blackness in every direction.

"Well Khalif, we know we were moving to the right, sideways, so we might as well keep going that way while we wait and hope the light regains some power if we give it a rest."

"Okay." His attempts to eke some light from the device unsuccessful, Khalif pocketed it and began sliding through the corridor after Dan.

It was terrifying to proceed without being able to see. Dan knew all too well the dangers of moving around in or beneath the pyramids, even when one could see. This was beyond dire, Dan thought. He struggled to keep his emotions in check. Also, he thought about Jami and how he had promised not to let the light get out of sight. *Oh well, nothing I can do about that now*, he told himself. They kept moving, very slowly, since it took extra time for Dan to reach out with his hands and right foot to test the support of each new step.

"Keep going, we're doing okay," he told Khalif, who only grunted in response. They kept going for some indeterminate time that felt like eternity, until Dan's right hand felt the cool touch of smooth stone. He brushed aside a momentary wave of panic at having reached a wall—what if it was a dead end? His other hand had already been trailing along the stone to his left, so he knew that way was not an option. Then he extended his right hand out to the right...

Open space!

Yes. He started to move that way and then remembered that Khalif couldn't see which way he was going. "It leads off to the right, here," he called back. "You'll feel the wall in front of you, and then you turn right."

Dan continued on into the blackness that led in this new direction. He had taken only a few cautious steps when he felt another stone barrier in front of him. The fact that it came so soon startled him and he stopped moving. "New wall up here," he called back to Khalif. He heard his feet stop shuffling. Dan reached a hand out to the right and felt another solid wall. Slowly, Dan reached his left arm out to the left, knowing that if he felt a wall there, they had reached a dead end. But by the time his entire arm was fully extended, he had still not come into contact with anything. He slid his left foot to the left, and was baffled to feel open space below it.

"Something's different here," he warned Khalif, whose shuffling came to a stop a few feet behind him. "Got some open space *down* and to my left."

"Can you walk down it?" Khalif wanted to know.

"Checking it out now." Dan leaned back toward the solid ground while dipping his left foot into the black void. Still nothing….He was about to withdraw his foot when the tip of his shoe bumped into something solid. He put more pressure on it, testing that it was strong enough to hold his weight. Reaching out to both sides, he felt smooth stone walls on the fingertips of each hand. "Nowhere to go but down," he said to Khalif.

"Sounds promising. I think."

Again, Dan probed the space below with his foot and found smooth stone a few inches down. "Steps," he clarified for Khalif. "These are steps!" He planted both feet on the next step and then repeated the process several more times, descending a stone staircase far beneath the Sphinx in complete darkness. Dan lost track of how much time passed, but he counted each step he touched in case they had to come back up. He had just counted to fourteen when he realized something was different.

"Hold up," he shouted back to Khalif, who promptly froze in place four steps up.

"What is it?"

"We're at the bottom of the steps, all fourteen of them."

"Fourteen. That number is a multiple of seven. The number seven was held sacred by the ancient Egyptians."

"Okay. I'm not sure how that helps us at the moment."

"I'm not either, except that it lends further credence to the notion that we are inside an actual ancient Egyptian structure. Not some natural cave formation or archaeological dig modifications, but a true monument to the Land of the Pharaohs."

"I've got space to move to the right."

"Go slow."

Dan began shuffling his feet with his hands out in front of his face. He had only taken a few steps when he felt yet another stone wall. "Left turn," he called out, following the maze. He wound his way through a few more lefts and rights, with Khalif following close behind. After putting one foot in front of the other a few more times, Dan ran into another stone wall. He paused to reach out an arm in either direction, feeling a tingle along his spine as both arms came into contact with smooth stone on either side of him.

Khalif bumped into him, thinking he'd be a few steps ahead already. "What's the matter?"

Dan's voice had a flatness to it. "I've got stone on all three sides—in front of me, left and right."

"I knew it. We are doomed."

Dan took more time examining the apparent dead-end he had come to, to the extent that the total darkness allowed. He started with the wall in front of him, held his hands high over his head and placed them on the wall. He felt shallow indentations, as though the block was carved with drawings or artistic decorations of some kind, but nothing that made a difference as to it being an impassable stone obstacle. He turned ninety degrees and repeated the process on that wall with the same results.

"Right's totally solid, too," he told Khalif, who muttered something unintelligible under his breath.

Dan turned his attention to the left-side wall, knowing that his perfunctory sweep of the hands was all that stood between them and having to retrace their steps without having met success. He placed his hands high up on the wall, and again, felt the intricate, light carvings that perhaps indicated some kind of artwork. With his hands as high as he could get them, standing on his toes, and still feeling only smooth stone, he began tracing his hands lower and lower on the cut rock. He moved them out to the sides and back toward the middle as he moved lower on the stone. He pushed slightly against the stone with both hands as he readjusted his stance when his hands got lower. To his great surprise, he felt the wall in front of him move.

Not move, exactly, Dan thought, but more like wobble. The entire thing tipped just a little bit forward, and then rocked back into place. Dan took a step back, not wanting to crush his feet. Then he pushed again, and no doubt about it, he felt it tip—farther this time—and then fall back into place with an audible thud that echoed inside the stone labyrinth.

"It's not really a wall!" Dan said, breathless with excitement more than exertion. "It must be a large block that's balanced on the edge of whatever this is."

"Can you tip it over?" Khalif was so close to him that Dan could feel his breath on his neck.

"I can try. Back up a bit, I'm going to want to move back fast after I tip it. Not sure what's going on in the dark. Count of three, okay?"

He heard Khalif's feet sliding on the stone as he backed away. Then he began the count. ""One, two, three..."

Dan heaved against the stone with both hands placed straight out in front of him at shoulders' width. He needed to push with his legs as well, but was mindful not to lean too far forward lest the momentum carry him over whatever precipice this was along with the stone block. He felt the block begin to tip, then flexed his calf muscles some more before straining his shoulder muscles to push the object out farther. "Here goes!" he said for Khalif's benefit.

Dan felt the block reach the tipping point on whatever edge it had been perched on for who knew how long. He gave it a final shove and backed up, waiting for whatever impact was coming. He didn't have to wait long.

Almost immediately they heard a loud cracking noise, like glass shattering. Following that was the splash of water. And then, at about the same time Khalif started to tell Dan he heard water, Dan began to realize that he could see.

The light was dim at first, and not white. Dull greenish, but growing brighter with each passing second. Dan realized he could see roiling water beneath him, and something else, something shiny. A broken clear dome of some sort, Dan knew it must be the object that shattered when the stone block hit it after it fell. He looked but could no longer see the block; it had fallen into deeper water after smashing the plastic or glass or crystal dome or whatever it was that was perched atop a pedestal of rock as if waiting for the stone block to someday smash it open.

Looking closer as the dull green light blossomed into a bright chemical glow, Dan could see that a river of the gooey green substance issued out of the broken glass dome and flowed through the base of rock on which he and Khalif now stood. He looked out on their current surroundings, eager to see....to see anything at all, really, after so much time spent in absolute darkness. The view from the ledge on which Dan and Khalif stood was perplexing, to say the least.

Dan stared out at a pond-sized body of water, now glowing green, with a low ceiling, about a foot over Dan's head. The pond itself was contained within a smallish chamber, far smaller than that containing the lake they had traversed to get here. Strangely, although he could now see the artwork inside the walls of the corridors they had navigated to this place, the walls and ceiling of the pond chamber were devoid of human markings. But there was one thing above all about the new water chamber that set it apart.

"I don't see any other exits or passages in there," Dan said flatly.

"How is it lighting up?" Khalif wondered aloud.

"The stone block crushed that glass bubble that released some kind of chemical into the surrounding water, which might also have a certain mineral composition. Kind of like those glow sticks the ravers use in Cairo?"

"I call them chem-lights," Khalif said.

"Yes, exactly. Chemical lights, and to use them, what do you do?"

Khalif eyeballed Dan in the ethereal green light. "Shake them up and then break the little glass bubble inside the tube by bending it…."

"Exactly. Once the bubble breaks, it releases a chemical that mixes with the solution outside the bubble, creating light as a byproduct of that chemical reaction. I think that's what happened here." Dan waved an arm at the glowing pond.

"You know what, though?" Khalif asked, but then answered without waiting   for   a   reply. "It's getting dimmer in here again. Look." He pointed to the pond, which, while still glowing, no longer held the forceful illumination it initially had.

Dan pointed to the hole under the stone they stood atop. "I think it's because there is a current flowing this way, and it's carrying the chemicals with it. So the glow is moving…" He pointed back the way they came.

Khalif's eyes opened wide. "Which means that after it all runs out, it will be dark in here again. Forever."

Dan nodded while glancing about the pond chamber. "And I don't see anything else to do in here, unless you want to get wet." He nodded to the pond.

"No thanks," Khalif said. "I'd rather get back to the lake."

"Let's go."

They began walking back through the maze, retracing their steps. They hadn't gone very far when they realized they could still see. A millimeter-wide crack, engineered to consistent width, ran down the middle of the maze floor. Beneath it, the glowing green water flowed, partially illuminating the corridor above. It wasn't much, but it was enough light to be able to walk fast through the twists and turns without fear of smashing face-first into a block of rock. In fact, Dan remarked, it seemed as though they were matching the pace of the flowing water exactly, keeping up with the glowing green light as they made their way back to the lake.

It didn't take long to retrace their steps. Khalif was in the lead, and Dan knew something had changed when he heard him say, "Oh wow!"

They emerged onto the veranda-like platform that fronted the edifice they had disappeared into. Looking out on the lake, they saw the same green glow they had witnessed back in the pond. It was faint at this point, but still enough to discern some details about the vast underground cavern in which they found themselves. And the illumination grew stronger by the second, as the chemicals flowed into the lake from the pond.

The jumble of flat stones nearest the lake shore prevented Dan from seeing Jami. He called out to her, knowing she'd be terrified at having been left in the dark with the injured Rashid.

"Here! Over here!" Her voice was faint but just loud enough to give him a direction to home in on—to the left. He turned his gaze that way and saw the green-backed silhouette of Jami standing and waving her arms.

"I see you! Hold on, we're coming to you!"

"What's happening?" she yelled back.

"Not sure! Be right there!" Then, to Khalif, Dan said, "C'mon, let's run along this until we're even with her, then we drop down. With me?"

But the Emirati was already in motion. The two of them ran along the stone walkway, noting the increasing green tinge cast about the massive cavern. The glow continued to increase until it cast enough light to see the cavern ceiling, high above their heads. Though he had seen glimpses of it before with the flashlight, now that he could see it all at once, Dan's perception of the cavern roof now changed. It was slightly dome shaped and roughly circular, but its shape wasn't what Dan found odd. It was the smoothness. From this distance, at least, the entire chamber ceiling seemed to be perfectly smooth. There were no stalactites, no irregularities whatsoever that one might expect to see in a natural cavern.

"I see drawings." Khalif pointed to the ceiling above them. Indeed, elaborate artwork of some sort was etched or painted into the rock. It seemed to depict a field of tall grass.

"Let's get down to Jami and Rashid, then we can check things out more carefully." Dan wasn't sure if the broken jumble of rock that led down from the edifice was the same path they'd taken to get up here before, but it looked like they could use it to get down and it was in line with where Jami was, so he picked his way along it. The ambient light made him want to go too fast. He had to deliberately slow himself lest he trip and be seriously injured. He could feel Khalif's footsteps right behind him.

Reaching the bottom of the pile where the ground became the lake shore, he picked his way toward the water. The radiance from the lake itself continued to grow brighter. When he was about halfway to the water and could see Jami's silhouetted figure facing him, he shouted to her.

"How's Rashid?"

CHAPTER 8

"How's Rashid?" Dan yelled again, and again he received no answer from Jami. She was clearly within hearing range, so he tried something else. "Jami, are you okay?"

"I am. Just get here and I'll tell you. This is so weird!"

Dan and Khalif made short work of the remaining rock jumble to reach Jami and Rashid. The going was much easier with the ambient light and not having to hold a flashlight in order to see at all. Dan could see from Jami's face that something was definitely not right. He followed her gaze as her eyes shifted to Rashid's inert form, laid out on the same flat stone as where they had left him.

"Rashid?" Dan ran to him and knelt down on the stone while Jami slowly shook her head with tears streaming down her face.

"He didn't make it. I'm sorry! I tried. I tried but I couldn't…."

Dan felt for Rashid's pulse, just to make sure. Felt the coldness of the arm and almost recoiled, but moved his thumb around until he found the depression inside the left wrist where he knew a pulse should be. Nothing. Even by the dim, eerie green glow of the lake, he could see that Rashid's eyes were gone, lifeless, in a soul-departed, dead and disheartening way. He tried for a pulse at the carotid artery on the neck, too, just in case, but found no sign of life there, either. Accepting the reality, he put his fingers on the dead man's face and gently closed the eyelids. Behind him, Khalif muttered some sort of a quick meditation to himself before kneeling to join Jami and Dan.

"He said something before he passed," Jami said. Neither of the two men commented, figuring it was of no significance other than a personal prayer, probably in his native Egyptian.

"He told me that we are supposed to do something with his body when he dies. That if we do, and he passes the test—that's what he called it—a test—that *we* would be shown the way out of here, as his 'shepherds'."

"Did he say what we need to do?" Khalif asked, staring at the deceased.

Jami shook her head. "Just something about a test. Oh…." She took a deep breath before continuing. "And he said that what we had to do might be gross, but we had to do it anyway, for him to be happy in death, and for us to get out of here." Then she broke down and began to cry. "But he didn't say what. He didn't say *what*! He died right after that!"

Dan moved to Jami and put an arm around her shoulders. "It's okay, we'll figure it out."

"Figure what out?" Jami half-sobbed, holding her arms out, palms up. "I don't know what he was talking about. What if he was just dying and said some random stuff because he wasn't right in the head? What if—"

"Unfortunately, I think I know what he meant," Khalif interrupted. Dan and Jami both looked at him. He stared not at them, nor at Rashid's corpse, but at a stone block perhaps fifty feet away, to the right when facing the edifice, and farther from the lake. He pointed to it. "That block is inscribed. Come, let's leave Rashid here for a few moments and take a look, shall we?"

The three of them stood and made their way to the raised stone, which was a slab carved with inscriptions sticking straight up out of the jumble of tilted rocks. "Look at what the drawing shows," Khalif said. The three of them focused on the inscriptions, which appeared black under the green light.

"It looks like a scale," Dan began. "With a human heart on one side, and a…"

"A feather on the other," Khalif said, nodding. "I know what this is."

"The test of Osiris?" Dan said, incredulity creeping into his voice.

"You know it?" Khalif asked, turning his head slowly to eye the American man.

"Of course I know it, I'm a tour guide at the pyramids. But I thought…"

"You thought it was just a myth?" Khalif finished for him.

"Not only that it was just a myth," Dan began, "but I've never heard of any kind of physical manifestation of it. Maybe drawings, I guess."

"Well this is a drawing," Jami said.

Khalif eyed the inscription dubiously. "In this particular case, I think we are dealing with much more than a drawing." The others appeared confused until Khalif cocked his head to the right, toward the edifice. "You see that other stone block there?"

They eyed the rectangular block a few yards away. "That's a picture of a human heart on it," Dan said.

"Right," Khalif said, pointing in a different direction. "Now look at that block over there. What's drawn on it?"

"A feather?" Jami asked.

Khalif nodded. "Precisely. The feather of Matt, Goddess of Truth and Justice. Let's take a look up on top of it." He started moving toward the block but Dan stared at him open-mouthed without moving.

"Are you thinking there's going to be a real feather on top of that block?" he asked, voice nearly at a whisper.

Khalif stopped walking and turned around, levelling his gaze at Dan. "Indeed I am. Come, let's find out."

The three of them made their way to the stone block inscribed with a picture of a feather. Dan found a section on one side of the block where the flat stones were in upheaval such that he could use them to walk up the side of the block, which was about six feet high. When he could see on top of the flat block, he held his breath.

"There is a feather up here!"

"Don't touch it!" Khalif warned.

"I won't."

Jami asked, "Is it just resting on the top of it or what?"

"No, it's a large feather, like it's from a raptor of some kind like maybe a hawk. And it's set into a depression in the stone, with the quill inserted into a slot, I guess to hold it in place."

"So I guess somebody really wanted it to stay there for good," Jami said.

"Exactly," Khalif said.

Dan climbed down from the stone block. "Maybe we should see what's on top of the other one?" He nodded to the other block, the one with a human heart inscribed on its base. The trio made their way over to it, the entire lake chamber now lit by the aqueous green glow. They reached the other block and appraised it while walking around its perimeter. It, too, appeared as though it had been thrust upward from below through the concrete slabs.

"I'll take a look," Dan said, finding another group of slabs thrusting high enough for him to climb up and view the top of the block. He poked his head over the edge and stared for a few seconds.

"Well, what's up there?" Khalif asked.

"A hole shaped like a heart."

"Can you be more specific?" Khalif asked.

Dan stared at the top of the block for a few more seconds before answering. "I don't mean heart like an 'I love you' heart. There's what looks to me like an anatomically correct cutout-- an indentation in the top of the block-- for an adult human heart."

"And nothing else?" Khalif asked, face tilted upward.

"That's it. Smooth stone top, just like the other one, except for the depression in the middle, which the other one also had, except that one was to hold a feather, with an actual feather in it. This one has a shape for a heart, but no actual heart."

"So the heart's missing," Khalif said.

After a pause, Jami said, "It's not missing, as in, a heart used to be there and now it's not. We're supposed to provide the heart."

Both men turned to look at her, including Dan from his perch atop the block.

"Say again?" Khalif asked.

"I said, *we* are supposed to provide a heart. Now I think that's what Rashid was talking about."

An even lengthier silence ensued as all three of them digested this.

"How could he have known…." Dan started but cut himself off as the truth dawned on him.

"He was a native Egyptian and pyramid tour guide for many years," Khalif said. "He would be very familiar with the legend of the so-called Trial by Osiris."

"But how did he know, if that's what he was referring to, that the actual Trial would be found here?" He eyed Jami.

"He implored me to take him to the 'test,' he called it."

"The Osiris Test?" Khalif wondered.

She shrugged. "I don't think he actually used the word Osiris. But he did call it a test that, if he passed, would allow all of us to get out of here. And he said it would be grotesque."

Dan and Khalif made uneasy eye contact. "Then I do not think there can be any mistaking it," Khalif said. "Rashid was telling us to sacrifice *him*—after his death---or more specifically, his heart, so that he may proceed to the afterlife."

"Through the field of reeds and all that?" Dan asked, referencing the Osiris myth.

"Yes, he literally wants to have his soul judged as being Good, so that he can then enter the heavenly realm through the field of reeds, for all eternity." Khalif motioned to the art adorning the cavern ceiling, featuring a field of reeds.

Dan laughed. "Look, to do that, we'd have to literally cut out his heart and place it on the scale."

"I think that's the gross thing he was talking about," Jami said.

Khalif pointed to first the heart block, and then the one with the feather. "If we look at those as the two halves of the scale, well, the feather is in place already. We just need the heart to weigh against it."

His gaze fell to Jami, who instantly recoiled. "Don't look at me! I'm not cutting his damned heart out; are you crazy?"

Dan swallowed hard and then pointed out, "We couldn't anyway, even if we wanted to. I'm pretty sure none of us have a knife."

"Don't be so sure," Khalif said, walking to the heart block. He traced his fingers along the drawings on the side of the block. "It depicts a ritual, you see: Here, the heart of the deceased is being removed for placement on the scale. And you see the other side of the scale already has the feather against which the soul of the departed—in the form of his or her heart—will be weighed."

Khalif continued to walk around the block. "And on this side, we see the field of reeds. Through these, the recently freed soul, deemed worthy, is allowed to pass through on their way to the afterlife, or what many people today might think of as Heaven."

Khalif held up a finger. "But to get there, they first had to undergo the Trial of Osiris." He walked to another facet of the stone block. "Here we have the god, Ammit, with the head of a crocodilian, waiting to devour the heart if the soul is found to be heavier than the feather, meaning it is not pure, but laden with sin."

"Would any of us really pass that test?" Jami wondered aloud.

"We're sure hoping that Rashid will," Dan said.

"What, like some magic thing is supposed to happen by putting his heart on there?" Jami said sarcastically.

Dan pointed to the green glow coming off the lake. "Well, that happened, so, who knows what else is possible? Besides, it was a dying man's last wish, so, I think that's the least we can do for him."

"Not *we*," Jami corrected forcefully. "I am not cutting anything out of anybody. No way."

"But you're a zoologist, right? Surely you've done lots of dissections and stuff like that?"

"Yes, and even vivisections, where the animal is still alive," Jami confirmed. "But not on people. I'm not a doctor, though I took all the same classes as the pre-med students. Grosses me out. I won't do it."

"I'll do it," Khalif stated flatly, looking at them both.

"Do it with what? We have no knives or tools," Jami reminded them.

"Ah, but we do," Khalif said, smiling mysteriously. He brought his hand to the knife depicted on the block, part of the image where Anubis is removing the heart of the recently departed. Khalif ran his fingers along the outline of the knife engraving, and then inserted them into a crack along the outline. But they heard a grating sound as rock rubbed against rock, and then Khalif's hand came away with a formidable looking stone knife, perhaps a foot in length.

"I think we're meant to do it with this," Khalif said, holding up the instrument, ornately carved with flourishing designs including ancient Coptic Egyptian runes.

"Let me see that," Dan said. "It's solid?"

"It's the real deal. A stone knife, well carved and…" He paused as he reached Dan to run his finger across the blade. "Quite sharp." He handed the blade to Dan, handle first. Dan noted that the butt of the handle was inlaid with gold. He flipped it over and caught his breath when he saw the gold inlay on the intricate designs. The rest of the knife was the same type of stone as that which was used to construct the block in which it was installed.

"Only one side of the blade is gold, I wonder if that means anything?" Dan posed.

Khalif shrugged. "Probably only that they didn't want anyone finding it who wasn't supposed to, but they also wanted a ceremonial knife of great beauty and function, and so they put gold on the only portion of the knife that wouldn't be visible when embedded in the stone."

Dan and Jami stared at Khalif. "You sure seem to know a lot about this stuff," Jami said.

Khalif smiled sheepishly. "I did some research in preparation for investigating the Prince's new dig site. I know how to do my homework." He looked out across the lake. "I also know how to trust my eyes, and they are telling me that the light produced by the lake is not quite as bright as it was a few minutes ago. The chemicals are fading, or dispersing to somewhere else underwater. Either way, it means we'll be in permanent darkness before too long, so what do you say we proceed with this....ceremonial necessity?" He made direct eye contact with Dan.

"So I guess I'm the one who's been voted to literally cut out Rashid's heart?" He looked at Khalif and Jami in turn. Neither of them said anything.

"I found the knife," Khalif said, holding it out toward Dan, an offering.

"Oh, so I'm not holding my weight around here, is that what you're trying to say?"

"Dan!" Jami cautioned, but it was too late.

"Fine," Khalif said, stalking away from them and toward the dead body. "I'll do it myself." He stopped suddenly and whirled around, pointing the knife tip at Dan as if it were his finger. "But the next unpleasant thing we need to do, you're up."

Without waiting for an answer, Khalif turned around and walked to Rashid's body. He took off his own jacket and laced it over Rashid's face. "Look away if you must!" he told Dan and Jami, who did no such thing.

"I don't see how it can do anything, anyway," Jami said, starting to sound panicky again. "I mean really, you're going to believe some ancient myth instead of logic and common sense?"

Dan placed a hand lightly on her arm. "We might as well try. Rashid wanted it that way, and who knows? There does seem to be some sort of setup, what with the glass chemical holder back there, and these prepared blocks….let's just see what happens."

They heard a wet punching noise and looked over to see Khalif kneeling over Rashid's chest, both hands on the knife handle. "The surgeon has begun his work," Dan said sourly.

"*Arrrghhhhh*!" Khalif yelled as he began to rip and tear Rashid's chest cavity with the stone blade. As Dan watched, flecks of blood, appearing black in the green light, splattered Khalif's face, though his concentration didn't waiver. They heard various popping and ripping noises as the stone edge sliced and pried its way through tendons and bone in the inexperienced hand of its user.

"Don't hack it up too much," Dan cautioned. "It needs to fit exactly into that pre-made cutout."

"I know." The Emirati kept at it with dogged persistence, and some minutes later, with a guttural yell, Khalif raised his dripping hands high in triumph.

"Osiris, this is for you!" he intoned, rising to his feet with Rashid's heart in his hands. The dense muscle, the former powerhouse of the deceased man's body, continued to drip blood as Khalif began to walk with it over to the stone block dedicated to the heart.

"Osiris is the God of what, again?" Jami asked Dan as the two of them began to follow Khalif over to the block.

"Lord of the Underworld, Judge of the Dead, the Great Resurrector." Dan watched as Khalif reached the heart block and began to circle it, looking for the easiest way up. "Left side," Dan called over to him. Khalif went to that side and began to climb up using only his legs, the heart held out above him in both hands.

"I do not want to drop it!" Khalif said needlessly.

Dan ran to the block and also climbed the slanted slabs, supporting Khalif with a hand on his legs, pushing him upwards until he could get a knee over the edge and kneel on top of the block.

"Scoot over, let me get up there, too," Dan said. Khalif shuffled to one side on his knees until Dan took his place kneeling on the edge of the block. For her part, Jami was content to remain on the ground, observing what she could from below. Dan looked over at Khalif, who was staring at the heart-shaped depression in the top of the block, Rashid's heart dripping blood and fluids that splattered off the smooth stone.

For a moment, all was quiet save for the sound of their labored breathing. Then, Khalif inched forward on his knees, arms extended. He turned the heart over in his hands, trying to reconcile the shape of the depression before him with the messy organ in his palms. "I think it goes like this," he said after turning it this way and that a few times.

"Looks right," Dan concurred.

"Then here goes nothing, as they say," Khalif pronounced.

"Here we go," Dan said, louder, for the benefit of Jami.

Khalif leaned forward and gently dropped Rashid's heart into the stone receptacle.

CHAPTER 9

Dan watched with rapt attention as the heart took the form of the perfectly matched indentation on top of the stone block. It slid into place with a wet slurping noise, quivered for a second, and then was still, occupying the entire heart space with form-fitting perfection. Khalif raised his hands from the heart and reared back on his knees, away from the centerpiece of the stone block.

"Did you drop it in?" Jami asked from below.

"It's in!" Dan yelled back without taking his eyes off of Rashid's heart.

"What's supposed to happen?" Jami yelled, even though all was quiet.

Khalif inched back a little further from the heart and said, "According to the legend, if the person's soul was not pure, not good, that is to say it was full of sin, then those impurities would collect in the heart, making it heavy, weighing it down. If on the other hand, the person lived a good and virtuous life, his or her heart would be free of impurities and therefore light as a feather." He turned and pointed to the other block, some meters away, on top of which the feather rested in its place. "So to answer your question, we want Rashid's heart to be lighter than that feather over there."

"Then maybe we should have squeezed all the blood out of it first," Jami said from below.

Dan took over the speculation. "Too late for that now. But if these two blocks are each one side of a balance—not a scale but a balance—then they should indicate which side is heavier by—wait! We have to get off!"

"What?" Khalif asked, momentarily stunned.

"What if our bodies are weighing down the—" Dan did not get a chance to complete his sentence, for at that moment they heard a grinding sound and then the stone block on which they were perched began to sink down into the ground. Dan looked over at the feather block and saw that it rose higher above ground.

"Is it counting our weight along with the heart?" Khalif asked.

"I think it is," Dan answered. "I sure hope so, anyway, because if not, Rashid's heart is way heavier than that feather, that's for sure."

"Something's in the water!" Jami pointed out onto the lake.

"More sharks?" Khalif started climbing down off the block.

"I don't think so. It's one gigantic thing, look!" She pointed again out onto the lake, where a sizable ripple—almost a wave—was visible rushing toward their shoreline in the form of an iridescent green line. But behind it, Dan could see as he looked out on the lake while waiting for Khalif to get down, was something else. Something sizable. Something moving. Something alive. Not a shark, Dan knew, for it had no fins he could see. But it was so damned huge! And coming right for them, he noted, or to their position on the shoreline, anyway. It was a big lake, and yet the creature made a beeline for the stone block.

"C'mon, get down, I'm off of it!" Khalif urged. Dan took his eyes off the unknown beast and scrambled to get down off the block. He took one last look at Rashid's heart as he lowered himself. It didn't look any different to him. He could feel the rumbling of the stone block as it lowered into the engineered recess, and wondered what would happen when it was completely sunken in. He dropped to the ground and took several steps away from the block to make certain he was completely clear of it and that his body weight wasn't anywhere near it. He, Khalif and Jami grouped together in a semi-circle and watched as the heart block slowed its downward motion and ground to a halt.

"It stopped!" Jami said.

And then the rumbling, the grinding, began anew. "Here we go again," Khalif said.

But this time, the block was moving back upward. "It worked!" Dan shouted. "It worked! It was our combined weight that was causing the block to be too heavy."

"Apparently Rashid was not too bad of a guy after all," Khalif said, smiling. "Bless you, my friend," he added while glancing over at the lifeless corpse sans a heart. The block continued to rise back up until it reached its former position, its top even with that of the feather block, which itself had lowered back to its former resting position.

"That thing is not stopping!" Jami reminded them, pointing at the onrushing beast.

"Looks like a crocodile!" Khalif said.

Dan eyeballed the animal, noting the sinuous movement of a long tail, and what appeared to be two basketball-sized nostrils at the end of a meter-long snout. "That's a croc, all right," he said. "Maybe a Nile Crocodile? Biggest one I've ever seen, by far."

While staring at the mega-croc, they failed to notice that the balance was once again in motion, only this time, it was the other block that moved.

"That's not a regular Nile crocodile," Jami said, gawking at the crocodilian.

"What is it, then?" Dan asked. "Now that I look at it, it does have weird purple glowing spots on it."

Jami nodded. "Bioluminescent glow. If I didn't know any better I'd say it's closer to a *Sarcosuchus imperator*—a prehistoric super-croc."

"Great," Dan said, with drawn out sarcasm. "As if Nile crocs weren't bad enough, now we—"

"The feather block is dropping!" Khalif said. "It's lowering into the ground!"

They turned away from the oversized reptile to watch the stone block. "Excellent! That means Rashid's heart is lighter than the feather."

Dan was skeptical. "But how can that be? We know Rashid's heart is heavier than that feather. I saw the feather. It's a big feather, but still. No way does it outweigh that heart."

Khalif turned to him with an appeasing expression, hands held palms upward. "It was a symbolic ritual. I'm sure they have it counterweighted such that—"

"Guys? Hey—hey!" Jami pointed back toward the edifice, where chunks of stone were crumbling from up high and falling to the ground. "What's happening?"

They all watched as the massive structure began to fall apart, to crumble before their very eyes. Then Khalif whirled back around. "We can't take our eyes off the croc."

Indeed, the oversized reptile was almost to shore. "Where to?" Jami asked, voice brimming with panic.

Dan watched the lake. At first he thought the wave of water about to inundate the shoreline came exclusively from the croc itself, from the movement of the big animal pushing water in front of itself as it moved. But now he realized that the entire lake shore was experiencing the same overflow of water. "I think the lake level is rising. Overflowing," he stated.

The others looked out at the water. "Higher ground, c'mon!" Khalif turned and started to run for the crumbling edifice. Jami and then Dan followed. They ran and climbed over blocks and ran some more and clambered over more blocks until they were some distance and elevation from the lake. They turned around and looked back at the water again. Still it rose, and at the same time, no longer glowed green as brightly.

"Getting dark again," Dan said. "We've got to find a way out."

"Only good news is I don't see the croc anymore," Khalif said.

"Maybe the rising water scared it," Jami offered. But Khalif shook his head.

"If we follow the myth, that croc was there to devour us if we didn't pass the test. If Rashid's heart had been heavier than the feather, that croc was to consume all of us."

"Good to know," Jami said flatly. "And now what, we're supposed to perish in floodwaters?" She eyed the rapidly rising lake with trepidation. "Rashid told me that his passing this test would be our salvation."

"The rising lake may be our way out. Come on!" Dan led the way, running toward the crumbling edifice. The rate at which the stone fell increased to the point that they could feel the rumbling through their feet whenever they were still on the ground. Various curses and exclamations of exertion were made as the three made their way toward the disintegrating building. So much material fell that clouds of dust became visible, roiling toward them through the subterranean air. "Pull your shirt over your mouth!" Dan shouted as he did so in order to prevent the incoming dust from inundating his mouth and nose.

"Lake water is still rising!" Khalif yelled. "Keep going!" The trio scrambled even faster for the higher ground the crumbling edifice represented. "Don't stop!"

They kept going, faster than was safe, sustaining numerous contusions, scrapes and pains, but making good progress. Before long they stood at the base of the causeway that fronted the mysterious structure.

"The water is still coming up!" Jami informed them. And indeed it was. A green translucent wall rolled up the stone blocks with ease, showing no signs of slowing as it ate up the remaining distance to the trapped trio.

"We've got to get up there. Let's go." Dan took off to the right to where he knew the access point he'd used before to ascend to the veranda was located. As he made his way toward it, behind him he could hear Khalif and Jami urging each other to hurry up.

"We got this, c'mon," Dan said as he reached the break in the wall that led up to the surrounding walkway. As he climbed and gained a little altitude, he looked back toward the lake and swallowed back a lump in his throat as his mind registered just how close the wall of glowing water was to them. Frightened at what was to be his likely fate should he not get out of the way, Dan scrambled the rest of the way up to the flat veranda-like area that fronted the edifice. He took stock of the situation while Jami and Khalif worked their way up to him.

The dust in the air now made it difficult to see very far, but he could make out enough detail to know that things were very different. The structure had been severely decimated by whatever it was exactly that the balance ritual had triggered in the underground realm. Where before they had needed to find a single break in the wall to enter the maze that led to the small pond chamber that had seemingly triggered this chain of events, now there was no wall still standing for much of the length of the veranda. Even with the severely reduced visibility, he could tell that much of the structure's walls had already come down, and still debris fell around them. Concerned that they could be hit, Dan knew they had to clear the area fast.

Looking back toward the lake, he saw Jami topping over the wall. He reached out a hand to pull her the rest of the way up. Khalif was next, and then Dan pointed to a segment of wall that had completely collapsed. He could tell that Khalif was utterly mystified at what had happened—or maybe it was what lay beyond the broken wall, for Dan had seen it, too, if only for a few fleeting seconds.

"The water's still rising!" Jami screamed.

"This way!" Dan grabbed her by the hand. They stepped through the cloud of billowing dust into the space on the other side of the wall.

"What are we looking at?" Khalif muttered. "What is this? How is it possible?"

CHAPTER 10

They looked out onto what was now level ground with the top of the veranda on which they stood. Beyond, past the field of very recently deposited rubble, lay a mystifying collection of architecture and culture. Greek-style buildings with marble columns opposed each other on either side of the revealed area. In between was a town or village layout with winding roads made of what appeared to be gold—or at least a gold-like substance. But the dust still swirled about miserably, making it hard to see in detail, as well as difficult to breathe.

Dan saw a hole in the ground created by a chunk of debris caving in part of the walkway, and waved an arm toward it. "Hunker down in here while the dust settles." Literally waiting for the dust to settle, the beleaguered trio crammed in together into the depression like World War I soldiers in a foxhole. While they waited, though they could no longer view the incredible vista they had seen, they talked about what it might represent.

"Did you see that stuff down there?" Khalif asked, eyes wide open, voice tinged with excitement while the dust roiled above their heads.

"From the quick glimpse I got, it looked like a bunch of Greek ruins," Dan admitted.

"How is that possible? This is ancient Egypt," Jami pointed out.

"Maybe the ancient Egyptians independently discovered the same kind of architecture?" Dan shrugged. "It's really a question for the scholars, but we discovered it, so we may as well be the first to check it out. Not to mention we need to find a way to get the hell out of here."

Khalif slowly shook his head while coughing into his shirt collar. "Just think, we discovered all this simply because an earthquake happened at the right time."

"Yeah, lucky us," Jami said, also hacking into her shirt. "Not gonna lie, I would have rather just read about it next month in National Geographic."

"I'm just glad Rashid's heart passed the test and we didn't get devoured by that prehistoric what's-it-croc?" Dan said, turning to Jami.

"*Sarcosuchus.*"

"Yeah, that's it. Wish I had a photo of it."

A few innumerable minutes passed in silence while the dust slowly let up. It also became quieter around them as the tumble of broken stone came to an end. At length, Dan shielded his face and head with his arms and slowly stood, surveying the transformed subterranean landscape.

"Well?" Khalif asked for both he and Jami, who still cowered in the relative safety of their stone pit.

"Good news and bad news," Dan said, after looking first out toward the new environs, and then back toward the lake.

"Aw great, here we go," Khalif said.

Jami tapped him on the back of the hand to quiet him down, while asking Dan, "What is it? Just tell us. Good news first, please. I need some good news right now!"

Dan spun around and faced the new area again. "The good news is that the dust has settled enough that we can move around freely." He paused and turned 180 degrees once again to face the lake.

"And the bad?" Khalif asked, rising to his feet.

"Bad news is that the lake water is rising fast. We've got to get out of here. C'mon!" He reached a hand down and pulled Jami up out of the hole.

"Oh my—" she started, but Dan led her by the hand toward the strange new area. As they walked along the perimeter of what used to be the stone wall blocking the view they now had of Greek-style buildings, Dan came to grips with the fact that they currently stood at the highest elevation he could see. Everything around them—from the lake to the new territory in front of them, was lower down. The new realm wasn't that much lower, though, Dan judged. It was a gentle slope down to what appeared to be a flat area, but if the lake water topped the flat walkway that had fronted the crumbed edifice, then it would run down into their newly discovered space.

"What's going on, Dan?" Jami asked, tugging at his shirtsleeve. But all Dan could think about was how this was happening, with the water. The dye pack in the pond had broken and triggered the chemical reaction that created light. It had run down through the rock to the big lake below, lighting it up. That much he could understand even though it was the last thing he ever expected. And the pond....He looked about to see if he could find it now. It had been a large depression on the other side of the edifice when it was still there. He looked left, then right, then back again. *It must be to the left...* There! Maybe fifty meters to the left, an egg-shaped depression in the ground a few feet from the veranda. The pond!

"Dan?" Jami interjected again.

"That's the pond me and Khalif found, except it's empty now."

"The water all drained to the lake, lighting it up," Khalif said, gawking at the hole in the ground that had been so different only minutes earlier.

Dan turned and watched the rising lake water. It still rolled up toward them, but the ferocity of the inundation was abating.

"But what made it come up here?" Dan wondered aloud.

Khalif shrugged and said, "Maybe when the stone block tipped over and crushed the glass, it did something else, too? Opened some kind of dam we can't see under the rocks?"

"Could be," Dan said, eyeballing the incoming wall of water that was now thinner and not as menacing as before. Then he pointed to the uprising of lake water, only a few feet away.

"Looks like it's stopping," Jami said, backing up a bit, nevertheless.

"Just stand here and wait," Dan said. "I think this is the peak of it. No point walking around in the water, let's wait it out."

They stood there while the water topped over the wall, just barely, not even rising to their ankles, and then rolling off the opposite edge and sluicing down into the gently downsloping new area. Much of the initial surge slid back down to the large lake.

"Looks like we don't need to worry about the lake overtaking us or flooding this whole place out," Khalif said, voicing the relief on all of their minds.

But Dan noticed something they did need to worry about. "The green glow is getting weaker, though, and the lake water being all the way up here was giving us more light. Now it's receding back down lower *and* I think it's getting weaker with time."

"And we have no more flashlight, right?" Jami asked, scared of the answer but knowing what it was at the same time.

"That's right," Dan said.

"Cell phones, I guess," Jami said. When neither of the two men said anything, she repeated, "Right?"

Dan shook his head sheepishly. "I just had one of those pay-as-you-go burner phones, and I forgot to put more minutes on it, so I didn't take it out with me tonight." The truth was that while Dan did have a pay-as-you-go burner phone, he had deliberately let it lapse as soon as he knew he would be leaving the country tomorrow. His Egyptian trac-phone would do him no good in the States. But it felt awkward to him that he hadn't yet mentioned anything to Jami about his going back to the U.S. tomorrow, even though now it looked as though none of them would be going anywhere unless they could figure a way out of here. Making their way back down to the lake in the pitch black and then swimming across the shark-infested waters while facing down the prehistoric crocodile didn't seem to have survivable odds.

"Oh," Jami said simply, but the disappointment in her voice was enough to crush Dan's spirits as she turned to Khalif with a hopeful look on her face. "What about you, do you have a phone?"

"Uhhh…" He fumbled around in his pockets for a few seconds and then pulled out a device. "Yeah, but it's an old clamshell model, no big bright touchscreen, I just use it to text and actually make calls. It doesn't even light up. No signal down here." He re-pocketed the device and then said to Jami, "What about you? You're a young person, you must have the latest iPhone or whatever, right?"

Jami exhaled sharply in a way that lifted her hair off her face, before pulling a modern smartphone from her pocket. "Battery's dead on my iPhone. I usually charge it when I go to sleep but last night I…" It was her turn to show embarrassment. "I was a little tipsy, okay, and I have one of those drop-on-top wireless chargers, and apparently I didn't drop it on straight enough, and so it didn't charge. Woke up in the morning and I was bummed because I saw it only had eighteen percent charge, but I had to get up and go do stuff. Of course I had no idea I'd end up here, beneath the Great Pyramid!" She shot a look that betrayed a touch of exasperation to Dan.

"Look," Dan said, "we still have *some* light left. We should remember what we came up here for—to either find materials to make a raft to be able to safely cross back over the lake—*or* to just find a way out of here altogether. With all this new stuff that opened up…." He waved an arm toward the expanse of architecturally remarkable buildings and the unknown beyond, "…I think the latter is a decent possibility."

" Let's go see what we can find!" Khalif said.

"Okay," Jami added, sounding less enthusiastic than Khalif.

Dan turned around to face the amazing new area, getting ready to look for the best route into it. But what he saw stopped him right where he was. All he could do was point. Down the gentle incline, a pool of the lake water that had run over the side had collected in a shallow ground depression. Were Dan to see it on the roads back home, he'd call it a pothole. But this pothole had a clearly defined and very unique shape, not to mention it glowed green with the shallow layer of water it had collected.

"Look at the shape of the water that collected there," Dan said, pointing. "That remind you of anything?"

Khalif and Jami both eyeballed the oddity, but after a few seconds, neither had an answer for Dan.

"I'm not sure what it is, either, but I know it looks familiar to me," Jami said.

Khalif narrowed his eyes at Dan. "Seriously, this is not the time to guess what kind of animal the cloud looks like. We need to get out of here!"

"You're right. I just thought it to be weirdly shaped in –"

"I know what it is!" Jami's outburst cut Dan off in the middle of his sentence. "I totally recognize it!"

"Do tell," Dan pleaded.

"It's….it's a country, or something from a map! Like Canada—but not Canada. Somewhere cold! It's mostly circular but has that funny tail section, a peninsula or archipelago, I guess."

"Alaska?" Dan asked.

"Hey, I don't see how this is helping us?" Khalif said. "Let's get down there. We'll pass by your weird puddle on the way."

"Fine, but the best view of it is from higher up, since it's pretty big. But I see what you're saying, Jami. It's an outline of a country—of a continent! Hey! Antarctica! It's Antarctica, isn't it?"

After a slight pause during which the crunch of Khalif's shoes on wet ground could be heard as he began walking down to the strange ruins, Jami responded, "Yes! Antarctica. You're right!"

"That is really weird," Dan said, beginning to walk down after Khalif while signaling for Jami to follow. "A puddle in the shape of Antarctica, who would have thought?"

He heard Jami's quick footsteps just behind him. "Okay, but let's get real here: it's not 'in the shape of Antarctica' like how Khalif was saying, when you look at puffy clouds or whatever and it sort of looks like something if you squint just right. No, I mean this appears to be an exact cartographic representation of the southern continent! How is that even possible? That's way too much for random coincidence."

"Sure is," Dan said, still trailing after Khalif down the gentle slope, toward the glowing continental pond.

Jami continued both walking and speaking. "But on the other hand, if you think about how amazingly precise the engineering would have had to have been five thousand years ago for all this to still work, my goodness!"

"Right," Dan said, "but that's exactly what everyone says about the pyramids themselves! So well-engineered, the precision, they must have had help designing them from a higher power, alien intelligence, whatever."

"So you're saying that the ancient Egyptians, the same ones who built the pyramids and the Sphinx, also built this intricate map—or drawing, whatever you want to call it-- of Antarctica that can only be seen after it floods with glowing green water—even thousands of years later?" The tone of incredulity in her voice left little room that she was skeptical.

"These buildings are most definitely not in the architectural style of ancient Egypt," Khalif said from up ahead. He was almost to the Antarctica puddle, beyond which the nearest building loomed, its majestic row of pillars beckoning in the dim greenish light. Dan and Jami walked in his direction until they all congregated at the edge of the strangely designed water feature. Dan walked slowly around the outline of the continent, while Jami and Khalif opted to stand in one place and observe.

The water still glowed green, and a greenish-tinged light was still visible from the big lake behind them, although it was definitely dimmer now. Dan studied the contours of the outline as he moved around it. The intricacy of the land mass' outline was nothing less than stunning. Of course he had no idea how accurate it was, not being able to reference a modern map at the moment, but it certainly seemed like it was hyper-accurate. He stared at the peninsula portion of the continent that Jami had mentioned. Indeed, its length was studded with countless tiny islands, each one of which was now highlighted by a small drop of fluorescing green water. He knew that Antarctica was the last major landmass on Earth to have been discovered and then mapped. So how, then, could the ancient Egyptians have known what its boundaries were with such precision?

He had made it about 180 degrees around the continental representation when a difference in coloration caught his attention. Part of the map, as he now thought of it, was a darker green—almost black now—than the rest of it. Stooping down to get a closer look, he realized that the water here was deeper—perhaps three or four inches deep rather than the few millimeters the rest of it was. This is what accounted for the darker coloration, he knew. But why was it that way? Was it random happenstance resulting from the topography of the ground here? He doubted it, since, as they had just discussed, the exacting engineering the ancients seemed to have been able to execute for everything else they accomplished would be at odds with such a degree of variation.

He called attention to the darkened area. Khalif poo-poohed the idea and said he was going to walk to the series of columns that marked the presence of the nearest building, reiterating their urgent need to find a way back above ground. But Jami remained interested in spite of the situation.

"Could it be a map?" she asked breathlessly.

"A map to what?" Dan wondered. He took note of his orientation to the map, if that's what it was. The peninsula was at roughly the 9 O'clock position, while the shaded portion of the map occupied the edge of the mainland at 11 O'clock.

"Got me," Dan admitted. "C'mon, let's check the rest of this place out."

"Good idea. Khalif's getting pretty irritated."

He smiled at her knowingly. "He must be worried about his almighty Prince again." Jami snickered and then they turned away from the map just in time to see Khalif passing between two massive marble columns.

"Khalif, where are you going?" Dan yelled. He didn't want them to get separated.

Khalif didn't stop, but called back, "The door's open! I'm going in!"

CHAPTER 11

Dan and Jami watched for Khalif to emerge again as they walked, but he did not. They increased their pace the rest of the distance to the columned building. When they were almost to it, they looked up and marveled at the height of the unexpected structure. It had to be at least three, maybe four stories high, Dan thought. Built into the rock wall itself, as was the opposite structure on the other side of the immense cavern, the building blended with its surroundings well for a Greek-style columned façade. But there was no time to dwell on details. Dan and Jami passed between two of the columns, as Khalif had before them, and into a covered vestibule-like area.

Dan called out for Khalif. "Where you at?"

"In here! This is incredible! It's almost dark in here, though."

"We're coming in," Dan alerted him. He and Jami walked into the vestibule area and immediately paused to let their eyes adjust to the dimmer light level.

"It is pretty dark in here," Jami said. "That's something whoever engineered this place all those years ago didn't think of."

"Maybe they thought whoever was smart enough to find this underground place way in the future would have their own light source with them?" Dan quipped.

"Good point. Sure wish even one of us did."

Dan heard the nervousness creeping back into her voice and decided to change the subject, to focus on the positive. "Khalif sounded pretty excited about something. Maybe he found a way out of here. Let's go find him."

Jami gave no argument, and so the two of them ventured deeper inside the marble vestibule. At least Dan had thought of it as a marble structure, but after watching carefully where he placed his feet for a few steps, it dawned on him that the floor tiles were actually made of some kind of dull metal, not stone. He knelt for a moment and felt the flooring. Smooth and cool to the touch. His retinas took in just enough photons of light to be able to detect a dull golden gleam. "Jami, I think the floor is made of gold," he said, rising to his feet.

"Can you chip me off a piece?" Even in the near darkness, he could make out the mischievous grin on her face. "Just kidding!" she added.

"You know I wouldn't do that. Right?" She smiled at him while pretending to dig the toe of her shoe into the gold floor. "I'm not a gold digger, really!"

"Right about now I'd trade all this gold for a rubber raft and a flashlight," Dan said, and then immediately regretted it. He'd finally taken her mind off their dire predicament, and now he'd just reminded her of it again. Then they both heard Khalif's voice, not far away.

"This is some other kind of civilization. Not ancient Egypt, or any period of Egypt!"

"Did you know the floors are gold?" Dan asked him.

"Not only the floors," Khalif returned. "This is amazing. Come over here. You are not going to believe this."

Dan had started walking toward Khalif's voice, deeper into the vestibule, when Jami surprised him by reaching out and taking his hand. She was frightened, he knew, but he still felt like maybe she was starting to like him. Dan told himself that she wouldn't hold Khalif's hand like this in the same situation. *Or would she?*

They reached the end of the entrance hall space and saw Khalif to the left, standing in front of some kind of elaborate display. It was so dim back here that it looked like little more than shadows to Dan and Jami, but they walked up to Khalif, who stood facing away from them.

"Wait a moment, and your eyes will acclimate. In the meantime, I will tell you what I believe we're looking at."

Dan said, "I see a lot of little structures or something."

"Yes," Khalif said. "The structures you see are miniature reproductions of the pyramids above us—not only the Great Pyramid, but the others as well."

"And the Sphinx?" Jami asked, pointing.

"Yes, yes!" Khalif said, voice warming. "But, while all other aspects of the…diorama, as I think of it, like the ones kids make in school, only this one is constructed, I think, from solid gold…while other aspects seem to be true to life—to modern day life—the exception here is the sphinx."

"Looks pretty true to life to me," Jami said, inching close to the display, which was situated in a depressed area of the golden floor. "It's even facing the right direction—east. And it seems to be to scale with the Great Pyramid."

"Yes, there is nothing wrong with that sphinx," Khalif said, "except that there are two of them."

"*What?*" Jami's single word echoed throughout the gold-floored, high-ceilinged room.

Khalif took a few slow steps out into the middle of the diorama and pointed straight up so as to indicate the world above their heads. "The sphinx you just saw here is in the same relative location as the sphinx we know up there. It faces east, while the pyramids themselves all have their four corners anchored to one of the four cardinal compass points—east, west, south or north. But in this representation, there is a *second* sphinx. Look…." He pointed down near his feet.

Jami stared hard into the shadows, where she saw a miniature version of the most recognizable statue in the world. "Oh yeah, I do see it! Wow, so what could that mean, two sphinxes?"

Khalif looked at her, grinning ear to ear. "What was it that got us to come down here in the first place? Rumors of a Hall of Records and possibly a second sphinx hidden beneath the first one, right?"

"But we're not beneath the first one. We went down the Osiris Shaft and then discovered the new passage uncovered by the earthquake, which led us some distance away to wherever we are now."

"Nevertheless, the existence of a second sphinx, wherever it may be exactly, is incredible news. As for where we are now…" Khalif reached out to touch the second sphinx. He placed a hand on its smooth, exquisitely detailed surface. "Perhaps this *is* where we are now? *Inside the second sphinx?*"

"And this is where we're going to stay if we don't find a way out, remember? Now who's getting distracted?" Dan levelled his gaze at Khalif, who turned away from the sphinx to look at Dan.

"Touché. But also note that these representations of the sphinx—both of them—differ from the actual sphinx up there in an important way. Do you know what it is?"

Jami and Dan stared blankly into the shadows. Khalif took the silence as a 'no' and continued. "Look at the faces. The face that is believed to be modeled after that of Khafre, the King and the most likely builder of the original sphinx." Again, he pointed up.

"So?" Dan said. "Khalif, we need to—"

"Bear with me. I'm working on it." He pointed to the nearest of the two mini-sphinxes, which was the easiest to make out detail on. "They have fully intact faces, without the nose missing as the life-size one above because it was shot off by Napoleon's army around 1800. The point being that these don't seem to be modern reproductions since most of those copy the sphinx as we know it now—sans nose."

"Most," Dan said, "but that doesn't mean no one makes sphinxes with a nose. Still, I'm not saying this stuff isn't old. It looks old, and it's made of gold, I think, so I'm guessing it could be very old."

Khalif smiled at him and leaned over again to touch the closer sphinx. "Feels like solid gold to me." He rapped on it with his knuckles, producing a dull thud.

"Have you ever knocked on something that big made out of solid gold before?" Dan asked, openly skeptical.

"Why yes, as a matter of fact, I have."

"Where?"

Jami had had enough. "Boys, please. Now who's wasting time?"

"Yes, let's finish up here," Khalif said, turning back to the sphinxes. "Besides the simple fact that they look old and materials-wise, could well be gold, and that they have been sealed down here in a section of underground labyrinth that was opened only today by an earthquake, there is something else about them that may be telling." No one said anything, so again, Khalif went on. "For a long time—and you can vouch for this, I'm sure, Dan--Egyptologists were of a consensus that the Sphinx was constructed at about the same time as the Great Pyramid it guards." Khalif paused long enough for Dan to give an impatient nod, and then continued.

"They agreed for the most part that its likeness was that of Khufu, the King who had the Great Pyramid built. Recent evidence, however, suggests that the Sphinx was constructed a great deal earlier than the pyramids, perhaps as much as 5,000 years earlier, or around 7,000 B.C.E."

"Yeah, I've heard that theory," Dan said, "but it's sort of a fringe thing as far as I know. Can we look for a way out of here now, please? I'm getting hungry."

"Me too," Jami chimed in.

"Me three," Khalif said. "But although as you point out, acceptance of the Old Sphinx Theory has been slow to gain traction in traditional archaeological circles, it has been attracting attention in light of new technology providing additional evidence that makes it harder to refute. But here's the thing that bothers me about this representation, here...." He pointed to the diorama. "According to the Amduat text, which is a well-known funerary text describing the underworld journey of Ra the Sun God, found inscribed on the inside of all pharaohs' tombs, the second Sphinx should face opposite that of the first. That is, since the first faces east, it should face west."

Khalif pointed to the second sphinx on the diorama. "Yet, as you can see here, both sphinxes are facing the same direction. So for me that brings up two questions...."

"How do we get out of here?" Dan reiterated.

"When can we eat?" Jami added, grinning at Dan.

Khalif frowned briefly but, recognizing he was running out of time, began speaking faster and with more urgency. "The questions are, One: why isn't the second sphinx facing east, as the known one *should* be?" He pointed at the first sphinx before hurriedly continuing. "And Two: which way is east?" He looked around the room, holding his hands up, for dramatic effect.

"How do we really know that the first sphinx, the one in the correct position, is really facing east?" Dan asked.

Khalif tilted his head while looking back to the diorama. "Good point," he conceded. "I admit that, without a compass, we cannot say for sure. However, if I had to guess, and I do, I think it safe to assume that, given the attention to detail here as well as the great lengths gone to preserving this diorama through the millennia, that the original designers and builders captured the proper orientation of all structures here, including *both* sphinxes."

Suddenly Khalif turned and walked out into the diorama, between the pyramid and the sphinx, until he reached the second sphinx. "Let me feel this one, to see if it feels the same as the first. Will only take a second." He knelt and again rapped his knuckles on the smooth, dull gold surface. It made the same sound as the other had. "No noticeable difference."

"C'mon Khalif, we need to see what else we can find around here. It's getting dark. The light is dying out. Whatever it is we're supposed to find, I guess it was only designed to take about this much time."

Khalif exhaled sharply, clearly irritated. "Fine, we'll go somewhere else. Let me see how easy it is to just take one of these with me. I would love to show it to the Prince..." He put both hands around the neck and chest of the sphinx and pulled, bracing his legs against the floor, grunting with the effort. Dan gently tapped Jami with an elbow, snickering ever so slightly at Khalif's mention of the Prince again.

"Don't laugh," Khalif said, somehow picking up on the communication. "You'd be surprised, gold has many unique characteristics, but tensile strength is not one of them." He continued pulling until his fingers slipped off the statuette and he fell hard on his rear end on the metal floor of the diorama. "Ow, that hurt!" he muttered.

"Be glad you didn't land on one of the pyramids," Jami said, eliciting hearty guffaws from Dan. Khalif got to his feet, dusting off his pants. "Well, I suppose I should give up on—Hey, wait a minute!"

"What? "Dan said.

"Look!" Khalif pointed to the sphinx he had just grabbed. "Look!"

"It moved!" Jami noticed.

"It did?" Dan asked, moving closer to the statuette.

"Yeah, look." Jami also walked over to it. "It was facing in the exact same direction as the other one—ostensibly east, as we were saying—but now it's been shifted more to the left, or northeast, I guess you would say. Look."

All three of them stared at the sphinx. Indeed, though still attached to its base, it had been rotated about twenty degrees. Khalif was the first to touch it again. "Maybe I loosened it. You know, like when a woman asks a man to open a jar and he tries, but it doesn't open, but when he gives it back to her she opens it easily? Maybe it'll be like that."

Jami looked at Dan while Khalif was facing away and rolled her eyes even though it was now barely light enough to discern the expression. Khalif knelt by the mini-sphinx and tried once again to yank it off its fixture, but once again, it remained stubbornly in place. "It turns, but it won't come off." The frustration was evident in his voice as he stood and backed away from the sphinx. Dan eyed it and mentally noted that it now faced in yet another random direction.

"Let me try something." He moved past Khalif and took his turn kneeling by the movable sphinx.

"This isn't like the jar thing," Khalif scoffed. "No way you will be able to pull it off."

"I'm not going to try to pull it off." Dan began to rotate the statuette. "I'm just going to face it in a certain direction. According to the Amduat text, it should be facing the opposite of the known Sphinx, right?"

"Right," Jami and Khalif said it at the exact same time. "Jinx!" Jami said, while Dan continued to slowly rotate the sphinx.

"So I'm going the long way around," he said as he spun the half-lion-half-man, "just to check it out, see how the movement works, or if there's any surprises….so far it's perfectly smooth." Jami and Khalif watched as Dan spun the sphinx until it faced nearly 180 degrees opposite its twin. "And here we go, this is about—whoa! Did you hear that?"

"Did it click?" Jami asked.

"Yes! It clicked into place!"

"Oh shit." Khalif slowly backed away from the diorama.

"What?" Dan asked, looking over at him.

"I don't know, exactly. But what if you just triggered some kind of trap?"

"That would suck," Dan said. He tried to turn the sphinx but it would no longer budge. "It's locked into position now."

"Stop. Just listen." Jami cocked an ear to one side. The others indulged her and they stood there in silence for one, two, three seconds, waiting to hear the first signs of…anything. But they heard nothing at all.

"Come," Khalif said. "There is another building across from this one. Let's check that one out before it gets completely dark."

They agreed, taking a last look at the strange double-sphinx display before walking away from the diorama. "Question for you, Khalif," Jami asked while they walked.

"Yes?"

They passed through the spacious vestibule, adorned in and constructed from gold.

"You said the architecture of the buildings here—this one and the one across from it that we're going to check out—are not Egyptian."

"Definitely not. Don't you agree, Dan?"

"I do. But at the same time, I can't place what else it might be—what other civilization might have built it. Very weird. Yet at the same time, my desire for survival is beginning to outweigh my curiosity about such matters."

"I second that," Jami said.

"I just use the history and speculation to keep my mind off of our predicament," Khalif said matter-of-factly. "And who knows? Maybe some of this conjecture will turn out to help us. For example, right now, as we walk to the next building and whatever it may hold, I am wondering about how *if* the sphinx—or sphinxes—were in fact built 7,000 years ago instead of about 4,500 years ago, what does that change? Who, in that case, could have built them, and why?"

"Romans? Greeks?" Dan threw out. "These buildings, at least the outsides of them, look like that to me, not that I'm an architectural historian, or any kind of architect, or any kind of historian."

"Romans came along much later," Jami said authoritatively. "I remember that from history class in college. They were after Christ. The Greeks were older, maybe as much as 2,000 years before Christ."

"Neither of those fit the timeline for even the pyramids, much less the older sphinx. Or sphinxes," Khalif said, picking up his pace as they exited the vestibule. Outside, it was slightly lighter, but not by much. Across a wide open space of gold interlocking paver tiles, another building, very similar in appearance to the last, beckoned. One difference, plain to see as they walked up to the open vestibule-like entrance set into the colossal wall of the cavern, was the doorway itself. It was adorned with two massive tusks framing the entrance, with a series of large bones arrayed on top of the tusks and extending all the way to the ground, where they formed a fence with an opening wide enough for them to pass through single file.

"Strange, but they look like elephant tusks," Jami said as they paused in front of the entrance.

"Were there elephants in Egypt?" Dan asked.

Jami shrugged. "Possibly. The climate could have been quite different back then, and this is Africa, where there are still elephants today, much farther south."

"What do you think is in here?" Khalif wondered aloud.

"Hopefully, it stays light enough to find out," Dan said, reminding them of the fading illumination. They stood in front of the bones, on the verge of the complete unknown, allowing their eyes to adjust to the darkness beyond. From out here the inside didn't appear much different than the previous building. Then they passed single file through the gate of bones and entered the building proper.

Right away they could see that this one, while it appeared to have the same physical layout, was much different in terms of what it contained. Shelves displaying many artifacts lined the walls. Some of them were in the open, exposed to the air, stone statues or perhaps tools of some kind. Metal objects, too, including strange coins and gold bars with unrecognizable stamps on them.

The walls themselves were adorned with murals and carvings. Dan pointed to one painting that depicted a tsunami or tidal wave inundating a village, its citizens either running hopelessly for their lives before the deluge of rushing water, or else being swept away by its unrelenting and indiscriminate fury. There were books, too, Jami pointed out, their stiff papyrus pages miraculously preserved, though their language was undiscernible to any of them. It seemed to be a strange pseudo-Cyrillic alphabet that none of them recognized, though they were not unaware of their lack of expertise in ancient languages.

"This is just incredible!" Khalif gushed, tracing his fingers over a gold engraving of a fisherman battling an unseen sea monster beneath the waves from a small boat with a harpoon-like weapon. "And yet, it's not Egyptian. It cannot be. This is something else. Not Roman, not Greek, not Egyptian, obviously not Far East...."

Dan wandered into the recesses of the space, where it was darkest. He paused in front of a group of shadowy objects. It took him a moment to realize he had found another diorama display. Only this one was not the same at all as the last, which depicted the recognizable pyramids and sphinxes. He could just make out what appeared to be an island community of some type, with concentric rings of canals surrounding a core landmass. Boats plied the canals, transporting seafood and crops, while a public gathering of some type could be seen taking place on a set of golden steps fronting an edifice in the same style of the ones they had found here.

"I know what it might be," Dan said, walking slowly around the new diorama, allowing his eyes to adjust. Khalif and Jami joined him in front of the 3D display. Khalif shook his head. "Again, I don't specifically recognize it. Looks marvelous, though, almost like something you would see in my native Dubai."

"Ah yes," Dan said, turning to Khalif. "That's it! Isn't there a certain luxury hotel in Dubai?"

"Well of course, dozens of the world's finest. There's the Burj Al Arab, the—"

"No, not those. But one that is part of a chain."

"Hilton?" Khalif asked, confused.

Dan smiled, pointing to the diorama. "You think whatever ancient culture built this had a Hilton?" Jami laughed and Khalif shrugged.

"I suppose not," he said with a smile. "But you are the one who brought up a hotel. So which one did you mean, and how does that make any sense?"

Dan pointed to the concentric rings around the island. "Atlantis."

CHAPTER 12

Khalif's eyes took on a wondrous expression as he stared at the island diorama. "Atlantis! Yes, the resort in Dubai. And the lost continent, no?"

"That's the one," Dan said. "Plato the ancient Greek wrote of it first. And here's the thing: According to Plato's account, Atlantis was destroyed by a flood about 11,000 years ago. The Sphinx was built about 9,000 years ago, so it is possible that surviving descendants of the Atlanteans could have built the Sphinx, or both of them, as the case may be, with this secret Hall of Records type thing below it to carry on their culture and way of life."

The stunned silence that fell upon Dan's ears when he completed his sentence told him that his audience of two was still processing what he had said. Jami was the first to recover.

"You mean to say that—assuming Atlantis was real—" she paused while Dan nodded, "—that *they* were the ones who built the Sphinx and the pyramids, not the Egyptians?"

At this, Dan and Khalif shook their heads. "No," Khalif said, joining in, "not the pyramids. We know beyond a shadow of a doubt they were built later than the Sphinx—too much later to be the work of Atlanteans. But the Sphinx—two thousand years after the fall of Atlantis—if we A) believe in Atlantis and B) accept the Older Sphinx Theory—the Sphinx is then within the realm of possibility that it was built by Atlanteans, or at least their direct descendants."

"I don't get it," Jami said. "The ancient Egyptians are really the Atlanteans?" She screwed up her features in a confused, doubtful expression.

"No," Dan said. "According to Plato's telling of the Atlantis tale, their Utopian society flourished for a time until its people got greedy and began straying from the path of purity or whatever you want to call it. They started to sin more, I guess. And so God punished them by sending a mighty tidal wave to flood their home permanently. So then if we accept what Khalif said about them existing in the first place and then also the Older Sphinx Theory, then it's plausible that in the end days of Atlantis, when it was flooded, that some of them set to sea on rafts or whatever, and survived. They would have needed somewhere to go. They would want to show the world that, 'Hey! We were here! We existed. We had a terrific society but now it's all gone except for this!'"

"Ahhh," Jami exclaimed, "so they ended up here, on the sands of Egypt, from wherever their island Home was in the first place."

"That's right!" Khalif said while Dan nodded along. "They came here, probably from somewhere in the western Atlantic—notice how it's very close to the name *Atlantis*?-- to demonstrate their technological prowess. Who knows, maybe they even built a blueprint of the Sphinxes in the form of that diorama to show the Egyptians how to do it? I don't know, but it's weird that there were two Sphinxes. Regardless, they built a pair of Sphinxes, at least one of which survives to this day."

"But then what happened to the Atlanteans?" Jami wanted to know. "Obviously, they didn't settle in Egypt, the land of Egyptians."

Dan's features brightened and it appeared that he was about to say something when they heard a scraping noise to their left, some distance away. Khalif held up a finger. "What's that?"

All of them froze. They heard the noise again. Sort of a dragging sound across the floor, or ground or whatever it was since they couldn't make out much detail in the vanishing light. Dan was the first to make any sort of statement.

"There, look! That statue! A door is opening in the wall!"

Indeed, a section of stone adorned with a bas-relief of a human-like figure was sliding upwards with an accompanying rumbling.

"That is the God Osiris, Lord of the Underworld, the Great Resurrector, on the door," Dan pointed out.

"I hear another noise." Jami pointed through the new opening. "Something's in there, moving!" Instinctively, she stepped closer to Dan and gripped his shoulder. For his part, Dan squinted into the space beyond as the door finished sliding up into the wall. The rumbling stopped and they could hear more clearly whatever was causing the approaching racket beyond.

"I don't like the sound of that, whatever it is," Khalif said, though he still stood in place.

"It sounds like running," Jami speculated.

"A whole lot of people running, stampeding, even," Dan clarified.

"Who says they have to be people?" Khalif posited.

"Are we just going to stand here and wait to be trampled by whatever the hell it is?" Jami asked.

At that moment, a chunk of stone landed three feet away from them with a heavy thud. Before any of them could ask, *What was that?*, two more dropped around them.

"This place is coming down!" Dan yelled.

"I think you triggered something when you spun the sphinx around!" Khalif said. He pointed to the diorama. "I do not think it an accident that that is happening." They took precious seconds to glance at the diorama of the concentric rings around an island. Water now flooded into it from below, spilling over the land portion of the island. "It's flooding."

"Here it comes!" Jami shouted. "Oh my god! There's a lot of it coming our way, whatever it is!"

Dan did a quick 360, scanning all directions. By the time he turned back around again, the first of many large boulders—golden boulders—was rolling toward them. Even in the dim light, Dan couldn't help but notice that they seemed to match the tile floor hue and texture.

"Boulder trap! This way!" Dan pulled Jami by the hand and checked to see that Khalif had heard him. The three of them moved erratically toward the vestibule entrance, dodging and weaving falling stone chunks while the river of golden debris rocketed out of the chute that had opened in the wall. Dan was hit in the head by a ping-pong sized rock that started a trickle of blood sluicing down his nose.

"Is this an aftershock of the earthquake?" Jami wondered aloud.

"More likely a trap triggered by our meddling, by turning the sphinx," Khalif said as he narrowly avoided being crushed by a falling segment of cavern ceiling rock. Dan had his eye toward the entrance and was about to suggest they make a break for it, back out the way they came through the tusk gate, when the entire front façade crumbled before his eyes in clouds of debris, dust and rubble. The way out was smothered in a mound of impenetrable material that also made it even darker inside. He began to feel like he was inside a tomb, which in a way he supposed he was, since after all that is what the pyramid complex was designed for.

And yet at the same time the river of golden boulders continued to spill forth from the revealed chute. They were trapped between the collapsed building on the right and the onrushing debris stream on their left. Jami shrieked, an ear-splitting wail, as she was peppered with small, sharp stones. The boulders started to pile up onto the island diorama, covering it even as it flooded with water.

"It's the fate of Atlantis!" Dan yelled. "This is it. The island diorama—it's flooding and getting besieged with earthquakes. But we came here to help. Turning the sphinx back to the way it was meant to be—how can they be mad at that—how—"

And then one of the golden rocks collided with another that had come to rest, and they heard a sharp *clack* as it cracked in half. The two pieces fell apart and something dark and large was left on the ground. With his arms over his head for protection from the falling material, Dan was about to yell for them all to turn and run when he saw the thing *move*.

"Hey, look!" He pointed to the dark, indistinguishable mass that had come out of the rock. Not only did it move, but it made a noise, a sort of snuffling or labored breathing.

"It's alive!" Khalif screamed, eyes so wide they were like two white beacons in the darkness.

"What's alive?" Dan asked.

"I don't know. Whatever that thing is!" Khalif sidestepped another chunk of falling rock. At that moment yet another of the roundish rocks collided with one that had come to rest against a mound of fallen stone, and it too, cracked apart.

"Something's coming out of that one, too!" Jami yelled, pointing.

Meanwhile, whatever had hatched out of the first rock started moving in a more pronounced fashion. "What are these?" Dan shouted. "This one's getting up!"

Jami paused amidst the chaos and forced herself to fix a hard stare on the movement emanating from the broken globules. "Some kind of animals! But how…"

"Osiris!" Khalif bellowed. "The Resurrector of the Dead—people *and* animals!"

More boulders rolled down into the diorama area and smashed into each other, breaking apart. Each contained a furry, indistinguishable shape that began to move after hatching.

"More of them are getting up!" Jami yelled. "What is going on here?"

"Way past that question," Dan replied, dodging a rolling boulder while shepherding Jami out of the way. Khalif, for his part, had made it to the edge of the boulder stream, toward the exit, when he was blocked by a downpour of stone building materials from above.

"What kind of animals are those?" Dan asked, pinned in place for the moment and uncertain as to which direction, if any, was safe. Jami was in the same situation, and so she forced herself to stand in place and bring out the zoologist in her as she stared at the hatching animals.

Not hatching, she told herself, for that term implied something being born. And these creatures weren't being born, she realized, looking at their full forms, but rather, they were being re-born. "Not sure. Maybe they are being released from some hibernation state?" she put forth with a helpless shrug. "Don't ask me how. I've never heard of an animal sheltering inside a solid ball of rock, I mean—" She cut herself off as one of the first animals to awaken and get to its feet—all four of them, she noted—began to walk with purposeful, intentional motion.

That was when she was able to formulate an idea in her mind as to what it was they were looking at. Her brain, after rapidly synthesizing all information available to it in the low light, came up with *bear*. The beasts had a matted hair look to them, and, when standing fully erect on four legs, seemed to be about the size of a large bear, perhaps a grizzly. But it was when she saw a second of the creatures move away from its halved rock that she gained a different perspective and knew instantly she had been wrong. Not a bear. An elephant.....*elephant*? That's when she made the connection with the entrance to this building, wreathed with large bones. Elephant bones, she had guessed. Now it appeared that she was right.

The noises the animal made further confirmed to the zoologist she was dealing with some kind of pachyderm-like organism. She was no elephant expert, but these bear-like elephants had long hair, and….Dan bumped into her at the exact same time her mind hit on the word, the word that made everything seem so impossible, and yet so correct at the same time.

Mammoth.

Wooly mammoth, she thought as Dan called out, "This way," before yanking her out of the path of one of the newly released creatures that had started to run past them, toward the exit. Khalif looked over his shoulder and promptly changed course, veering off to the right while shouting something unintelligible amidst the din of crumbling rock and stampeding feet.

More of the animals rose to their feet and ran after the others, in a confined herd formation, a line one or two animals wide, breaking up and shifting occasionally to avoid falling rock. Dan and Jami battled their way toward Khalif and the exit, bouncing once off a marauding quadruped before leaping over a slab of fallen stone to continue on.

"Mammoths! I think they might be wooly mammoths! Either mastodons or mammoths, pretty sure the latter. Mastodons didn't have the huge curly-cue tusks like the ones on the door," Jami said as they ran.

"Aren't mammoths prehistoric?" Dan huffed as they dodged and weaved.

"Not really, no. You might get a kick out of this: wooly mammoths still roamed the Earth during the same time the Egyptian pyramids were being built!"

"But not here in Egypt, though, right?" Dan asked, kicking a loose rock out of the way that posed a tripping hazard. Next to it on the floor, he noticed a small, pool-ball sized chunk from one of the golden boulders and quickly bent down and scooped it up before dropping it into his pocket.

"I think they were in Siberia, but not positive. We should have taken the hint with the bones on the door. Mammoth, not elephant, or mastodon. But tusked mammals aren't my specialty, especially not extinct ones."

"These don't look very extinct," Dan pointed out as the procession of rampaging beasts passed them by.

"At least they're not trampling us," Jami said.

"Not us," Dan added, "but what about Khalif? Hey Khalif, watch out! They're all coming your way!" He wasn't sure Khalif heard them, for at that moment terribly large chunks of the building structure itself began dropping in front of them.

"Gonna have to find a different way out!" Dan yelled as all hell broke loose around them. Terrifyingly, he had just pulled Jami out of the way of a wobbling boulder when a large crack opened up in the tile floor in front of them. They stopped short of it, staring down into a yawning, dark maw. As they watched, one of the wooly mammoths ran from the side into the opening and out of sight down an incline that appeared to level off just before the animal ran from view. Before they could say anything about it, a second of the animals charged into the yawning gap in the floor as they backed cautiously away.

"If it doesn't lead anywhere, they'll come back out," Dan speculated.

"If it doesn't cave in on them first," Jami added.

But after a few tense seconds during which they watched as Khalif was forced to retrace his steps to avoid being crushed by collapsing stone, neither of the mammoths had re-emerged from the tunnel that had opened in the floor. In fact, a third elephantine beast joined the first two, disappearing into the rocky chute. The grinding and shifting of rock and stone, peppered with rock shattering as it fell from great heights, made it difficult to hear one another, even huddled together.

"More mammoths, incoming!" Dan pointed back toward the diorama where a small herd of the creatures galloped in their direction. He looked around and spotted a small rise created by two slabs of stone tented together where they fell. He knew they wouldn't have much time before they were overrun by the beasts, which, for some reason, were all heading for the floor chute. He tugged on Jami's arm. "Up here, quick!"

He led her by the hand as he hopped up onto the smooth but inclined slab, pulling her behind him until they reached the top of the rise, which afforded them a head-high vantage point from which to survey their surroundings. Small bits of rock and stone rained down on them and all around, but looking up, they saw no major sections about to let loose, unlike the portion of the structure under which Khalif now stood.

The Emirati was frozen like the proverbial deer in headlights with his arms over his head in a futile attempt at saving his skull should a chunk of stone weighing innumerable tons fall on it. Dan shouted to him: "Khalif! Over here! This way, now!"

His voice was barely audible over the collapsing building, but it was just enough to get Khalif's attention. Dan saw him turn and look his way, confused and terrified, but searching for the source of the voice. Dan waved his arms. "This way!" He certainly hoped he wouldn't get him killed by moving him into harm's way, but there was much more falling rock where he was now. Even if he didn't become injured or die over there, Dan knew it was best at this point that they stay together as a group. To be lost in here now would likely mean to remain lost forever.

Khalif bolted for Dan and Jami's perch, sacrificing agility and defensive protection for raw speed. Dan watched, thinking *Don't trip, don't trip,* the entire time he ran. Somehow he made the dash without sustaining major injuries, but he reached the base of the perch at the same time as a pair of wooly mammoths shuffled around the entrance to the chute, battered by their own primal brethren that poured into the opening in the floor. Khalif's eyes and mouth opened wide in complete shock and disbelief. When trying to pivot, he went down to the floor instead, landing on his side. One of the two massive elephants stepped right over him, two of its clubbed feet hoisted in motion over his prone body, leaving him to feel like a small animal crossing a road that is passed over by a car without being touched.

Jami pointed to the oncoming herd, shattering Khalif's illusion that he had time to take a breather and reflect on his near-death experience. "So many more coming!"

Dan cupped his hands over his mouth and shouted to Khalif. "Get up! Khalif, get up here now. You're clear but not for long!"

The Arab heeded the advice, rolling over and then pushing up with one hand and one knee until he was upright again. He glanced over at where Jami was pointing, saw the onrushing mammoths and then turned and sprang up the inclined blocks until he stood at the small pinnacle next to Dan and Jami. Dan steadied him with a hand on his arm until he was sure his footing was established, then pointed into the chute in the floor, where more mammoths disappeared, bumping and snorting as they went.

A massive section of stone ceiling dropped to the floor scant feet behind them, showering them with a cloud of dust and bits of stone shrapnel. By the entrance, from where Khalif had just returned, heaps of rubble continued to pile up on the floor from both the walls and ceiling.

"This entire place is falling apart right now!" Jami warned.

Dan made brief eye contact with first Jami, then Khalif, before pointing down the chute. "I think that's our only way out!"

Jami whipped her head to the side, away from the marauding mammoths, to eyeball Dan. "We'll be crushed in the stampede if we try to walk through there."

"Who said anything about walking?" Dan asked, while staring into the tunnel.

"Walking, running, whatever—"Jami began, but Dan interrupted, recognizing that time was of the essence as more and more of the building disintegrated around them.

He stared down at the living train of hairy flesh that passed by them before the mammoths began their descent into the tunnel. Because of the incline of the chute, the backs of the mammoths were a couple of feet lower than the pinnacle of the humans' perch. "We need to catch a ride," Dan said, pointing to a pair of mammoths that managed to squeeze down the chute side by side.

"What? No way! You've got to be—" Jami was interrupted by a chunk of marble landing on her shoulder. She cried out in pain and then said, "Fine. I've got no better ideas. I hope we don't die."

Khalif was also doubtful. "Wait a minute, that's your plan?"

"Jump!" He took Jami by the hand and leapt from the perch onto the back of one of the resurrected beasts. He gripped its long, coarse hair with the hand not holding onto Jami. He felt her wrap an arm around him as they jostled along on the back of the running behemoth. The giant elephant, for its part, seemed not to notice or care that it had taken on a pair of human riders. It continued running along with the herd, down the chute. The smell was the thing that struck him most—it was an awful stench, like a combination of mold and body odor and something else altogether unfamiliar.

Dan looked back and saw Khalif still standing on the perch, watching them with horror as the procession of mammoths continued to run headlong into the chute. Soon they would be out of sight of each other as they rode the elephantine convoy deep into the tunnel.

"Now, Khalif! Get on one!" Dan yelled, but his words were lost as a massive section of ceiling collapsed over most of the room they had been in. Through a cloud of roiling dust, Dan saw Khalif leap from the perch, and then he was lost from sight.

"What do we do?" Jami asked as they rode their mammoth deeper into the tunnel. If anything, the beasts ran along even faster as they progressed into the passageway.

Dan squeezed her side to show that he was holding onto her and looking out for her.

"Hold on!"

CHAPTER 13

Dan had ridden camels before, but this was nothing like that. They were at least twice as high off the ground than any dromedary he'd ever ridden, and after living in Egypt for a year, he'd had plenty of opportunities. The gait was different, too, somehow slower but because of the huge legs, smoother with longer steps.

Right now they were moving fast. Dan wasn't sure exactly how fast, but he thought they might be travelling along at twenty-five miles per hour. All around them, many more mammoths also galloped into the chute. Dan knew that were either he or Jami to fall from their oblivious steed, they would surely be crushed by the other beasts behind them. The ground was now just that, Dan noted—actual ground, no longer smooth, tile floors. Loose clods of dirt and sand with the occasional rock mixed in pelted the mammoth riders as dozens of the prehistoric pachyderms crashed through the underground tunnel, now in complete darkness. He could hear the animals' breath as they labored to run through the narrow space.

What were they evading? Dan couldn't help but think. He turned around, hoping to see Khalif, but it was pitch dark back that way, too. He and Jami had no choice but to hang on for the ride and be transported to wherever it was the mammoths were heading. Hopefully, the beasts knew of a way out, but then again, they'd just hatched or broken out of hibernation a few minutes ago after who knows how many thousands of years—so what could they possibly know that would send them into such a frenzied run? Dan voiced his concern to Jami, who surprised him with her answer.

"There are animals that sometimes have an instinctive urge to return to a remote ancestral homeland—there's even a term for it that I somehow remember from zoology classes, called *nostophilia*."

"It is crazy that you remember that stuff, especially at a time like this," Dan said loudly into her ear.

She gave a brief laugh that was nearly lost amidst the thundering of the herd. "Some things have a way of coming back to you later. So I'm trying to apply it. Now, I've never heard of nostophilia in connection with mammoths. Usually the examples involve birds or fish. For instance—ooooh, and you're really going to like this—there's an area of Atlantic Ocean south of the Azores Islands—"

"A possible resting place for Atlantis!" Dan spat. The words came out a little choked since their mammoth stumbled a bit as it collided with another to their left while he spoke, but the ancient beast regained its footing and they were back on track, enabling Dan to continue. Even as he spoke, he scanned ahead in the dark, but the pitch black gave him no warnings of what was ahead, good or bad. He wanted to shield his face and head by at least holding an arm out in front of him, but with one hand gripping the mammoth so as not to get thrown off, and the other holding onto Jami to stabilize them both on the bouncing paleo-pachyderm and simply because he liked holding onto her, that was impossible.

"Believe it or not, I've heard a fair amount about the lost continent during my time as a pyramid tour guide. You wouldn't believe the conspiracy theories people throw around. It makes me wonder how they even have enough money to come all the way here on vacation!"

"Probably ad revenue from their wacky YouTube videos explaining stuff like how they know the Earth is flat, or how the pyramids are so advanced that they must have been built by aliens." Dan laughed heartily and then Jami went on, her tone more serious.

"There have been verified reports of birds—and not seabirds, either—flying around and around an area of open ocean where there is no land for hundreds of miles, until they get so tired they can no longer fly, and they fall into the water and drown."

Dan held up a finger. "Because their instincts, or their genes or whatever, are telling them that their home is there, except that it's not there anymore. It's been flooded, and is way underwater. Or maybe slid into the water after a huge earthquake."

"Exactly," Jami agreed. "And that kind of thing could also possibly explain why lemmings engage in their mass suicide behavior of jumping off cliffs *en masse*."

"Jumping off cliffs *en masse* about sums up what it feels like we're doing right now!" Dan shouted back to her, tightening his fingers around the matted mammoth hair.

"I sure hope not! Like you said, how can they know where to go?"

"Must be by design," Dan said, noting the barest flash of dull white denoting one of the massive, curled tusks catching some faint light. "Whoever built this place made it in such a way that they knew the mammoths would hatch out back there and then have to run to…..here!" Dan shouted, his muscles tensing around the mammoth. "Brace yourself, big gap coming up! I see light!"

Indeed, while the chute began to grow almost imperceptibly lighter, they had no time to drink in the details it provided because the mammoth they rode began to gallop faster than ever, jostling them hard.

"Don't let me fall, Dan!" He felt both of Jami's arms encircle his waist, gripping him hard. Dan used both hands now to clutch the mammoth's thick, knotted hair while straddling the broad back by squatting on his knees, as Jami also did.

Ahead, Dan saw something but wasn't sure what. A profusion of light, but was there really a change to the contour of the tunnel they'd been travelling? With all the dust in the air and the general pandemonium, he couldn't be sure. It didn't seem like they had made any turns or taken any kind of side passages.

They kept on riding until the cadence of their unlikely steed became startlingly unpredictable. A normal gait for four or five steps would be followed by a leap that would have them in the air for a few terrifying seconds, and then a few more steps before some new obstacle required a jump. "Hold on!" Dan yelled, feeling Jami tense up against him.

All the while, it grew brighter and the air became more turbulent around them. Like being in a micro-tornado, they were buffeted by winds in a tunnel. But to Dan the air smelled fresh and clean compared to the stale air of the chute reeking of reanimated elephantine bodies running for their lives. They must be near some type of physical connection to the outside world.

But where was it? Chaos reigned. Nothing more than a swirling maelstrom of fur and mud and faint light and sensory overload in every way. All Dan knew to do was to grip the mammoth and hold onto Jami when he could, while she held onto him for dear life. Everything else ceased to exist as they floated through an ethereal, high velocity dreamworld. The cries of the mammoths were undeniable. Dan had become accustomed to them about halfway through the chute, at first thinking it was a wind-related noise or even a figment of his overworked imagination. But now they were louder than ever, a constant presence in his ears making verbal communication impossible.

As the wind picked up, so did the presence of what Dan recognized as sand. The coarse granules pummeled his face and pelted his eyes, causing him to lower his head. He didn't know where it was coming from, whether it meant the entire tunnel system was falling apart or what might be happening, but it was a change, and one that made the going tougher for all of them—humans and animals alike.

"Sand!" he thought he heard Jami shout, but with the constant din of the stampede he wasn't sure she had said anything at all. The progress of the wooly procession grew more erratic. He had to fight constantly to keep both of them on their steed. Near-misses and collisions with the other mammoths became more frequent. He saw the bone white of a massive, curled tusk careening toward his left leg and raised his foot. It cleared the tusk by inches, and the mammoth on which he rode bore the full brunt of the incoming ivory. The impact was like that of a traffic collision between small cars, giving him a kind of sideways whiplash as the wooly mammoth was shoved to the right by the tusk of its comrade.

Dan found the whipping sand to be too much to bear, and combined with the lateral impact that had turned him halfway around anyway, he decided to spin all the way around so that he faced Jami. He couldn't see anything facing forward anyway, so thought it best he could see her and make sure they stayed together on their wild beast. Still the sand came, thicker than ever. It poured around them from every direction. Dan flashed on the entire sandy desert collapsing in on the subterranean space that they had disturbed after who knew how many eons, smothering them in untold millions of tons of silica grains. And yet the mighty beast somehow continued moving through it, until they felt it fall. Shifting their bodies to avoid impact with the ground, they felt the mammoth lose its footing and yet it continued to be carried along in the river of sand, its non-stop gyrations no longer controlled by its own brain, but instead by the physical forces of the powerful flow of sand that now threatened to choke all of them out of existence.

Dan forced himself to clench his mouth shut and hold his breath for long periods until he thought it was safe to snatch a quick breath. He hoped Jami was doing the same, for their ride was now so tumultuous, so beyond their control, that it was all he could do simply to hang on. Then he heard her, calling out to him from right beside him on the mammoth, though her voice was still barely audible. He could feel the exertion of her breathing more than he could hear the words.

"Dan? Dan!"

"Jami, hold…." He choked on some sand and had to spit it out and then waited for a particularly brutal sandblast to pass before yelling again. "Hold on!"

As he finished spitting out the second word along with another mouthful of sand, Dan felt the odd sensation of a lack of feeling on his face. Like an abating of the sensory overload of millions of tiny glass particles power-washing his skin. Then, as quickly as he felt it, it passed. Then it happened again, once more for only a second or two, but this time it was enough to recognize that the constant pelting of sand was letting up just enough to where he could actually feel the absence of it on his face for a split moment. He dared to open his eyes during one of these sand lulls, and thought he could see light—daylight—but then he paid the price for having his eyes open with a face full of fresh sand. His eyes stung so bad that he risked taking his hand off the mammoth's coat in order to reflexively wipe at them, but without water, it wasn't very effective. He couldn't see anything. He braced for the inevitable, forceful bashing that would no doubt put an end to he and Jami. All it would take was for one of the other mammoths to momentarily smash against their own animal at the right angle, and the frail humans would be instantly crushed to death.

He clutched the mammoth's fur tightly, still maintaining a firm grip on Jami's arm. Even with his eyes closed amidst the turmoil, he could tell the world was somehow brightening around them. He still heard Jami's wails, but they were muffled by the thundering of wind, sand, and wooly mammoth cries, not unlike those of African elephants. Dan didn't know how long this kaleidoscopic limbo period went on, nor did he understand what caused it. He considered that this may be punishment for disturbing the ancient site that had gone undiscovered for so long, until he got there. A trap or curse. But he had meant no harm, had no intentions of profiting personally off of the discovery. He wanted only to survive.

He took a chance and opened his eyes again, and this time he saw a patch of brown hair fly by—a mammoth running faster than their own-- and also something else. A face? A human face? Was it Rashid? The eyes were closed and skin pale. He told himself to forget it, his mind was playing tricks on him.

And then something most extraordinary happened. He thought he had died, that he was literally seeing the light at the end of the tunnel. But the pain told him he was still very much among the living, like it or not. For how long was another matter.

"Don't let go!" he cried out to Jami, and was surprised to hear most of the words leave his mouth as intended. What he really meant was, *Don't let go of each other*, since their mammoth was now simply tumbling along, no longer under its own controlled locomotion. It was only a matter of time before—and then it happened. Dan felt the mammoth's dreadlocked hair be torn from his fingers as it bashed into something hard and unforgiving—most likely another mammoth. Dan and Jami were pitched forward off of the beast and Dan barely had time to tighten his grip on Jami's arm before they went flying.

He felt snatches of open, clean air for a few seconds at a time before being sandblasted, but kept his eyes and mouth closed as his body somersaulted through a series of high energy gyrations. At any second he knew he could be impaled on a tusk or pulverized between two mammoth bodies or even hurt by Jami's head smashing into his own. He tried to curl up into a protective fetal position as much as possible and simply go along for the ride, like a surfer underwater during a wipeout on a huge wave. When he felt as though he were about to pass out, he took a quick breath again, which he held for nearly a minute. He repeated this process an untold number of times before he felt his body slowing down. He took the opportunity to pull Jami closer to him. *Don't lose her.* Sand slid off of his body and his head broke free into unfettered air.

He heard Jami gasp for breath and he squeezed her arm to let her know he was still with her. "Breathe, Jami, breathe! We're in the air. I see the sky!"

And it was true. The sight of clouds had never been so appealing to him. It was light out, but not fully so. Must be dawn, he thought, as his body came rolling to a stop in a hillock of warm desert sand. He cradled Jami in his arms while looking around for what might be about to smack into them.

But he saw nothing. No mammoths, no other people, no....*no tunnel*, he realized with a jolt of confusion.

Where were they?

1

CHAPTER 14

Once he was certain the air was truly clear, that they were no longer amidst swirling, raging sand, Dan took a few deep breaths, gulping air like a drowning person finally reaching the surface of the water after being held below. Jami also gasped her way to the top. When they had both reoxygenated their bloodstreams, they began looking around in more detail at their new surroundings.

Featureless desert sand lay in all directions. The Great Pyramid loomed in the distance, but the area in which Dan and Jami found themselves was unbroken by any type of entity other than sand, living or otherwise.

"Khalif?" It was the first clear word Dan had heard from Jami in a long time. Dan looked around, slowly and carefully scanning the flat sands for any signs of another human besides Jami. "Don't see him."

Jami hung her head. "He must still be down there."

"I saw him jump from the same platform we leapt onto the mammoth from, but I couldn't see if he landed on a mammoth or not."

"The mammoths…" Jami tilted her head to look across the desert floor. "All of them buried?"

"I guess so." Dan rose to his feet, dusted off his pants and looked around. He knew that once the sun came up, it would get unbearably hot out here. There was no water in this desert, and they had none. "It's too bad, really, because we could use a ride right about now." He gestured toward faraway Giza. "Looks like we're going to have to hoof it ourselves before the sun gets too high in the sky."

Jami leaned back on her elbows, face to the sky, still breathing heavily. "Normally I'd complain, but right now I'm just happy to be alive."

"I hear you." Dan moved next to her in the sand and also lay back on his elbows. They could afford to rest for a few minutes, he told himself. "Let's take five."

They lay there in the early morning on top of the desert sands. Jami reached out and grabbed Dan's hand and he held it while neither said anything. They lay there staring up at the cloudless sky, moon setting over the Sphinx in the distance. Then Dan released her hand and stood up, hoping she would get the message. It was time to go. Jami reached up and Dan pulled her to her feet.

"Which way?" she asked softly, and Dan pointed back towards the Sphinx.

"To our old friend." Jami nodded and the pair set off walking side by side. They trudged along in silence, each lost in their own thoughts about what they had seen underground, about their own mortality, about how real what they had witnessed really was, and of how much they truly understood about the world in which they lived.

* * * * *

"Taxi!" Dan hailed the cab from one of a congregation that had parked nearby a feeder road to the Sphinx tourism complex. Now late morning, the pair of explorers were drenched in sweat and would draw attention with their torn and soiled clothes and bruised and cut bodies. "Hopefully, we can get into a hotel and get cleaned up before anyone notices us," Dan said, alluding to the fact that they had snuck into unauthorized parts of the Sphinx and pyramid with people dying as a result. It made him nervous since they were being chased by authorities right up until when they disappeared down into the Osiris Shaft.

One Egyptian cabbie immediately put his car into gear and reversed to where the bedraggled pair stood. The driver exited the vehicle, walked around and opened the back door of the older sedan, which, although it looked like it had seen better days, was nonetheless a step up from their previous modes of transportation. Dan took a final look around, especially back towards the desert, hoping against hope that somehow Khalif would come walking up, as worse for wear as they were, but alive. But after a few seconds of glancing around, the cabbie asked him, "Ready, Sir?" while tilting his head toward the back seat of the vehicle. If he thought their condition was alarming, he didn't comment. Jami, her once bouncy, frizzy curls now matted with dust and sand, slid in first, and then Dan followed, resigning himself to the fact that Khalif would not be coming back to town with them. As they drove off, Jami slumped lower in the seat and leaned her head on Dan's shoulder.

"Where to?" the driver asked, glancing in the rearview mirror.

Dan gave him the name of his own hotel in Giza. He was supposed to check out today, but now that somehow seemed like the least important thing in the world. Like Jami, he was still processing what had just happened to them, what they had just seen, the sheer improbability of it all combined with an ethereal sense of deep discovery. He looked out the window and saw the same scene he'd been a part of nearly every day for the last year: tourists milling about the Giza complex, touring the Great Pyramid and the Sphinx. Nothing looked any different, despite the earthquake and all the commotion he had witnessed beneath the sands. All of that was subterranean. And he knew, looking at the lines of tourists being led into the sanctioned parts of the pyramid and Sphinx, that these were not the first tours of the day, so if any significant damage had been observed by the guides on the morning's early tours, those routes would have been closed for the day while the cause of the damage was investigated by authorities. That could only mean that everything they had seen down there had so far gone unnoticed.

Dan stared blankly at the pedestrian and vehicle traffic as they rolled onto the road that would take them into the city. How many of these people knew there was something else down there, below the complex, which has gone unmentioned all these centuries? Only he and Jami? He turned his head and watched her sleeping against his shoulder. *Could we be the only ones? The only ones alive, anyway*, he thought bitterly, reflecting on the loss of both Rashid and Khalif. The thought that it could all be for nothing gnawed at his very soul. What did he know that would prove to the world that those people had died for something extraordinary, not for some stupid, impetuous accident?

He supposed the only course of action in that regard was to approach archaeological authorities and recount what they had seen, and then to let the chips fall where they may. But he knew the way amateurs were generally perceived by professional academics in the field of archaeology. They'd be polite, but the end result would be a brush-off, not worth their time and grant money to even verify, much less investigate. Dan sighed and looked out at the traffic as they merged onto a major artery that would take them into downtown Giza. Maybe he was ready to go home after all.

The cab reached Dan's hotel and he was amazed to find he still had his wallet with enough cash in it to pay for the ride. He gently tapped Jami until she woke and looked around, startled. "It's okay," he told her. "We're at my hotel in Giza. Let's go get cleaned up and get some food." This seemed to rouse her somewhat and she sat up straight, rubbing her eyes while looking out the window.

The driver got out and opened the curbside door for them, all smiles and exaggerated courteousness despite their shabby appearance. Dan gave him the very last of his cash as a tip, not that it was a lot, but it was all he had and he was grateful for the ride out of the Giza complex. The driver took the tip and pulled away from the curb, leaving Dan and Jami standing on the sidewalk in front of the hotel, where another cab was already pulling up with new guests.

Dan took Jami by the hand and they walked through the revolving doors into the hotel lobby. Dan fumbled in his pocket and once again was astounded to find that his room key card was still there, after all he'd been through. *Why couldn't it have been a penlight?* he thought. They ignored the curious stares of the other guests and walked straight back to the elevators. They rode a car up to the third floor and Dan led Jami by the hand to his small room.

"I know, there's only one bed, but I'll take the couch. But first let's get something to eat. I'll call room service so we don't have to go anywhere looking like this."

"Good idea. I'll take a shower while you order. A cheeseburger would be awesome. Also, ask them if they can bring me some women's clothing from the gift shop. I'm happy to pay for it. Believe it or not, I still have my credit card and ID after all we went through." She gave him her sizes and then retreated to the bathroom while Dan ordered room service from the hotel restaurant and ordered the clothes while Jami took a shower. When she was done, he did the same, and afterwards, Jami had already changed into her new outfit that had been delivered, as well as set their food out on the small table by the window.

"Ready to eat?" she asked him. He caught his breath as he looked at her, so different now that she had literally cleaned herself up and put on fresh clothing.

"Absolutely." The two sat and dined in comfortable silence, savoring the taste of their first real food in many hours, washing it down with bottled water on ice and chilled bottles of Stella beer. When they had finished, both admitted they were beyond exhausted and ready for sleep. Dan retired to the couch with a pillow and blanket while Jami fell into the bed.

* * * * *

The next morning found them up with the sunlight streaming through the window, the curtains of which they had never closed. Both agreed that they were ready to venture back out into the world now that they had eaten, showered and slept, and so they made plans to go get some breakfast and then bring Jami back to her hotel. They ate first at a nearby sidewalk café, since the weather was beautiful and it was the first they had been outside in daylight in what seemed like a very long time. They were more talkative now, but still stuck to "safe" topics like how nice it was to be above ground, literally and figuratively, and laughing at various passersby who looked odd or did silly things. Dan avoided mentioning that he was supposed to return home today, that he was basically out of money, and that although they had just gone on a fantastic, though dangerous and even horrifying at times, adventure together, he couldn't help but wonder what, if anything, was next for them as friends. He was about to ask her how long she planned to stay in country when she shook her head and mentioned something about a lack of closure on not knowing what had happened to Khalif.

"We saw what happened to Rashid," she said, "but without actually seeing what became of Khalif, it just makes me feel so guilty to be here, walking around, eating, laughing, having fun....*living*, you know? Like, I wish there was something we could do for him."

Dan tilted his head to one side while he thought about this. Then he said, "I guess we could at least stop by his hotel and report him missing. Let them know that we were with him and we got separated, he didn't return."

Jami's face brightened. "Yes, good idea! Because he might have family or friends who called his hotel looking for him. Do you know where he was staying?"

Dan thought back to their night in the bar. It seemed like a lifetime ago, but he pictured Khalif's face, his swagger as he came walking into the place with his flask, and overhearing their conversation next to his table, and it came back to him. "He said he was at the Nile Ritz-Carlton."

"Of course. I was going to book myself there but it was full." She rolled her eyes. "Not to mention I could stay for two weeks at my place instead of one night there."

Dan laughed. "Right."

"Okay, let's go as soon as we're done here."

The two finished their breakfast and called an Uber while waiting for the check. Their driver was an Egyptian man perhaps ten years their senior who spoke good English, and he asked them if they were Americans. They told him yes, and he said, "Ah, let me guess, you are on your honeymoon?"

Dan and Jami exchanged glances and giggled. Dan found himself replying, "Yep, I wanted to go to Bora Bora, but she was dying to see the pyramids, so here we are!"

"Excellent choice!" the driver beamed. "Your better half will always be right, get used to it! Happy wife, happy life!"

And so the ride went, with them all joking about married life, and before they knew it, they were pulling up to an expansive circular drive lined with date palms and high-end exotic sports cars. Khalif's hotel. Dan was able to pay the driver with a credit card he'd had in his hotel room, and then he and "Mrs. Dan James" were turning down porter requests for their non-existent luggage and walking up to the grand lobby entrance.

"Hopefully, the front desk people will be helpful," Jami said. "I know they're not supposed to give out information, but in this case…"

"Like you said, we can at least leave a message with them to call us if he returns."

The two entered the hotel and walked in until they were clear of the entrance before pausing to look around. The place was elegantly appointed and spacious, with multiple restaurants, bars, cafes and shops occupying the sprawling interior environs. Dan pointed out the lobby and they started walking toward it. They passed a bar on the right called The Tap East, and Dan glanced over at it, noting the open layout with no doors to enter. A long bar occupied the wall of the place while numerous tables and chairs were spread throughout. Not a bad place to grab a drink, Dan couldn't help but thinking as he checked out the huge selection of beer taps behind the bar. He was about to suggest to Jami that they stop in for a pint after they talk to the hotel staff, when a man seated at the bar turned around and Dan got a look at his face.

He stopped walking and grabbed Jami's arm without looking away. The face was unmistakable. The thick, black hair, the beard, the olive skin. His mind could scarcely believe it and yet at the same time would give him only one word: *Khalif.* And at the same time, Khalif was staring right back at him, his own eyes widening.

"Khalif!" Dan said to both Khalif and for the benefit of Jami, who was puzzled as to why Dan had stopped walking.

"What?" he heard Jami say, and at the same time, he saw a neat red circle appear in Khalif's forehead. The Arab fell off his barstool to the floor, where he lay unmoving in a crumpled heap. Dan spun around, thinking the shot must have come from his direction, but behind them was only wide open space with numerous people milling about. No loud report accompanied the shot, so Dan knew that a sound suppressor must have been used. Even so, panic began to ensue as patrons in the bar shrieked at the sight of the gunshot victim on the floor of the high-end establishment. Guests cleared the lobby in a panic, running both for the elevators and for the main exits. Head on a swivel, Dan spotted a man tucking a pistol into his suit jacket and starting to run.

"Jami, we have to be careful. If whoever shot Khalif knows that we were with him under the Sphinx, then we have to assume that we're targets also."

"Should we hide or run?" she asked, clutching him tightly while glancing all around. Dan unfortunately made eye contact with the shooter, who then appeared to speak into the lapel of his jacket.

"Run!" He took Jami by the hand and they beat feet toward the exit, but Dan realized the throng there was starting to be a bottleneck and that they would have to stand there in the crowd like sitting ducks while they waited for people to exit. "No, this way!" He turned left and they ran instead for the rear of the lobby to the elevator bank. A smaller crowd was gathered there waiting for the four cars. By the time they were almost there, one of them opened and the waiting throng surged into it, pinning a couple inside who had unknowingly come down at the wrong time. Dan saw that the right-most elevator was descending from Floor 5, and so would be next to open although the crowd had yet to notice since they were all jostling for position in front of the currently open car.

"C'mon." Dan pulled Jami to the right, behind the throng. They reached the elevator when it was on Floor 2. Others quickly started moving toward that elevator, realizing it was about to open. Dan knew they would be able to get in, and he mentally prepared himself to hit the 'Close Door' button as soon as he did. He was thinking of this when the door to the stairs opened to their right, and he cursed himself for not thinking about taking the stairs in the first place. He was just opening his mouth to suggest it to Jami when the man who had emerged from the stairwell walked up to him and stuck a sound-suppressed pistol into his gut.

"Both of you: with me now up the stairs, or you get a bullet." The voice was in English, but with an Arabic accent. Dan knew that no one would hear in the midst of all the commotion if he was to get shot with the silenced handgun. He also didn't want Jami to do anything rash that would cause the gunman to pull the trigger.

"Okay," he said, loud enough for both the gunman and Jami to hear. "We'll do it, just relax."

The gunman nodded toward the stairway exit at the same time the elevator they stood in front of opened. Dan led Jami to the stairwell door followed closely by the gunman while a herd of people behind them, oblivious to the weapon in their immediate midst, invaded the open elevator. Dan opened the stairwell door while Jami entered first. The gunman indicated for him to pass through next, which Dan did, and then the gunman slipped inside behind them. "All the way up."

"Roof?" Dan asked, getting worried. He started climbing, knowing there had to be at least twenty stories, maybe more.

"No, penthouse. Now shut up and move. No more talking until we get there. And no games, or I shoot."

"You're the boss," Dan said, wondering where all this was going. He knew his answer lay at the top of about twenty more flights of stairs, so he resigned himself to the workout and started pumping his legs, as did Jami. As they ascended, they occasionally heard doors open and close, and even a voice in the stairwell, but by the time they reached Floor 15, according to the stencil on the wall, they had still encountered no other people. As they continued to climb, Dan's mind whirled into overdrive with possible outcomes of this unlikely encounter, most of them not good. He found it difficult to think clearly with the constant exertion of pounding up the steps. After a few more flights he decided to simply focus on reaching the top. They had just made Floor 18 when the door opened and a family of three, including a small boy, peered into the stairwell.

"Don't come down—stay on your floor, there's an emergency in the lobby. Stay put!" the gunman yelled. The door promptly swung shut. The three of them continued up without further incident until reaching a floor marked with a letter "P".

"This is it. Open it," the gunman commanded. Dan pushed the metal bar on the door and it swung into a carpeted hallway.

"Turn left and walk to Suite 22," the gunman ordered.

"Sounds good," Dan said. "C'mon, Jami. I'm sure this is all a huge misunderstanding."

"Shut up." The gunman stepped into the hall and the door clicked shut behind them. Dan and Jami walked side by side down the empty but well-appointed hall, looking for #22. Plush carpeting, fine art on the walls, soft music playing. The doors with numbers on them were far apart and they found 22 after passing two others. Dan and Jami stopped in front of the door while the gunman, pistol still in hand and pointed at Dan, approached.

"Knock on the door precisely five times in a row."

Dan thought about asking what would happen if he only knocked four times, or if he knocked six times, but the old phrase, "I've got the gun, I'll ask the questions," popped into his head and he thought better of it. He rapped his knuckles loudly on the door five times in quick succession.

"Step back from the door," the gunman said. Dan and Jami complied, stepping back a few paces, halfway to the opposite wall. The gunman spoke a few unintelligible words into a mic attached to his jacket lapel. A few seconds later, the door swung open.

CHAPTER 15

A swarthy-complected Arab holding a snub-nosed machine gun greeted them in the doorway. His expression was blank but his body language said, *watch yourselves*. He held the gun rock-steady with one hand, the other having been used to open the door. Some ten feet behind him, another armed Arab levelled a sound-suppressed pistol at Dan's chest.

"Inside," came the order from the gunman in the hallway, who waved his own pistol toward the suite entrance. Dan and Jami shuffled into the suite. In spite of the dire circumstance, Dan couldn't help but be taken aback by the splendor of the place, how grand it was. It dawned on him at that moment that he had never been inside a penthouse level suite before. The ceilings were higher than those of a normal room. That the entire place consisted of several rooms, like a large condo or a small house, was in itself a revelation to Dan. Opulence was everywhere, from the plush carpeting to the quartz countertops on the color-changing LED-lit wet bar to the crystal chandeliers hanging over the dining room table, to the floor-to-ceiling-windows in the living room offering stunning views of downtown Cairo and Giza in the distance.

"Sure beats Motel 6," Dan quipped.

"No doubt!" Jami couldn't help but reply. She, too, was impressed by the surroundings to the point it took her mind off their predicament. But Dan knew that the banter also had the effect of humanizing them to their captors, which would make them less like objects and hopefully just a little more difficult to extinguish the life out of, should it come to that. And Dan knew that it might. This same group had just shot Khalif dead on the spot, after all.

"Continue into the living room and sit down on the couch," the escort gunman behind them said.

"Is that Italian leather?" Dan asked, following up with a low whistle. "Look, I don't know what it is you guys want, but if you can afford to stay here, there's nothing we have that you—"

He didn't see the butt of the sub-machine gun coming, and its impact to the side of his head literally knocked him the rest of the way to the couch. He could feel the blood running down his face and no sooner had he put a finger on the wound and then looked at the blood dripping from his hand than a high thread count towel was thrown at his face from one of the gun-toting thugs.

"You will shut the hell up and only speak when spoken to from this point forward. Is that clear enough?"

Dan put the towel to the side of his head and nodded with narrowed eyes. Jami took a seat on the couch next to him, her face a study in consternation. The gunmen backed up from the couch as another man walked into the room. He was also Arab and perhaps somewhat younger than his security team. He wore cloth head gear and a flowing white robe. He carried nothing in his hands, but a gold-handled scimitar in a sheath hung from the golden rope that cinched his robe around his waist. He stared intently at first Dan and then Jami before addressing them.

"My name is Prince Abdullah Mohammed. I am from the United Arab Emirates. I have long held an interest in ancient cultures, and for many years have been trying to secure permission from Egyptian authorities to sponsor an archaeological dig beneath the Great Pyramid."

"Khalif showed us the entrance to your dig site," Dan said, cutting to the chase. "But none of us went in there. We didn't touch it whatsoever."

"There were other people down there besides us," Jami added. "We thought they were police, but we never actually saw them. They chased us."

The prince took a step closer to them and eyed Jami intently. "Are you saying they are the ones who sabotaged my dig site, and not you?"

"I'm saying it wasn't us, and they were there, so it could have been them." Her tone of voice was matter-of-fact, as if she were stating something that couldn't possibly be any other way.

But the prince answered her in the same tone. "Or perhaps the path you took into the Osiris chamber eventually led into where my dig would have led. *Regardless*," he said while holding up a finger to ward off the objection he could see forming on Jami's lips, "even if it was them, they were there because of you. They chased *you* down to my site. *You* were the ones who called attention to it in the first place." Dan flashed on his removing the barricade in front of the prince's dig site before retreating into the quake-opened passage, to throw their pursuers off their trail. He held his best poker face.

"You don't know that for sure," Jami spat.

"I know enough!" the prince shouted, his face contorting into a mask of genuine anger.

"You're both forgetting something," Dan said.

The prince turned to look at him. "Did that little bump on the noggin refresh your memory? Do tell."

Dan ignored the jab and responded. "There was an earthquake. You must have heard about it on the news by now."

At this, two of the gunmen behind the prince exchanged glances. "Go on," the prince said.

Dan did. "That quake opened up a new offshoot of the Osiris chamber that wasn't accessible or visible at all before. The same tremor is probably what disturbed your site."

"Khalif told me you found things down there. Tell me everything! Be thorough and leave nothing out. If I sense one of you is lying, I will make one of you shoot the other."

"I'll go first," Dan said. He proceeded to relate how they found the new passage opened by the earthquake beneath the Osiris chamber, and then the underground lake and the test of the afterlife with the scale, including Rashid's death, and the giant crocodile in the lake. He deliberately left out the details relating to Atlantis, but described the general surroundings and structures discovered, including the gold flooring. Through the recounting, the prince paid rapt attention, not interrupting and occasionally pacing in front of them while his bodyguards kept their weapons trained on Dan and Jami.

With Jami frequently chiming in, Dan explained that the last they saw of Khalif was right after they had jumped from the slab onto the wooly mammoths, and that he saw Khalif jump as they rode the beast out of sight into the tunnel.

"Why did you kill him?" Jami asked point-blank, while on the subject of Khalif.

The prince shot her an icy stare. "Khalif is from my country. He has long been interested in archaeological treasures, particularly those associated with Egypt and the pyramids. On more than one occasion, I issued him a directive—verbally, face-to-face—*not* to interfere with my dig site in any way. I specifically warned him not to come anywhere *near* it. And yet he disregarded my order. Not only that," the prince continued, on seeing the disgust still present in Jami's eyes, "but even upon being confronted in the hotel bar on what he had done, he refused to cooperate. He would not tell me anything about what he had found or even seen. He was nowhere near as descriptive as you two Americans."

"Great, so does that mean you're not going to kill us?" Dan asked. He wasn't sure if being American was helping or hurting them in this context. At this question, the prince spun on a heel and walked in the other direction. He nodded to one of his bodyguards, who took his place in front of the couch, automatic weapon levelled at Dan's chest.

"Unfortunately, no," the prince answered. "You have seen too much. You know too much. It is nothing personal, but both of you are now casualties of war in my royal Emirati quest to locate the planet's most alluring cultural treasures. Antiquities of such import that I am competing with individuals and institutions with resources similar to mine. I cannot afford any loose ends." He directed a single Arabic syllable to the bodyguard in front of the couch, who nodded and fine-tuned the aim of his weapon on Dan's chest.

"I know where to find something of incomparable value that you will never locate without us," Dan said.

The prince held up a hand to the bodyguard before turning back around to look at Dan. "And what is that?"

"The lost city of Atlantis."

Dan expected the prince to laugh, but he did not. He merely stared hard at Dan and Jami, his gaze alternating between them before replying in a calm and measured voice. "Is this knowledge of Atlantis connected to your sojourn into the pyramids today?"

"It is," Dan said, with Jami nodding along with him.

The prince held out his hands. "I would be remiss were I not to ask, how do I know you're telling the truth?"

Dan shrugged. "Right now, you don't. You can't. But I can take you to it, and if we find it, or at least find proof that it was there but is no longer, then would you be willing to let us go?"

The prince reared his head back with a wildly skeptical expression. "I'll indulge myself and play along for a minute. Without giving away the exact location, how long does it take to get there?"

Again, Dan shrugged. "It's on the continent of Antarctica. I know approximately where based on something I saw down under the pyramids. The evidence that conveyed the information to us has now been destroyed by the events that I told you about. But you have the financial resources to take us all to Antarctica. Once on site, I will explain everything I know, and you will be satisfied that I am telling the truth based on how I came to know this—and hopefully--on what we find when we get there."

"Antarctica?"

"That's what I said, yes. Did you listen to anything I said after that, or…?"

The prince stroked the stubble on his chin, apparently considering his captive in a new light. He said something in Arabic to his bodyguard, who lowered his weapon and retreated to the edge of the room, although he continued to keep a watchful eye on the Americans.

The prince nodded slowly while drawing his scimitar with a raspy metallic clang. The silver blade gleamed. "So you expect me to finance an expedition more than halfway around the world, to Antarctica—based on the words of a man who thought himself, along with his woman—about to die?" The prince took two steps closer to Dan, holding the tip of his long blade out towards Dan's neck.

"If you want to find Atlantis, then yes, I expect you will do it. And since you said you're interested in finding the world's most noble treasures, or however you put it, and Atlantis is known for its streets paved in gold, and having an advanced civilization with many great artworks, then yes, I expect you will finance the expedition."

The prince took one step closer to Dan, so that he was now only one blade's length away. "I could simply have you tortured until you tell me."

Once again, Dan shrugged. "If you like wasting time. Everybody knows that someone being tortured just says whatever they think will make the torture stop. So it's like I'll say, 'It's here!' And you either go all the way to Antarctica yourself, or send your goons, and wait for them to say, 'It's not there.' Then we start all over again."

"No, then I just kill you."

"You could kill me if I tell you the truth, too. So it's to my advantage to give you just enough information to show that I have something, and then when we get there—we all figure out the exact location together. I realize that you could kill us at that point, too, in Antarctica, after we find Atlantis. It's not like there's a big population there. But I'm hoping that a businessman such as yourself is a man of your word, and that if I make this deal with you, that you will honor it. I know we will." Jami nodded in a show of solidarity.

A lengthy silence ensued that Dan found unnerving. Was he going to refuse the deal in his mind and simply have them shot on the couch?

"Do both of you still have your passports?"

CHAPTER 16

Later that night, Dan and Jami were sequestered in Dan's hotel room after checking Jami out of hers and informing Dan's hotel that he'd be staying one more night and checking out in the morning. The prince had released them, but not before confiscating both of their passports with the icy statement, "You will get them back when you meet my envoy tomorrow morning in the airport." Dan had managed to hold back a snide remark about never having met an envoy before, and he and Jami had been unceremoniously released from their penthouse prison.

On the way back to the hotel, they'd picked up some basic first aid supplies to treat Dan's head wound and some of the other scrapes and bruises sustained beneath the Giza Complex. After patching each other up and ordering room service—they'd decided dining in was probably the safest option for now—talk turned to their immediate future.

"I can't believe we're going to Antarctica tomorrow," Jami said. "So exciting—as a zoologist, I've always wanted to go there. But of course, not under these circumstances. Do you really think we can trust him to let us live at the end of this trip? I mean, Antarctica—it's desolate, there's nobody there. He could kill us so easily and nobody would ever even know! And that's even if we find Atlantis! What if we don't find it? How much will he care about us then?"

"You saw that map down there, Jami, with the green water, remember?"

"Yes."

"Well, how could that be anything else but a map? A map to show where in Antarctica the Atlanteans relocated to. I made a mental note of the fact that the peninsula was at roughly the nine O'clock position, while the shaded portion of the map occupied the edge of the mainland at 11 O'clock."

"We need to look at a real map of Antarctica. Hold on…." Jami went to her bag and pulled her laptop out of it and lit it up. She brought up a map of the roughly circular continent, and then picked up the laptop and rotated it on screen such that the peninsula, Queen Maude Land, was at about the 9 O'clock position, as Dan had indicated. "And so you said the shaded part of the map—where the deeper water was that made it look darker—was at approximately 11 O'clock?"

"That's right," Dan said, not taking his eyes off the screen.

"So that should be this general area, right about....here." She touched the tip of her pointer finger to the image. "That could still be a pretty big area, you know?"

Dan shrugged. "Yes, but it's something at least semi-concrete to go on. I didn't know what else to say. I was literally at gunpoint and had to come up with something. But hey, we'll just have to enlist His Royal Highness' vast resources to help us search the area carefully, almost like a professional archeology dig, now, wont we?"

She gave him a weak smile that carried a lot of doubt.

He held his head in his hands for a moment and then levelled a stare at her. "Look, Jami, I'm really sorry I got you into all this."

She reached out and squeezed his hand. "Not your fault. You couldn't possibly have known all the crazy stuff that would happen."

"You don't have to go to Antarctica if you don't want."

Her eyes widened. "I don't? You mean, instead I could go to the U.S. embassy and hide out in Egypt until I can have my passport replaced? Then fly back home and look over my shoulder the rest of my life? Every time someone gets behind me in a store line I'll think I'm about to be shot with some silenced pistol? No thanks. I'll take my chances with His Royal Psycho in Antarctica. Besides," she said, batting her eyelashes, "so far it's been pretty fun hanging out with you. Far and away the most exciting first date I've ever been on."

Dan felt his cheeks blushing red. "The feeling is mutual. We have to get up super-early, while it's still dark out. We should probably get some sleep. I'll take the couch."

She smiled at him. "I think the bed's big enough for both of us. For *sleeping*. I want the window side. Let's get some shut eye, fellow explorer."

CHAPTER 17

At 5:30 A.M. the next morning, Dan and Jami exited an Uber ride at Cairo International Airport. They had awoken to a text from the prince to be at this specific location at this time. "We need Hall 4 in Terminal 1," Dan said. Jami pointed to a sign over an entrance not far from where they stood. "Less crowded than I thought it would be," she noted. A puzzled look took over Dan's face as he nodded in agreement while looking around. "Let's go in."

Inside, they located Hall 4 and Dan pointed to a sign reading, "Private Jet Terminal."

Jami smiled. "Should have known."

"Lotta private planes in this part of the world," Dan acknowledged, glancing around at the semi-crowded terminal.

Soon they were greeted by an Arab man in a suit wielding a sign with the printed English words, "Prince Abdullah Mohammed." They approached and said they were told to meet him in Hall 4. The envoy lowered his sign, made momentary eye contact with each of them, and said simply, "Come with me." He dropped the sign into a trash can as they walked through the terminal to a walkway that led out to the tarmac.

"That is your plane." He pointed across the asphalt to a waiting Gulfstream G650 jet.

"Whoa!" Jami couldn't help but exclaim. "I guess if you're going to be forced to ride on a plane, this would be the one." Dan lightly tapped her on the foot, a gesture meant to be a low-key way of telling her to "cool it" in front of the Prince's employee.

"Please, make your way to the boarding ladder. A flight attendant on board will show you to your seats. The prince and I wish you a most pleasant flight!"

The emissary beamed at them while waiting for them to walk toward the aircraft, which they did without a further word. When they were halfway to the plane, Dan turned around to see if anyone was following them, perhaps other passengers, but they were the only two making their way to that particular luxury jet. Upon reaching the boarding ladder, a female flight attendant in uniform waved to them with a bright smile and beckoned them aboard.

"Welcome to your flight! Please follow me." When he and Jami reached the top of the stairs and stepped onto the aircraft itself, Dan glanced to the left, at the cockpit. Unlike commercial airliners, where passengers could usually see into the cockpit and sometimes even say hello to the pilot, the cockpit door here was shut all the way. The flight attendant, a Lebanese woman in what Dan guessed to be her mid-thirties, led them off to the right. The plane's cabin was testament to Middle-Eastern opulence. Unlike a commercial airliner, which was basically a tube crammed with as many rows of seats as possible, this Gulfstream had been modified to accommodate up to a dozen passengers in extreme style. Plush carpeting, high-end furniture, and even beds awaited those who flew with, or for, the Prince.

"You will find an office at the rear of the jet, complete with high speed Internet, teleconferencing and a computer station featuring all major business productivity software. We also have a full kitchen and bar with menus for your perusal by scanning the QR code on your portable device, as well as printed should you desire." The flight attendant paused to extend an arm toward a row of leather reclining seats in the middle of the plane. "Please be seated and fasten your seatbelts for takeoff. Once we're at cruising altitude, we'll let you know it's safe to move about the cabin. Enjoy your flight!" With that, she bounced off toward the cockpit, leaving Dan and Jami to seat themselves amidst the lavish splendor. They flopped into the oversized seats, which they found to be extraordinarily comfortable even in the full upright position.

Dan pointed to the office area at the rear of the plane. "I guess they want us to research Atlantis while we're underway."

Jami nodded. "Yeah, I took that as a subtle hint, too." She shrugged before continuing. "And it makes sense. I don't want to waste my time, either. If we can narrow the search down, let's do that once we're up there."

Soon after they had buckled their seatbelts, a male voice speaking English came over the intercom. "Good morning, passengers, welcome aboard Prince Mohammed's Gulfstream 650, for our flight all the way to Punta Arenas, Chile. We will have several refueling stops along the way. Our first layover will be in Portugal, before we cross the Atlantic Ocean to New York. From there we'll head south to Miami before making our way to the South American continent. We'll keep you updated with each stop along our journey. At some of the refuel stops you may be permitted to stretch your legs by disembarking the aircraft and visiting the airport facilities. We are of course fully stocked with anything you might need for a pleasant voyage, so don't hesitate to let any of our crew know of your needs. We'll be in the air in a few minutes. Please remain seated with your seatbelts fastened until the crew tells you it's safe to move about the cabin. Enjoy your flight!"

The aircraft began to roll as it taxied down the runway. It paused at the end of the takeoff stretch and then the jet engines roared to life. Jami reached over and gripped Dan's hand. "Never been on such a small jet," she said, squeezing hard.

"It'll be pretty smooth, I think . And fast." Dan had no idea what he was talking about, but he turned out to be right. Following a powerful but brief acceleration, they were wheels up in no time, the golden sands of Egypt spreading out below them. They stared at the endless vista until clouds obscured their view out the window. Then, realizing that they had a full menu at their disposal, Dan's thoughts turned to food. He ordered a bottle of Moet champagne, to Jami's surprise, and a dozen oysters Moscow on the half-shell. They ate all kinds of food, from exotic appetizers to hearty surf & turf entrees, and when they could eat no more, they lay back in their seats and grew tired. They had arisen early, after all, and despite a good night's sleep, they were making up for lost hours with the previous day being spent underground. Dan suggested they try out the beds for a nap, and they found them behind a door at the rear of the plane. They took bunks opposite one another and promptly dozed off.

When they awoke, Dan looked at his watch and saw that about seven hours had passed. He raised the shade on the nearest window and saw only white clouds beyond it. He glanced over at Jami, who still slept soundly in her bed, fleece covers pulled up to her neck. He got out of the bunk and exited the sleeper section, wanting to find out what their current position was. A flight attendant—a different female from the one before—approached and asked him if he needed anything. He told her he wanted to know where they were, and the crew member pointed to a screen mounted on a bulkhead.

"We're about to land in Miami," she told him matter-of-factly in what Dan was surprised to recognize as an American accent, northeastern. "I came on board at JFK. Is there anything else you need? Because real soon we're going in for a landing and for that, you need to be either in a seat or in a sleeper." She finished with a winning smile that, while friendly, also suggested that the conversation was over.

"Okay, thanks. Could I get some food?"

"Sure, you can order from your phone or else use the touchscreen on the back of the seats."

As Dan turned and walked over to the sleeper area, he realized he was completely taking her word for their location. "Sure kid, you're in the sky over Miami, yeah that's it!" How was he to know? They could be anywhere in the world by now. But then he decided there was nothing he could do about it anyway. He was groggy and just wanted to get something to eat and drink. He found the nearest empty seat, noting that he was now the only passenger in sight, and ordered a breakfast consisting of *huevos rancheros*, fresh squeezed orange juice, Colombian coffee and a side of cut melons. He didn't have long to wait, and by the time he finished eating, there were breaks in the clouds allowing him to see a sprawling urban environment below with a lot of water around it, including a fantastic looking white sand beach lined with skyscrapers. Miami, he guessed, now feeling more relaxed.

The flight attendant returned to clear his plates right before the fasten seatbelt light came on, accompanied by the pilot's voice announcing they were beginning descent to Miami International. Dan watched as they flew over a long but thin stretch of golden sand and palm trees, which was soon replaced by skyscrapers and highways. When the plane landed, Dan waited for the seatbelt sign to click off and then headed back to the sleeper car to check on Jami. Still asleep, he decided there was no reason not to take a nap himself, rather than deplane to hang out in the airport. He thought about Atlantis, about what he had seen beneath the pyramids, until sleep overtook him.

So the time passed, across too many time zones to keep track of, the hours a blur as they flew ever closer to the bottom of the globe. Dan lost track of where exactly they were after a while. It was just a repeating cycle of sleep, ask for food that was always great, eat it, do some reading about Atlantis and Antarctica, then go back to sleep, wake up to find they had already landed and refueled somewhere and were now in the air again. Most of the time Jami was up with him and they ate and drank together, researched together.

They were almost used to the travel routine when the pilot's voice came over the intercom informing them that they were preparing to land in Punta Arenas, Chile, where the current temperature was 37 degrees Fahrenheit. Looking out the windows, they saw only white sky until the plane began to descend. They emerged from a layer of clouds to see the blue-and-white ocean spreading out beyond Land's End. The airport itself looked like a collection of metal roofed huts, although the runways were big, but it definitely didn't look like a large JFK-style international airport.

The landing was as smooth as the rest of the journey, and then they were informed that in a few minutes, they would be deplaning to meet waiting ground transportation. Dan and Jami grabbed their bags and thanked their flight attendant on the way out, noting that the cockpit door was still shut. Standing at the top of the airstair, Dan could see an identical looking G650 jet parked nearby. He pointed it out to Jami. "Wonder if His Royal Highness took his own separate plane from us?"

Jami shrugged. "Good for him if he did. Were you really looking forward to hanging out with him all that time?"

"Good point! Looks like that's our ride. Let's check it out." They descended the airstairs and walked to a black limousine idling close by with the trunk and rear door open, a uniformed Argentinian driver standing at attention. He bid them a warm and friendly greeting in Spanish before taking their bags and placing them in the trunk, and then closing the door and taking his place behind the wheel.

Inside the limo, Dan and Jami found that they were to be the only occupants for a short ride to the Punta Arenas seaport. The parts of town they passed through on the way were modern with a certain quaint charm. Paved streets with colonial style houses, a smallish business district including a row of inviting-looking hotels that Dan and Jami couldn't help but ask about.

"We're not checking into one of these?" Dan asked the driver, who shook his head with a smile and replied in accented English.

"No, you're going to the seaport."

"I hope the hotels there are as nice as these," Jami said, gazing fondly at a luxury hotel where guests were having their luggage carried through a revolving door by porters.

"You are not staying in a hotel," the driver told them with a smile.

"A house?" Dan asked, getting a little worried. Again, the driver shook his head.

"It is best I save it for a surprise. We are almost there. You will see!"

Dan and Jami had to content themselves with a little mystery as they rolled the rest of the way through Punta Arenas to the seaport while they speculated about staying in a nice, waterfront resort with views of boats passing by. They pulled into the port and saw a long dock jutting out into the harbor with numerous ships, both commercial and private, tied up to it. Traffic, both vehicular and pedestrian was moderate, and a few coffee shops and seafood places maintained outdoor seating areas in spite of what Dan considered to be chilly air. When they turned off the street into the parking lot of the seaport, they could smell the fish market through the limo's closed doors. Flocks of gulls hovered in the air, divebombing when they saw opportunity.

Their transport rolled farther and farther out along the port, and buildings became fewer and farther between. They passed a row of berths where large ships were docked, and after passing dozens of these, the driver coasted to a stop in front of one of the bigger ones. He honked the horn a couple of times before exiting the vehicle to open the door for his passengers. "This will be your lodging for the evening, the *Antarctic Queen*."

"I guess we're going right to the ship that will take us to Antarctica," Dan said to Jami, staring at the vessel. It was large, definitely a ship and not a boat, but not gigantic like a modern commercial cruise ship or oil tanker.

"I guess we should have known," Jami said with a sigh. "I was hoping for a quaint little bed and breakfast or something like that."

The door swung open and the driver beckoned. "A crewmember is waiting for you at the gangway to show you to your quarters." With that, the driver got back behind the wheel and drove off, just as a crewman walked down the gangway, waving in greeting. Dan and Jami walked with their few bags to the top of the gangway, the massive ship looming behind it.

"Welcome aboard the *Queen*, my name is Antonio Contreras, and I will be happy to show you aboard the finest icebreaker in all the Southern Ocean!" He spoke in accented English with a bright and seemingly genuine smile. Dan was beginning to suspect that not everyone the prince did business with was privy to the seedy underbelly of his dealings. It seemed that the prince kept his business compartmentalized. This crewperson likely only thought he was doing his duty managing the charter guests and helping to run the charter. At least Dan assumed it was a charter, since there was no good reason for someone from the Middle East to own an icebreaker ship. He wondered if perhaps some of these people could be persuaded to help them, should the need arise.

"Thanks," Dan said, shaking the man's hand and then waiting for Jami to do the same before asking, "When do we set sail for Antarctica?"

"Weather permitting—and it looks like it will be—at first light. You'll have plenty of time to get a good night's sleep tonight. Chow time's at 5:30. Right this way, please."

Dan and Jami dutifully followed their guide around for a tour of the ship, but their heart was not in it after all of the travel and due to the general uncertainty surrounding their fate. They heard phrases like "converted icebreaker," "special modifications," and "cutting-edge technological capabilities," but mostly it was just a whirlwind walking tour of expansive decks, ladder-like stairwells and catwalks, a peer into the currently unmanned bridge festooned with LCD monitors and high-end electronic equipment. They saw a few other crewmembers along the way, who ignored them as they went about their work, but like their guide had said, there were not many people considering the size of the vessel. They passed by numerous mechanical apparatus such as cranes, winches, cabling and smaller support vessels that they were told would be used to get them ashore once they neared the Southern Continent.

At the end of the tour, as promised, they were shown to their quarters—blessedly private—a very small cabin with bunk beds. Their guide reminded them dinner would be at 5:30 in the mess hall, and that someone would be there to show them the way shortly before that. After he left, Dan closed their door and dropped his backpack on the floor. The accommodations were Spartan but clean.

"Not gonna lie, I would have preferred a hotel," Jami said, flopping onto the bottom bunk's thin mattress.

"I'm sorry," Dan managed, shaking his head as he looked around the basic confines of their quarters. "We don't have to stay in here, though, we are free to move about the ship."

"I feel like we should maybe hit the library they showed us, and use the Internet to tell people where the hell we are."

Dan pondered this for a moment before answering. "You don't think the Prince's people will be monitoring those communications?"

Jami shrugged. "Even if they are, so what? I still want my family to know where I am, what is happening to me."

"Now that I think about it, what's the worst that could happen? We get kidnapped and taken to Antarctica? Let's go do some research in the library before din-din."

Jami smiled at him warmly and they left their quarters. Doing their best to recall the ship's layout from the tour they had just received, the pair made their way topside from the belowdecks quarters area. They encountered a crewmember here and there as they made their way toward the ship's superstructure, in which the library was housed. Most of them paid them no mind, and those who did only broke away from their work long enough to give a cursory wave or nod. Upon reaching the superstructure, they entered a maze of stairwells and catwalks which eventually led them to an inside area several floors up from the main deck affording a commanding view of the surrounding seaport.

Dan couldn't help but glance over at the roads and parking areas for any signs of a stretch limo or any other kind of ostentatious transportation that might herald the arrival of the prince, but he saw nothing out of the ordinary. He supposed he would arrive for dinner, and wondered what they would talk about. He told Jami he thought it best they get to the library before the prince did arrive, since they intended to try and get a sensitive email out. They tore themselves from the view and continued down the hallway until it rounded a corner, looking for the library / media room they had been shown very briefly earlier. They passed a radio room, but not the actual bridge, and then a machine shop, a break room where a group of men played a game of table tennis. It occurred to Dan that they certainly had the run of the ship. He wondered how long their unfettered access would continue.

They found the media room and ducked inside, closing the door behind them. The small space was blessedly unoccupied. Two computer workstations were set up on a desk, with a conferencing telephone on top of a small table. A single shelf offered books on non-fiction, such as oceanography, maritime history and seamanship.

"We better get to work before someone decides to check up on us," Jami said, taking a seat in front of one of the computer workstations. Dan glanced back at the door, noting that whoever sat at the computer station would have their back to the room's only door. Nevertheless, he took a seat next to Jami at the other computer. "How about you try to send an email and I'll do a little web research on Antarctica and Atlantis?"

"Sounds good," she said, already clicking the mouse to open an Internet browser. But her initiative was short-lived. "Uh-oh, here we go." She pointed to her screen, where a message was displayed. "Enter employee login credentials."

Dan sighed as the same message popped up on his screen. He tapped enter to see if it would work with the field left blank, but an error message was displayed. "I'll try 'guest'." But that, too, was ineffective.

Jami got up from the computer. "We could just ask the same guy who welcomed us aboard and ask him if we could get a guest login."

"Yeah, my hacker skills aren't what they used to be," Dan joked. They left the media room and began walking back down the superstructure's ladder-like stairs. "Reminds me a little of the stepwells under the Sphinx," Dan said as they plodded downward, their footfalls reverberating with dull metallic thuds.

As luck would have it, as soon as they emerged from the superstructure to the main deck, their tour guide, Antonio, was there. He smiled warmly and asked them how they were liking the ship so far and if they needed anything. Dan flat out told them they tried to access the Internet but could not. "Is there a guest login we could use?"

The crewman shook his head and held his hands apart. "I apologize, but our Communications Officer is the one who would need to set that up. But he won't be aboard until early tomorrow morning, in the middle of the night, basically. But once he's here, I'll let him know you would like access. Anything I can do for you right now? Chow-time in about..." he paused to consult his oversized dive watch... "one hour!"

"I think we're good, thanks," Dan said. He looked at Jami, but she had nothing to add, so they parted ways with the crewman and began to walk along the ship's deck, which had white-painted, chest-high tubular guard rails along its length. After a minute of walking, Dan asked, Jami, "You think he's giving us the runaround?"

Jami shrugged as she paused to look out over the seaport's moderately busy waters. "Probably. But hey, we'll ask the Communications Officer once he gets here, right?"

"Right, and if he gives us the runaround, then I think we know what's up."

They continued walking the deck of the ship, at once pleased with and surprised by the seemingly mundane tranquility of it all: a few ship workers going about their business, light traffic around the port, taking a stroll on the ship's deck as if they were about to embark upon the cruise of a lifetime. Which in fact they were, but not in the way they would have wanted. The uncertainty of it all was soul-crushing.

Dan stared out onto the water, eyeballing an unattended dinghy tied to another boat within swimming distance of their ship. How hard would it be to slip overboard, swim to it and commandeer it, rowing to shore at some other part of the seaport and then just disappear into the city? But even if they managed it, Dan knew, Jami's earlier words haunted him. Something about looking over her shoulder for the rest of her life, never knowing if she (and it applied to him, too, he was aware) was about to be assassinated in cold blood by some highly paid hitman. No, he wouldn't even mention the possibility of escape again. They had made up their minds to complete the voyage, for better or worse, whatever that may entail, and that's what they were going to do.

Dan brought up Atlantis, and he and Jami discussed various theories that would explain its presence in Antarctica, and what they might expect to find there. He found that in spite of having no choice in the matter, he was genuinely interested in uncovering the secrets of the lost continent, particularly after what they had witnessed firsthand beneath the Egyptian sands. He was actually looking forward to the expedition, despite its unusual and coercive circumstances.

By the time they slow-walked all the way around the ship, pausing here and there to look at some piece of equipment, it was time for dinner. He and Jami weren't sure what to expect, but it turned out not to be the formal or even semi-formal affair they had anticipated. A few introductions were made, but most of the crew chatted in groups of twos and threes, eating quickly before returning to their duties or retiring to their quarters for the night. No one so much as asked them why they were going to Antarctica. It seemed they had already been told they were part of an archaeology expedition, and that was that. No additional curiosity was expressed. But Dan and Jami found the food—a Chilean sea bass dish--to be good, even great, and a welcome change after their stint in

Egypt. While they ate, Dan surmised that most, if not all, of these men—and they were all men—would not be on the expedition itself, and possibly not even leaving the ship to set foot on the continent.

"So where is the prince?" Jami wondered. "He said he was going with us."

Dan shrugged between forkfuls of the flavorful fish. "If he doesn't show up, that could be a good thing."

Jami nodded. "Maybe he changed his mind about the whole thing!"

With much amusement, the pair discussed what their plans would be should newfound freedom be unexpectedly bestowed upon them here in Chile. Seeing Antarctica for fun, touring Patagonia, maybe even an extended sojourn throughout South America…the possibilities were endless and provided a welcome diversion while they finished eating.

The rest of the evening was quiet and uneventful, with the pair retiring early to their quarters, knowing the ship was scheduled to depart early the following morning. Dan took the top bunk and while Jami fell fast asleep, he read articles and books on his laptop about Atlantis until he fell asleep.

His watch alarm woke them up in the pre-dawn hours. Remembering a little coffee maker in their quarters, he fired it up and dressed into a pair of long pants and a fisherman's style sweater, shoving a wool beanie cap into a pocket. Out at sea it would be even chillier than it was already on the southern tip of South America. Once he had the coffee made and was ready to go himself, he gently woke Jami. "Up and at 'em, girl. Coffee's hot." As if to underscore his message, they both heard and felt a rumbling in the steel walls and floor indicating that the big ship's diesel engines were starting up. Jami swung her feet onto the floor.

"We're leaving?"

"Sounds that way."

"How long ago did you get up?"

"Few minutes ago."

"So you don't know if the prince is on board?"

Dan shook his head. "Let's go see who's out there."

Out on deck, the sky pinkening with the new day, the pair were unsurprised to see a few crewmen going about their business of readying the ship for the Southern Sea. By the time they made their way all the way around, they had still found no sign of the prince. As the ship slipped out of the seaport to the open ocean, they watched the buildings of Punta Arenas recede into the distance. Jami turned to Dan. "I guess His Royalness won't be joining us. What a shame."

But her face told him that she was quite happy. They stared out over the water for a minute, unsure of what this meant. The prince had not shown up for his own expedition. Now what?

And then they heard it. A rhythmic thumping that grew louder, at first imperceptibly so, but then with each passing second it became unmistakable.

"Is that a…." Jami wondered aloud.

"Helicopter?" Dan finished for her.

She frowned while tipping her face skyward. "I'll be damned. Sure is. And it's coming this way."

They continued to watch as the aircraft beelined out over the harbor toward their ship. Dan pointed out that it was definitely a commercial craft, not military, nor was it designated as police or medical. Then a male voice issued over a loudspeaker system. "All personnel and passengers clear the helipad area for landing. Repeat…"

Dan and Jami exchanged surprised glances. "I guess we have a pretty good idea of who the drop-in is," Dan said. Jami nodded. "No sleeping on the ship in port for him."

They walked to the stairs of the superstructure and took them to the second level where they could observe the landing from above without being in the way. The ship itself did not slow down or alter its own course as the chopper descended over the helipad. The landing was smooth, and almost immediately a crewman was opening the helicopter door and assisting passengers onto the helipad. Several men of Middle Eastern origin emerged first, followed by a few women wearing headgear that completely covered their faces. A gaggle of children came next, and finally, an adult male wearing white robes with a gold sash.

"Ah, the prince," Dan said.

"So nice of him to make an appearance," Jami added.

"Looks like he brought the whole family."

"And entourage. Gotta be twenty people altogether. I wonder if he kidnaps people on all of his family vacays, and if his family even knows?"

Dan shook his head as he watched the new arrivals file down the stairway leading to the ship's main deck. They were all smiles and joviality, waving to the crew and making small talk with each other as they made their way onto the ship. Dan noted that the helicopter pilot shut the motor off and exited the craft himself while the ship's crew secured the chopper's skids to the helipad, fixing it in place. "I guess the chopper's going with us," he noted aloud.

Jami shrugged. "Why not? It can't reach South America from Antarctica, but it could help transport the expedition around."

"Whatever it takes," Dan said unenthusiastically. He heard the vessel's engines increase in pitch. He turned and looked out on the water, where there was now only open ocean, the seaport firmly in their churning wake.

CHAPTER 18

The days at sea passed in quiet desolation. Dan nor Jami saw anything of the prince and his entourage, other than occasionally from a distance, and that was fine with Dan. He and Jami were doing a job, completing their end of a forced bargain, and he wanted nothing to do with such a person other than to be rid of him. If finding Atlantis was what it took, then he was going to do his damnedest to do just that. He and Jami wiled away the hours reading more books on Antarctica and the lost city. The ship's Internet connection was mysteriously down, and although technicians were purportedly working on it, they were given no guarantees it would work on this trip.

"Just enjoy the solitude of Mother Nature," the crewman who had initially welcomed them on board told them when he broke the bad tech news. But they learned that the "library," besides books, also had a great selection of maps and charts, including many of Antarctica. Long hours in their quarters and in the ship's library were spent together learning all they could about the topography of the southernmost continent. They discussed animals, too, and what they might have to do with the ancient Atlanteans. Jami explained that in Antarctica, on land, anyway, there weren't many megafauna—large animals, at least in present day-—but that underwater was a different story.

"We won't be going underwater," Dan said, wrapping his arms around himself as if to ward off the chill just thinking about it. "Too freaking freezing. Even with a drysuit, no way. We have to have some safe limits. He can't just make us do suicidal stuff."

"We'll see how it goes. I have to admit, I'm sort of looking forward to this now, after all of our studying. I mean, we're *going* to Antarctica to look for Atlantis! What if we actually find it? Have you thought about that?"

"Not beyond what it might mean for us as far as the prince."

"It would change our lives forever, Dan. Already I've been thinking about all the papers I could write about the role animals played in Atlantean society, and in guarding their legacy…."

Dan stared at a chart of the Antarctica coast, an enlargement of a particular stretch of coastline containing the peninsula of interest, the section of the ice continent that was briefly called New Swabia during the Second World War. He tried to envision it in his head, the actual landscape, and that drove him from his quarters up to the deck to take a look at their progress across the Southern Ocean. He had to convince Jami to come along with him. They'd gotten used to sequestering in their cozy quarters for much of the day. They bundled up and made their way topside, where instantly, the chill in the air bit at what little exposed skin they dared to leave uncovered. But it was the visual that truly arrested their senses, for the seascape had changed dramatically since their last viewing.

"Is that… ice?" Jami said through chattering teeth.

"Icebergs," Dan nodded. "We've obviously been heading south." A fog-like mist obscured visibility beyond a couple of miles, such that they still had no view of the white continent itself.

"Good thing this ship is an icebreaker," Jami said, before turning away from the rail as a piercingly cold breeze cropped up. "Let's go back inside."

They retreated once again to their quarters and spent the night feeding their minds, learning, absorbing, contemplating and reflecting. They spoke in hushed tones of unknown monsters swimming below their ship in the icy waters, and of the known human monsters with whom they shared the expedition. They talked, too, of the fabled lost city and its Egyptian connections. Heads swimming with these pregnant thoughts, they drifted off to sleep, maintaining the early-to-bed, early-to-rise routine of seafarers and explorers the world over.

*****

The next morning after breakfast, Dan and Jami went topside and took in the view they had been hoping for. "Land!" Jami exclaimed, genuinely excited. "I hadn't realized the effect that not seeing land for days on end would have on me," she admitted.

"It's icy and it's freezing, but it's land all the same," Dan said. "The bottom of the Earth!"

As the ship drew nearer to the continent, their speed diminished in proportion to the increasing pack ice. Although land was within sight, a full day's travel awaited them before they would reach the frozen shores due to the slow speeds and abundance of navigational caution needed to safely traverse the continental ice pack. They passed much of the time remaining on deck, bundled in their parkas and mittens and hoods, taking in the frigid beauty of the southernmost continent's outer fringes while at the same time acclimating to the frozen clime. Droplets of seawater carried on the wind all the way to their skin told them that the ocean was extremely salty—and cold. Leopard seals basking on icebergs and seabirds diving for fish hinted at the lush nature that inhabited this land. Jami pointed to one of the toothy seals.

"Did you know that leopard seals are the only known natural predator of killer whales?"

Dan smiled at her. "I did not. I learn something new every day. Trouble is, I forget something new every day, too."

"As long as it's not me."

"No chance of that."

As they neared the land mass it became clear that the terrain was varied just as with any other continent. They passed cliffs of ice and flat cobblestone beaches leading to plains with mountains in the distance. They knew that during the Antarctic summer, the visibility was much better than in winter when snowstorms frequently led to whiteouts. Their expedition would not even be one worth attempting during the winter season.

The nearer they got to the coastline, the more activity there was on deck. Crates were moved around with cranes and heavy machinery, and small boats prepared for launch. Staring out at Antarctica beyond it all, Dan shook his head to himself that all of this activity was to facilitate the discovery of Atlantis, based on his and Jami's discoveries. But meanwhile the continent was so vast, so huge—how would they be able to locate the lost civilization—or evidence it did not exist here—with such meager clues?

As Dan and Jami continued to watch the expedition equipment be staged on the aft deck, they realized that this was shaping up to be a serious undertaking—strange circumstances or not. The equipment was high-end, including numerous vehicular resources at their disposal, not the least of which was the helicopter. In addition to the chopper, however, there were drones, small boats, snow trekkers, and even...

"What am I looking at?" Jami asked, pointing to the largest of the crates that now had two men on either side of it, prying it apart.

"Some kind of vehicle. Snowmobile, perhaps?" Dan guessed.

But it was clear he was wrong the moment the crate boards fell away and an acrylic bubble dome with highly reflective surfaces caught their eye.

"Got to be kidding me!" Jami said. "A mini-sub."

Dan emitted a low whistle in appreciation. "Our expedition backer is not messing around."

*****

The rattle of the *Antarctic Queen*'s anchor chain dropping into the frigid waters of Seal Bay echoed across glassy water that was studded with icebergs. A light fog hung above the Bay, extending inland to where the land rose to higher elevation. Dan and Jami entered the cafeteria for lunch, knowing that following the meal, they would be leaving the ship for the ice continent.

Upon entering the hub of activity, they were surprised to see the prince and his entourage seated at several tables that had been pushed together to accommodate the large party. The prince himself beamed upon seeing Dan and Jami enter, beckoning them with a friendly wave.

"Wow, look," Dan said, "we're being asked to sit at the cool kids' table in the cafeteria!"

"High school all over again," Jami said, "only this time if they don't like us, they kill us!"

"Just smile and act cool," Dan said as they walked over to the assemblage of tables hosting about twenty people, many of whom wore Arabic robes and head gear.

"I don't even care, I just want to eat," Jami said with a sigh of exasperation. "Last ship's meal for some time, right?"

"The woman is correct." This from a middle-aged Arab man who turned around from his seat at the table in order to say it. "Greetings. My name is Habib Saroohd. I am the expedition leader for this sojourn. Is this the first trip to Antarctica for you both?" And then, with the gesture of an arm, a woman appeared at his side and said something discreetly to two men who had been sitting next to him. Whatever she said, it caused the men to move, thereby creating two empty seats next to Habib, who then gestured to the Americans. "Please—sit. Let us discuss our journey."

The prince, for his part, seemed not to notice the interaction taking place, instead wrapped up in jovial conversation with the men and women seated on either side of him at the head of the table some distance away. Dan sat directly next to Habib, with Jami on his other side, while a scarfed Arab woman on Habib's opposite side doted on a young girl, encouraging her to try the food.

"So you've been to Antarctica before?" Dan broke the ice with.

"This is my third trip," Habib answered with a nod. "And the first I have been the leader of. I intend to run things smooth as ice, ha ha!"

"As smooth as the hunt for a mythical lost continent can be, anyway, right?" Dan said with a smile. He could feel Jami holding back an outright laugh.

At this, Habib was unpredictably calm, and shrugged while answering in a matter-of-fact tone using his heavily accented English. "My job is simply to enable the expedition archaeologists..." he paused while he literally poked Dan in the shoulder with his finger... "That's you....to safely operate within their area of investigation." He paused to let that sink in while making eye contact with both Dan and Jami in turn, and then he went on. "Whether or not you succeed in locating your archaeological quest is not really my concern. I am here simply to facilitate your search in the safest and most expedient way possible. Does that make sense?"

Dan and Jami both nodded. Feeling bold, Dan leaned into Habib and asked, "And can you guarantee our safety, meaning we will be able to return to our country after this expedition?"

Habib's expression was unreadable as he replied, "I can guarantee your safety insofar as I will do my utmost to lead you and your entire group through the natural perils of this harsh land. If the team members turn on each other—and believe me I have seen it—I may or may not be able to intervene."

Dan made prolonged eye contact with the explorer, but could detect no undercurrents to what he was saying. If he was aware of the dynamic at play between the prince and the American couple, he was keeping that knowledge to himself. Dan decided it best to change the subject.

"We noticed all the uncrating of vehicles and equipment going on today. Seems like you're very well outfitted."

At this, Habib nodded vigorously and his eyes brightened somewhat. Apparently, he too was glad for the change in subject. "Indeed, in addition to the helicopter, which has an extra supply of fuel brought in with the crates, we also have not one, but *two* Hagglunds snowtrackers. They're treaded vehicles that can carry a dozen people and literally tons of gear through the most inhospitable terrain, including ice."

"And I do believe I saw a mini-sub?" Jami piped in from between forkfuls of what she found to be quite the robust chicken pot pie. Habib nodded with a wide grin.

"Ah yes, how could I forget?"

"You literally spared no expense!" Dan couldn't help but add.

"You have the prince himself to thank for that," Habib said, nodding toward the robed figure holding court at the head of the table. "I told him the submersible was probably not necessary, but he insisted we bring it anyway, just in case. And in addition to the exotic vehicles," Habib continued, "we also have with us state-of-the-art expedition personal gear, including cold weather clothing, tents—what you might think of as camping gear, only suitable for Antarctica and very high end. We have sufficient technology as well—rugged radio and GPS units, laser rangefinders, artificial lighting, portable generators, solar arrays and the like. If this expedition fails, it will not be for lack of preparedness."

Dan and Jami nodded slowly as they digested this along with the meal they consumed. It hardly seemed real that they were about to set foot on Antarctica for an extensive expedition in search of the lost continent. And yet Habib's next words made it that much more apparent.

"After lunch, we'll be landing ashore to set up base camp. We won't be doing any actual exploring for the day. Just going to acclimate and get set up. We'll also conduct briefings to hash out our strategy. I understand you two will be an integral part of those conversations," Habib said.

"We sure hope so," Dan admitted while Jami nodded vigorously.

Habib eyed them seriously. "I am told you have highly specialized knowledge from a recent archaeological dig in Egypt, of all places."

"Correct," Dan said. "Quite specialized indeed. How helpful it proves to be is another matter entirely. But we think we can be of assistance."

"I have no doubt that you will be." Habib levelled a serious stare at Dan before saying, "Please, you two, enjoy what will be your last shipboard meal for some days. I will see you later at base camp in Antarctica!" With that, Habib turned away to the Arab seated on his other side and engaged in conversation in his native language.

"Okay," Dan said in his direction, though he knew he was no longer listening.

Jami helped herself to another glass of white wine from one of the carafes on the table, and dug back into her meal. Dan was momentarily lost in thought, pondering all of the resources at their disposal for the expedition. He tried his best to put the journey into a positive light, but couldn't help but sense that Habib was loyal to the prince above all, including he and Jami. It wasn't a comfortable feeling. But they were committed, and he would make the best of it.

His mind pictured the watery map of Antarctica under the sands of Giza. *Could it be? Is it really here?*

CHAPTER 19

Dan and Jami stepped onto the Zodiac Rigid Inflatable Boat runabout that would transport them from the ship to the shore of Antarctica. They rode with eight other expedition team members, though not the prince, who they were told would be going to shore on a later transport. In addition to the team members, loads of gear occupied deck space on the boat. A steady wind whipped the sea into a light chop that made for a bouncy ride as the inflatable boat motored away from the ship toward shore. They landed on a cobblestone beach occupied by seals and penguins.

All of them helped unload gear and carry it up the beach, with the exception of the boat pilot, who, after the gear was offloaded, headed back to the ship to transport another load of expedition personnel and equipment. Dan had to admit that feeling the crunch of the round stones beneath his boots made coming to Antarctica all the more real, and yet it was seeing the boat launch depart—leaving them here with no way back to the ship, which caused his new reality to really hit home. He and Jami helped load multiple backpacks of gear, crates of food and drinking water, as well as scientific and industrial tools onto a treaded snowmobile that towed a small trailer behind it. It was operated by an expedition member named Ermin, who hailed from somewhere in South America, Jami had gleaned from the ship's cafeteria chat.

Neither Dan nor Jami spoke much while they worked to move the mounds of gear and supplies that had been dropped on the beach up to the campsite on higher ground. All around them, sea birds wheeled overhead, penguins loitered off to the sides of the rocky beach, the occasional splashy water indicating fish activity caught their attention off the beach, and unseen seals barked in the distance. The place was full of life.

Dan unzipped his parka despite the 30°F temperature. All the lifting and moving things around was heating him up. The sun was exceedingly bright as well, and he was still getting used to the fact that during the Antarctic summer as it was now, the sun was almost always in the sky. He knew from his research, though, that the closer one got to the geographic South Pole itself, in the center of the continent, the colder it became, the stronger the winds blew (200mph was common, even without a storm), and that during winter, it was inhospitable for any human--more like the surface of another planet than that of Earth.

The remainder of the day passed in a whirlwind of focused activity as the camp was set up. Much more substantial than a collection of tents, there were actual pre-fabricated buildings with generator-powered electricity. The Hagglunds tracked vehicles were brought over separately on a larger, barge-like boat that was also used to transport the rest of the snowmobiles and the submersible, which was small and light enough to be transported over ground by one of the Hagglunds. By the end of the day, the newly established compound looked like an exotic vehicle show, with glass and plexiglass and metal gleaming in the polar daylight.

Dan and Jami were fortunate to have their own tent. "I guess we don't rate one of those fancy plastic igloos," she said, but Dan told her to be glad they had their own private quarters, and that it would only be for one night, since tomorrow they would be setting off into the continent's interior, looking for Atlantis. And they were being treated as a couple, and he was fine with that, as was she. A campfire was set up, even though there was a small portable building to serve as a kitchen, but most of the team preferred to dine outside as long as the weather held. They enjoyed a clear view of the bay as the sun went down. Jami pointed out how the water seemed to sparkle with blue-green trails. "Bioluminescence," she noted. "Bio-lights from single-celled algae called dinoflagellates." The effect was stunning combined with the waning sun and rising moon. They had just finished eating when the whine of the helicopter starting up on the ship shattered the stillness of the Antarctic evening.

"Look who's decided to make an appearance now that base camp is set up," Dan said, watching the whirlybird lift off the ship's deck into the chilly air.

"Prince Charming himself," Jami answered, unzipping their tent flap. Most of the camp watched as the chopper made the brief hop from the ship to a flat spot of ground high up on the beach where the aircraft set down. The door opened and from it stepped two Arabic men carrying nothing followed by the prince, also carrying nothing, with three more men following behind him carrying bags.

"I'm guessing the first two guys are bodyguards," Dan said, watching a flock of penguins scatter in the wake of the noisy helicopter. Suddenly, Jami grabbed Dan by the hand and began walking toward their pup tent.

"C'mon, let's go to bed for the night. We know the deal is to be up at first light to start the search. I don't feel the need to sit around the campfire and toast marshmallows with these guys, do you?"

Dan had no arguments, and together they retreated to the protective confines of their tent. Outside, the light wind that had buffeted them while they set up camp began to intensify.

*****

The next morning found them up at what would normally be considered before dawn, only it was already light out owing to their extreme southerly latitude. Outside the tent, Dan and Jami found the camp to be a beehive of activity, with men loading the Hagglund snowtrackers and using the onboard cranes those vehicles featured to efficiently move and lift heavy loads, including snowmobiles. The two had barely poured themselves a cup of coffee from the kitchen igloo pot, which was thankfully a robust Chilean bean and piping hot, when none other than the prince himself approached them with what Dan had to admit was a genuine-looking warm smile.

"We are going to scout ahead in the helo while the rest of the team makes their way inland to the general search area in the Hagglunds. Liftoff in ten minutes." And with that, the prince waved an arm toward the waiting chopper and began striding purposefully toward it.

Dan and Jami gathered their backpacks and took a last look around base camp while they cinched their parka hoods down a little tighter. "Couldn't imagine being here in winter, knowing that this is summer," Jami said.

"I wonder what the Atlanteans did here in winter?" Dan posed the question while looking inland to the great ice-topped mountains that dominated the distant skyline.

"Hunkered down somewhere," Jami said.

But there was no time to dwell on the mystery, for the whine of the helicopter's engine reminded them that it was time to start the hunt.

CHAPTER 20

Dan and Jami pulled their sunglasses tighter against their faces as the helicopter lifted into the bright Antarctic morning sky. Sunlight glinted off the ocean below, off the superstructure of the *Antarctic Queen*, and most of all off the ice fields that extended from just inland of the cobble beach to the mountains rising majestically in the distance. They sat in the back with their backpacks, while the prince rode up front with the pilot, a man of Arabic descent who was not introduced to them.

They arced out over the bay, flying over their ship before turning inland and passing low above base camp. They returned the waves from those below who watched them fade into the distance toward the looming mountain range. Dan noticed that the pilot and the prince wore headsets with microphones to communicate, while he and Jami did not. Although he could see them talking, he could not hear what was being said due to the ambient noise of riding in the chopper. Once the initial liftoff was complete and they had settled into a straight course toward the mountains, Dan pulled out one of the paper maps he'd been working with and unfolded it across his lap. He tried to reconcile the topography they approached with what he saw on the map. Then, once he was satisfied he was able to do that, he examined the small outline he'd made during their nights sequestered in Punta Arenas.

He held the map out toward the cockpit, shaking it until he caught the prince's attention. The prince immediately lowered his headset and took the map while glancing back at Dan, who said loudly, "I think somewhere in that area I outlined is where we should start looking."

The prince gave him a hard stare without eyeballing the map and then nodded, snatching the paper. "We will fly over the area if it is in range. If it is not in range, we may have to wait for the terrestrial team to reach us so that we can refuel the chopper, and then resume our aerial survey."

Dan nodded and then shrunk back into his seat. It was literally out of his hands now. He and Jami held hands while looking out the windows at the majestic landscape whizzing by below, and increasingly, in front of them as they approached the white peaks that marked the beginning of Antarctica's true interior. The helo steadily gained altitude as they climbed in elevation along with the upthrusted land itself. As he watched the landscape pass by, Dan thought about the combination of risk and the long odds of finding Atlantis.

Helicopters weren't widely used for travel in Antarctica, although the continent featured twenty airports altogether. They were used for shuttling supplies between bases and from ship to shore as they had done. But landing on snow was not good for copters, and the higher the altitude and colder the air became, the more problematic safe flight became as well. So much to go wrong, Dan thought as he looked out the window.

And yet, as the landscape changed around them—not only below, but also above them as they neared the mountain—he felt a certain calmness take hold of him. Sort of an internal reassurance that he did not consciously initiate that told him he not only knew the answer, but that he alone was part of the answer. The watery map beneath Giza. The incongruent architecture there. These mountains up ahead that thousands of years ago may have been green and verdant rather than covered with ice. To him it all added up to the fact that they were here now and this was it. His own personal journey in life had led him to this point, this moment that he was somehow guided to by the ancient Atlanteans. Something else both bothered and made sense to him, too. That he had somehow been paired with a zoologist, who had the knowledge base to understand the animals they had encountered on their journey. It was all so surreal, and flying over the never-ending polarscape, he could feel that beasts must have been a part of the Atlanteans' saga here, as well.

As they ascended higher into Queen Maud Land, Dan again mentally pictured the map of the area he had spent so much time studying. Then, outside, he took in the towering vertical spires of rock, which he knew by now to be called the Drygalski Mountains, named after a German polar scientist. He was also aware that many of the jagged, spiky peaks were unnamed, and that further, some of the glaciers, mountains, and certainly peaks in this area had never seen human footprints, while some to this day had never even had human eyes laid on them.

Certainly, if they were to discover Atlantis, they would be the first eyes there, in modern times, at least. And then a darker realization struck Dan as a small chunk of ice struck the window level with his eyes, obscuring his vision somewhat: *unless someone found it before and didn't survive to tell the tale.* He thought of the German presence here he had read about, when they sent expeditions during WWII to what is now Queen Maud Land, but back then had been called New Swabia, in a bid to claim this part of the Southern Continent for Germany. *So people have definitely been to this general region in modern times*, he reflected. And then there were the recent accounts he'd read online of rock climbers and mountaineers travelling here for sport, to climb pristine faces previously untouched by human hands. But even with this documented, limited presence, no one had ever claimed to have found Atlantis.

Dan shifted his head slightly to the left to see around a window smudge left behind by the ice. He scanned the steep mountain formation they now skirted the base of. He closed his eyes and envisioned the watery, green-tinged relief map. He opened his eyes and looked at the outline formed by the base of the broad glacial mountain supporting the jagged, tall peaks. This was it, his inner voice screamed. *This is it!* He must have stirred in his seat or possibly even muttered something, because now Jami was tapping his shoulder asking him, "What, what is it?"

"Look for a place we can land," he yelled, loud enough for the prince to hear him up front. "There is no reason not to begin the search right here."

The prince turned around swiftly, but calmly. "What makes you so certain?"

Dan did not hesitate. "Look at this place." He waved an arm toward the ship side of the craft, where miles and miles of nearly featureless, bleak ice stretched out to their left until it met the frozen sea. "When the Atlanteans arrived here from the other side of the world, even if it was unfrozen and green, what do you think would have really grabbed their attention? This flat expanse or…."

He turned dramatically toward the other side of the helicopter where the majestic peaks stretched vertically for a long, impressive row. Then he continued. "Not only that, but I saw when flying over that we're on a crack that runs along the base of these peaks. And we're looking for a chasm of some kind. A large crack in the ice, maybe, I don't know exactly what. But that's the only way any kind of architecture as significant as what the Atlanteans would have had could survive all this time without being seen. And based on my map studies after what we witnessed in Giza, I'm confident that we are in the right place, or at least on the edge of it."

The prince stared at the map himself for a long moment before turning back to Dan. "Very well. I will instruct my pilot to land at the nearest feasible location. Then we will investigate boots-on-the-ground and see if it merits further exploration."

Dan nodded his agreement and the prince turned back around to confer with the pilot, who first shrugged, then nodded, and finally pointed through the windscreen somewhere out in front of them. Apparently, he was not outright refusing to land, at least. Jami leaned in toward Dan and spoke close to his ear.

"Are you really sure this is the place?"

He shrugged. "I think so. If not exactly here, then somewhere along this ridge of peaks. We'll find something that shows Atlantis or some kind of ancient civilization was here. Then we can leave." She placed a hand on his shoulder for a second and then turned away.

Suddenly the chopper banked sharply to the left, down the slope and away from the base of the row of rocky peaks. Dan looked but couldn't see any trace of the ground party in the distance on the flat plain. He figured he should take a last look while he still had the vantage point of being airborne. The chopper descended rapidly, toward a smooth oval of dirt and rock covered with patchy snow. Finding no traces of not only the ground party, but of anything at all in the distance, he shifted his focus to their landing zone. It was almost level ground. He was thankful enough for that. He wasn't sure exactly how flat a helicopter landing area needed to be, but this looked mostly flat, especially given that they were well up a sloping mountain and near the base of a series of near-vertical peaks.

The pilot himself turned around and yelled at them, "Seatbelts on!" Jami and Dan stared at each other, somewhat alarmed, but although he looked down at his lap to make sure, his seatbelt was already fastened, since he had never undone it during any point of the flight. Same for Jami. He gave the pilot the thumbs up, but the aviator had already turned his attention back to his flight controls as he made the final approach to the landing area. It surprised Dan how small a patch of smooth ground was actually needed on which to land, for there wasn't much available. At the base of the mountain, exposed beds of loose rock lay next to snow-covered ground—which could contain hidden boulders—along with sheets of smooth ice. Almost all of it was on some sort of slope, and yet the pilot managed to eagle-eye a patch of smooth, nearly flat rock a bit larger than the footprint of the helicopter's skids themselves.

The skids touched down on the ground and they all felt a jolt. "All good," the pilot called out, his hands busy on his control panel. They heard the whine of the engine decrease in pitch. Dan looked around outside. He couldn't believe it. Here they were at the base of an Antarctic mountain range, about to search for the mythical lost continent of Atlantis. And the weather was good, for Antarctica. A stiff breeze, but no precipitation, at least at this altitude, and it wasn't deathly cold, either, hovering around 20°F. The pilot turned around and spoke to them.

"I will need to stay in the cockpit and do a post-flight systems check, but the rest of you are free to start off-loading the gear and set up a rendezvous area with the ground team." With that, he turned back around to his instrument console once again, as well as sending a radio message to base camp with their landing zone coordinates.

Dan and Jami began the process of unloading the chopper, first gathering their personal belongings and then scoping the area immediately outside the chopper for a stable patch of land on which to set the equipment. They also needed to set up a mini-camp while they waited for the terrestrial team to catch up, which the prince and pilot informed them would be four-to-five hours if the weather held. "If not," the pilot said, turning his hands palms up, "Who knows? Half a day? One day? Never? It's Antarctica. So make yourselves comfortable."

They finished unloading all of the equipment from the helicopter, noting that the pilot remained in the cockpit while the prince used a satellite phone, presumably to communicate with the ground team. Still, the chopper was not a large cargo-style air vehicle, and it took less than an hour for the two of them to have all of the gear neatly piled some distance away from the aircraft, up against the base of the mountain. They set up polar pyramid tents, their shape reminiscent of the shelters used by early polar explorers. They also installed a perimeter of brightly colored flags to make themselves visible after the helicopter left back to base camp, which would happen after the pilot refueled from the extra gas cans on board, and then once the ground team met up with them.

Dan spotted a shadow moving quickly across the ground and paused to look up above the mountain peaks. He sighted a large bird of prey, a raptor he knew from his research while in lockdown on the ship to be called a petrel. The large bird gracefully soared through the air high above them, swooping low toward the ground before looping back up into the sky, skirting close to the majestic peak walls above. He watched it for some time, longer than he should have, he was beginning to think, but then as time passed he began to notice patterns within its swooping arcs. It would disappear for a few seconds at the top of its arc before coming back into view laterally and farther away from them. Then it would divebomb back toward them, and start the pattern anew by climbing back into the sky against the background of the ragged peaks. His mind lit on the inscriptions in the tunnel walls beneath Giza, the hieroglyphics his brain had somehow registered and preserved in memory even while running for his life beneath the concealing sands. He thought back to the Osiris chamber and more crucially, the Test of Osiris with the scale and the heart and the...feather. He stared up at the bird again, watching it swoop up into the high part of its cycle, where it disappeared for a time.

Could it be?

He heard the whisper of her parka fabric against his as she brushed up against him. "Watcha looking at?" Jami implored, tipping her head skyward to eye the petrel.

"Just checking out that petrel to see where it goes." He didn't feel he could go into the details of his collage of thoughts without derailing the momentum in his thinking that told him he might be onto something. "I think we should take a little walk around our immediate site and check it out. Let's tell the prince."

"You mean ask the prince?" she said, lowering her voice and making steady eye contact with him.

"Right. But I'm sure he won't mind. It's not like we could run away from here without dying of exposure."

"True." She pulled her parka collar up higher around her neck against the steady winds.

They found the prince still sitting in the helicopter, door open, his satellite phone to his ear. Outside the craft, the pilot was in the process of refueling the aircraft. The prince lowered the phone on their approach, and Dan said, "We're going to take a look around while we wait for the terrestrial team."

The prince nodded. "Stay within sight of the helicopter or you could be lost if weather conditions deteriorate. Also, beware of the katabatic winds which flow from up high to down low in Antarctica. They seem not to be active now, but that could change."

"We'll be careful," Jami answered.

To that, the prince shook his sat-phone and said, "The terrestrial team has been given the coordinates of our landing zone. They have already left base camp in the Hagglunds." Dan thanked him and reiterated that they would stay within visual range of the helicopter.

Then he and Jami, taking only their small day backpacks, set out walking along the base of the ridgeline, away from the helicopter.

CHAPTER 21

Dan knew by consulting a handheld compass that they were walking in an easterly direction. They continued to move east while the petrel flew above them. Wordless for now, and with the helicopter's engine off, they heard only the sounds of their boots crunching a thin layer of snow and loose rock, along with the wind rustling down through the rocky spires toward the distant coastline.

After a few minutes of walking during which Jami joked they hadn't found Atlantis yet, the bird changed its flight pattern. "It's circling the same spot now," Dan observed.

"Pretty far up there."

"Not anywhere near the top of the peaks, though. We could probably walk up there if we wanted, but I guess it's just hunting a rodent or whatever."

Jami appeared thoughtful while continuing to watch the circling raptor. "Actually, Antarctica has no naturally occurring terrestrial mammals."

"I keep forgetting you're a zoologist. Well then, why did it suddenly stop right there?"

Jami shrugged. "It could be resting in an updraft. Sometimes birds find air currents that hold them up and they can just stay there in one place without having to exert themselves by flapping their wings."

"But there's a strong downdraft right now," Dan said, tightening the drawstring on his parka hood. "So it's actually expending energy to stay there for some reason, even though you say it can't be because of a prey item."

She eyed the bird again, which still wheeled tightly in a particular spot. "There is a little cleft of rock up there. And looking up ahead, if we just keep walking the way we've been going, I don't really see anything different, do you?"

Dan looked that way and shook his head. "No, it looks the same if we keep going straight. I say we go up and check out that cleft of rock by the bird."

"Let's do it, then. After you, explorer boy."

Dan smiled but was looking back at the helicopter. He saw nothing unusual. The prince and his pilot sat in the cockpit, while the ground party was still a long way off. No reason not to go. He turned around to face the incline again and looked up to see the bird, still circling high above them, but not anywhere near the apex of the peak. Then he trailed his gaze downward along their intended route, looking for obstacles, points of interest, anything that might be of note during the ascent. This was Antarctica, after all, and even minor accidents could turn out to be very serious. Qualified medical help, meaning base camp, was a long way off, and transportation off of Antarctica, even when one had helicopters and ships at their disposal, was far from guaranteed at any given time.

Everything looked fine though, even placid, like something he'd watch on a nature TV show and mention casually how he'd like to go there someday. They started up the incline. It was odd, Dan thought while making his way up, listening to Jami's footsteps crunching the steep ground behind him, that there were almost no land animals here. Not on the ground anyway. Even the petrel above was also a seabird. Which took him back to the quandary of, what was it doing here, maintaining its position over this one spot? Or even doing this far inland at all, knowing there was no land mammal prey for it to eat?

"Maybe the petrel eats small birds, or bird eggs out of nests," Jami said from behind him. Dan paused his leading foot on the vegetation-covered incline.

"You are literally reading my mind. I was just thinking about what else it might eat that would explain its presence here."

"At this point," Jami said, exhaling sharply as she made her way up the incline, "we may as well just see when we get up there."

"We'll be there soon enough." Dan resumed the upward trek, still able to ascend using only his legs. The biggest danger were the patches of ice that lurked here and there, some hidden beneath mats of vegetation. Jami also had little trouble making her way up, slipping now and then before making an easy recovery.

"After what we did in Egypt, this seems like a cakewalk," she said, followed by, "I hope I didn't just curse us!"

"Bird's still there. Let's keep moving." And they did, higher and higher, against the downwind that poured down from the peaks high, high above. Dan had just lifted his right foot and was about to plant it down again when he spotted a glint of metal in a small recess in the ground, next to a rock.

"Hold up!" He stopped moving and held a hand up.

"What is it?"

"Not sure yet, but I think it's something metallic. Let's take a second to check it out." He stripped off his backpack and set it next to him on the ground, taking a moment to be sure it wouldn't roll or slide down the hill away from him. "Yeah, definitely metal. Like a pole or a rod, maybe?"

"Sounds like climbing or camping gear? Maybe a tent stake or a piton for hammering in a line?"

He turned around to look at her. "Like if they were climbing these peaks and dropped it on the way? Because that kind of gear isn't necessary right here. As you can see, we got this far with no ropes. But you're right, they may have just dropped something along the way up. Let's see."

He lay almost in a prone position to be able to extend his arm farther down into the recess. His hand was just able to grip the end of the rod.

"Ouch! It's sharp."

"Careful, don't hurt yourself up here, please."

"I've got it. It's loose." Unable to pull the object straight out of the ground, he wiggled it back and forth a few times until he found a more manageable angle. "Think I've got it." He slowly pulled the rod out and slid it into the open air.

"Oh wow, I see color--red and black paint." He pulled the object completely free and rose to a sitting position while holding the find in both palms. It was long, over a meter in length, and Jami sucked in her breath as she took in its detail.

"Oh my God!"

"What the..." Dan trailed off in stunned amazement as he, too, stared at the incredible artifact. "It's an arrow!"

Indeed, the metal rod was sharpened to a point at one end, with three metal stabilizing fins on the other. These fins were painted with the infamous Nazi swastika.

"What's up with the Nazi stuff?" Jami asked.

"I read about it," Dan said, turning the arrow over in his hands. "They did an expedition here in WWII to claim land for Germany, and also—get this—to search for Atlantis in order to seek out proof that the Aryans are the purest race."

"Wow. But why an arrow?" Jami asked. "Did they think there would be game here to hunt?"

Dan shook his head while handing Jami the arrow to hold. "No, they just dropped them out of their plane to mark their territory, because they would stick into the ground. They dropped a bunch of them, and from what I read none were ever found."

"Until now!"

"Right. And it was a little ways underground but still just visible enough. This means there may be more around here, too. They probably dropped them at predetermined intervals as they flew a pattern."

"We should show it to the prince. It's an artifact of sorts."

"Definitely. And it lends credence to our own search. The Germans were looking here, too." Dan turned and looked back toward the helicopter, which they could still see sitting in the landing zone. "We should probably head back now, actually. The arrow is some good work for such a short time out."

"I agree. It's getting a little chilly, too, I admit it."

Dan took another look up and saw the petrel still there, in its same flight pattern. A lip of rock ran parallel to the hill, at the base of where the true mountain began, which culminated in the steep, thin spires high above. The lip of rock where the raptor flew wasn't all that high up, perhaps another 100 feet.

"You want to go up there, don't you?" Jami queried.

"There is some interesting topography up there, and we would still be in sight of the helo."

Jami took a deep breath. "You really don't know when to quit, do you?"

Dan shrugged and looked back up the hill. "I want to be able to tell the prince that we checked it out. Combined with the Nazi arrow, it could be that he's satisfied we've done our job already and we'll have completed our forced obligations."

"Fine. I hope you're right. Let's do this. You carry the arrow." She handed it back to him and they set out upwards once again. The incline grew steeper as they progressed, and occasionally they had to use their hands in order to steady themselves on the terrain, but they kept going until they reached the base of the rock lip. They paused there, standing side by side, assessing the layout.

"We'll have to climb just a little bit to see what's over the edge," Dan said.

"I'll wait here. I can help boost you if you need. Then you can take a look over the edge and see what's there."

Dan took his pack off and lay it on the ground at Jami's feet. He studied his route upward for a few moments and then placed his right foot into a small crevice and tested it for leverage. "Give me a boost so I can make this first little ledge, okay?"

"You just want me to put my hands on your butt, don't you?"

"Yeah, that's it. I could jump, I guess."

"I got it, here goes...." Jami boosted him up and he sprung off the foothold. When he felt his fingertips curl over the lip of rock as he rose away from Jami, he gripped down hard to make sure he wouldn't fall backwards. He hung there for a moment, resting before making the final pull to top over the rock lip.

"Whoa!" Dan exclaimed immediately upon gaining his new view.

"What is it?"

"Big chasm. Starts here but runs far to the east. Maybe even to the west, too, once you get down, there, I can't tell. It's pretty dark."

"Don't go down there!"

"I'm not." On top of the rock, Dan sensed a change and lifted his head. "Where'd the bird go?"

"Don't see it."

Suddenly Dan heard a squawk from below. "It's down there! The petrel, it flew down into the chasm. With some of the climbing gear the ground team is bringing, I'd say it's possible to check this out."

"Okay. But not without that. We should get back to the chopper and report what we found."

Dan could sense Jami's anxiety. He definitely didn't want her to think he was about to do something stupid—something else stupid, he reminded himself, after all he had already put her through. Carefully, he faced the mountain and hung from the rock lip to begin the trek back down to their field camp.

CHAPTER 22

Back at the chopper, Dan and Jami relayed the news of what they had seen. They presented the prince with the Nazi arrow. Upon handling it, his face took on a wondrous expression that appeared genuine. "Astounding! Excellent find!" he praised them. "The Nazis sought to find evidence that Aryans were the superior race. Atlanteans, as light-skinned, blond-haired and blue-eyed people, would have fit into that narrative."

Dan and Jami nodded, eager to have sufficient evidence to be able to leave freely, whenever that became feasible.

"But this in itself is not proof of Atlantis," the prince said, tossing the arrow onto the helicopter's back seat. "It is proof of the Germans' exploration here during World War II, nothing more."

Dan nodded, having predicted this reaction. It was true, after all. "And yet we and the Nazis independently came up with this Antarctic location as a possible resting place of Atlantis. Anyway," Dan segued, not wanting to belabor the point, "we also found something else that bears further exploration." The prince eyed him expectantly without saying anything, so Dan continued.

"I climbed up to that rocky lip, there." He paused to point up to the base of where the rocky spire peaks began. The prince nodded as he eyeballed the geographic landmark, and Dan went on.

"It marks the opening to a deep crevice that runs a long distance—out of sight—to the left and right of the opening—that's east and west, respectively." The prince nodded, and Dan knew that his map research had paid off. "With the climbing gear the ground crew is bringing, we can probably check it out to see if there are hidden structures, or any kinds of artifacts down inside."

Suddenly a walkie-talkie squawked and the prince unclipped the handheld unit from his belt. "Remote Base Camp to Hagglund 1, I copy you. Go ahead."

"Roger that, Remote Base. Listen, Hagglund 2 ran into a problem, literally. The right-side tread is wedged into a crevice between two rocks. I think we'll be able to extricate it, but it's going to take some time, over."

There was no hiding the look of outright disgust on the prince's face. "What is your position, over?"

"We're about an hour out, still down on the plains."

The prince eyed Dan for a moment before replying. "Which one of the Hagglunds carries more climbing gear?"

"That would be Number 2, the stuck one."

"Transfer the climbing gear into Hag 1, and proceed in 1 up to our position at Remote Base."

"We were standing by with Hagglund Number 2, sir, in order to be able to render assistance if needed until they are up and running again, over."

Dan watched the prince's face take on a subtle shade of red. Clearly he was not used to answers he didn't like. "Leave them any equipment they might need to be able to extricate themselves, and you bring us that climbing gear now. Understood?"

"Yes, sir. Will comply. Over and out."

The prince tossed his radio onto the chopper seat and turned to Dan and Jami. "I'm tired of sitting here. You feel like taking another look up there while we wait for the Hagglund?"

Dan looked at Jami, aware that it showed hesitation on his part, but his eyes were locked on hers and he saw the subtle shrug of her shoulders. "Sure, why not," he said, as Jami nodded and said, "Yeah. Give me a minute to use the ladies' room, but I'm up for it."

The prince grinned. "Yes, let me confer with our pilot. He will hold down the fort, as you say in America, right, while we investigate the new site. I am excited!"

With that, the royal ventured around to the rear of the chopper where the pilot was conducting a post-flight mechanical inspection on the tail rotor. While Dan heard him engaged in conversation with the airman, he walked with Jami a few feet farther away before speaking softly to her. "We don't have to do this, you know. We could say we changed our minds, we're too tired, we'd rather wait for the Hag to get here."

"Who you calling a hag?" she grinned at him to show she was joking.

"I'm glad to see you haven't lost your sense of humor, in spite of our situation." Dan couldn't help but glare at the prince, who looked away and pointed in the direction from where Dan and Jami had just returned.

They set off in a line, the prince out front with Dan behind him and Jami behind Dan, walking easily over the almost flat terrain until they reached the base of the steep incline. Dan looked up and no longer saw the petrel, which had flown down into the chasm up above. He wondered silently if it was still down there. They had mentioned nothing to the prince about the bird. Even without it, he knew he was in the right spot from their own boot prints in the rocks around the base of the incline they had climbed.

"This is where we go up," he told the prince, who merely nodded while staring up at the incline he had said he wanted to climb. "I'll go first," Dan said. He heard no arguments and so started his ascent, repeating the boost process with Jami. It dawned on him that she would have to boost the prince up as well. When Dan had been boosted and made his way up the incline to be clear of the prince's entry point, he stopped and looked down, where he could see Jami reluctantly preparing to brace for the prince's weight. He was tall but slender, and Dan estimated that he and the Arab royal weighed about the same.

The prince pulled a coil of climbing rope from one of the pockets of his parka. "This single rope is the extent of our climbing gear until the Hag gets here, but I think it will be simpler for me to pull myself up if you can secure the rope to something up there, than it would be to have the young lady bear my weight. Also," the prince continued as he worked to unravel the rope, "it will enable her to be able to join us, since she would have no one to boost her after I was boosted."

"I don't mind waiting for you all down here," Jami said.

"It's not safe to leave you there alone," the prince countered.

"Let's see how it goes with the rope first. I guess if I can get up there I will."

The prince nodded at her and then tipped his face upward toward Dan, who was settling into a crook of the incline suitable for wedging himself in. He turned around to look down on them.

"Tell me when you're ready and I'll toss you the rope." The prince shook a coil of rope and feigned a throwing motion. Higher up the incline, Dan made the okay sign. "Go ahead." The prince tossed the rope up and Dan caught it. He then wrapped the line around a butt of rock several times before also gripping it with both hands to make sure it would hold. He pronounced it ready, and then the prince dropped the slack end of the rope down to Jami, who grabbed it and approached the rock wall.

"Wrap the rope around your waist a couple of times and then grip it above your shoulders with both hands," the prince instructed.

"You have climbing experience?" Dan asked the prince from above. It was obvious he did, but he also recognized an opportunity to get to know the man himself a little bit, since he knew very little of him as a person.

"Not as a professional, but I have climbed Mount Kilimanjaro in Africa, been as far as Base Camp in Everest, and a few other peaks that do not necessarily require highly technical skills."

"Okay great, then we should be fine for now, but I'm sure even you will be impressed by the crevice up here."

"Can't wait to see it," the prince said with genuine enthusiasm. "Let's do this!"

Jami set herself up with the rope and planted her right foot on the wall. After testing the rope and gaining confidence it would hold, she placed her other foot on the rock and began "walking" herself up the short vertical section until she was able to grab ahold of the rocky protuberance Dan and the prince had used. From there she was able to basically hike the rest of the way up to the prince. A few minutes later the three of them were gathered in the same spot, with a short distance remaining to the rock lip marking the edge of the crevice.

Before making the final move higher, they took a look down toward the chopper, where they could just make out the tiny figure of the pilot standing nearby his craft. Beyond that, on the plain covered with patchy snow and ice, they could discern motion on the otherwise still wilderness expanse.

"That's the Hag," the prince said, pointing. "By the time we check this out and get back down to camp, they'll be just about here."

"Let's get started, then," Dan said, eyeballing the rocky lip he had grabbed onto earlier to reach the chasm. "I did it by jumping, but you two can use the rope if I get up there first." Dan jumped up to the edge of the chasm and pulled himself up onto the narrow rocky promontory as he had done before. The prince tossed him the rope and he wrapped it around a rock outcropping. Then he lowered it down to the prince, who easily made the jump and hauled himself up next to Dan without really needing the rope. Jami then hand-over-handed herself up the rope until the two men each gripped one of her arms and pulled her up beside them.

Dan turned around and eyed the darkness down in the chasm. He took off his small pack and removed from it a simple flashlight that he used to aim down into the narrow opening. Not to be outdone, the prince took a light from his pocket that was much smaller than Dan's, and yet proved to be many times brighter. They began moving slowly along the edge of the crevasse, with Dan's light illuminating a wider swath higher up, and the prince's probing a narrower, brighter cone deeper down.

"Whatever you do, don't lean over the edge," Dan advised, rather needlessly.

"I don't see a bottom," said the prince. "But the wall on this side of the crevasse appears to curve or turn concave far down there—maybe a couple hundred feet down?"

Dan and Jami paused to follow the prince's light beam and look at what he was talking about.

"Yeah I see that," Dan said. "It still drops straight down out of sight, but the wall itself curves back toward us. Like maybe there's a cavern way down there?"

"It could—"

Suddenly Jami's boot scuffed on a loose rock and she stumbled, a little scream issuing from her lips. Instantly, Dan reached out and clamped a hand around one of her calves, steadying her. She had not been in real danger of falling over, and yet it was still a scary moment, for none of them were tethered with any sort of safety gear. "You're good, take it easy."

Although none of them had noticed it, the rock Jami had slipped on ended up rolling into the crevasse. But they all heard the splash it produced far below.

"Hear that?" the prince asked, edging closer to the precipice.

"Yes," Dan answered in nearly a whisper, cocking an ear toward the crevasse. "Sounded like a splash."

"I kicked that rock over," Jami said.

"Now we know there's water down there," the prince said.

"Sounded pretty far down, too." Dan aimed his flashlight into the upper reaches of the gash in the mountain, but saw nothing telling. The prince focused his beam farther below, straight down into the crevasse.

"I see something." The prince's words cut through the scene like the proverbial hot knife through butter.

"What is it?" This from Jami, who cautiously made her way over to the prince, as far from the edge of the precarious drop-off as possible. When she reached him, he was down on his hands and knees, peering into the abyss.

"I swear it looks like a structure of some kind. Something metallic. I thought I saw a glint of metal." He shined his light this way and that, varying the angle at which he held the flashlight.

Dan looked down on the prince, who crawled a little closer to the edge and bent his head even more forward, engrossed in what he was seeing. Dan looked back at Jami, who also stared down into the royal's light beam. It was clear to Dan that neither had an inkling of the dark thought forming in his mind. But could he really do it? Should he? He eyeballed the prince again and confirmed that he was not tethered in any way. Then, in a rush of streaming rationalization, logic and self-preservation all wrapped into one lightning-fast bolt of decision-making, Dan acted.

He wheeled around and took two steps toward the open crevasse before planting his right boot on the kneeling prince's backside. He shoved hard, hard enough that he was concerned his momentum could carry himself over the edge along with the prince, who was definitely going over. But the royal Emirati's reflexes were much sharper than he had anticipated, and as his mind dimly registered Jami's forceful shriek while watching the prince plummet, he felt a strong hand encircle his left ankle.

The prince intended to take Dan with him.

Jami reached out and grabbed Dan's outstretched arm. She provided just enough resistance to slow his dragging by the prince to allow him to gain better traction with his other foot. He dug in with the foot not gripped by the prince's desperately clawing hand while Jami screeched in some combination of shock, horror, surprise and fear. Dan threw the only object he had at his disposal—his small flashlight—at the prince's dangling head. He hit him square in the face, and he saw the prince's eyes—wide open in fear—close shut with the impact that produced a red bloom on his nose. Dan stomped the foot that had the prince's hand gripped around it, and felt the clutching fingers slip away.

The prince fell silently into the chasm, without a last scream, but his eyes were as wide open as can be, and they locked with Dan's until he fell beyond their line of sight. Dan stared back at him, both horrified at what he had done and unable to do anything about it.

But the sound of a gunshot shredding the relative silence of this most remote area was enough to shake him into reality. The shot missed. Had the falling man's aim been lucky enough to be true, Dan would have been hit, for he did not manage to move a muscle as the bullet came into contact with the lip of the chasm, not a foot beneath where Dan stood frozen.

"Get down!" Jami followed her own advice, not knowing if more shots might somehow be coming. She hit the ground in a prone position. Dan stood there, still shell-shocked. Jami tugged at his ankle and again told him to get down. Again, she repeated herself and pulled at his boot before he went to his knees.

But no more shots came.

The next sound they heard was an indistinct, low rumbling.

"Dan, let's—"

She was interrupted by the sudden trembling of the ground and then the crumbling of the lip of rock that Dan clung to. He started to slide down into the gaping opening. She moved toward him and extended her other arm. He grabbed her hand but more ground gave way beneath them.

"Rockslide!" Dan shouted as more and more rock removed itself from the formation it had been a part of and fell down into the abyss. "We're going down!"

No sooner had he completed his sentence than Dan began to slide out of sight into the crevasse. Jami held onto him and was dragged toward the edge, which was no longer a smooth rock lip but now a jagged, irregular affair. She dug herself into the ground, entrenching herself with her boots wedged into the frigid soil, but the very earth itself dissociated beneath her feet and then she was falling, tumbling, still clutching onto Dan's leg.

She and Dan screamed as they plummeted, certain they were about to die.

CHAPTER 23

The next couple of minutes would forever remain a hectic, horrifying blur to Dan and Jami. Darkness, pain from being besieged on all sides by rock and ice, confusion and the stinging realization that this time, they had gone too far and put themselves in a situation from which they could not recover. Their warning had been in the subterranean labyrinth of Giza, and they had ignored it, instead following the trail literally to the end of the Earth.

Their only solace during this chaotic fall was that they managed to keep a grip on one another. They had gotten into this together, and now they would die together. As it was, they could hardly be more isolated than this desolate fractured mountain crevasse on the lonely continent of Antarctica. Darkness enveloped them as they fell deeper into the crevasse. They suffered countless striations, contusions and scrapes until they slammed to a stop on something hard and solid.

Dan and Jami grunted with all-encompassing pain as their downward momentum came to a sudden and cruel stop. Neither could move or even say anything for minutes following the impact. They just lay there— wherever *there* was—entwined with each other's battered bodies, hoping that the respite from the maelstrom of falling rock was more than temporary. More time went by while they lay still, with arms shielding their heads. Save for the occasional single clack of a small rock landing somewhere, no further landslide activity ensued.

Dan extricated his limbs from Jami's and made the first attempt to determine if they were somewhere stable enough to be able to stand up and move about. With no light, this was a difficult and treacherous task. They had no idea if they had landed on a precarious lip of rock about to dash apart at any moment, or if they had settled on a stable shelf.

"Dan?" Jami's voice was feeble and full of fear.

"Don't move. Let's try and figure out how much room we have, wherever we are." He looked up, but saw only pitch darkness. "Look around. See any light coming from anywhere?" A few seconds later Jami reported that it was black in all directions. Then Dan heard her rummaging around, looking for something.

"Do you still have your pack?" she asked. He told her that he did. "Do you still have your little flashlight?"

"No, I threw it at the prince."

"That's great, Dan. Really! Why did you even do what you did?"

"I don't believe he was going to let us live. It was what I saw as our only chance to neutralize him as a threat and hopefully get us out of harm's way."

She laughed, snorting, a sarcastic outburst in the darkness that hurt Dan just as much as the physical pain he currently felt. "Out of harm's way, huh? Is that what you call this? *Is it*? We're going to die down here."

"Look, I felt like we were in danger. The fact he was armed proves I was right. I didn't even know he had a gun on him, or that he would be able to get a shot off, or that that shot would trigger a landslide, okay?"

"But it did, and now what? We can't even see to get out of here if there's even a way."

"The Hag team will be here soon," Dan said, his voice weak.

"How will they find us?" Jami screamed, panicking now. "We're caved in deep inside a crevasse, part way up a mountain for God's sake!"

"They'll see our chopper, and the pilot saw where we went. Remember, the prince told us not to go out of visual range, and we didn't until we fell down here."

"Oh, I'm glad you listen to the prince now, after you decided to kill him! Who are you, anyway? A murderer? Is that who I've been traipsing around the world with? I should have gone home from the bar that night."

"I did what I thought I needed to save our lives," Dan said through clenched teeth. "What I thought I *had* to."

"Well now look what we have to do: we have to make our way up in pitch dark through an avalanche of collapsed rock...IN THE MIDDLE OF ANTARCTICA AFTER YOU JUST KILLED THE GUY WHO BROUGHT US HERE!"

"Then we better stop arguing and get started!" Dan shouted. The words came out more harshly delivered than he'd intended, and he reached out to put a hand on her shoulder. She recoiled and lost her balance, flailing her arms. "Hey!" she screamed, eyes widening in fear and confusion.

Dan lunged forward to grab her outstretched arm, but just as they contacted each other she went off the edge of whatever precipice they had been perched on. He had no choice but to go with her. Together they tumbled further into the dark unknown depths. Hands and feet occasionally came into contact with sheer walls of ice and rock, slowing them down some, but then they would freefall through open space. This went on for a terrifyingly long, and yet at the same time unknown amount of time, until they hit a solid platform even deeper into the crevasse.

"Jami, are you okay?"

"We're definitely dead now," came her weak reply, little more than a whisper. Dan fought back the rising tide of desperation her words elicited by sweeping his hands and feet around whatever surface it was upon which they'd landed. He consoled himself with the small victory that he detected no edges, and therefore had enough space to stand without worrying about falling over an edge. He told Jami he was going to stand up, then slowly got to first his knees, and then, reaching a hand over his head to probe for overhead obstructions, he rose to his unsteady feet.

Wishing they could see, he searched his pockets to take inventory of what little possessions he might have. He carried no backpack—not that it had much in it that could help in this situation anyway—but it had been ripped away during the fall. In his pockets he found a small penknife, a half-eaten granola bar, and an AA battery, but no light source. "I don't have a light, do you?"

"No." Her voice was flat and unemotional, and somehow that scared Dan more than if she'd sounded frightened or angry.

"Radio?" he continued, hoping against hope.

She answered in the same toneless way. "No."

They lapsed into silence at the realization that with no supplies or equipment, with none of the rest of the team knowing exactly where they were and with no way out in pitch blackness, they were all but doomed. During that silence, their glum thoughts were the loudest thing. Loudest, that is, until the ruminations had run their course and began to repeat— the same dismal fates over and over, when even a new way to die besides starvation or dying of thirst or falling into the abyss or being crushed in a crevasse collapse was a relief from their bleak reality. When all those things had been painfully exhausted, Dan registered a new sound, and it wasn't only in his head. Instantly recognizable, it was at once strange and familiar, because although he'd heard it countless times, he wasn't expecting to hear it here and now.

Water. The lapping of water against…the rock walls of the crevasse, he supposed. It was too dark to tell. But it was definitely water, and almost surely ocean water, since they were far down in a crack in the Earth near the South Pole, meaning it would be too cold for freshwater that was not in the form of ice to exist here, permanently out of reach of the sun's rays. Saltwater wouldn't freeze, so it must be the ocean.

"Water," Dan said flatly. "It's water down there."

"Maybe we should just jump in and die quick instead of slow," was Jami's response. Dan tried to think of something uplifting to say, but he could not. The situation was getting to him, too. Maybe they should just give up. The thought of dying down here like this was awful. Their only chance of survival was for the Hag team to find them down here in time. He supposed it was possible, but with the rock-and-ice-slide caused by the gunshot, who knew if they were even reachable anymore? How deep were they buried?

And then suddenly, a stab of bright light from off to their right, and slightly above. Bright, artificial light, accompanied by a familiar voice.

"Perhaps if we all work together we can make it through this." The prince. The direction of the light changed such that it illuminated his own face, some meters away, haggard and blood-streaked. "I forgive you for what you did, Dan. I understand you acted out of fear, and I myself am at fault for letting my own guard down as well as for precipitating this situation in the first place. It should not have been allowed to happen. I mean both of you no ill will. My intentions have always been to make sure you leave here both very much alive as well as enlightened."

Dan was indignant despite the hopeless situation all three of them were in, although the light was literally a ray of hope. "Yeah right, you kidnapped us at gunpoint to bring us here. If we found anything of value, you were just going to kill us and leave us out here in the middle of nowhere, or probably have your hired thugs do it for you."

"Again, my American friends, I can see how you would think that way, which is why I am willing to let bygones be bygones and work together from this point forward. As you can see, I do have a strong light." He aimed the beam briefly at them before sweeping it along the ledge on which they had landed. In itself it was unremarkable—a small outcropping of rock. But then he played the light downward, which illuminated a choppy body of water. It appeared black and foreboding, as well as deep. Then the prince shone the beam upward. This was the most heart-wrenching view of all, for it showed them that they had landed at the bottom of the crevasse, several hundred feet down. Furthermore, the uppermost portion appeared to be sealed completely.

"We're screwed no matter what," Dan said.

Surprisingly, the prince shrugged. "With that attitude, yes. But instead, if you wish, we can try to work together for at least a chance at survival. The choice is yours."

Dan was quick to reply, while Jami continued to sit in sullen silence. "You're the one who actually caused this cave-in, anyway, with your gun, another reason why we don't trust you. Why would you even bring one with you if you meant no harm to us?"

The prince played his light beam around the water below while he replied. "As a person of considerable means, I learned early on that it pays for me to look out for myself. I could elaborate but now is not the time or place if we wish to have any hope of survival. Instead, I hope that this gesture will suffice as a token of my trustworthiness."

With that, the prince held out his pistol, swung his arm a couple of times in an underhand fashion before tossing the firearm over to Dan and Jami, where it landed at their feet. Dan picked up the weapon and used the light the prince shined to open the chamber of the Ruger 9mm. "Six rounds left."

"Yes," the prince said. "Quite enough to eliminate me now if you wish. I am trusting you as well. I thank *Allah* for the life I have gratefully lived up to now, but if He chooses, I will extend it further. You now have your own choice to make."

"Maybe we should ask the prince to shoot us," Jami interjected without warning. "Might be better than slowly starving and dying of thirst and freezing to death down here in the dark after the light goes out."

"Never give up," Dan said, thinking of a favorite song.

Too far away to hear their low-toned conversation, the prince shouted across the gap: "I have a radio that works. I will try to reach our pilot. He knows we are down here because he had a visual on us until we dropped into the crevasse."

Dan's face brightened in the darkened surroundings. "You see," he said to Jami, "there is hope."

They heard the blare of white noise static as the prince turned on his handheld radio. "I will try to get a message out," he called over to them before speaking into his transmitter. "Chopper One, Chopper One, this is Mobile One in distress. Repeat: this is Mobile One in distress, do you copy, over?" As soon as he released the talk button, they heard a wash of static no different than before. He tried again, repeating the message several more times, but after each try only dense, indecipherable static came back.

"Let me try a channel scan," he said, fiddling with the unit's controls. "If a strong enough signal occurs on any frequency, we will hear it." But for the next few seconds all they heard was more impenetrable white noise.

"Probably too much rock for the signal to make it through," Dan guessed.

The prince shrugged. "You may be right. We can try to move around, see if we can get to a higher vantage point that perhaps would offer better signal propagation?"

"Let's see," Dan said, taking a look back down toward the freezing water not far below. "Is that really an option?"

Taking the hint, the prince directed his flashlight's beam to the slab of rock Dan and Jami occupied. A roiling body of water lay scant feet below them, with the other side of the chasm too far to reach by jumping across. The prince then scanned the light from Jami and Dan's platform out along the chasm wall at the same height. Dan followed the beam's progress with his gaze as it played out away from the ledge he occupied. More featureless rock, the bottom strata of it wet with seawater. The prince would occasionally jump the light upwards, but this revealed only more featureless walls of rock. *There's nothing down here*, Dan began to think. *Nothing that will lead us back to the world above.*

And then they heard it.

A cooing noise. The bird. Dan knew it was the petrel he had sighted earlier, the one that had led them down into this hellish place. It must be trapped down here, too, he thought. The sound of its call reverberated off the rock and water, making it impossible to tell from which direction it came. Nothing was visible outside the cone of the prince's flashlight, but he wanted to know where the bird had gone. It must be stuck down here, too, he reasoned, or it would be flying out by now, wouldn't it? He voiced his concern that maybe they should try to find the bird so as to watch it and see if it found a way up, so that at least they would know where an outlet to the outside world waited.

In response, the prince began directing his light around the walls of the crevasse, scoping the daunting environs for the raptor. He aimed the beam up high at first, figuring that a bird would be as near the top of the crevasse as possible, but that turned up nothing. He began shining the beam progressively lower down toward the water, scanning from left to right on the wall above Dan and Jami.

Suddenly they heard the bird screech again, but louder and closer this time. And then there it was, flying lower over the water towards the prince. It passed directly in front of Dan and Jami's precarious perch—actually below them—gliding fast without flapping its wings, straight at the prince's flashlight. Dan's head turned as he watched it fly—barely able to register that it was in fact the petrel he'd seen earlier before it was out of sight past the prince's ledge. The bird was moving *fast*, Dan thought.

But why?

And then the entire body of water beneath them, whatever it was, began to brighten.

CHAPTER 24

"It's getting so bright!" It was the first time in quite a while that Dan detected any emotion in Jami's voice whatsoever. And she was right. The surface of the water, or just beneath it, now appeared a dull white color.

"What is that?" the prince called out. He shone his beam on Dan and Jami, possibly to see if they were somehow causing the strange glow, before shifting the light back to the water, and in so doing Dan noticed that he could not see the white glow while the flashlight was not trained on it. This told him that whatever it was underwater, it wasn't a source of light on its own.

"We're getting wet!" All of a sudden Jami was on her feet, and then Dan felt it, too. Water splashing over his boots. He freed his mind enough from the task of *watching* the disturbance in the water to actually be able to *listen* to it, and then he heard the sound of the wave that was being generated as the object moved through the liquid space. It was past the prince now. The Emirati royal's back was to Dan and Jami as he aimed the light at the retreating spectacle. Dan and Jami clung to each other as the wave of water rolled over their platform. Dan knew there was nothing to hold onto on the featureless plateau except each other, and that if they were swept into the freezing water they would not survive.

The water rose as high as their knees, causing him to squat in order to lower his center of gravity while Jami did the same, clutched in his embrace. They held on and in a matter of a few seconds, the water was receding, pouring off the platform in a great sheet, while they remained standing. Eyeing the fleeing raptor silhouetted in the prince's flashlight, Dan watched as the unknown light-colored force overtook the gliding bird.

The fleeing avian, probably feeling a rush of air on its feathers from the oncoming wave pushed by the unknown submerged force, flapped its wings in a frenetic burst of energy meant to gain altitude fast. As it rose higher into the narrow air column defined by the walls of the caved-in crevasse, so too the whitish shape began to rise from the depths. Dan watched as its broad, white form broke the water's surface. Unbelievably, it rose higher and higher from the water until more of its shape was exposed, and then Dan's mouth dropped even further open in heart-stopping, stunned recognition.

"It's a shark!" he stammered. "A massive freakin' shark!"

The prince backed up away from the edge of his narrow ledge. Jami moved closer to the end of their ledge for a better look. "It's too big to be a great white. If I didn't know any—"

But she cut herself off as the massive fish breached into the air and opened its jaws wide—visible to her by the head rearing back. It happened in a flash of time—one second the bird was there and the next, there was a gigantic splash as the gargantuan fish fell back into the water. A few feathers drifted in the cold air as the shark disappeared into the unknown depths.

"It ate the bird!" the prince shouted.

"I guess swimming out of here is out," Dan said. "What kind of shark was that?" He looked to Jami, but she only shook her head in shock while staring down into the roiling water the leviathan had left behind.

"Great white?" Dan prodded.

"No," Jami finally answered at length. "The Southern Ocean is too cold for *Carcharadon carcharias*."

"Then what is *that*?" Dan asked, his gaze probing the dark depths.

"I...." she trailed off without answering.

"It's okay if you don't know. You're more than smart enough in my book already." He nudged her arm.

"It's true that I don't *know*. But I have a guess—what my intuition tells me—but that's what's making me feel weird."

"What is it?"

"If I didn't know any better, I'd swear it looks like a *Carcharadon megalodon*."

Dan made eye contact with her in the dim light of the prince's roving flashlight beam, which still sought the shark. "What? A megalodon?"

"I told you it was crazy," she said, turning away with a sheepish expression.

"Aren't those extinct?"

"I thought so—along with everybody else. But look how big that thing was. I don't know what else it can be. The only other known living shark bigger than a white is maybe a whale shark, but those only eat plankton. That was no whale shark. And even if regular white sharks somehow did manage to adapt to the polar waters down here, that specimen we just saw was far too huge."

"I found something!" the prince's excited voice cut through the shark talk. Dan turned to see him aiming his beam behind him, at the wall bordering his own ledge prison.

"We can't see it from here," Dan shouted over to him. "What is it?"

"It's a drawing," the prince said, still facing the same direction, away from the water.

"Of what?" Jami asked. Dan was glad to see a spark of the old curiosity and thirst for life returning for her. The prince hesitated before answering, taking a few steps closer to the wall.

"It's a cave-type drawing, done with crude white lines, of Osiris."

To Dan, it meant one thing: "We saw that in Giza!" The connection chilled him even more than the subterranean Antarctic environment in which he now found himself.

But to Jami it meant something else, something much more specific: "The *resurrector* of animals. Do you see?"

Dan looked at her blankly.

"I don't see any animals in the drawing, or any other drawings besides this one," said the prince, not realizing she hadn't been addressing him.

"The animal I'm talking about is the one swimming down there somewhere," Jami replied, turning around to face the water once again. "The one that ate the bird."

"The megalodon?" Dan asked, a spark in his eye

She nodded. "Osiris brought animals back to life as well as humans, remember?" Dan nodded while the prince did the same as he inched even closer to the drawing. "So perhaps Osiris worked his magic on the megalodon and reanimated it, like with the wooly mammoths."

"What for?" Dan wondered aloud. The prince turned around to face them.

"Yes, why would an Egyptian god wish to do such a thing?"

Jami walked a few steps out toward the edge of the platform and peered first down into the water, and then up and around the crevasse walls, which the prince illuminated for her with his light. "Why, to guard the Atlanteans' treasures, of course! Why else?"

"Guard them?" the prince asked, his voice rising in pitch with his growing excitement. "Guard them from what, or whom?"

"From anyone who seeks to plunder the secrets of Atlantis. From the Nazis. From the likes of *us*," she said. Both Dan and the prince were formulating a reply when the prince's radio crackled, startling them all with its unexpected clear voice, fragmented as the transmission was.

"...read? Hag 1 at Remote Base One...."

The prince scrambled to remove the radio from his belt. "Remote One to Hag One: I read you. Do you copy, over?"

They all waited breathlessly for a reply. It wasn't long in coming, though still somewhat broken up.

"...top of ridge. Pilot ...you went....crevasse not penetrable.....yet....copy?"

The prince's face brightened almost enough to light the caved-in crevasse by himself. He yelled over to Dan and Jami, "The Hag team is here. They are up there!"

"Yes!" their cries of rejoice were cut short by a loud, heavy splash coming from the left of Dan and Jami's ledge. Immediately they looked in that direction while the prince trained his light, but none of them saw anything conclusive. Then the radio refocused their attention once more.

"...looking for an entry point. ...--ck in touch...--er."

"Copy that!" the prince yelled into the transmitter. "Please hurry!"

"Shine your light this way!" Jami called. The prince complied and soon they were looking at an anomaly beneath the surface of the water. That was all it looked like so far, from their distance away and the prince's flashlight from even father, it was simply something incongruous with the natural surroundings, a few feet down underwater on the opposite wall.

"Something's down there," Jami said, pointing.

"The shark?" the prince asked.

Dan shook his head and pointed off to the left. "No, the shark is right over there."

"So then what is it?" the prince inquired.

Jami walked toward the closest edge of their platform and stared out at the anomaly. "A large opening of some kind, like maybe a cavern, a few feet below the surface."

"*Below* the surface?" the prince called over.

"Yes," Jami answered. "Totally submerged. Too far down to be exposed by either tidal movements or wave action."

"What good can it do if it's underwater?" the prince pressed.

"I don't know, I'm just pointing out that there's something there, is all."

A loud splash off to Jami's left caused them all to whip their heads in that direction. A second later, a couple of smaller splashes happened in about the same place. "Rocks, coming from above," Dan shouted.

"Another cave-in?" Jami asked.

"It's our team, looking for a way in." The prince scrambled to bring his radio to his lips. "Hag 1 team, you are close! You're knocking rocks down to us. Do you copy?"

To Dan and Jami, the noise issuing from the radio sounded indecipherable, but apparently it meant something to the prince because he spoke animatedly into the transmitter in response. When he paused and looked over to Dan and Jami, Dan yelled across to the prince, "Did they hear you?"

They could see the prince's nod before he replied by pointing up toward the distant roof of the crevasse. "They're about to break through! Be careful of more falling rock."

Dan and Jami both placed their arms over their heads as they looked up toward what they now knew was their rescue team. As they did, they were stunned to see a sliver of bright light open up as the sky became visible through the collapsed crevasse.

"I see light!" Jami cried out exuberantly.

She had barely finished speaking when they saw a large object fall through the crack and down through the crevasse.

CHAPTER 25

If not for the scream, they would have passed it off as yet another large rock falling into the crevasse from above. Agonizing, hair-raising, spine-tingling, and above all, distinctly human.

"That's a guy!" Dan said a half-second before the man struck the water.

"He could still be alive!" the prince yelled while waving his light around the area of the fallen team member. "Yell to him, tell him to swim to you!"

Dan and Jami did so, waving their arms while jumping up and down and shouting at the top of their lungs. They saw splashing. "Over here! This way." All of them knew from their expedition briefings that a human falling into Antarctic waters—which are actually below freezing due to the high salt content—had mere seconds to get out and get warm before hypothermia would render them non-functional.

The fallen team member turned his head toward Dan and Jami for a second and then started to swim. It was a slow, clumsy stroke, no doubt impeded by the life-sapping water temperature, but he did manage to make some progress towards his wayward expedition-mates. Until, about halfway to them, he suddenly stopped swimming and began treading water instead. He rotated in place until he faced the crevasse wall on the opposite side to Dan and Jami. He stared down into the water without moving. Dan feared his energy was sapped and he was about to slip under for good.

"Keep moving! Don't stop now!" Dan shouted. "Swim to my voice, come on!" Behind them, the prince waved his flashlight to create a visual target for the swimmer to home in on. Still the man only treaded water, but now he spoke, loud and clear enough for all of them to hear, his voice echoing throughout the aqueous crevasse bottom.

"It's beautiful!" he shouted. "Unbelievable! Have them bring—" He would never finish his sentence, for at that moment the same massive shark that had earlier consumed the petrel now engulfed the man, and with about as much ease. He was lifted explosively from his vertical posture, catapulted by the leviathan's mouth. The man's eyes, impossibly wide with fear, shock and disbelief, would be forever etched in Dan's brain as the prince illuminated them with his light as he gyrated within the shark's jaws. It was all over in a second when the shark returned to the water and dragged its defenseless prey with it into the unsurvivable depths.

The resulting silence weighed so heavily it was hard for Dan, Jami and the prince to comprehend.

"He's gone!" Jami choked, breaking into a sob. Dan put an arm around her but she pulled away.

"Hold it together!" the prince called over. "The rest of our team is up there." As if to underscore his point, his radio blared. The message was unintelligible to Dan but he could tell it contained an actual human voice and not merely static. The prince held the radio to his mouth while looking up to the top of the caved-in crevasse. After a brief two-way exchange, he yelled over to Dan and Jami.

"They're going to try to knock out some more rock to clear an access point. Back up to the wall and cover your head with your arms!"

The prince heeded his own advice on his island ledge, preparing for an onslaught of falling rock and ice. High above, they could all hear the grinding of rock against rock, as the team worked to gain entry into the sealed crevasse. Meanwhile, a small wave travelled across the narrow expanse of water as the unseen leviathan travelled somewhere silently below.

They didn't have long to wait before another onslaught of geological material poured into the subterranean space. Great sheets of rock sliced all the way down into the water, with lighter fragments and dust drifting down after them through the air. But with the debris came light. Lots of it. The pitch blackness was now merely a pervasive dimness that seemed bright as day to the trapped trio after being in the dark for so long.

They hugged the walls of their respective ledges for a few more minutes until they were sure no additional rockslides were forthcoming. Dan and Jami craned their necks to look up at the new opening in the caved-in crevasse. They heard the prince say something into his radio, and then the handheld crackled back with something unintelligible.

"Something's down there!" Dan said to Jami, excited. "Before…." His tone softened while remembering the horrible death of an expedition member they had just witnessed. "Before the shark took him, he said there was something amazing down there, underwater?"

"The same thing we were looking at before. Not all that deep."

Dan looked out toward the end of the shelf as he thought about it. "Doesn't really matter how deep it is though since the water's too cold for us to get into at all. Not like we can go swimming around."

"Not without a full drysuit, anyway. I know you said we didn't bring dive gear."

Dan shook his head. "No SCUBA. Oh but…we did bring dive gear!" The smile on his face perked up Jami's spirits a bit.

"Really, what?"

"The mini-sub! How could I forget?"

Jami laughed. "Mini-sub, okay. How are we going to get it down here?"

Before Dan could answer, the prince shouted over to them.

"Heads up: a team member is going to try to rappel down to the shelf you're on to see if we can establish a way to get us all out of here."

"Copy that!" Dan shouted back over to him. He turned to Jami. "They're coming for us!" In response, she put her arms around him and told him that she was freezing.

"Won't be long before we're sipping hot chocolate in the tent wrapped up in sleeping bags," Dan said, wanting her to focus on the positive. But as he heard some sort of commotion high above, some sort of shouting followed by the sound of more rocks bouncing down the crevasse walls, he reminded himself that they weren't out of the proverbial woods yet. "Right now, let's just pay attention and do what we can to help them help us."

"Okay," Jami said with a sniffle, but she turned her attention to first the prince, who stood on his ledge with his radio to his lips, and then to the top of the crevasse, where a pair of legs could be seen in silhouette preparing to drop down into the subterranean space. They heard a voice over the radio in English say something about needing more slack, followed by something indecipherable and more small rocks falling. Then the rappeler began his descent.

He proceeded slowly, not knowing if the wall he planted his feet on would hold or break away causing yet another chain-reactive crumbling. On some sections he was out of sight of Dan and Jami due to concavities in the wall, or sections where the rock wall flared out. But he would reappear lower down and continue on his path. When he was low enough, he called over to Dan and Jami: "I'm going to toss you a rope. I need you to grab it. Okay?"

Dan nodded and then the rappeler gathered a coil of green climbing rope in one hand. He swung it a couple of times and then released his grip, and the rope partially uncoiled as it flew through the air and landed on the ledge a couple of feet away from Dan, who stepped on it before it could get away from him. He picked it up and recoiled it so that it was organized and ready to use.

"Good job," the team member called out. He wore a helmet with a headlamp built in making Dan unable to see who it was, not that he cared. "Now just hold onto it while I make the rest of the way down to you. I don't want to hit the water, okay, so hold onto it so that I can slide over onto your ledge."

"I've got it." Dan hoped his voice inspired confidence. In his mind he flashed on the last team member who fell into the water, getting swept up in the jaws of that hideous goliath that was still down there somewhere. He resolved himself not to let go of the rope at any cost.

"Ready when you are!" he reiterated. The rappeler, for his part, seemed to harbor no undue fears. He did not hesitate as he kicked off the rock wall and began a zipline-like slide down the rope fastened by himself to the wall and held in place on the ledge by Dan's boots. The prince followed his through-air progress with his noticeably dimmer light beam while Jami positioned herself to be out of the climber's way when he landed but close enough to render assistance if need be.

The climber zipped along smoothly until he landed surefootedly on the ledge, bringing himself to a halt within a few steps smack in the middle of the platform, a perfect landing. He unclipped himself from the rope and extended a hand to Dan and Jami in turn. "Well hello there! We'll have to get you topside for some proper care, but in the meantime…." He paused while he removed a couple of water bottles that had been clipped onto his waistband and handed one to each of them. "This will help." He even had a third bottle which he tossed to the prince with a warning of, "Catch, my friend." The prince caught it and the three of them chugged in silence for a few seconds while the climber radioed his team topside.

"One rope in place to the nearest ledge with Dan and Jami and now myself. The prince is on a separate ledge about twenty meters away. Easiest way to get him to us is probably to lower a raft, over, but given what happened to Ben, I'm thinking that's not a wise option at this point." Both Dan and Jami nodded vigorously. "It's too far away for the steel ladder," the climber said, resuming his radio exchange, referencing how climbers in Everest and other icy locations sometimes used actual ladders to traverse ice chasms. "But we may be able to make a rope bridge." The climber then engaged in additional radio banter about the equipment they would need to make the rope bridge happen.

The next hour or so saw the chasm transformed into a beehive of activity as the team worked together to transport men and equipment to Dan and Jami's ledge. Another team member made the descent and together he and the first were able to create the rope bridge to the prince's ledge by anchoring two ropes to Dan and Jami's ledge and tossing the ropes from up high over to the prince's ledge. They then tossed the prince some metal stakes and a rock hammer for him to anchor into the rock, which he did, before giving the thumbs up sign that he was ready to cross.

The newly arrived climbers lit the prince's way with their own lights so that he was able to have both hands free. Dan eyed the water beneath the bridge, which was about fifteen feet up. He thought back to the behemoth's breach and wasn't sure it was high enough, but it was better than being on the water in a raft, and certainly better than being in it. The prince tentatively placed his weight onto the first rungs of the horizontally placed rope ladder, testing it. Satisfied it was holding, he then crawled out on all fours until he was no longer over the ledge at all.

Slowly but surely, while alternating looking down through the rungs at the choppy sea below and eyeballing his path straight ahead, the prince made his way across the gap between the two ledges. The ladder was wobbly, and once the prince even flipped all the way over, but he clung on and was able to right himself and continue his way across. Dan eyed the sea for signs of the mega-beast, but the waters remained empty as the prince completed his crossing. He was helped onto the occupied ledge by the two climbers who had rigged the ladder bridge. They pulled the prince to his feet and asked him if he was okay.

"Thanks to these two, yes, I'm quite fine!" the prince beamed, making eye contact that Dan found most uncomfortable. Was he going to mention what had happened to cause the crevasse collapse? The talk immediately turned to the logistics of extricating them all out of here, but then the prince interrupted. Dan caught his breath because he thought the royal was going to bring up the fact that Dan pushed him into the crevasse, but instead he pointed to the strange underwater region.

"There is something there worth investigating." He looked to Dan and Jami. "Am I right?"

Dan looked at Jami, who was already nodding. "Before Ben was...."

"Eaten," Dan finished for her. He was so exhausted, mentally and physically, that he didn't have the energy to sugarcoat anything. Jami eyed Dan briefly before turning back to the two climbers.

"He told us while he was sill in the water that he saw something down there that was extraordinary."

"I saw a glow of some sort on the way down," the second arrived of the two climbers said. "I passed it off as a dropped light or something from you guys."

The prince, Dan and Jami all shook their heads. But the first climber appeared irritated. "Look everyone, as the Terrestrial Team Lead, I have to insist that we make our ascent out of here without delay. We can talk up there. But we know that the stability of this area is an issue, so let's get everyone back above ground, okay?"

There were no sensible arguments to give, and so they all turned their full attention to making the ascent to the top of the crevasse. Within the hour, more rigging was put in place to safely allow all of them to ascend to the lip of the crevasse. As Dan climbed above the ledge, he couldn't help but look down into the choppy water across from their ledge, where the odd glow persisted. The higher he rose, aided by team members from above pulling him up by an additional rope, the more he thought about the anomaly, and how they might access it. By the time he reached the opening to the crevasse, he had formulated a plan.

CHAPTER 26

To Dan and Jami, emerging from the top of the crevasse was something like being reborn. The fresh, moving air was beyond invigorating. The pervasive light, uplifting. But to Dan, something was incomplete. Unfinished. Fragmented. As he was helped out of his climbing harness by a team member, he stared back down into the crevasse, mentally picturing the hellishness that had already transpired down there.

And yet, he already felt an indomitable urge to go back. After all, there *was* something down there. Something that now even more people had died in pursuit of. Dan walked over to the prince who had also just removed his climbing rig. All around them was talk about the logistics of packing up and getting everyone and the vehicles back to base camp so that they could terminate the expedition. People had died, it was time to pack it in, was the consensus.

"So that's it, we're giving up?" Dan asked the prince.

The prince took another step closer. "I am not aware we had options. Please tell me, what else can we do? Or are you just looking for an excuse to finish what you started earlier?" His eyes appeared like brown steel as he met Dan's intense gaze.

"Just the opposite of that. I'm trying to make it up to you by giving you what you came here for, or at least the best possible chance for it."

"And how do you propose to do that?"

Dan pointed down into the crevasse, the intimidating opening only a few feet away from their feet. "The strange...." He hesitated as he searched his mind for the right word, "...object...that was underwater. The Unidentified Underwater Object—like a UFO only underwater, get it?"

The prince nodded but did not appear amused. Dan continued.

"We should investigate it. See what it is."

The prince shrugged. "It's underwater, as you said, and at the bottom of the crevasse we just barely made it out alive from."

"We have a small, two-person submersible."

At this the prince tipped back his head and laughed uproariously, causing a few of the other team members, including Jami, to look their way. When he finished guffawing and composed himself, he looked at Dan and said, "The submersible was meant for coastal exploration, ideally from the support ship, although we did load it onto a snowtracker just in case."

Dan saw an opportunity to jump in. "Right, and this is just that case! This is it—right down there!" He pointed dramatically down into the crevasse. The prince frowned.

"I think you missed the part about the sub being for *coastal* exploration. In case you haven't noticed, we are halfway up a steep mountain and the UUO, as you call it, is down at the bottom of this very narrow chasm. So how would the submersible be able to access it?"

Dan turned and pointed down the mountain. "As you said, the sub is already here. We just need to get it down into the crevasse."

The prince snorted. "Oh, is that all?"

"Hear me out," Dan said, making a placating gesture with his hands. "I said I know a way to get the sub *down* there. I didn't say we'd be able to get it back up." He let this sink in while eyeing the prince, whose expression became more serious.

"Go on," he told Dan.

Again, Dan pointed down the hill. "We use the helicopter to airlift the sub up over the crevasse and drop it straight down the middle so that it splashes into the water below." Dan could see the prince's eyes widening far beyond what is natural, and so hurriedly continued before he could be interrupted. "And then, we rappel back down into the crevasse, board the sub, and take it down to investigate what is there. We document it, whatever it is, and then resurface, leave the sub down there and climb back out. But the sub will have to be left behind," Dan said. "Dropping it in is okay—and I admit that it might not even make it—if it hits the side on the way down, it's toast, I know. But on the way up would require too much lifting power to overcome the suction of the water and it's basically a needless risk at that point. You're just going to have to eat the cost of the sub if you decide to go through with this."

There was a long, pregnant silence during which the prince said nothing, but appeared to be lost deep in thought, perhaps judging Dan in some way.

"Well, what do you think?" Dan prodded.

"I'm starting to think you are crazy," the prince said with a straight face. "Really crazy. You expect me to just give up a multi-million-dollar vehicle because...."

"Because it might show us the answer to Atlantis! What is that down there? Don't you want to know? You were willing to literally kidnap two people at gunpoint all the way around the world and now you're afraid of losing some fancy toy?" Dan stared as hard as he could at the prince, hoping his gaze was burning right through to the man's brain, his very soul, even.

Slowly, the prince turned his head and looked down the mountain, where the helicopter waited out of sight. "Assuming this stunt of yours is even technically feasible—and that my pilot will even attempt it—who is going to make the dive? The sub is only rated for two persons, and one must be the qualified pilot, who happens to be me."

Dan did his best to display a poker face, but he had to admit to himself that he had not considered the possibility that the prince and he would end up in the mini-sub together. But before he could ask himself if he still wanted to go through with it, the submersible pilot spoke again. "I would do the dive with you. That is not the issue. The real issues are the viability of doing it safely, and of losing my *toy*, as you put it. I would not stay wealthy for long if I constantly threw my money away. So allow me to consult in private with my helicopter pilot—and again—this part of the operation is entirely in his hands--I am not a certified pilot of any kind beyond this particular submersible."

Dan made extended eye contact with the prince and then nodded his agreement. It was the best that he could hope for. "Just one more thing," he said, causing the prince to turn back around with a raised eyebrow.

"Yes?"

"If we do this—go down there in the sub and find out whatever it was that Ben saw before he was eaten—then me and you—and Jami and you—are even, fair and square, all debts settled, we owe you nothing and you us nothing, agreed?"

The prince nodded. "Yes, of course," he said, before starting to turn away. But Dan persisted.

"No, I mean really, for the rest of our lives, you will not chase us down or pester us; we will have settled our obligation to you even if we do not find evidence of Atlantis. This is my best effort to give you want you want. Agreed?"

The prince allowed a few beats to pass, but then nodded amiably. "Let me discuss things with the pilot to see if it is really even an option before we go too much further."

"I want to go with you."

The prince had no immediate reply, so Dan continued. "I want to hear for myself what the pilot says."

The prince shrugged. "You think I will say he said no when he said yes, is that it? Let's go, then. Personally, I put the odds of him going along with it, even with additional financial incentives and assuming that the chopper does in fact have sufficient lifting power—at 70/30." Dan started to ask a question but the prince cut him off. "70 that he won't do it. But let's go find out."

"Where are you going?" Jami's voice pierced the polar air.

"Come with us," Dan invited her. "I'll update you on the way down." The prince had no objections and Jami fell into step beside them as they began walking along the ridgeline toward the section that they had used to climb up to the crevasse. It had since been shored up with climbing gear—rope and pitons—making the descent much easier than it had been the first time. When they got to the chopper, the pilot was standing in front of it, having been told by radio they were coming.

"There's nowhere for me to land up there, if that's what you're going to ask," he began without preamble, a lit cigarette dangling from his lips. To Dan, he looked like a Hunter S. Thompson type, big, mirrored sunglasses, leaning casually on the chopper with a weird furry hat on and smoking a cigarette. In response, Dan and the prince both shook their heads.

"For what we want to do, we don't need to land," the prince said, taking the final steps up to his pilot. "Yet it is not without risks, all the same." He proceeded to outline the plan, with interjections from Dan, all the while the pilot making alternately bemused and outraged expressions.

At the end of it, he asked them, "Is that all?"

"That is all," the prince confirmed.

The pilot glanced at his chopper, then up the mountain to the edge of the recently reopened crevasse, then back to the prince. "It's not a bad day to die today, is it?" He plucked the cigarette from his mouth and tossed it onto the snow-covered ground, where it sizzled out.

"Do we really need to pollute the last pristine environment on earth?" Jami asked in an exasperated tone.

The pilot sighed heavily. "I can keep the butts in an ashtray in the chopper, but then it'll smell up the cabin for our passengers."

He eyed the prince, who said, "Here in Antarctica, that should be the procedure from now on. Now, what do you say as to the operation?"

Jami smiled at the pilot, who, after a lengthy pause, said, "I'm in, under two conditions."

Dan beamed while Jami remained impassive, and the prince, used to people asking him for things, merely shrugged and said, "And what are those?"

The pilot did not hesitate. "One: I will require hazard pay, similar to the job I did for you in Iraq last—"

The prince waved a hand. "Say no more. Agreed. And your second condition?"

The pilot nodded. "My second condition is that I will *try* it, but I am in complete charge of the entire airlift operation from start to finish. If at any time I feel that lives are in danger—particularly my own—then I reserve the right to abort the mission, even if it seems to you or others like it may still be able to be carried out. I will do my best to complete it, but there are no guarantees. Do we understand each other, boss?"

The prince gave a slow nod and said, "We are in agreement." He extended a hand and the two shook on the deal. "Let's get started, then, with the understanding that we will likely need the rest of today's daylight to prepare. Then, assuming all goes well enough today, we can begin the mission tomorrow morning." The prince paused and the others nodded to indicate their agreement. "Go ahead and direct the team to what you need done to make it happen," the prince ordered.

The pilot nodded. "First thing we'll need is to construct a special harness for the mini-sub so that I can lift it with the chopper. I think the cargo straps used to hold the gear on the Hag should work. We also have to make it so that it has some sort of quick-release mechanism so that someone riding in the chopper with me can jettison the sub at the exact right moment—a crucial aspect of the operation."

The prince nodded. "While you're doing that, I'm going to brief Mr. James, here, on how to be an effective submersible co-pilot." The helicopter pilot nodded and turned away while grabbing his radio from his belt. "Let's do this!"

* * * *

Near the end of the day, though it was still light out, they set up camp in between the base of the mountain wall and the parked Hag and chopper, so that they were shielded from the wind, which had begun to pick up even more. This latter fact worried the pilot to no end, who was seen alternately staring at his satellite weather radar app and the top of the crevasse. The preparations had gone well, however, including construction of a harness for the sub that the pilot had deemed suitable, along with a corresponding release mechanism.

Dan's head was swimming with the technical details and logistics of the operation that he himself had conceived. They had gone over it all day. All he wanted to do now was get a good night's sleep.

He and Jami zipped into their pyramid tent and burrowed into their sleeping bags.

"I'm worried about tomorrow," Jami admitted.

"Why, what could possibly go wrong?"

They laughed until they were too exhausted to talk and fell into a deep sleep.

CHAPTER 27

Dan and Jami were awakened in the pre-dawn dark hours by the flapping of their tent. "What's going on?" Jami asked groggily.

"Tent stake's come undone," Dan said. "Means it's super-windy." The frenetic manner in which the loose tent corner flapped around indicated this was true.

"Can you fix it?"

"Yes, dear," he said in a mocking tone. It still came as a surprise to Dan that he and Jami had only known one another for a few days. He pulled on a pair of gloves, unzipped the tent door flap and then crawled outside. He saw the smoldering embers of the previous night's cook and campfires, around which they had sat briefly, discussing the upcoming mission before retiring early to their tents, exhausted. He crawled around the tent corner and found the uprooted stake, still attached to the tent fabric and flapping in the wind. Dan grabbed the stake and used a rock to punch it back into the frozen ground, which took some effort. Task accomplished, he turned around to crawl back into the warmth of the tent when his eye caught a gleam of fire reflected off the acrylic bubble dome of the mini-sub.

It sat propped on the Hag after being uncrated earlier that day in anticipation for use. He had even spent a couple of hours inside the cockpit, at the prince's insistence that he familiarize himself with the controls and the general layout of the complex machine. As he looked at it now, a thought suddenly overtook him. He wasn't sure where it came from or why he had it, but knew only that it somehow made sense. It was something that, if he was going to do it, would have to be done now, in the fleeting hours while the polar summer light was weakest, and while he was still the only one up and about the camp. He crawled back into the tent and pulled his boots on.

"What are you doing?" Jami asked. "The tent's fixed, right?"

"Yeah, but I see something I need to fix on one of the supply tents— it's loose too. It'll just take me a couple minutes to stamp it down. I'll be right back." He found his pack and grabbed an item out of it before tucking it into a pocket of his parka.

"Hurry back."

"I will." He kissed her on the forehead and slipped back outside into the chilly, blustery Antarctic air. He paused for a moment just outside the tent to scan the camp. No activity detected, he proceeded at a normal walking pace toward the cradled mini-sub. He mentally reviewed what he would say he was doing up at this hour should someone happen to see and question him. He still hadn't seen or heard anyone by the time he reached the underwater craft.

He stared up at the bubble, knowing that opening it by himself—quietly—would be the difficult part of this clandestine op. Taking one last look around, Dan scrambled up onto the Hag. He knew that once up here, off the ground, it would be very difficult to convincingly explain his reasons for being here at this time. From the cargo bed of the Hag he climbed atop the sub's deck, which was the rear metal portion of the craft behind the bubble dome cockpit. Only the cockpit was dry once underwater, while the rest of the craft was designed to be wet. He was about to start moving toward the sub's cockpit when he heard coughing come from one of the tents. He crouched and remained still for a few seconds, watching his breath in the frigid air. When he heard no further noise, he began a crouched walk, ducking low behind the sub's body to shield him from view of most of the tents.

When he reached the acrylic bubble, he rested, for he knew he would need strength to complete the next step. Today he'd seen the cockpit opened, and it took two men, both exerting significant effort, to raise it to its fully open position where it locked into place to allow safe boarding. Once all passengers were inside, it was designed to be closed by topside crew. But tonight, Dan was the sole passenger and crew, and so he was going to have to do it all on his own.

He crept to the side of the dome where he knew the first of three latches securing the dome would be. He used both hands to carefully unsnap the first one, mindful not to let it snap back and make any noise. The latches weren't as heavy duty or hard to fasten and unfasten as he expected. The prince had explained to him that it was because once underwater even a few feet, the water pressure kept the dome sealed tight against the sub's frame.

Dan rested on his heels for a few moments, knowing that the next step would be difficult. Looking east, he thought he could already detect the first brightening of the sky, which even now wasn't completely dark, but was about as dark as it would get this time of year. It was time to move. He stood and placed the fingers of both hands on the edge of the acrylic dome. Bending his knees, he put all his leg strength into pushing up while his arms pulled upward. The dome slowly lifted from the cockpit frame and he slowly rose with it. He knew he had to move fluidly to be able to enter the cockpit. It was too heavy for him to reliably prop all the way open, but he thought that if he acted fast enough, he should be able to slither inside without the heavy dome falling back down on him.

When his arms were fully extended, elbows locked, Dan slowly let go with his right hand to make certain only the left would hold the heavy dome aloft for at least a few seconds. Instantly, the remaining arm bearing the load began to tremble. But it held as he swung a leg under the dome into the cockpit. From there, he slipped his second hand back under the lid as it came back down and was able to slow its downward motion enough so that it made only a soft thud when contacting the frame.

He was inside the submersible. Now it was time to do what he came for. He reached into the pocket of his parka and removed the pistol that the prince had tossed to them down in the crevasse. He knew that it still contained six rounds. He also knew that when it was time to board the sub tomorrow—today, rather, he reminded himself, noting it was almost dawn—he would be wearing the provided thermal jumpsuit. The prince had told him bulky cold weather polar gear would not work in the sub, and so the "technical exposure wear" as he called it, was a requirement. For Dan, it meant that the tight-fitting outfit would not allow him to conceal the weapon on his person.

So here he was. He had already made good use of his time in the sub earlier by identifying what he thought would be a good place to hide the gun: under his co-pilot's seat. The funny thing was, he realized, the entire cockpit was a see-through acrylic sphere, such that anyone viewing the cockpit from below—possibly when they lifted the sub into the air, would be able to see it from below. But that was a chance he'd just have to take if he wanted to buy into his little insurance policy, as he thought of it.

He had just finished reaching down and placing the pistol there when the brilliance of a flashlight stabbing the pre-dawn darkness threatened to ruin his night vision. *Who's there?* He hunched down in the seat, making his profile as low as possible before freezing in place. Whoever it was with the light was walking around with it because the direction of the beam was changing.

Dan had no idea what he would say were he to be seen in here. *Just psyching myself up for the dive later*, was all he could think of. And in a weird way, that wasn't far off. It dawned on him now, as the new day's light began to dawn over the Antarctic continent, that in a few hours' time, if all went well, he would be sitting in this very bubble underwater, staring into the greatest of unknowns.

But right now, he had other issues, such as getting back to his tent undetected. The night-walker continued about the camp with the light, walking on the opposite side of the sub and the Hag from Dan and Jami's tent. That was so far a blessing, because once on the ground, the large, high-profile vehicle would hide him from line-of-sight on the other side of it. The team member drew nearer to the sub. But when he reached the firepit, he stooped and stirred its embers with a stick. Was he testing if it was all the way out or looking to start it up? Being this close to dawn, Dan guessed the latter. The man's efforts sent only a couple of sparks skyward, and it was clear the fire wouldn't be rekindled by mere stirring.

Dan hoped this meant he would give up and turn away, and he was right. The early-riser abruptly turned and strode purposely toward the KP igloo, where the fire-starting and butane supplies were kept. Dan knew that he had a couple of minutes, at most, to make his escape from the sub before his expedition-mate returned to the campfire. There was no way he could open the dome unseen if anyone was at the fire. He got into position to raise the hatch from the inside, which was difficult because it was not designed to be opened from the inside, but with topside support, so there were no handles or grips on the inside.

Dan knew he had to do it, though, so he put all the upper body strength he could muster into it and found he was only able to raise the heavy acrylic lid perhaps two or three inches. *Not gonna do it*, he thought, panic swimming in his gut. He redoubled his efforts and tried again, this time succeeding in raising the dome about six inches. Still insufficient to let himself out. He glanced over at the kitchen and saw a light switch on inside. The firestarter was looking for what he needed. It wouldn't be long now.

He stared intently at the edge of the dome where it contacted the frame and thought about how he needed at least two feet of clearance to be able to worm his way out. He had nothing with which to prop it open, and so his own body would have to do. Taking one more deep breath, Dan heaved as he lifted the acrylic hemisphere yet again, this time placing his head beneath the lip as he did so. Keenly aware that if the dome fell back on his neck he could easily asphyxiate or break his neck, he summoned what he hoped would be a superhuman burst of strength, in the way that mothers were known to do when lifting wrecked cars off of their babies or similar situations.

The effort was successful in that it gained him two more inches of clearance—enough to wedge his right shoulder beneath the edge of the acrylic. The weight of the dome pressing down on him took his breath away, though, and he winced while staring down at the bed of the Hag, trying to recover enough from the sudden force to be able to take another deep breath. After multiple tries, he found that he could not take more than a normal breath. Also, it made him nervous that now he could only look straight down and would not be able to see when the team member would emerge from the tent.

He took a long, slow breath, willing himself to slowly fill his lungs all the way up in order to oxygenate his muscles for his next attempt. Fighting the pressure of the dome on his upper back, he filled his lungs. Then he lifted up with his arms, now thankful for his off-again, on-again weight training hobby. He raised the insufferable acrylic two inches, then three more before he hit a wall and his arm muscles began shaking uncontrollably. He sucked in half a breath more and then forced his arm muscles to contract one more time. The dome raised another half an inch, and Dan knew that was all he was going to get. He jammed his body further through the opening, and was rewarded by the feel of the acrylic lid moving up along his upper back. He began to slip through the gap between the dome and the sub frame, his head inching closer to the bed of the Hag as he struggled through.

But he *was* slipping through, that was the important part. Dan felt the dome pinch painfully against his thighs and the metal sub frame, but at the same time he knew it meant that he was going to make it. As he got closer to the ground, he was no longer able to lift the dome with his arms and had to simply allow gravity to pull his legs out as he dropped toward the bed of the Hag. When his palms came into contact with the frigid metal, his ankles were beneath the crushing grip of the dome, and he had to suppress the urge to cry out in pain. His boots snagged a little and he had to twist his body to free them, but he managed to extricate himself from the sub and flop to the deck of the Hag in an exhausted and relieved heap.

Normally he would have lay there and taken some time to collect himself, but he knew that every second was precious if he was to get back to his tent undetected. He pushed up to his knees and then peered down over the edge of the Hag. He was thankful that the vehicle used treads and not wheels, since it meant there were no gaps to peer through underneath the vehicle as with a truck.

The sound of boots crunching on the ground alerted Dan to the fact that the early riser had just left the kitchen and was now approaching the cookfire. *Time to go!* Dan dropped himself head-first from the bed of the Hag onto the frozen soil. He tried to let himself roll limply in order to minimize any sound, but to his ears he was like an elephant stampede. A wooly mammoth stampede, he corrected himself.

He raised his head and eyed his tent, what seemed like a long distance away. At least he was shielded from view of the rest of the campsite. He needed only to make his way quietly back to the tent, *back to Jami*, he thought. He crept back to their shelter while the expedition member was preoccupied with starting a breakfast cookfire. He zipped the tent door flap and slipped back into his sleeping bag.

"How'd it go?" Jami asked. He had thought she was asleep.

"Good." At least he hoped it would turn out good. He knew he had at most one hour before he would be roused by the general morning activity of the camp, and so he used a military technique he had read about that purportedly allowed soldiers to fall asleep anywhere within two minutes. He knew he would need whatever sleep he could get for the upcoming day's events.

CHAPTER 28

The morning was the coldest of the expedition yet, even without the. windchill factor from the strong gusts that began to whip through the campsite, bouncing off the mountain only to churn right back though the camp. The smell of strong coffee and the whistle of teapots signaled the day was officially underway and that Dan, for his part, was not yet a part of it. "Come on, sleepyhead," Jami cooed to him. She held a steaming mug of coffee close to his face as if they were smelling salts. "You can do this. It's time to rise and shine."

Dan opened his eyes and quickly looked around to make sure that Jami's face and the tent were real and not a dream. Only minutes earlier he was inside the sub....*objective completed*. Recalling that he had successfully hidden the gun under the co-pilot's seat buoyed Dan's spirits enough to rouse him from bed. He propped himself up on an elbow and took the mug from Jami. He sipped it a few times, reveling in the rich Argentinian brew.

"Did you get everything done out there?" she asked.

"Everything?" Dan asked, scrambling to recall what he'd told her.

"Yeah, did you fix the supply tent?"

"Oh yeah," he said, rubbing the sleep from his eyes. "I did." After what had happened in the crevasse, he felt uncomfortable about telling her he'd hidden the firearm. She would worry about it the whole time he was down there, assuming the sub drop was even successful. He pulled the sleeping bag off of him and rose to his feet.

"Let's go see if we can drop that sub down there!"

"That's the spirit!" Jami exited the tent with him, and the two went to the kitchen igloo where they grabbed a simple but hearty breakfast of bacon, eggs, potatoes and biscuits before gathering around the now well lit fire. Almost everyone they had interacted with, including the prince, was there around the fire. Conversation was lively and the anticipation of the upcoming day's activity was palpable in the air. The Emirati shot Dan a serious look, and for one withering moment he thought that somehow he knew of his clandestine sojourn mere minutes earlier.

"After much discussion and revisiting of particulars, I think it best if we have a drop team—a rappelling unit-- that will be ready on top of the crevasse, *before* the helicopter drops the sub. This drop team will of course include you and I, as the submersible crew, so that as soon as the sub contacts the water, we are ready to rappel down to it and recover it before it is carried away out of sight by currents or bashed against the rocks."

"Noted," Dan acknowledged. "I'm looking forward to the mission."

"As are we all," the prince said. "Let us review one final time the details of the drop operation—Operation Drop? I feel as though we should give it a name," he said.

Dan looked at him now, this cultured individual of elite wealth from a world so much different than his own, and wondered if he had somehow misjudged him. But then he flashed on the horrendous way he and Jami had been treated by him and his people, and cautioned himself never to forget.

"After breakfast," the prince went on, "we dive to Atlantis!" He raised his silver tea chalice in a toast which was enthusiastically met with a show of various insulated tumblers.

After the meal, the Hag was driven to a flat, open patch of ground away from camp and closer to the chopper, from which the physical link-up between chopper and sub would be made. Dan, Jami, the prince, the helicopter pilot, the Hag driver and two men from his team convened at the massive vehicle, the submersible's acrylic bubble gleaming in the bright morning sunlight.

The sub's harness was checked and re-checked, as well as the cable connecting it to the helicopter and the winch that could pay out or reel back in the cable, raising or lowering the heavy payload as needed. Technical details were reviewed, discussed and verified. When all seemed ready to go, the prince removed his outer layers of heavy parka and fur to reveal a simple navy blue jumpsuit with a patch bearing the name of the sub, *Deep View*.

He told Dan, "It's time to suit up."

Dan shed his outer layers as well, checking the pockets to make sure he wasn't leaving anything important behind. This was why he had planted the gun. The form-fitting jumpsuit wouldn't have offered sufficient concealment for the weapon. But he was ready now. He eyed the climbing team, half of them at the base of the mountain leading to the crevasse, and the other half already in position out of sight on the edge of the crevasse itself.

Dan handed his garments to Jami while the prince gave him a utility belt containing a few just-in-case items they had discussed as hopefully not needing: handheld radio, flashlight, multi-tool, a couple of energy bars, a canteen of water.

"Be careful, Dan!" Jami reminded him, looking deeply into his eyes. He could almost feel the warning, not just about the environmental dangers they had already witnessed firsthand, but about his sub pilot, whose threats they had also already witnessed directly. He told her he would. The prince smiled at them patiently, waiting, while Jami leaned in and kissed him on the lips.

Then he turned to the prince. "Let's do this." A chorus of cheers went up from the team as those going with them to the crevasse opening began to walk. Dan and the prince fell into step, and he knew he was underway on the most dangerous, and most exciting, mission of his life.

CHAPTER 29

Dan marveled at how trivial the hike back up to the crevasse opening was compared to the first time he'd ventured up here with Jami. Then it had seemed so foreboding and somewhat perilous. Now, it was like walking out to the rocket pad to board for a trip to space. Inner space, that is. Dan told himself that it was okay, that this was perfectly normal, he was going to ride in a submarine that was dropped by a helicopter into a sliver of ocean deep down in a chasm….and then look for Atlantis. All in a day's work.

While they made their way up, they heard the helicopter's engines whine to life, warming up for the Herculean task ahead. Once the sub was harnessed to the helicopter, the pilot planned to do a short test run by lifting the sub straight up into the air a short distance, to make sure the harness system would actually hold before he ascended all the way up to the crevasse, where the winds would be trickier, and the rock face a clear and present danger.

Near their destination at the lip of the crevasse, the wind was much stronger than on the ground below. Even on foot, they had to watch their steps carefully, and briefly discussed the possibility of using safety lines as a precaution against falls, but decided they could make it if they continued slow and steady. Cold and windy, Dan thought. He'd actually be glad to be down in the crevasse where at least the wind wouldn't be so much of a factor. Or so he thought—*it could just be another case of out-of-the-frying-pan-and-into-the-fire*, he told himself, Or...*more like out of the freezer and into the ice pond, or something like that*…His rambling musings occupied his thoughts until they reached the crevasse entry point, where a four-person climbing team awaited.

They had already rigged the harnesses and safety lines for rappelling so that Dan and the prince would be ready to go. All they waited on now was for the helo to drop the sub into the water. Dan stepped up to the lip of the crevasse and gazed down into the chasm that he had only just escaped from. *Back in it one more time*, he thought.

They heard the chopper's engine change in pitch as it lifted into the air. Turning away from the mountain face, Dan looked in time to see the aircraft come into view as it lifted high enough to be even with their position. He could see the harness system around its undercarriage, and could hear the strain of the engine as it struggled to lift an obviously heavy and cumbersome load. The entire craft rotated slowly as it gained altitude, a couple of hundred feet away from the mountain face.

Dan heard the prince's walkie-talkie crackle. "Whoa, nellie," came the pilot's voice. "I'm off the ground with this mother but boy is she wobbly! The sub looks nice and steady, though, not twisting around or anything, over."

The prince nodded before speaking into his walkie. "Copy that. Your bird just came into view for us at the rappel site."

"Copy. I'm going to drop down lower one more time, just to get a little more feel for the handling, and then I'm going to track up above you guys and try to hover over the drop site, over and out."

"Good luck, out!"

The prince walked over to Dan. "We may as well suit up into our climbing rigs. Once the sub hits the water, we'll want to get right down there." Dan stepped over to the climbing team, two of whom would be descending with them. They helped him rig up while the helicopter rose slowly into the air beyond their ledge. After tugging on ropes here and adjusting carabiners there, Dan and the prince stepped back from the crevasse to watch the chopper pilot maneuver with the submersible in tow.

Ever so slowly, and with a higher-pitched than normal whine from the engine, the heavily burdened machine rose into the sky adjacent to the frigid mountain. Soon the submersible itself came into view, its gleaming bubble dome rising into the morning sun like a strange UFO. Dan stared at the watercraft, trying to make sense of it being so out of its element. Hopefully that was about to change, he thought. He knew there was a decent chance that the pricey craft was about to be dashed to pieces on the rocks, but the prince was a gambler, and like him, he hoped it would pay off. And that if it did not, that the prince would honor his word and allow him and Jami to peacefully return to their normal lives. *Whatever that meant anymore*, Dan thought, still watching the chopper rise with its perilous payload.

The wind worried him the most. Still it picked up, and without the goggles he wore, his eyes would be pelted with freezing air and tiny particles of ice. But they were committed now, at least until the helo pilot called it off out of personal safety concerns. As if reading his mind, the prince's radio warbled with the pilot's voice.

"Big Bird to Climb Team: Yeah listen, I don't know. It's *really* dicey up here. I feel like a hummingbird trying to carry away a cantaloupe. My only hope is that over the crevasse itself, a little closer to the face, I might not be in the slipstream as much as I am now. Only one way to find out. But if it gets any worse than this as far as controllability, I'm going to have to abort mission, over."

The prince turned to make eye contact with Dan, checking that he heard. Then he pressed his transmitter button. "Understood, Big Bird. Thank you for trying and good luck. We're all watching down here and standing by. Good luck! Over and out."

This was it, Dan knew. It all came down to this last effort. Their shared dreams of Atlantis, the team's dreams of an augmented payday from the prince, Dan and Jami's dreams of freedom and returning to a normal life…all of it hinged on the piloting that would happen next. He watched as the submersible swayed in the buffeting winds while the helo climbed still higher, well above them now.

From a shaky, semi-controlled hover, the helicopter's nose began to turn toward the face of the mountain, the sub swaying about twenty feet beneath it. As Dan watched, a large bird, wings spread wide but not flapping as it caught an updraft, glided up toward the strange aerial ensemble. "Jami!" he said, "is that another petrel?"

She squinted behind polarized sunglasses as she watched the progress of the winged animal. "It looks like a petrel. It's about the same size as the one the shark ate, too."

"Probably never seen an aircraft in its life," the prince commented.

Dan wondered how the man who had demonstrated such a capacity for cruelty and violence could now participate in such casual conversation with them, but he kept the commentary to himself. No need to rile things up now. The situation was tense enough without adding human drama into it.

Overhead, the chopper began moving laterally, toward the mountain, taking it over the open crevasse. The prince's radio blared with the pilot's strained voice: "Get your climbing team in position, I'M GOING FOR IT!"

A French member of the climbing team they knew as Jean Paul strode purposefully up to them. "Raul and I will be rappelling down with you and Dan," he said to the prince, while also eyeing Dan to let him know he was talking to him, too. "Remember that once it hits the water, it will be critical to gain control of the sub as soon as possible, or it can drift away or be damaged against the rocks." Both Dan and the prince nodded. He gazed nervously up into the sky to check the aircraft's progress before addressing them again, speaking rapidly.

"Remember, there are handling lines with buoys attached to be able to pull it to us once we get down to the ledge. And the drogues—the sea anchors--bags, basically--that slow a craft from drifting—they should deploy and slow down any movement, but you will of course need to detach them before beginning normal submersible operations." He glanced up again. "Looks like he's about to lower it."

At that moment, the radio crackled. "We're lowering the payload. Here goes nothing. Or everything."

Jean Paul motioned them closer to the lip of the crevasse. "Let's get roped in and be ready to drop, but remember: We need to be able to move in a hurry if things go south."

"That's funny because we're already about as far south as you can get," Dan quipped.

The Frenchman smiled for about a millisecond and then waved toward the crevasse. "He's coming down!" Dan looked up and saw the sub's underbelly—its two yellow pontoons—looming larger. The chopper descended faster than he would have expected, and he realized that it was about to happen.

The entire climbing team watched spellbound as the unwieldy payload was lowered toward the opening of the great chasm. The engine noise increased as well as the rotor wash, the lower the aircraft descended. Several of them waved their arms like someone guiding a car backing out of a driveway, indicating that it looked okay for the chopper to continue on its current course, but Dan knew that the pilot was ignoring that.

Lower and lower the helicopter descended, but now, closer to the chasm's narrow opening, Dan could see how much difference the seemingly minor sway the submersible was subject to could really make. The sub had to not only stay within the walls of the chasm on the way in, but remain that way all the way down to the water. If it was dropped at the right moment, it should work. They'd verified it with a laser pointer by stringing a rope ladder across the entire chasm, then having a climber midway across shine the laser down. He was able to verify that the unbroken beam was visible on the water below. They also knew that there was perhaps ten feet of space on either side from center from which to make a clean drop, just wide enough for the sub.

Now they were about to find out if it was going to actually work. The wind showed no signs of letting up as the chopper edged lower to the chasm opening, about fifty feet to their left. The sub rocked back and forth in its cradle until it was ten feet above the gap. The team member in the helicopter with the pilot whose job it was to release the sub from the harness appeared in the open door, helmeted head leaning out to look down on the chasm yawning scant feet below. They saw his blue-jacketed arm reach briefly outside the craft—a signal that he was about to release the payload. Watch out below.

But still the helo dropped lower. A tremendous gust of wind ripped down the mountain face and started the sub swinging on a wild arc, bordering on out of control. Two of the climbing team closest to the sub ran to it and physically pushed against the dome bubble with both hands to swing it away from the jagged rocks and out into the open space above the crevasse.

"Once the sub gets below our level," Jean Paul yelled over the rotor noise, which was louder as it echoed throughout the crevasse, "start rappelling. Got it?"

Dan and the two others on the rappel team said they understood, and they resumed watching the sub. At this point, the helicopter could no longer get any closer to the ground without risking collision, and so it began letting out the winch cable that was clipped to the sub at the other end. The idea was for the chopper to maintain position while the sub was lowered into the crevasse, but something went wrong because the chopper was pulled into the ground. The pilot was able to compensate and lifted back up into the air, and the submersible swung in a long arc, barely clearing the soil at the bottom of its swing.

He lifted the chopper up some distance and restabilized, fighting a confusing maelstrom of crosswinds while everybody on the ground wondered if it was going to work. Then the wind let up the slightest bit and the pilot lowered his chopper sharply, plummeting it until the acrylic sphere of the sub dangled below the lip of the narrow chasm.

"Go, go go!" they heard from the climbing team, but Dan was too spellbound to react much at all. He only stood in awe of the spectacle unfolding before his very eyes. He half expected the chopper to pull back up again, but lower and lower it moved until the undercarriage was within jumping distance of the ground. Then the winch operator began paying out cable, and now the entire sub was down into the chasm, out of sight unless they stood on the very edge of the crevasse to look down on it.

Jean Paul motioned for them to move toward the crevasse. "Let's be ready!" Dan and the prince ran with him to the planned rappel site. They leaned over and watched the sub dangle from the chopper and be lowered deeper into the chasm. The rest of the climbing team was nearer to the helicopter to watch the sub drop.

Jean Paul motioned for his rappel team to begin the descent. "We go now that the sub is below us!"

With that, Jean Paul leaned out backwards over the crevasse and released his grip on the climbing descender that gave him the necessary slack to slide down the line and then lock down tight when pressed. His first jump took him ten feet beneath the lip of the crevasse before he planted his feet on the icy wall. The prince was next, and then Dan.

With a last look up at Jami's concerned face peering down from above, Dan followed them back down into the chasm.

CHAPTER 30

"Here goes nothing!" They all heard the pilot's energized voice over multiple walkie-talkies at once, including Dan, via the prince's radio as they roped down into the crevasse.

"Sub's got a clear line to the water!" one of the climbing team nearest the sub radioed the pilot.

There were no further radio exchanges, for at that moment the submersible was released from its cable. It plummeted straight down to the water at the bottom of the chasm. Dan and the other rappelers paused their descent down the wall to watch the sub's fall. This was it. If the underwater craft didn't cleanly hit the water—right side up--hundreds of feet below, then the mission was over. Dan was trying to discern the splash the sub made when he heard excited radio chatter that told him others up above were looking at something else.

From his position with two legs ninety degrees to the wall and hands on his rope, Dan looked up in time to see the helicopter careening wildly upwards in the narrow sliver of sky their vantage point from down in the crevasse afforded them.

The helicopter was in trouble. As soon as it had ditched its heavy payload, the sudden subtraction of weight caused it to shoot skyward. This movement was amplified by a sudden gust of katabatic winds rolling down from the mountain peak, causing turbulence in the narrow chasm. The sudden imposition of opposing forces proved too much for the pilot to control against, and the chopper careened toward the mountain face immediately above the crevasse opening.

Seeing the aircraft was about to hit the rock, the winch operator, desperate to survive, abandoned both duty and craft, leaping from the open doorway. Both fortunately and unfortunately for him, he was exactly midway over the crevasse opening when he jumped. This meant that he would fall all the way to the freezing water below. If he had been a few feet back when he'd jumped, he would have landed on the ground, but this would have certainly spelled his instant demise, since the chopper continued on to smash into the rock face even with the top of the crevasse.

The crunch of metal and shattering glass pierced the polar serenity. Then, as the entire smashed helicopter began to slide down into the chasm, it erupted into a fuel-fed fireball. Dan saw the flailing body of the winch operator plummet past them, frighteningly fast, about a hundred feet away. The doomed airman's screams echoed throughout the chamber, as they would in Dan's thoughts for a long time to come.

"Chopper down!" came the radio warning.

"Hug the wall!" Jean Paul yelled. Dan, the prince, Jean Paul and Jean Paul's climbing assistant, Raul, all flattened themselves against the rock wall, one arm over their heads, as the helicopter slid down the far side of the crevasse. They felt the heat of the explosion and even their closed eyes registered the bright flash of the fireball that trailed from the ruined aircraft as it plunged downward. Face flat against the craggy rock, Dan dared to open one eye in time to see debris from the smashed chopper dropping past them.

But then his half-open eyes registered something else, too. Something about the debris that was falling just didn't seem right. It was...*moving* too much. And although it was almost lost in the unreal sounds of the echoing explosion and twisting and scraping metal and screams of the onlookers above, he heard another sound, too: a human voice, shrieking as the person fell from up above. Then he felt himself being pelted by rocks and dirt.

"Heads up, possible cave-in triggered by the explosion!" this from Jean Paul, who then said, "Let's get to the ledge, where's there's an overhang we can duck under!" The four rappelers continued their way down the face, moving fast, taking long leaps before their feet hit the wall again. More debris and for all any of them knew, more bodies fell past them from high above. The radios crackled with so much frantic activity that none of it was comprehensible to Dan. He just kept working his way down his line like the rest of them. *This is bad*, he kept telling himself, *this is real bad*...But he kept rappelling, as did the others around him, deeper and deeper into what was fast becoming an unwelcome tomb.

"Gap coming up!" Jean Paul warned. They all knew what it meant: the wall stopped abruptly at the roof of the ledge Dan and Jami had been stranded on earlier, creating a twenty-five foot drop to the ledge floor where there would be no wall on which to put their feet. Executing a controlled rope slide, they timed their last push off the face so that they wouldn't swing inward too much and instead allowed themselves to drop straight down, using the rope's resistance to control their speed with the climbing descender gear.

Dan felt no relief as his feet hit the ledge. He and everyone around him was still in great danger, and by the looks of things, more people had died. But the prince had a one track mind. He shone his flashlight onto an object bobbing in the water about fifty feet from them to their right.

"There's the sub!"

"Look for the trailing grab lines," Jean Paul urged. The drogue seemed to be doing its job, since the sub wasn't changing position much, floating in about the same spot. "Should be a yellow buoy at the end of each line," Jean Paul added. "Four of them."

"I see one!" the prince yelled, pointing off to their right.

"Okay," Jean Paul said, unfurling a grappling hook tied to the end of a thin line. "I'll snag it."

"Are we really continuing on with the mission?" Dan asked. "What about the people who need help?"

"Look around!" Jean Paul said as he tossed the hook out toward the yellow buoy. "Use the radio. Let's do what we can, but meanwhile, we may as well retrieve the sub if we can. We might even be able to use it as a rescue vehicle to pick up people in the water."

Dan, now outfitted with his own light, directed his beam around the narrow slice of water between the chasm walls. He had seen people fall in, so now where were they? He knew that they could have been dead before they fell, from the blast or from hitting rocks higher up, but he had to at least look. Even now, more debris still rained down sporadically from above. He swept his light in a zig-zag pattern from one side of the chasm to the water and back. The water was choppier than last time he was down here, due to the falling debris, but as his eyes got used to the pattern of it, he was able to tell what was normal and what was not, and that was when he saw it.

A swimmer. No, wait—two swimmers, far to his left. He quickly realized that they must have fallen from where the team had been standing to observe the helicopter dropping the sub, and that when the chopper exploded, they had been caught in the quick-crumbling rockfall.

"Two people in the water!" Dan yelled, but at the same exact time, Jean Paul bellowed, "Hooked it!"

"What?" Dan asked, not taking his light or his eyes off of the fallen expedition members.

"I've got the sub!" Jean Paul shouted. "I'll pull it to us while you two look for survivors!"

"I said I found two survivors!" Dan yelled, frustration cracking his voice.

At this, Jean Paul turned to look over at Dan, who promptly waved his light back and forth on one of the people in the water. Two arms waved frantically above the sub-freezing seawater. Jean Paul immediately dropped the rope tethered to the sub and ran to Dan while unclipping a coil of climbing rope from his utility belt. The prince glanced over toward the running Jean Paul and then turned back to the dropped rope and picked it up. He began hauling the sub toward them, hand over hand.

"There's somebody right there!" Dan pointed at a swimmer while aiming the light. He knew the person only had seconds in such low temperature water—colder than that of the night the Titanic sank--before they succumbed completely to hypothermia. Dan aimed his light while Jean Paul, also wearing a headlamp, prepared to toss a line to the stricken swimmer.

Dan saw a change in the water surface pattern. An all too familiar change, he recognized with an adrenaline spike in his gut. He'd seen it before, and not all that long ago.

"Hurry, Jean Paul!"

"I'm doing the best I can! Don't want to—" And then Dan could see from his facial expression that he saw it, too. The eerie white glow in the water. The rising wave pushing ahead of it, toward the swimmer.

The shark was back. The *megalodon*, Dan thought, recalling Jami's speculation. Informed speculation, he corrected himself. He didn't want to cause a panic, but at the same time, quick action was imperative and he knew that there was a single word that would get his message across to both Jean Paul and the swimmer: "Shark!"

To his credit, Jean Paul shifted his gaze quickly to the swimmer and back again to his rope throw preparation, not allowing it to distract him while taking in the information. The swimmer, on the other hand, showed no noticeable change in behavior, probably already unable to move well as a result of being injured during the fall, along with the water temperature.

Jean Paul completed his preparation and tossed the line out to the swimmer. It was a near-perfect throw, the end of the line landing with a splash mere feet in front of the rescuee.

"Grab it!" Dan yelled to the hapless swimmer. To his credit, the man moved his arms, scratching at that sub-freezing saltwater in an attempt to reach the line. But it was far too little, too late, for at that moment, the leviathan struck. The aquatic beast launched itself out of the water in a tremendous breach meant to scoop the prey in its mouth, but somehow it missed, nudging the human out of its way. For a split second Dan held out hope for the person, because surely such a large creature would take a few seconds to turn around, and he was right. It did take a few seconds, the water churning and bubbling with its exertions, while the swimmer grabbed onto the rope.

But no sooner had Jean Paul started hauling the line in, hand over fist, than the swimmer was suddenly and violently yanked underwater. Not by the mega-shark, though, since they could still see it thrashing about on the surface, but by something else entirely.

A second shark? Dan's mind was now a confused blur trying to process incredible events at a rapid pace. *A second megalodon?* But as the hapless swimmer suddenly appeared at the surface again, Dan was afforded a partial view of what it was that had dragged him under, and it was clear that it wasn't a shark. It was big, though, whatever it was, but sort of brownish colored. And it had teeth, Dan could tell, by all the blood that now stained the water around the stricken swimmer. But then the creature struck again, this time breaching enough to raise its entire, massive head above water before striking it back down on its human victim. To Dan it looked like a giant alligator, except he could see that it had fins. He wished Jami was here to tell him what it was they were dealing with. Some kind of crazy sea monster was all it was to Dan. Didn't really matter, he told himself. Whatever it was, it was deadly and had likely just killed an expedition member.

Jean Paul was still screaming for the victim to hold onto the rope, but it was clear that he was now beyond help. The water around him churned frothy red, and his choking and gurgling noises echoed in the narrow chamber. Huge chunks of rock continued to slide down into the water, some of it at a slow, crumbling pace, and others dropping all at once all the way down. Dan could barely make sense of it all, but when the head of the victim went underwater again and didn't come up, he understood that the situation had gotten far out of control.

The prince called out to them. "I have the sub!"

Dan turned his head to see the submersible floating next to the ledge, the prince's hand on one of its tether ropes. He hardly saw the importance of the sub anymore. Surely the mission had to be aborted. More people dead, more rockslides, the whole body of water down here teeming with bizarre creatures....it was time to value his own life above finding Atlantis. He was taking a breath with which to give the prince his opinion when he somehow heard a faint voice—a new voice-- coming from the opposite direction—on the water.

CHAPTER 31

"Jean Paul, stop! Hold on a second." Dan put his hand out toward the rope the climbing team leader was hauling back in after losing the swimmer to the strange mega-predator. "I heard something."

"What is it?" Jean Paul stopped pulling the rope and looked around. Behind them, the prince inspected the sub with his flashlight.

"A person!" Dan said.

"Oh c'mon. He went under. We saw it. If you—"

"No, I mean *another* person in the water!" Dan insisted.

Both of them looked around, using their flashlights to parse the water's surface. After thirty seconds they spotted activity in the middle of the channel, but on closer inspection, it was clear that it wasn't human. A sailfin of some sort sliced the water's surface before disappearing below.

"What is with all the creatures down here?" Dan wondered aloud.

Jean Paul shook his head while first staring at the water and then turning to look at the prince, who was finishing the process of tying up the sub's tether to a protrusion of rock. "Unexplored territory. Who knows what else is here? But listen: I've got to get back up there to see what's going on and help. The submersible is under control. I assume the dive is on hold for now. I'm going to fast-rope up there and check the status. I'll be in contact by radio." He held his walkie-talkie out and conducted a quick check to make sure Dan could hear him on his. That done, he returned to the ledge wall, stepped into his climbing harness, and began spidering back up the crevasse wall. Dan watched him until he was out of sight over the concave ledge section, and then turned back to face the water. The prince still stood by the tied sub, so he yelled at him, "Shine your light on the water. Look for survivors!"

But most of his words were drowned out by more debris falling, and the sound of rock cracking against more rock as it fell. He saw the prince looking up at the crevasse wall and knew he was just now realizing that Jean Paul was making his way above ground. He'd been so obsessed with tending to the sub that he hadn't paid attention to what was happening around him. Now he looked all about as though seeing the place for the first time.

Bits of rock streamed down the chasm sides, while the water roiled with activity—sea monster predation and rockslides—while high above, the rest of the team looked down in shock on the tragedy befalling their expedition. And then, from the water, they heard a voice. Muttering incoherently. Dan aimed his beam not far from the target of their submersible investigation—the opening below the waterline, and saw another person struggling in the frigid water.

"There!" Now wishing he still had Jean Paul with him, it dawned on Dan that he would need to do this rescue himself. The man's life was in his hands. But as he gathered up a rope to throw, it happened again. A massive set of aquatic predatory jaws opened from below and tugged at the person, ripping and gnawing at him until he disappeared beneath frothy, maroon water, deathly screams reverberating about the hellish space.

"We've got to get out of here!" the prince said. "Abort mission!" He then spoke into his radio, something about a request for climbing assistance, but most of what he said was drowned out by a new set of shrieks—this time from far above—followed by the low rumbling of sliding rock.

"We better start climbing," Dan said. He scanned the water one last time, to make sure there were no other fall survivors. Seeing none, he turned and strode to the ledge wall to don his climbing rig. The prince followed suit. He had almost completed setting up when both of their radios crackled.

"Look out below, the whole crevasse looks like it's about to come down!" Dan and the prince exchanged concerned glances. In their current position, they were beneath a thick overhang of rock at the base of the ledge. Dan knew that should it come down, they would perish instantly, being crushed beneath tons of hard earth. Yet the overhang, as long as it held, also provided shelter, for beyond its reach now rained a steady procession of rock and ice.

"We can't go now," the prince said.

"I agree. But I hope it doesn't mean we're about to be buried alive in here."

"Or just buried."

Dan shrugged. It certainly was a possibility. And then he heard a scream that chilled him more than the sub-freezing waters below ever could.

A female scream.

Knowing that Jami was the only female member of the expedition told him all he needed to know about who was in danger. The prince had women and children who had accompanied him to the continent, but all of them stayed at base camp the entire time, some experiencing snow for the first time in their lives. Jami was still high up, at least, that much was evident from the direction of the sound, near the opening of the crevasse, but what was going on up there? He keyed his radio to ask for a report when suddenly a fresh onslaught of rock cascaded down from above. It covered a wide swath of the crevasse, from where the helo had crashed all the way to almost the second ledge adjacent to them where the prince had been stranded earlier.

"It's all coming down!" a male voice under heavy exertion came over the radio. "…entire mountainside is unstable. Some slid down already, the rest of us are running downhill back to camp!"

Dan turned to look at the prince who was already staring at him, his radio in his hand, his body frozen. Both men knew that they were likely about to die. But it was not over yet, Dan knew, even as massive chunks of rock came sliding over the roof of the ledge like a waterfall, mere feet from the sub. Worse, across from them, the chasm wall was falling off in entire sections.

"This whole thing is coming down. There's nowhere to hide!" the prince exclaimed.

Dan looked around one more time, saw it all coming down, and could hear nothing above the din of falling rock. Where was Jami? Undaunted, he took a few steps closer to the edge of the ledge, as close as he dared to the onslaught of falling earth, and probed the water's surface, now peppered with debris, making it difficult to distinguish specific outlines. Detecting movement off to his right, he turned to see the prince undoing the latches on the sub's bubble dome.

"What are you doing?" he called over to him. The prince waved for Dan to come his way. "Come on, let's get in and ride this out! We'll be safer underwater until the rockslide stops!"

Dan briefly considered whether this was some kind of trap. It did have some merit to it, he reasoned, watching the steady avalanche of earthen material pour into the water from above while his radio blared unintelligible static.

"Let's go, before the sub is damaged!" the prince pressed. A soccer ball-sized piece of stone fragmented into shrapnel a few feet from him and he felt a sting on his cheek, followed by warm liquid running down his face. He didn't need another warning. Dan ran to the sub and helped the prince undo the rest of the dome latches. As he did, he couldn't help but flash on his covert activity of the previous night.

The latches undone, the two of them raised the hatch to the open position, and Dan noted to himself how much easier it was with two people. The prince hopped into the sub, which bobbed boisterously in the waters made choppy with falling rock. He began flipping switches on the control panel and Dan saw a sea of LED lights blink to life.

"Untie us from the ledge," the prince said without looking up from his controls. Dan moved to the rope where it was cleated off on the sub and undid it, wondering if he would ever set foot on land again once he got into the underwater craft.

"Push us off and jump in!" the prince commanded. As the volume of falling rock increased, Dan put one leg on the edge of the sub and pushed off with the other from the edge of the ledge. As the craft was shoved away from the ledge, Dan jumped into the open sub. His sudden weight added to the small craft caused it to tip, and the choppy waters splashed inside the cabin.

"Quick, let's close the hatch before we get a boulder in here," the prince said, standing from his pilot bucket seat. Together they gripped the edge of the dome bubble and pulled it closed down over them. As in his brief and hurried co-pilot training held the day before, he felt the pressure wave on his ears as the cabin's two-inch thick acrylic dome was sealed shut.

"Activating forward thrusters. I'll get us out away from the side a little before we dive." The prince pressed a button and Dan both heard a faint hum and felt a faint vibration as the sub's electric motors whirred to life. They were propelled slowly out from the ledge toward the middle of the chasm, where the water became noticeably choppier as it sloshed around in the narrow channel.

"Think I feel some sea-sickness coming on," Dan said. Then he felt bad for voicing concern about so trivial a malady while people—possibly even Jami—were dying around him.

"When we submerge it'll get better," the prince said, now turning the sub toward the left side of the chasm. Suddenly a large splash erupted scant feet away right in front of them, eliciting a shout of surprise from both submariners as a large chunk of rock dropped into the water from high above.

"We better dive," the prince said. "Even a few feet of water will make a big difference in force of impact if a rock does hit us."

Dan had no arguments, and the prince pressed a button that began venting buoyancy tube air. The cabin started to sink below the waterline and Dan saw the white frothy water sloshing over the acrylic dome. Looking down, he could see the dark depths of the aquatic realm with not a hint of bottom in sight. And then he spotted some color—dark color—moving fast below them, and then it was gone. *Sea creature*, Dan surmised. A substantial one.

"Are we clear down there?" the prince asked, his gaze roving over the sub's control panel. "No obstructions?"

"I only see water and maybe a giant sea creature," Dan said truthfully.

The prince cast a sidelong glance at him to see if he was joking or cracking up under pressure. Apparently satisfied with his answer, he said, "Commencing dive." The sub began to drop lower from the waterline, when Dan spotted fast movement coming from above—something that had some color to it and was obviously not a rock.

It was to the left of the ledge, nearer to where the chopper had exploded. A high fall, giving him enough time to track it through the air and focus in on the details. He saw the unmistakable outline of arms flailing high above a head. Of *hair* fluttering in the wind, and then he knew that the person was female. The person was Jami. He thought he had heard her scream before, and maybe he did even though she was higher up. Possibly she had been stranded on an outcropping before falling the rest of the way. But he had no time to speculate.

"Somebody just fell into the water! We have to get over there to pick them up!" he told the prince.

But the Emirati shook his head. "This sub is only rated for two people. Not only that, opening the canopy to pull them in in this choppy water is too dangerous. We run the risk of being swamped and sinking or being crushed by rock. We need to ride out the avalanche down below and then come up when it subsides and help people then!"

Dan continued to watch Jami as she hit the water. He knew she was still alive because he saw her immediately start to swim. Knowing she was suffering unbearably at that moment in the sub-freezing water almost threw him into an uncontrollable rage. He wanted to throw himself at the prince and throttle some sense into him, but knowing that wouldn't accomplish anything, he forced himself to calm down.

"That is Jami! She's swimming now. We have to help her at least get to the ledge."

"I'm sorry but the answer is no." With that, the prince continued jettisoning the sub's air, and they began sinking below the waves. Dan watched him for a moment as he purposefully worked the controls, submerging them into the water. Then he looked over to see Jami still swimming. He knew that if the water temperature didn't get her soon, the oceanic predators or collapsing crevasse would. He had to do something. He turned his attention back to the sub, glanced down at his feet and the dark waters below them visible through the clear dome, and he remembered.

The gun!

Dan reached down beneath the seat to grab it from where he'd placed it the night before. His hand felt down along the wire underframe of the bucket seat, but where he expected the comforting feel of the firearm's cold steel, now he encountered only the smooth, curved metal of the sub's undercarriage.

The gun was gone.

CHAPTER 32

Dan frantically swiped his hands beneath the seat one more time, searching for his hidden firearm. It must have been jarred loose from its hiding place during the drop from the helicopter. But where did it end up?

"What are you doing?" the prince inquired.

Dan wasn't sure what to say. "Going crazy, I guess. I need to get out of here. Let me out!"

"Calm down! We need to be underwater to be safe from the rockslide."

From his hunched over position, Dan turned his head in the prince's direction to face him, and that's when he saw it: the pistol underneath the pilot's seat, near the edge on the right side, closest to Dan. Without waiting for the prince to register that he was looking at something and give him the chance to catch on, Dan leaned over and snatched the gun out from under the seat. Surprisingly, the prince never took his eyes off the sub's controls, so intent was his focus on submerging the craft. Water now lapped over the top of the dome.

Dan withdrew to his seat and quickly examined the gun. Having seen too many movies where the bad guy removed the bullets and gave the gun back, Dan opened the chamber and checked that it was actually loaded, which it was. He held the gun in his lap with both hands on it, concealing it. "I'm going to ask you one more time: please take us over to the person in the water so we can pick them up."

"I am not willing to risk my life for that. I'm sorry."

"Then I will risk it for you." Dan raised the gun and levelled it at the prince's chest. He waited a few seconds for him to look over, taking satisfaction in the complete look of surprise. To his credit, the prince recovered quickly, raising both hands in the air.

"It seems I underestimated you, Mr. James."

"Shut up and take us to the surface. Now!" Dan shook the gun for emphasis.

"Very well." The prince put his hands on the sub's controls. They heard the hiss of compressed air inflating the sub's buoyancy tubes that would allow it to remain buoyant without using battery power. Dan watched through the top of the cockpit dome as water sluiced off of it until he was once again looking up at the now all too familiar point of view of the narrow chasm walls stretching up out of sight into what was only…darkness. Had there been a complete cave-in? He didn't know but remembered that Jami had mere seconds to live.

"Now take us that way. Fast!" He pointed to where he had last seen Jami. Panic welled up within him as he scanned the choppy water. Where was she? Had she already slipped beneath the waves forever? The prince activated the forward thrusters and the sub's motors propelled it in the direction Dan had indicated. As they motored over, water splashed off the dome constantly, like a rainstorm on a car windshield, only they had no wipers.

And then, directly in front of them, he saw it: two massive arms culminating in giant webbed hands, and a long neck stretching out of view. Dan recognized it only as some sort of prehistoric aquatic creature. Jami would know what it was. Where was she? He wished they could put the dome up and just cruise along the surface like a boat, which would give them more visibility, but it was plain to see that the conditions wouldn't allow it. They'd be swamped with water in here in no time, not to mention the electronics getting wet. Of course they would have to open it to let Jami in, but they had to find her first.

Dan couldn't help but glance down to see the monster creature dart out of sight below. What if one of those had already taken Jami? He had no choice but to kick thoughts like that aside and push onward through the chop, searching for her hopefully living body. "A little more that way," he said to the prince, guiding him closer to where he'd last seen her.

"She's got to be here, got to be here," Dan muttered under his breath as the little sub bulled its way through the waves. Another chunk of mountain splashed into the water nearby, tipping the watercraft violently to one side before it righted itself.

"You see, it's getting bad in here," the prince felt the need to point out. "We need some depth to be safe."

"We're almost to where I saw her," Dan replied. He sat higher in the seat, head on a swivel as he looked for any signs of a human in the water. If she was still in there, Dan couldn't help but think, she didn't have long. The prince kept the sub motoring along at a clip that allowed them to make progress through the soup but wasn't so fast or bouncy so as to make looking for survivors impossible. He knew his craft well, Dan couldn't help but notice. He even tried turning on a floodlight mounted outside in front of the sub, but they found it caused too much reflection off the waves and actually made searching more difficult, so he turned it off.

Dan was about to admit to himself that it was too late, that she had slipped below the waves, when he spotted motion off to their right, out more in the middle of the channel. "There, I see something!"

"Okay, turning. Just don't shoot me."

"Always worried about yourself, as usual. Just get us over there." Dan was done taking any kind of flak from the arrogant billionaire. He wanted only to rescue Jami and as many other expedition members as possible, and then get out of here so that they could resume what he now thought of as a normal life. Funny how before this escapade he had thought his life was so unusual and full of adventure. Now he had seen enough of that for a lifetime, should he make it through this.

"I see her." The prince's voice was flat and emotionless as he pointed through the cabin dome and then maneuvered the craft in that direction. Dan aimed a pocket flashlight through the acrylic and caught his breath when it highlighted Jami's form, her long brownish hair plastered to her ghostly pale face.

"I see her too!" Dan was exuberant. He thought she had been lost.

And then his heart sank when beneath their feet he registered motion. He looked down to see the ghostly white shape of the mega-shark knifing through the water, effortlessly smooth. It was actually headed away from Jami at the moment, but Dan knew that it could turn in an instant, and may be attracted to the electrical activity emitted by the submersible.

"Slow down, let's get right up to her." Dan didn't take his eyes off her but also leaned more to the right in his seat, aware that the prince could possibly make a lunge for his gun. He wasn't sure he needed it at this point, since they had already gotten to Jami, but if the prince had proven anything up to this point it was that he was unpredictable. But he did slow the sub down and, from what Dan could tell, did his best to ease the slow but heavy craft as near as the stricken swimmer as possible without putting her in danger of being hit by the multi-ton vehicle as it bounced up and down in the landslide-induced swells.

Dan saw Jami's eyes open wider in recognition that the sub had come for her. She took a couple of strokes toward them, but they were ineffective. She could barely hold her head above water and sputtered saltwater from her mouth.

"We've got to open the hatch long enough to let her in!" Dan said.

"Okay, there are two latches on my side, two on yours." Dan had already undone one of his and was working on the other. The prince followed suit and then they were lifting the hatch. "One, two, three," the prince counted off. The rocking motion of the sub made it difficult to maintain a solid hold, and they had to let it back down once before trying again. The second time they had it almost to the tipping point when a small rock landed on Dan's head, gashing his temple and causing him to lose control of the hatch.

"Is it not possible? We could throw her a rope and tow her to the ledge…" the prince began, but Dan shook his head.

"One more time! Let's go!"

"Hurry, one big rock in here and we are all dead," the prince reminded him.

They raised the hatch yet again, grunting with the effort of maintaining their balance in the rocking sub while extending their arms and pushing with their legs to move the heavy acrylic dome all the way back. This time, they were able to do it, and they felt it latch into place onto the sub's metal body.

But Jami had drifted some distance from the vessel. The current took her further from them. Worse, Dan could see an imposing fin breaking the water not far from her.

"Jami! Swim to us!" In response she moved her arms, but it was clear she had been sapped of all usable energy.

Dan turned to the prince but he was already activating the sub's thrusters, pushing them on the surface toward the woman in jeopardy. "I will come up to her on your side," the prince said. He deftly maneuvered the sub to within a few feet of her. Then Dan leaned out over the sub's open dome, extending a hand. She was less than five feet away, but the massive fin approached her and was gaining speed.

"Swim to us, Jami!" She made attempts to move her arms, but the sub-freezing water had sapped her of all functional strength. Then, as if in a slow motion horror movie, Dan saw the maw of the massive shark emerge from the water, with teeth that looked over a foot long hanging from its upper jaw. Without thinking, he raised the gun and squeezed off two shots straight into its throat. He had no idea if it was due to the projectiles, but the great fish dropped off to the side, away from Jami and the sub. Jami still treaded water, paralyzed with cold and fear.

Taking no more chances, Dan shoved the gun into his waistband—he didn't want to leave it for the prince—sharks in the water, landsharks out of it, he thought—and then dove toward Jami into the treacherous hidden pocket of polar ocean.

The shock of the water was like nothing he'd ever experienced before. It was a physical force contracting his lungs and paralyzing his muscles at the same time. He couldn't move at all, but the momentum of his dive carried him the short distance to his friend. Somehow in the chaos he heard the stirring of the sub's motors, and it occurred to him that the prince could leave them here now and that would likely be it for the not-so-long-running Dan & Jami Show. He could shoot at him, but would the gun even still work now that it was wet? Those thoughts were in the back of his mind, but would have to wait, because when his head broke the surface, he was staring into her eyes again.

"Jami, I'm here! I've got you! Let's get in the sub!" She didn't try to speak, but reached an arm out to him. At that moment, the water all around them was pelted with rock and dirt. A tremendous rumbling ensued as great formations of the crevasse walls began to slide down from the chasm high above. Dan put her into a rescue hold—one of his arms hooked through her underarm-- and began scissor-kicking and paddling with his other arm toward the sub. The prince thankfully had motored almost to them. The submersible see-sawed up and down over increasing swells as he struggled to keep it in position. They heard the clanging sound of smaller rocks bouncing off of the sub's metal frame. Were one of them to crack the acrylic hatch, Dan knew, it would no longer be a submersible, but merely an inefficient small boat.

Dan somehow reached the sub, nearly drained of all his strength and thankful that the prince moved to his side of the craft and that he didn't have to ask for him to help. The prince reached down and pulled Jami, who was completely limp, dead weight, up and over the lip of the frame and into the sub, with Dan pushing her up from the water. Then the prince reached down and hauled Dan in. The prince moved back to his pilot's seat while Dan helped Jami get settled into the co-pilot's seat with him.

"Help me close the hatch!" Dan said.

Dan and the prince gripped the dome's handles and pulled. Again, they had bad timing as the craft went over a wave, causing them to lose control of the hatch. It dropped back into position and they had to try again, but this time they were successful, latching the dome into place. Immediately they felt more protected, out of the elements of wind and sea spray. But the falling rock intensified.

"Diving!" the prince yelled. "I'm taking us down or we'll be smashed." They heard a mechanical sound as the prince vented air from the sub's buoyancy tubes, and it began to sink beneath the waves. Dan saw a white trail of bubbles, like a comet through inner space, as a chunk of rock plummeted through the water next to the sub. Slowly, the submersible followed it downward, the light rapidly fading away with each foot of depth.

"Let's switch on the exterior lights." The prince hit a button and twin halogen floodlights came to life on the front of the craft. Dan and Jami were still trying to get comfortable sharing the single co-pilot seat, with Jami ensconced in Dan's lap. At least they were keeping each other warm, Dan thought, since they were both deathly cold from the twenty-eight degree water soaking their clothes. Having nothing else to change into, they would have to make the best of it.

Dan eyed the compass bubble mounted in the middle of the dash and studied it for a moment. "While we descend, let's head that way," Dan said to the prince, pointing to a spot across from their old ledge.

"Why that way?" the prince asked as the sub sank lower into the depths.

"It's where the anomaly was sighted. Might as well check it out while we're down here."

The prince aimed the sub in that direction. Around them, the water was peppered by small rock missiles and larger boulder bombs. As they neared the target, Dan even saw what looked like an entire expanse of cliff wall sliding into the sea.

"I think this whole place is coming down," he said, voice flat. No one had a response. The situation was too depressing, for it seemed they were all about to be buried alive, entombed in a metal and acrylic capsule for all eternity, deep in the bowels of Antarctica where even their bodies would likely never be discovered.

And then he saw it. The entrance to...to whatever it was, he thought, reminding himself that despite the sighting, they had no idea what it might be. Though the water was now cloudier from all the rock falling into it, the strange glow was still visible.

"There it is," he said, mostly to the prince, since Jami was still recovering, nearly asleep from shock, and still mildly shivering. But she was alive, Dan reminded himself, as were they all. They just had to figure out how to stay that way.

"I'll see how close I can get to it," the prince said. He had barely finished his sentence when the gigantic, long-necked creature Dan saw earlier swam into view from the direction of the unknown underwater feature.

"What is *that*?" the prince inquired.

"Not sure, some kind of ancient sea monster by the looks of it." At that, Jami stirred and then turned her head away from Dan's chest long enough to take a look out the cabin's bubble.

"Mosasaur," she said without emotion. "Late Cretaceous aquatic lizard. This place is lost in time."

The creature swerved and headed for the front of the sub, its long snout opening to reveal formidable rows of long, pointed teeth. "Watch it!" Dan instinctively held an arm out in front of him and Jami, despite realizing how silly that was. Like the mother of a young child in a car, he thought. Yet the threat was real. The beast rammed into the sub, opening its mouth wide, top and bottom rows of teeth scraping against the dome bubble as it attempted to grasp onto it with its unimaginably powerful jaws.

The submersible was pushed back but the creature was unable to gain purchase on the smooth, curved acrylic. The prince turned the thrusters on full power and they heard and felt the motors increase in pitch as the sub veered away from the sea monster and back toward their goal.

"Shark, dead ahead!" Dan intoned. He couldn't even muster the excitement to raise his voice. Even yet another massive sea predator no longer phased him. It was just how it was down here. Jami opened an eye and looked out the cabin. "Megalodon. How surprising."

"How is this possible?" Dan wondered aloud as the prince cursed to himself in Arabic, fretting over his controls.

"Osiris the Resurrector at work again," she nearly whispered. "Atlantis must be near."

The prince pointed into the murky distance. "I see an opening in the cliff wall, about twenty foot depth." The barrage of rockfall intensified in the water around them, and Dan saw the massive shark get pelted with a stone slab and turn away from them. Then they felt a dull thud as a projectile landed on the cabin roof. Even with the buffer of about twenty feet of seawater over the sub, the impact was still significant. Dan eyeballed the contact point.

"Damage?" the prince asked, voice brimming with a nervous edge.

"Just a scratch," Dan reported. "I'd worry a lot more about the prehistoric menagerie of aquatic death machines."

Then they heard a dull metallic *thunk* as another chunk of rock nailed the sub's steel chassis. "Lot more rock falling!" Dan said. "Seriously looks like this whole place is coming down around us!" Indeed, the water became cloudy to the point of near-zero visibility as it became laden with dissolving rock.

"I'm going in!" The prince aimed the submersible into the aperture in the side of the cliff, the faint glow the only thing keeping him on target. As they were about to enter, the colossal mosasaur swam up from below and to the right, knocking the sub off track so that it bumped into the cliff wall, to the left of the intended opening.

"Backing up!" the prince yelled.

"Is there anything we can do to fend off these monsters?" Dan asked.

"I can flip on every external light," the prince said, fingers dancing across the control panel as it became brighter outside. "Might make it harder for them to see."

"Or might attract them more," Jami muttered.

"Drains our batteries quicker," the prince said.

"At this rate we're not gonna last long enough to worry about battery life," Dan pointed out. "Anything else we can do?"

"We have a mechanical grab arm. I guess we could extend it to give them something to have to get around. They might just break it off, though. Here's the joystick for it, I'll leave it to you."

Dan took control of the stick and took satisfaction in controlling a four-foot long metal articulating arm with a grabber claw at the end. As it extended to full length, he swung it so that it was at a right angle to the sub's cabin. He was rewarded by seeing a large predator, only partially visible in the murk which now consisted of scattered light from the suspended particles reflecting the floodlights, dart away.

"We're lined up again," the prince said. They felt another significant thud as a chunk of cliff fell onto the sub's rear framework.

"Go!" Dan urged.

The prince set the sub's thrusters to full power and the little submarine propelled itself into the faintly glowing opening in the side of the cliff.

CHAPTER 33

A tunnel. To Dan, that's what it looked like they had entered. A roughly circular opening about ten feet in diameter that continued into the underwater cliff face as a tunnel. When the sub was barely one length inside, they felt an impact on the rear of the craft, like being stopped at a light in a car and being rear-ended by another going 30mph, enough to induce whiplash.

Dan turned around to see the snout of the gigantic shark wedged into the tunnel so tightly it appeared it might be stuck there. The prince did his best to counteract the sudden movement but the sub careened into the right upper wall of the tunnel after being bashed by the shark.

"You have time!" Dan told the prince. "Shark is too big to fit through here."

"I need to put us into reverse to get back into the middle of the tunnel without scraping. Make sure I don't back up too much, meaning into the shark's mouth."

"You got it." Dan tried to pretend like he was just a guy standing in a driveway somewhere guiding a driver trying to back into the garage. "You got room. Keep going, c'mon. That's it. And…stop!"

The prince's hands deftly swept over the controls, counteracting the sub's reverse momentum with forward acceleration while simultaneously aiming the craft's nose back down the middle of the tunnel. Dan stared back at the megalodon as the sub slowly left it behind.

"It can't fit through," he said.

"Is it stuck in the opening?" the prince asked. "Because we will probably need to get back out that way after the landslide calms down."

"It's thrashing around, but—oh! There it goes. It's back out into the channel."

"Good," the prince said, hand on the sub's joystick to keep them in the middle of the tunnel, both with respect to the side walls as well as the ceiling and floor.

With the toothy threat gone at least for now, Dan turned his attention to the details of their immediate surroundings. The prince was fully occupied with his piloting duties, and Jami was still only half-conscious from shock. He eyed the walls of the tunnel, then the ceiling, and even the floor in front of them. Then it hit him.

Gold.

The tunnel they travelled through was constructed of solid gold. Dan pointed to the compass mounted on the dash. It spun in crazy circles, completely off kilter. "All the metal must be messing it up."

"Let's see if it leads anywhere," the prince said. "But even if it does, I don't want to get too far from the opening, and we certainly don't want to get lost. The oxygen and battery power are only good for a couple of hours max. And the oxygen less so, because now we have three people in here and it's only rated for two. So we have to be very careful."

"I'll breathe shallow," Dan joked.

"How about we just keep conversation to a necessary minimum," the prince intoned.

Not a problem, Dan thought. The idea of dying while in close proximity to the prince was not exactly a fate he looked forward to.

They continued their way along the tunnel, which was remarkably featureless but for the fact it seemed to be made of pure gold, and not natural gold ore, but polished, perfectly smooth gold, Dan noticed. The only perceptible change was that after travelling for several minutes at a speed the prince had said during Dan's training was about 7mph, the tunnel began to slope gradually upward. They still encountered no offshoots or even variability in tunnel width. To Dan it seemed impossible this could be a natural formation. It wasn't perfectly uniform, like it had been bored or drilled out of the Earth with a machine, and yet at the same time nothing about it seemed natural.

When the incline was pronounced enough that Dan noticed he was tipped back in his seat (with Jami still in his lap) facing upwards, like they were in a roller coaster going uphill, the prince informed them that battery power was one-third drained. "According to the rule of thirds, we need to turn back now. It's one-third power or oxygen out, one third to return, which leaves one-third for emergency contingencies, which I'd say we are bound to encounter."

"Can we even turn around in here?" Dan asked. The walls of the tunnel seemed too close to allow it.

"No," the prince confirmed. "But we could reverse all the way back."

"To me it looks like something's different not too far up there," Dan said. "A change in the look of the water, the lighting, I think. Maybe we could follow it for two more minutes tops and then go back?"

"You really like to live on the edge, don't you, Dan?" the prince asked, taking a moment to look away from his controls and make eye contact. "Hope for the best and worry about the consequences later?"

"Something like that. But I really think it may be worth checking out. I think I see a change in something up ahead. Visibility looks like it's getting clearer."

"We'll give it a couple more minutes while we hope the megalodon leaves the area," the prince said, directing the submersible up through the golden tunnel. "But I'm pretty sure you'd rather take your chances up there rather than suffocate."

This created a somber mood of silence as they motored up the inclined passage, the only sound being the hum of the submersible's electric motors. As they progressed, the prince squinted at the controls, forehead wrinkled. Dan thought that the water might be changing in color up ahead, but wasn't completely sure, so he turned to look at the prince and saw his look of consternation.

"What is it?"

Suddenly the hum of the motors came to an abrupt stop, with the world completely silent around them. "Motor cut out?" Dan asked. Jami stirred in his lap.

"Negative," the prince returned. "I switched it off because I noticed our speed increasing even though I wasn't giving it more power. It's the water current. It's getting faster and it's taking us along with it."

"So we're drifting *up*?" Dan asked, incredulous.

"Indeed we are," the prince confirmed, making a show of lifting his hands up and off of the console while the sub continued along at its brisk pace up the chute.

"How is that possible?" His question was answered with a deep rumbling that vibrated the craft itself. Dan stared at the tunnel walls, studying them for signs of movement. "Walls look to be holding solid," Dan said, scouting in all directions outside the sub.

"What's going on?" Jami asked, suddenly more alert.

"We're in the golden tunnel being swept upstream to...somewhere," Dan told her.

"The cliff walls outside of the tunnel must be caving into the narrow sea chasm below, causing the water level to rise. So as it pushes more water into the tunnel, the water in here flows through the tunnel faster," the prince hypothesized.

"I'm scared," Jami said.

Dan was trying to think of something comforting to say when he saw something different up ahead. Literally *up* ahead, as the chute through which they travelled was now nearly vertically oriented. He couldn't yet tell what he was looking at, only that something was different. The endless column of blackness they had been shooting into now had color at the end of it. A golden color.

"Something's changing up ahead," Dan announced.

"I see it."

"Can we go slower?" Dan asked, trying to contain the edge in his voice so as not to scare Jami even more.

"I already have no thrusters engaged, but I can put them in reverse to counter the current." The prince put a hand on the joystick and pressed a button, and they heard the whirring of the motors coming to life. Their upward progress slowed but did not stop. "I can give it a little more," the prince said through clenched teeth, his hand moving again with the joystick. Again their speed slowed, but still they were carried inexorably upward through the gold-walled tunnel.

"We're full reverse," the prince said, eyes widening as he stared up at the fast-approaching anomaly that they could now see was some kind of golden obstruction.

"I see a solid object up there," Dan said, pointing up. This far up in the tunnel, the water clarity was good, and so he was indicating something perhaps fifty feet away, straight up.

"Nothing I can do. We're going to hit it, whatever it is." The prince eyeballed the controls but made no further adjustments to them.

"So we're reaching a…." Jami began but then faltered, "…a dead end in here?"

"We don't know yet for sure," Dan said, ever seeking to maintain the calm. This was definitely not the time and place for panic. But inwardly, his mind was reeling. *There has to be a way out of here. There has to be…*

"Brace yourselves!" The prince's warning ended Dan's brooding. He put one arm around Jami while the other gripped the bottom of his seat. Looking up, he could see now that they were indeed heading straight toward a dead end.

But an interesting looking one.

CHAPTER 34

The impact was more substantial than Dan expected. The time spent travelling underwater had inured him to the actual forces involved. Although it seemed like they were floating peacefully through molasses in slow motion, in actuality their two-ton vehicle was being propelled at a rate measurable in meters per second by a sum of tremendous forces into what appeared to be a solid metal wall.

A large gold disc. The way ahead, or up, was blocked by a solid-looking gold disc that covered the entire diameter of the chute they travelled through to reach this point. But Dan could see that the central portion of the disc had some sort of feature, some relief to it. About the size of a manhole cover, it was raised from the main disc with a textured surface of some sort.

Crack. The forward-facing top of the sub's bubble dome collided with the gold cap. Dan held onto Jami as they hit, staring at the acrylic dome separating them from untold billions of gallons of sub-freezing water. He half-thought it would spiderweb and then implode, instantly crushing them all. And that might be the most merciful death, he thought fleetingly, given what actually might be in store for them based on what they'd seen so far.

Yet the integrity of the sub held, at least for now. But they had a new problem.

"We're pinned up against the ceiling," the prince barked, grappling with the sub's controls to no avail. "The water current is too strong to move against."

Dan and Jami looked into each other's eyes, each knowing that this truly looked like the end. "It's not budging at all?" Jami asked at length. Dan eyed the gold disc through the dome and shook his head. They were wedged up against the top portion of the disc. By looking down and slightly to the right, he could focus on the center portion of the circular cap, where the raised component was. His eyes widened as he now recognized easily discernible features.

"Hey look at that! Looks like a gold bug raised up from the rest of the disc. Like a little statue, very ornately carved." Even Jami craned her neck to look at it, while the prince aimed one of the sub's external lights at it.

"It looks like a scarab," she said flatly.

"Oh!" Dan said. "Wow, I didn't even see that. You're right!"

"What is the significance?" the prince asked.

"Dung beetle," Jami answered. "Representing renewal, rebirth, and resurrection."

A moment of silence ensued while the three of them digested this. "So it would seem that resurrection is our only hope for continued existence," the prince said.

Around them, despite the great forces pinning them to the golden ceiling disc, all was incredibly quiet. Dan stared at the scarab, at its ornate design, wondering why someone would put something that obviously took much effort to create in such an inaccessible location. Or if tens of thousands of years ago this location was perhaps not so inaccessible? But it had to be in a narrow tunnel, regardless of whether it had been underwater. He ruminated on the matter for a few moments while staring transfixed at the golden beetle. A new idea came to him.

"Since we're just sitting here, let's try something." Without waiting for a response, he continued by pointing to the protruding golden carving. "Maybe we could use the external manipulator arm to pull or turn the scarab."

The prince faced him, eyes wide open. "What, you think it may be a....like a door handle to open this …this golden hatch that could lead somewhere?"

Dan nodded. "That's what I'm hoping. It's just a guess, but unless someone else has something better to try…"

No one said anything, nor did they show any excitement. Jami continued to stare forlornly out of the cabin, seeing nothing, while the prince's gaze roved from the instrument gauges to Dan. "We can try it," the prince said, his tone far from hopeful.

But Dan perked up, hoping that his enthusiasm for the idea would be contagious. "Great! So I take it you're probably better at working the manipulator arm than me, but let me know if there's anything I can do to help."

The prince nodded and pressed a couple of buttons on the control panel. "I don't think it will take long to at least see if your idea has merit. First of all, is the arm in working order after bumping up against the ceiling? Second, is it long enough and articulate enough to reach the scarab and do its work?"

Dan could see that the pilot required no response, since he wasted no time in putting his hand on a different joystick from the one that steered the sub. The high-pitched servo motor whirred somewhere outside the cabin and beneath their feet, which were currently above their heads in their upside-down orientation. He saw a glint of silver metal and then turned to see the grab arm come into view above his feet.

"Now to test the grip of the mechanical claw." The prince pressed a button and outside the windows they watched a four-pronged claw close and then open again.

"Looks like it's working," Jami said. Dan was glad to see her participating.

"Yes! Let's try this!" he said.

"What is it you say in your country? Here goes…. nothing?" the prince said.

All three of them turned to watch out of the cabin as the grab arm began to extend toward the scarab. The sub remained fixed against the gold cap by the water current, allowing the prince to devote all his energies to operating the arm. After extending the arm to nearly the end of its reach, he paused and leaned closer to the acrylic to get a careful look at the end of the arm. "Rotating the claw to face optimally for gripping the …."

"The carapace of the scarab," Jami interjected. "The topmost part of the dorsal shell." She pointed, and the prince nodded.

"I didn't know it was called that, but I think I can grab it. Here we go."

A faint mechanical hum ensued while the claw approached the top of the beetle. The prince made a minor adjustment to the claw's angle when it was a few inches above the carapace peak, and then proceeded to open the claw to nearly its full grabbing width.

"Here we—" the prince started, but was cut short as the sub itself suddenly moved against the grate before coming to rest again, a reminder they were still being pinned against the golden ceiling cap by untold tons of rushing water. They waited for a few moments, slowly looking around to see if their craft would suddenly roll out of its current position. After it held for nearly a full minute, the prince put his hand on the controls again and began readjusting the arm's position. "And here we are again," he announced after bringing the claw into readiness above the scarab.

He hesitated just a moment before pressing the button that began closing the claw's grasp around the golden carapace. The metal rods of the claw closed around either side of the scarab. He moved the base of the arm somewhat while keeping the claw gripped in place. Then he began to lift the entire arm away, in the opposite direction from the scarab's back.

"The claw's not slipping," Dan said with his gaze glued to the mechanism outside the cabin.

"The entire scarab is holding, too," the prince said from beneath a veil of sweat on his eyebrows and forehead. "If it's like the handle on a lid that's supposed to pull off, it doesn't appear to be working," he finished.

"Hold on, keep the claw there, let's think about this for a minute."

"Not like we can go anywhere at the moment," the prince reminded them.

Dan was unfazed. "We tried pulling it. What about turning it?"

"Turning what?"

Dan looked at him. Seeing his sweat made his own that much more noticeable. The air in the sub grew increasingly stale as Jami turned restlessly in his lap, burying her head in his chest. "We need to do something now, Dan," the prince said in a low voice.

"Keep the claw right where it is. But instead of pulling it, try to turn it so that it might spin the entire disc underneath."

The prince studied the disc and the scarab and the claw for a moment before raising an eyebrow. "Which way? Counter-clockwise, left?"

Dan shrugged. "I don't know why it wouldn't be."

"Hopefully, the whole thing's not rusted shut," the prince said.

"I don't think so," Dan replied. "Gold doesn't rust or corrode. That's why it's used in high-end electrical conductivity applications like spacecraft."

"It can still have marine growth on it, though," Jami half-mumbled from behind the hood of her sweatshirt. "But not algae, I guess, since there's no light here," she said reminding them of the fact that if the sub's power ran out, they would still be pinned here, but in complete darkness.

"Looks pretty clean to me," the prince said.

"Agreed," Jami said, "but it's not impossible that there are other types of growth underneath, like boring worms or barnacles, stuff like that. Depends on if there's spaces with water under the circular part."

"That would make it hard to turn," Dan said, "but let's just try it and see how it goes."

"What could go wrong?" Jami asked. Nobody laughed.

"Give me a minute to adjust the arm position." The prince manipulated the grab arm controls some more, until the two-piece articulated extension arm swiveled into place such that the claw could be turned rather than pulled. "And now," said the prince, "here we go." He moved the control stick to the left, causing the arm to torque the scarab carapace in a different direction than before.

At first nothing happened. All was quiet in the sub except for the mechanical arm's motor straining to overcome the forces presented to it. Around them they could still hear the muted sounds of a thousand rocky collisions as the mountain continued to slide apart somewhere outside of their tunnel. And then it happened.

The sub suddenly lurched as resistance broke for the grab arm and the scarab itself rotated a bit atop the golden circular seal.

"It moved!" Dan yelled. "Not much, just a fraction of an inch, but it moved! That thing turns! Keep it up!"

"Need to stabilize the sub," their pilot said, turning away from the arm controls and to those that controlled the underwater vehicle itself. "The arm will rip off the sub if I let the whole craft just hang. We need to be fixed in place within the arm's reach of the scarab."

"You're clear on the starboard side," Dan said, peering out of the cabin around Jami's head.

"The arm is okay for now," Jami said.

"Okay, I'm reversing the starboard thruster while activating the port thruster forward at full power." They felt the sub's undercarriage scraping against the tunnel wall beneath the gold cap along with the vibration of the straining thruster.

"It's turning again!" Jami said, her voice sounding full and energetic for the first time in a long time.

"Holding position," the prince said, "but that was an accident. The arm turned the scarab by brute force. My hands weren't even near the grab arm controllers. I can't keep the sub in place and do that at the same time. I'm going to need one of you to operate the grab arm."

"I'll do it," Dan said, shifting his body in the co-pilot seat with Jami on his lap. "I was okay using it to fend off the sea creatures, right?"

"I'll monitor what's happening outside the sub while you guys are on the controls," Jami said.

"Holding position while Dan takes up the manipulator controls," the prince confirmed.

"So I push the joystick left to have the arm turn the scarab to the left, like before. Right?"

"That's right," the prince said, a hint of irritation in his voice. "Hurry, I don't know how long I can keep us in this position." They heard another distant dull boom somewhere outside in the bowels of the mountain.

"Okay, turning arm left..." Dan pushed the joystick left, tentatively at first, then moving it slowly all the way left.

"It's turning!" Jami said, face close to the cabin sphere. "It's really turning!"

The prince continued to operate the mechanical arm joystick while the sub remained pinned in place. The entire golden disc in the tunnel ceiling turned counter-clockwise, propelled by the sub's arm that gripped the scarab extension.

"Have I gone all the way around once with it yet?" the prince asked.

"Almost," Jami answered. "I can tell because of the way the scarab's nose was pointing. I'll tell you when it's all the way 'round." The disc continued to spin very slowly, but before Jami said anything, they heard a piercing click. And then the golden disc fell from its position in the ceiling.

The massive slab of heavy metal plummeted straight down, now obviously unconnected in any way to whatever forces had been holding it in place. None of them even had time to scream. They heard a metal ripping noise as the base of the mechanical arm was torn from the outside of the sub, its claw still gripping the scarab as it fell. Then came a jarring impact as the wayward disc sliced right through an assemblage of external lights. Half of the exterior lighting blinked out.

The next thing they all knew, the sub was spinning crazily, in spite of the prince's attempts to counteract the unpredictable movements. They felt another heavy thud as the acrylic dome in front of them collided with the edge of the newly created opening vacated by the fallen disc, already out of sight far below them. Even more horrifying, they watched as a spiderweb of cracks appeared along much of the clear protective dome keeping them alive.

"We're going up through the opening in the ceiling!" the prince yelled. Dan and Jami hugged each other as the submersible rolled off the edge and up through the middle of the opening. Immediately something felt different since they were no longer pinned in place by a current of water. But it wasn't only that, Dan noticed. The motion itself was very distinct. And that's when it hit him: they were bobbing along on top of the water, floating on it, instead of diving through it.

Which meant, Dan thought, still unable to voice these incredulous realizations, that they were now in air.

CHAPTER 35

The mini-sub bobbed atop the waves in whatever unknown body of water they now found themselves. Wherever they were, it was still dark all round them. A high-pitched alarm blared inside the cabin. Jami jolted against Dan. Both looked to the prince, whose hands were already smashing buttons. The alarm ceased and the prince said, "Low battery warning. Next will be—"

Yet another audible alarm sounded, this one lower in pitch and slower. "And that would be the low oxygen warning," the prince said, again moving quickly to kill the electronic braying. "We need to get the cabin open right away. The CO_2 scrubber is about to give out, as well as all of our systems when we lose power." As if to underscore his point, the remaining set of operational external lights blinked out, being a non-essential power drain.

"I can help get the latches open," Dan said, "but it'll be a little tricky for space with Jami up here, since the other times I did it I had more space or was by myself." He immediately recognized his slipup and couldn't believe he'd been that stupid.

"I can open the latches if you show me where they are," Jami said. Dan certainly appreciated her moving things along, for the prince ignored Dan's previous comment and said, "I've got the set of two latches on my side, and Dan can show you where the two are on that side." They set to work unclipping the hatch latches, with Dan and Jami each unlocking one. They looked to the prince, who appeared to be struggling with a latch. "I got one of them, but something seems to have caused some damage to the other that's preventing it from opening. Not surprising, really."

"Will it open enough for us to get out with only one not working?" Jami asked. As much as Dan hated to quash her hopes, he knew the answer was no and shook his head right along with the prince's as their sub pilot said, "No, all four latches must be free and clear for us to get out, and this acrylic is not breakable by us."

"I can lean pretty far over there to push up on the hatch," Dan offered. "Maybe that'll be enough to break it loose."

They decided to give it a try. Jami sat in the co-pilot seat while Dan leaned as far over to the left as he could and still get good purchase with his legs to be able to push the canopy open. They both strained to their full extent, but the stubborn hatch remained closed.

"Maybe if you break the latch mechanism on this side?" Dan suggested.

"With what?" the prince asked, holding his hands up in frustration.

"This might do it." Dan reached beneath the pilot's seat and pulled out what he knew would be there from his training sessions the day before, which now seemed like years ago. A small red fire extinguisher, which he handed up to the prince, who nodded enthusiastically.

"That might work. Let me see...." He took the metal cylinder and hefted it a couple of times in his hands, testing its weight. For some reason Dan's mind went to the gun. What if the Emirati royal suddenly turned on him, just went crazy and told him he was using too much oxygen, how there'd be more without him, and then smashed him in the head with that thing? He had to be prepared. He didn't think the prince would do something that half-cocked, but they were in a highly stressful situation in a very enclosed space. Stranger things had happened, he told himself.

The prince slammed the butt end of the extinguisher into the stubborn canopy latch. They heard something fracture and then the extinguisher clattered to the bottom of the cabin. "Got it!"

The prince put both hands on the inside of the curved dome and began to exert pressure. "Push on your side!" he grunted. Dan and Jami scrambled into position to be able to both push on the canopy. Dan immediately saw stars as his vision dimmed with the extreme effort in the low oxygen environment. As he was about to pass out, he felt the suction let up as the dome lifted from its frame.

At once they felt the chilly rush of Antarctic air streaming into the cabin's depleted atmosphere. They all gulped the air greedily as it seeped into the cabin, even while they continued to push up on the dome hatch until it reached the tipping point and began to fall back.

"Just let it go!" the prince shouted. "We can't dive anymore, anyway." The dome fell back against the rear structure of the sub, where it made a loud *clack* that reverberated in whatever space it was into which they had come up.

"So where the heck are we? Who's got a light?" Jami asked.

"I could flip the sub's lights back on for a few seconds so we can see where we are," the prince said, shifting his weight back into the pilot's seat. "Flipping them on in three, two, one..."

Inside the open cabin they heard the snap of a switch. In the wash of light that followed—each of them looked around at their new surroundings. They were speechless at first as they took it all in, and then the lights blinked out with a snap as the power failed. The prince spoke. "That's it for the lights. But I saw what looked like flat land—maybe a shoreline?—straight ahead at the far end of this subterranean lake."

Dan dipped his hand outside the cabin, getting it wet and then licking his fingers. "Saltwater."

"No surprise there," Jami said.

"Don't worry, I'm sure we'll be surprised some way or another," Dan said. "Can we motor over to the shoreline?"

"We can go as far as we can until the battery dies. Enjoy the ride. Here, use my flashlight for light since I can't hold it while piloting." Dan shone the beam straight ahead to brighten their immediate path forward while the prince motored along at a sedate pace. A wave of ripples spread out all around the mini-sub as it plowed along on the surface of the lake like a small boat. "Keeping our speed slow because the battery will last longer that way," the prince said of their painfully sluggish progress.

"That's fine, it's better to make it all the way across and not have to swim," Jami said. As they plowed through the lake, Dan tried to illuminate more of their surroundings but without the external lights all they could see was water in every direction, and up, there was only darkness. As they settled into the rhythm of travel, they quieted while listening to the faint motor hum and the lapping of water against the sub.

"Seems like there's no creatures in here," Dan said.

"I wish you had not said that," the prince responded with a groan. "Knock on wood, as they say in your country."

"There's no wood in here," Dan said.

"What, no joke about what's in your pants?" Jami quipped. Dan cackled but saw the prince was not laughing, and figured it was a cultural thing. He was glad to see Jami in higher spirits. They were not going to suffocate to death in the sub's cabin, at least. That was something. Dan continued sweeping the flashlight beam in front of them, still illuminating only the same rippled, black water.

"How are we for batteries?" Dan asked, straining to see ahead of them in the flashlight's weakening beam.

The prince glanced at a gauge and shrugged. "According to the gauges, we're already out of power. Basically, the remaining battery life is below the threshold that the instrumentation can detect, which means that we could come to a stop at any second."

"Or we could keep going for who knows how long," Jami hoped aloud.

"That is also correct," the prince said. "For now, we are moving along. See anything over there yet?"

Dan swept the beam slowly out in front of them, probing for signs of the opposite shore they had seen for a few seconds with the external lights. He saw nothing but water in the beam's path, and nothing outside the beam but darkness. It would be a shame to have made it this far, Dan thought to himself, only to be lost here, floating in perpetuity on the surface of a subterranean sea in a dead sub. And he hadn't actually seen the "land" the prince claimed to have seen, it occurred to him. But it was something to go on and this space couldn't be boundless. Or could it?

He was about to check the compass again to see if it might be working now when Jami tapped his arm. "I see something in the light!"

CHAPTER 36

Dan strained his eyes through the darkness beyond the flashlight's beam to see if he could corroborate what Jami saw. The water was calm enough that the motion of the sub was not an issue. And then, when he was about to ask Jami if she still saw it, it registered in his own vision. A sort of brownish expanse at the edge of the light beam.

"Land ho! Keep going," he said to the prince, who frowned in response.

"She's slowing down. I'm afraid we truly are down to the last gasp of battery power. But I'll keep us pointed this way and try to keep her going as long as I can."

The trio sat in silence as they labored slowly on. The brownish mass became more distinct, and now Dan clearly recognized it as an actual shoreline of sorts. The sub's rate of progress became slower and slower until they could barely hear the motor. The craft moved forward slower than a swimmer would, were the water not so frigid. "We're closer," Dan said. "Keep us going!"

"We are moving under the lowest possible power. Once this goes out, that's it, I'm afraid."

"We can see the shore," Dan said, excitement rising in his voice. "Looks like it goes back for a little ways." The submersible continued to thrust its way toward the unknown shoreline even as its power center entered its death throes. Dan kept the light on shore, pleased with every meter closer to it they came, for that meant one less meter they would need to swim, should it come to that. More detail became visible as they approached the ethereal coast.

"What I can see looks reflective," Jami said.

"I think it's all metal," Dan added. "Probably gold."

The prince shook his head and laughed. "You mean those...those sort of towers—rectangular looking towers?"

"Yeah, they do look like they might be rectangular," Dan said.

"If those are gold," the prince said, finishing with a low whistle.

"I wonder if they're solid gold or just plated over on the surface with gold."

"Either way," the prince shook his head. "I've heard that all of the world's existing gold, if compacted into a cube, would measure about eighty square meters. So if all that is gold, then the very price of gold itself would crash because the known supply would have increased many-fold overnight."

Suddenly they heard a soft scraping noise. "What is that?" Jami whispered, looking around.

"It's the sub!" the prince said, sounding happy. "We've hit bottom. Look around. How deep is it?"

Dan leaned over the edge of the open cockpit and shone his beam straight down. "Yes! I see the bottom. It's right there, probably only about a foot deep. And the bottom—it's metal, too. More gold!" The sub's undercarriage bumped every so often on the lake bottom as they motored on, going very slow now, toward the metal shore. The bottom scraping became more frequent, until, a few minutes later, the sub came to rest on the aquatic floor, moving forward no more.

"That is it," the prince announced, hand still on the throttle control. "We've officially run aground. This vessel is stuck right here."

Dan aimed his beam toward shore. "Not too bad," he said, tracing the beam from a golden shelf some distance away across the expanse of shallow water that gleamed with the gold beneath it. "We'll have to walk the rest of the way, but it's shallow enough."

"Let's gather everything of use--make sure you have your flashlight, whatever gear you have. There is a first aid kit in here—I'll bring that."

A couple of minutes later, the group had gathered their belongings and prepared to abandon the sub. Dan noted that, while very cold, the air was warmer here inside the mountain than it was outside, especially given it was sheltered from any kind of wind. He was the first to drop from the sub's open cabin. He landed with a splash in water up to his ankles.

"Not gonna lie," he said, taking a couple of cautious steps away from the sub, "the water's freezing cold. But at least it's only our feet."

"What's the bottom feel like?" the prince asked.

"Solid gold, baby," Dan said with a smile. "Seriously, like I'm standing on a regular smooth floor. No aquatic growth, and just a few pieces of regular rock here and there," Dan finished, looking around near his feet. The prince jumped out from the pilot side, and then Jami, on Dan's side. The prince activated his flashlight and then the three of them stood for a moment, surveying the water from their current position to the golden shore. None could detect any obvious threats.

Then they started to walk. Their splashy footfalls seemed incredibly loud as they trudged toward the metallic shore. Dan kept his light shining directly in front of them to make sure they weren't about to walk into anything, and that the water remained shallow. The prince kept his beam focused farther away, trying to pick out features on "dry land."

While they walked, Dan asked, "Do either of you think it's weird that there was an Egyptian symbol—the scarab—that we used to get into this place?"

"The Egyptians obviously knew about the Atlanteans. That map. The two sphinxes. That's how we got here, after all," Jami said.

They continued to slosh through the shallows to the beach. "That's not impossible," the prince said. "The Nazis thought the Atlanteans might be here, too, and we know from the arrow we found that they were a stone's throw from this very spot!"

"So if the Atlanteans did rebuild their civilization here," Jami said, still putting one foot in front of the other, "then we should see evidence of that soon, right?"

"Besides the golden tunnel, the scarab portal to enter this place, and the fabricated sheets of gold that we appear to be walking on right now?" the prince asked.

Dan found it amusing that now the prince seemed to accept they had pretty much found proof of Atlantis, while Jami remained skeptical. "We're about to find out whatever it is that this place has to offer," Dan replied from his point position a few feet ahead. "Water's edge is right up ahead."

The beleaguered trio walked up onto a metal beach, perfectly flat, as if it was machined. Set on a slight incline, the "beach" was angled such that the metal beneath their feet became dry after a few steps. The surface was textured, which made for better traction with their wet shoes. They gladly left the frigid water behind, walking away from the lake and up the slight incline. After some minutes of walking, the incline transitioned into a flight of broad steps, so large as to be almost a set of small step plateaus. They would walk forward for a minute or so, then climb up a step, walk forward for a minute or so, and climb up to the next step. The exertion helped keep them warm as they fought off the cold.

As they gained elevation from the lake, they began to see a blue-green glow up ahead. They still needed the flashlights to walk with, but when they shut the lights off for a few seconds, they could see a faint glow of illumination ahead. They ascended a few more broad steps until they realized the newest step was different.

Inlaid with a complex series of line engravings that created some sort of pattern, the three of them walked across the step, which extended farther than the others. "This pattern," Dan began. "There's something weird about it." They stared at the floor as they walked.

At length, Jami said, "I don't think the pattern ever repeats. It's always the same type of thing, but never exactly the same."

"A non-repeating pattern?" the prince asked.

"Non-repeating, non-periodic, whatever you want to call it," Jami said, "but it's different."

"Not seen in ancient Egypt," Dan said. "Their patterns are all repeating, and usually with shapes that fit together with no gaps. I've heard architects call them 'tessellations'."

"Yes," Jami said, "interlocking polygons like bee honeycombs. They're hexagonal tessellations. But you're right, these seems to be just randomly intersecting lines."

"Sort of looks like an electronic circuit board to me," the prince interjected.

As they walked, the platform narrowed and also grew lighter. They still had plenty of room to walk three abreast, but it was no longer the great expanse of metal they had walked on to get here.

"Does it seem like the cavern walls are closing in on us?" the prince asked.

"It does," Jami said.

"But it's also getting lighter," Dan said, adding, "Up ahead it looks like real light."

Walking onward for some indeterminate time, the trio came to a buttress of sorts, after which the roadway, if it could be called that, became narrower still. Two trails of bluish-green light were directly visible. Their length began just ahead of them, behind two stone statues that flanked the path forward.

"It's weird, but they look sort of Mayan, or maybe Aztec," the prince stated, as the three of them came to a stop at what appeared to be a gateway.

"And they're stone, too. Everything else around here is metal, especially gold," Dan pointed out.

Normally the statues, each one of which was as tall as the lanky prince, would command their full attention. But it was the illumination system that took their breath away. Two long tubes—one on either side of each statue—ran for a long distance ahead. Each tube was perhaps six feet in diameter, and placed on a rail system that elevated them about six feet off of the gold paved walkway. For that's what it was now, they could see: a narrow walkway, barely wide enough between the pair of tubes for the three of them to walk abreast. The tubes were clear, appearing to be glass, which permitted them to see the strange liquid inside of them.

Bluish-green water glowed with sparkling pinpoints of color as it flowed through the tubular conveyance system. "Bioluminescence," Jami said. "Same exact color as we saw on the ship coming into shore in the bay."

"I was going to say, it's not quite as green as whatever it was beneath Giza," Dan said.

"Different species of algae, probably," Jami said. "That was warm freshwater from the Nile, this is sub-freezing saltwater from the Southern Ocean."

"It's lighting our way!" the prince marveled.

"As it has for who knows how many centuries," Jami said.

"Whoever built this must have intended for people to walk this way," Dan said, pointing ahead along the narrow, lit walkway. "Let's check it out."

The three of them walked the golden pathway between the tubes. Dan felt the side of one of them and it was cold to the touch. "There must be an intake for the seawater somewhere," he speculated, gazing down over the side of the walkway into a black abyss he could not see the bottom of. For a long time they walked the elevated golden path in silence, contemplating where it was taking them, what it all meant.

They didn't have long to wonder. After a distance they estimated to be one mile (two kilometers, the prince said), while it grew lighter in the distance, the vista changed dramatically. A large break appeared in the walkway a few meters in front of them where the bridge ended abruptly in twisted gold ruins. They stopped walking while aiming their flashlights on what they could now see for certain was damage that had occurred to the walkway.

"What happened here?" the prince asked, eyeing the massive gap in the golden span.

"Maybe it broke when the crevasse fell apart?" Jami asked.

Dan swept his flashlight beam back on the walkway. "There wasn't a single bit of rock or ice or debris of any kind on the entire way here," he pointed out. "So I'm guessing that whatever caused it happened a long, long time ago."

Perhaps an eighth of a mile further on, they could see that the span resumed, but the missing section meant for them that they would be walking no farther, even though ahead of them lay an awe-inspiring vista.

CHAPTER 37

The dramatic damage could not hold their attention, for in the distance towered a city of gold, illuminated by towering conduits of bioluminescent liquid. Far enough away that they couldn't make out details, it was nevertheless clear that the structures were buildings that gleamed weakly in the eerie, bluish-green light.

"I don't see any way to get over there," Dan stated without emotion, for what should have been an expressive moment. They were, after all, simultaneously confronted by very good and bad news. A lost city of gold was little more than a literal stone's throw away. But on the other hand, they had no hope of reaching it. The black void between them and the city was an insurmountable obstacle. There was no going back the way they came. They could walk back to the lake, but without the sub, retracing the route they had taken to get here through the lengthy underwater tunnel was not an option.

"Is that...." Jami trailed off.

"Atlantis," the prince finished for her. His voice sounded detached like he wasn't even listening to what he was saying as he gawked at the golden marvel. "What else could it be?"

"I wish we could see it up close," Jami lamented.

At length, Dan said, "Maybe it's best to let it be." He sat down on the golden walkway, near the end of the broken span. Weary, the others sat as well, and for a while there was defeated silence in spite of the magical view and what it represented. After a time, conversation began again, this time about their prospects for survival.

"We have no climbing gear whatsoever," the prince said. "All we have are the most basic survival items that we brought, just—"

At that moment they heard a noise that baffled them because it was at once familiar and, in this setting, strange. A radio, blaring static. What made it odd was that neither the prince nor Dan's radios had been turned on. While in the sub, they'd had no need for them; they were stored as part of their emergency kits the prince had made them take on the sub.

"That's weird," the prince said, eyeing Dan.

"My radio must have flipped on by mistake when I sat down," he said, reaching to pick it up. As soon as he did, the static stopped. "That's weird." He set it back down again the way it had come to rest, with the antenna on the gold walkway. Immediately, the static resumed.

"We are buried inside innumerable tons of rock," the prince said. "I am surprised you even hear static. In fact, I turned my radio on shortly after we landed ashore, just to check that it didn't work—and sure enough—complete dead silence. Let me try it now." The prince grabbed his walkie-talkie from his small bag and turned it on. "Nothing," he said, staring once again at Dan's radio, from which strong white noise continued to erupt. Dan picked up his radio again, and again the noise ceased.

"The antenna needs to be touching the metal," Dan said, placing the unit back down on the terminated bridge inside one of the etched grooves that made up the non-repeating pattern. The static resumed again. "You see, gold is such a great conductor, that—"

He was interrupted by a human voice. Not from one of the other two people in his company, but one issuing from the electronic device itself. Male voice, speaking English. Still partially obscured by static, but overall intelligible.

"...leave field camp...base camp breakdown.....ship tomorrow..."

"That's Habib Saroohd, my Expedition Leader!" the prince explained, moving near to Dan's radio. Dan recalled the man from breakfast aboard the ship before leaving to set up base camp. It seemed like eons ago.

"Who cares who he is?" Jami yelled. "Talk to him! Tell him we're down here!"

Reflexively, Dan snatched up the radio and brought it to his mouth to transmit, but as soon as he lifted it from the metallic surface, it once again emitted only dense static. He carefully placed it back down onto the gold surface, this time actually into one of the depressed grooves that formed the non-repeating patterns, and was rewarded once again with an intelligible transmission.

"...mark the position then rendezvous with Hag....no time...."

This time there was even less static, although to produce the clear signal while also being able to transmit meant that Dan had to awkwardly position his face next to the radio such that the antenna remained in contact with the etched groove, and then depress the transmit button.

"Hey! Field team! Hag team, Habib! Anybody! This is Dan, do you copy, over?"

"It sounds like they're getting ready to leave!" Jami said.

The prince nodded. "Dismantling base camp. Try again, Dan! If they depart Antarctica without us...." He knew there was no need to complete the sentence.

Dan repeated his message a few more times, then listened to the channel.

"...say again. I repeat, say again. Dan?"

"They heard you!" Jami squealed. The prince clenched a fist.

Dan repositioned his hand around the radio so that its antenna would remain firmly positioned in the etched metal groove. Then he pressed the transmitter again. "Yes, it's me, Dan James! Do you copy?"

"We copy you, Dan. This is Habib. Where are you, over?"

"Deep inside the mountain. The prince and Jami are with me."

"Alive?"

"Yes, we are all alive!" The prince and Jami both shouted "Yes! Yes!" in the background of the transmission.

"What happened?" Habib asked. Dan proceeded to relate a short version of their voyage through the tunnel across from the ledge in the mini-sub. He said that they surfaced in a lake in a massive cavern, omitting mention of the scarab. He didn't want to risk losing the connection by relating details that did not pertain to their ability to be rescued. He explained only that they were now out of the water, deep inside the mountain somewhere, and that they had weak light in the form of aquatic bioluminescence.

"How can we get to you?" Habib asked, breathless. "We can try to drill down if we know where—"

"Let me talk to him!" the prince yelled. Dan looked up at him from his awkward hunched over position and explained that they shouldn't risk repositioning the radio. "Just tell me what you want to say," he said. The prince eyed Dan and Jami in turn.

"I can have a second submersible identical to the first shipped here. And another helicopter. I have the money and the contacts to make that happen. It would take a couple of days, meaning that—"

"We can't stay here for a couple of days!" Jami objected.

The prince held his hands palms up. "Look, in the meantime, they can try to reach us, but wouldn't it be nice to know that if they can't get to us from the top down, that a rescue is on the way?"

Dan nodded agreement. "And we do have some food—the Power Bars, and we have drinking water."

"That's right," the prince said.

"Dan?" Habib's concerned voice came over the frequency. "Still there?"

Dan keyed the transmitter. "Copy that. We have an idea..."

He proceeded to relate the prince's plan for obtaining and transporting a second sub to the site, as well as a second helicopter. At first, he was understandably reluctant, but the prince relayed the details of how the transactions would be carried out, along with the contact information, as well as the need for a new pilot who understood the risks. He supplied the name of one he said would do it ("Owes me big from an escapade in the Red Sea a few years ago"), along with specific payment instructions. At the end of the radio exchange, Habib ensured them that the new vehicles would be brought to the site, and that in the meantime they would attempt to locate the missing trio. Knowing that the radio batteries would not last if used continuously for days, Dan told them that they would check in every two hours for a quick status update.

Dan turned off the radio, and then they were left with only each other and the stark realization that they were most likely going to be down here with very little food and water, in the cold, for at least two days. They laid out their collection of PowerBars and their small canteens of drinking water, and devised a ration plan. They would be constantly hungry and thirsty, but they had enough to survive for two days.

They wiled away the hours at first by more thoroughly examining the golden span and the magnificent city in the near distance, checking and re-checking to see if there was some way over to it they had missed during their initial assessment. But there was only an impassible gap.

They slept a lot, at first right there on the end of the broken span. Later, they decided to make their way back to the lake, since that was where the new sub would be to pick them up if all went well. During the walk back they discussed what could go wrong. What if the sub didn't have enough battery power to make it here and back? What if the next helicopter pilot crashed also when bringing the sub? The prince did his best to assuage their concerns by pointing out that the rescue sub would not have to expend energy while opening the scarab portal, as they had done, and would be bringing extra batteries because they know what they're up against. They would be better prepared with equipment specially suited to the task, rather than having to improvise as his last helicopter pilot had to do.

They walked slowly back across the golden bridge, back down the metal stairs, and back down the series of steppe plateaus, until they reached the metallic lake shore. There they established the most basic of camps, leaving their gear and supplies there, napping there, and leaving occasionally to walk back to the gold walkway in order to check in on the radio.

Habib reported that the climbing team was looking for access points higher up in the mountain to see if there was another crevasse or some kind of entry point, but that so far they had not found any.

The three of them had plenty of discussions, as well, about what they would tell people they had found down here. If they ever got out, that is. The uncertainty surrounding their future was as palpable as the weight of the mountain threatening to entomb them for all eternity.

*****

Time lost meaning for them. Day and night did not exist down here. The most meaningful measure they had was their dwindling food and water supply. Hunger and thirst gnawed at them, punctuated by radio updates from the team on the outside. Habib informed them that, though they still had a climbing team scouring the slopes for a way inside the mountain other than the underwater passage, they had yet to find one. The only good news was that the sub, helicopter, and respective pilots for each were en route from various parts of the globe.

As the beginning of their third day underground began, Dan left his two dormant companions to make the now well-worn trudge back up to the golden span for their radio update. He knelt on the gold and assumed the now practiced position of placing the radio antenna in contact with the metal etchings before talking into the device.

"Good news!" Habib's impossibly ebullient-sounding voice told him.

"Tell me." Dan's own words were flat and lifeless.

"The sub and chopper are here!"

"Here at the mountain?" Dan perked up a little.

"No, here in Antarctica at base camp. But the sub is being loaded onto one of the Hags now, and the chopper is being prepped for flight to our field camp. The sub pilot will be on it, too. The biggest delay now is the Hag trek to bring the sub. We do have a little storm cropping up that's making things difficult."

Dan pressed his forehead hard into the cold gold floor. "How much longer are we looking at, Habib? We can't hold out much more."

"I am sorry, but you're looking at least another twelve hours or so altogether, if everything goes well."

Dan's heart sank a little lower in his chest, if that was even possible, but he supposed he should be glad simply to have a chance. But deep down he knew this would be their last possibility for rescue. If something went wrong with that perilous sub drop into the chasm—there simply would not be time to try it again, except as a body recovery mission.

Exhausted, Dan trudged back through the incredible surroundings that he now barely noticed, to their sorry camp. Jami and the prince still slept, and although he had actual news to tell them, he decided to simply lay down and take a nap rather than waking them up only to say it would be at least another half-day. He slept for a long time. At some point later on he did wake up to find the prince also awake, lying on his back and staring up at the dark cavern ceiling. Jami still slept, her breathing very shallow. He checked his digital watch and realized he had slept through what should have been three more radio check-ins. He was in the process of telling the prince about the last radio update, when they heard a splashing noise coming from the lake.

Dan and the prince struggled to their feet and aimed their flashlights—now quite dim—out on the water, searching for the disturbance. Dan found their now useless sub, drifting about on the surface where it would likely reside forever, hatch open. And then he saw it. On the far end of the lake, a patch of bright yellow announced the arrival of their rescue submersible.

"They're here!" He and the prince waved their light beams at the sub to show the newcomer where they were. The sub pilot blinked the exterior lights at them three times and then began to motor slowly toward them.

Dan ran back to their camp and shook Jami awake. "They're here for us, baby! We're getting out of here!" She rubbed her eyes and stared in dazed disbelief at the yellow submersible, its exterior lights blazing brightly in the dim cavern as it approached their shore.

"I gotta go make a radio call to Habib!" Dan said, as he started jogging up the metal plateaus for what he knew should be the last time. When he got out along the gold span, he placed the radio antenna into a groove and made the transmission. Habib responded at once, excitement brimming over in his voice.

"Dan! What happened? I thought maybe your radio died. Listen—the sub is on the way right now. Should be there soon, over."

"It's here now! It just surfaced in the lake. Sorry, I fell asleep. I just wanted to let you know that the sub is here. I've got to get back down to the lake, over."

"Copy that, get back down there and have a good sub trip back topside. The climbing team is already in place to assist you out of the crevasse. Over and out!"

Dan staggered to his feet and looked out on the glowing lost city for a final time. He was about to turn around for the hike back to the beach when a blinking light near the center of the forgotten metropolis caught his attention. It was blue-greenish, like the rest of the bioluminescence, but brighter, and the only one he'd ever seen blink. As he stared at it, a shadow of some sort passed in front of it, obscuring it for a moment before the blinking resumed. Then the bright light itself winked out.

Dan stared for a moment more, now seeing nothing else unusual. *Probably just a trick of the weird light on my tired eyes*, he thought. He turned and ran toward the lake.

EPILOGUE

One week later
Persian Gulf off Dubai, United Arab Emirates

The Sikorsky S-76D helicopter banked into a sharp turn that followed the outline of an island a few hundred feet below. Dan, Jami and the prince were seated in the rear of the luxurious craft on leather seats as they looked down on the sprawling excess of the wealthy region. They sipped champagne from crystal flutes as they took in the majestic views. An array of 300 manmade islands stretched out below them, tan wafers on an azure sea, but it was the unusual pattern in which they were arranged that elicited the eye-popping stares from Dan and Jami.

"Welcome to The World," said the prince. But his face was impassive as he looked down on the scenery, which depicted a series of islands arranged in the shape of the planet's major land masses. "As you can see, we are currently flying over North America. Do you recognize it?"

Dan and Jami nodded their recognition. "That's so cool!" Dan said. But the prince shrugged.

"Sadly, they represent one of Dubai's few large-scale failures. After the real estate debacle of 2008, and then the oil crash of '14, much of the building was abandoned. Units on the islands were not sold. Some of the islands themselves began to sink back into the sea from which their sand was dredged."

"Wow," Dan said, shaking his head. "So it's sort of like Atlantis— abandoned and left behind to be reclaimed by the sea."

"Exactly," the prince answered, nodding with a hand on his bearded chin. He was dressed almost exclusively in white, including flowing robes and headgear. Only the sandals he wore and the golden scimitar Dan had seen before on his waist betrayed the color scheme. "But like what the Atlanteans did, known only to the three of us in the back of this helicopter, Dubai also hopes to rebuild. The World may one day rise again. But in the meantime," he said, turning away from the window to face Dan and Jami, "I want to reiterate what I believe we already agree on."

"And that is?" Jami asked.

The prince indicated the islands below. "That we are to remain forever silent about what we found in Antarctica. I myself have mentioned it to no one, including the expedition members who were there."

Dan nodded, recalling how he, Jami and the prince had remained silent upon being rescued that fateful day last week. The submersible pilot who effected their rescue saw the cavern, but did not see the scarab portal since it had already broken off, nor did he see the golden span or the lost city itself. Fortunately, the rescue effort, with multiple submersible trips back and forth to get the three explorers and the rescue pilot back above ground, took constant effort and coordination such that there was not time for talk of what they had found. Even once they were at base camp, no one had pressed them about what exactly they had seen, instead giving them space to recuperate from their traumatic ordeal. Later, on the ship voyage back to Chile, they had spoken of the large cavern containing the lake, and the metal shore, since it was viewable by the sub pilot, but that was the extent of what they revealed to the public.

"I think we can all agree on that, am I right, Jami?" Dan said, looking to the woman he now thought of as his girlfriend. Their time in Dubai since the prince had flown them here for "discussions about a business proposition" had been nothing short of exhilarating. She smiled as she made eye contact with first Dan and then the prince.

"Absolutely. Let it rest. Let it be guarded by the creatures that we know have kept it safe for all these millennia."

Then, with a spark in her eye, she asked, "Do either of you think it strange that during the entire rescue process to get us back above ground—all those sub trips, the climbing teams hanging out on the ledges again—that the creatures never bothered us? I mean, we never even *saw* one."

It was true. The megalodon, mosasaur, and whatever other unknown creatures they had seen, had never appeared again. "It was as if they knew they had fulfilled their purpose," Jami continued. The three of them rode along through the sky in silence while sipping their sparkling wine.

At length, the prince changed the subject by saying, "So, I know I told you I had a business proposition…"

"Uh oh," Dan said, and the three of them laughed heartily as the chopper flew over the forgotten islands.

"I wanted to give you some time to decompress after our ordeal, to relax and enjoy yourselves for a few days so that you may consider my idea with clear and refreshed minds. I would like to ask if you two—and this offer stands for either or both of you, though I do hope you stick together as it seems you've taken a liking to one another." The prince paused while Dan and Jami smiled at one another. Then he continued.

"I would like to go into business with you, running a company that searches for lost civilizations and, when appropriate, reports on our findings to both the public and scientific research communities. I feel there are many ancient societies that have been all but forgotten, and that with my resources and your skill, knowledge and abilities, that the three of us—along with a trustworthy support staff—could do much in the way of shedding light on these overlooked accomplishments of humankind."

After a long pause, Dan said, "But Atlantis is off-limits, right?"

The prince nodded. "Yes, we have already agreed that Atlantis is off-limits. But I think we all know based on what we have seen in Antarctica, and on what you two have seen in Egypt, that there may in fact be even more to the story of the Atlanteans. Perhaps even more to the ancient Egyptians, as well."

"Perhaps a lot more," Dan said, removing a piece of paper from his pants pocket and unfolding it. "Remember the piece of metal from the mammoth hatching orb that you told me to have analyzed at a lab?" He also pulled a small hunk of metal from his pocket, holding it up so that it reflected the sunlight through the helicopter window, revealing a perplexing mix of iridescent hues.

"You got the results back already?" the prince asked, eyeing the paper.

"You carry that thing around everywhere you go?" Jami asked with a laugh. He addressed her first.

"Hey, some people carry a rabbit's foot. This is definitely my good luck charm." Then he turned to the prince.

"Yes, I chiseled off a tiny piece of this and sent it to them. This is the detailed lab analysis. And it indicates that the metal ore that comprises the mammoth hibernation pods was not of this Earth. Literally, not of this Earth, as in the metal comes from a meteorite."

"Astounding!" the prince replied. "So much to investigate!"

Dan thought back to the twinkle of light he'd seen in the golden city just before he turned back for the last time to return to the metallic lake shore. He had mentioned that to no one, not even Jami.

"Yes." He put the meteorite back in his pocket. "So much, indeed."

THE END

www.ingramcontent.com/pod-product-compliance
Lightning Source LLC
Chambersburg PA
CBHW060425180626
46817CB00007B/2664